FUTURISTICA

Volume 1

Metasagas Press

Published by Metasagas Press
411 Walnut St. #6797
Green Cove Springs, FL 32043

Cover art and design by Kanaxa Design

Interior layout and design by Chester W. Hoster

Edited by Chester W. Hoster and Katy Stauber

First published in 2016. Printed in the United States.

ISBN: 1-939120-07-1
ISBN-13: 978-1-939120-07-6

FUTURISTICA
Volume 1

Bo Balder — James Beamon — Marina Berlin
Stephanie Burgis — L Chan — Megan Chaudhuri
L. H. Davis — Ciro Faienza — Anne E. Johnson
E. E. King — Gary Kloster — Mary Mascari
Mike Morgan — Robert Lowell Russell — Patrice Sarath
Holly Schofield — Wole Talabi — Nancy S.M. Waldman
And

Darina Yakusha

Metasagas Press

This book is dedicated to Duncan, Noah, Peter, Rory, Teyasia, and Zara.

Table of Contents

Sterile Technique
by Megan Chaudhuri

From every wall of the sitting room, the dead stared down at Rubaiyat. Daguerreotypes from the British Raj frowned beside polaroids of smiling women in saris. A digital morph-portrait—fashionable among wealthy survivors—looped behind Mrs. Mukherjee and her grandson. Within its gold frame, an infant grew seamlessly into a college student, graduated to a plump young man at a wedding, and then shrunk back to chubby infancy.

"I hope contamination is not an issue for you," Mrs. Mukherjee was saying from the rosewood couch. A gold charm, shaped like a healthy human brain, glittered at her wrist. "Our last vitrist... God knows where the old fool ran off to! Couldn't grow anything trickier than chicken sausage without yeast contaminating the culture."

She's upset about only eating sausage, Rubaiyat marveled. She shifted on the Persian rug, feeling every centimeter the orphaned scholarship student from Hyderabad's slums. *Focus. Jaya needs you to get this job.*

"I have three years' experience culturing meat, Mrs. Mukherjee," Rubaiyat said. The air conditioner's soft whine nearly drowned out her voice. "In accordance with halal standards and—"

"Excellent," Mrs. Mukherjee said, glancing at her grandson. Except for his scowl and new-looking polo shirt, he resembled the man in the slide show.

She turned back to Rubaiyat. "What's your status?"

"P-pardon?"

"Your test results, girl."

Rubaiyat's skin goosebumped beneath her formal kurta tunic and threadbare leggings. There were privacy laws; but then, there were laws about vitrists culturing meat for private consumption. Between those laws and what would happen to Jaya if she didn't break them, Rubaiyat had squirmed as she traveled from Hyderabad to Calcutta, from the light rail station to the Mukherjees' townhome.

The question was ridiculous, anyway. Even if she was positive, prions could only infect the cultures if Rubaiyat biopsied her nerves and grew them into the meat itself.

"I am negative," Rubaiyat said. Taking out her battered phone, she forwarded her last university screening to Mrs. Mukherjee. The woman pulled Tata's latest phone model from her purse.

"Good," Mrs. Mukherjee said. "Why haven't you finished your degree?"

Rubaiyat hesitated, staring at Mrs. Mukherjee's brain-shaped charm. *Because my sister will die if I don't pay for her treatment by next Friday.*

Jaya's call had come during class last week, telling Rubaiyat of her diagnosis, her need for postexposure monoclonal antibodies, the clinic's demand to be paid up front. *I just had a bit to drink after my shift, Baiya. They said the lamb was c-clean*, Jaya had said, her face doll sized on Rubaiyat's phone screen.

Focus. Rubaiyat's gaze flickered from Mrs. Mukherjee to the scowling Basu to the portraits of the dead. Under their long-dead eyes, the significance of the prying question and the charm sank into her, as silently as misfolded prion proteins slipping into the gut's nerves. *She fears anything and anyone associated with infection.*

"B-because I'm getting married next year, in twenty fifty-four," Rubaiyat said, looking down at her feet. The sandals had been Jaya's, and were so small that Rubaiyat's toes stretched a centimeter past the front. "I'm taking a term off to earn money for gifts to my fiancé's family."

She jumped at Mrs. Mukherjee's sharp clap.

"How fitting!" Mrs. Mukherjee smiled for the first time. "Basu, too, will soon be married. That's why we need a vitrist so fast. The girl's parents are coming next Thursday to meet him, and it would be wonderful to serve them tenderloins." It *must* be wonderful, her expression said.

Tenderloins. Rubaiyat ran a hand through her close-cropped hair. The complicated meats normally needed nine days, from seeding the progenitor cells onto a printed cartilage matrix to layering adipocytes to developing enough muscle.

But then she realized she was hired.

"I can make tenderloins for your future in-laws, Mr. Mukherjee." Rubaiyat grinned at Basu.

Without replying, Basu stood and stalked out of the room. The door slammed, rattling the daguerreotypes and stuttering the morph-portrait.

In the tense silence, the air conditioner shut off. Rubaiyat heard Mrs. Mukherjee's brain charm tinkle as the woman adjusted her gold-embroidered sari.

"He's nervous," Mrs. Mukherjee said. "But the Khans are genetically resistant to prions... at least *his* children will be safe." Over her shoulder, the plump young man's image smiled, his resemblance to Mrs. Mukherjee clear.

She looked straight at Rubaiyat. "He must be in a good mood for the visit. I will expect sausage for his breakfast and another meat at supper, starting tomorrow."

Rubaiyat stared. "That would take three vitrists..." But she swallowed her words, feeling them settle in her stomach like a lump of badly cultured chicken sausage. "I will try. And I will be paid before next Friday?"

"You young people!" The couch creaked as Mrs. Mukherjee stood. "Always concerned about money." She pressed a button on a table. Deep in the house's bowels, a bell rang.

"I will pay you next Thursday," she said, waving a hand. "Now, go with Susmita. She will show you the culture room in the kitchens.

"But try to remember, girl," Mrs. Mukherjee said, her gaze on the gold-framed portrait of her dead son. "There are more important things than money."

∞

The windowless basement kitchen smelled of deep-frying, chat masala spices, and strawberry Pop-Tarts. Dull yellow light pooled on the range and island at the center of the room, reflecting off an ancient smartphone blasting Radio Bhangra. Everything was old and worn and cramped. Much like Susmita, Rubaiyat thought as she trailed after the child-sized cook.

"Meat in there, please, once you've harvested it," Susmita said, rapping the fridge's insulated door as she circled the island. She looked nearly seventy, but Rubaiyat had to work to keep up with her rapid pace and words.

Next came the range, its heat as tangible as Basu's glare.

"Probably best if you don't wander about." Susmita paused long enough to adjust the flame roaring beneath a pot. "And don't turn off the phone. I hate missing *Kittie Party*."

"Yes, Auntie," Rubaiyat said, rubbing her forehead. Between the hot, noisy kitchen, her thoughts of Jaya, and the interview with Mrs. Mukherjee, she was developing a headache.

"Bleach and ethanol in here." Susmita opened the closet. Rubaiyat glimpsed an old-fashioned whisk broom for wet-sweeping before she shut it. Susmita shuffled quickly to another door and opened it a crack; the distant roar of traffic and the close stench of rotting vegetables flowed inside. "Come in and out through the alley here, not the front door. Compost digester and trash're at the corner."

Rubaiyat heard dull thumps that sounded like bad plumbing as they rounded towards the final door and the hallway beside it. Her heart sank when she spotted the old plastic streamers draped across the hall. With these conditions, no wonder the old vitrist had had contamination.

"This is my room next to the culture room," Susmita said. She picked up the phone and tapped it with a tiny bent thumb. Radio Bhangra's techno grew even louder, drowning out the dull thumps. Susmita shouted, "Not enough space to board you here, unfortunately."

Damn. "I'll stay in a hostel."

"What?"

"A hostel," Rubaiyat said louder, looking at the phone pointedly.

Susmita didn't take the hint. "Dangerous. You really want work that bad?"

"I won't be here long," Rubaiyat said, a little sharply. This was all she could get; Jaya only had seven days before the antibodies wouldn't work anymore.

"That's what Vasudha said when she started twenty-three years ago," Susmita said, turning back to the stove.

"Who's…" Rubaiyat started to say. *Vasudha. Must be the old vitrist who disappeared.* "What happened?"

Radio Bhangra cut off. But the blessed silence was shortly interrupted by the formal, familiar recording from India's Health Ministry, cautioning all desis to avoid animal-grown meats and report numbness, delusions, and unexplained deaths.

The bad techno resumed.

"Too much contamination," Susmita said.

"Contamination happens to every vitrist, even with sterile technique," Rubaiyat said, rubbing her head. Sweat was beading on the short bristles of her hair. "They just fired her, after twenty-three years?"

But then common sense silenced her. Words always got back to rich people; Rubaiyat had learned that as a scholarship Muslim amidst rich, Brahmin-caste classmates. "P-pardon, Auntie."

"You're fine, girl," Susmita said gruffly. Covering the soup, she turned to face Rubaiyat, her skin moist with steam and sweat. For a moment, her mouth opened and her throat worked, as if she was trying to shape words.

—just like how Rubaiyat's mother and father had tried, their lips wriggling like worms in the sun, cut off forever by a billion misfolded proteins gutting their brains, by a single cheap snack of contaminated lamb dumplings from a Chinese food cart—

Rubaiyat jumped as the phone blasted a commercial for weight-loss pills and anti-prion vitamins.

"Don't take all day," Susmita said.

Rubaiyat nodded. She took a breath of air thick with old grease and fresh spices. Turning, she faced the opaque streamers draped over the dark hallway. For one minute, her mind gnawed at the whole deal: the cramped, claustrophobic kitchen; the need to stay at a crowded, dirty hostel; and the history of contamination. If she'd come here for any reason other than Jaya eating some damned animal-grown lamb when she knew better, she would have left right then for Hyderabad.

But no. Jaya needed rescuing, like she always did since their parents died.

And Rubaiyat was the one to rescue her only living relative. Like she always did.

The plastic streamers crackled as Rubaiyat entered the hall.

∞

The Mukherjees' private culture room was nothing like her university's sleek labs. Whitewash coated windowless brick walls built during the British Raj. Boxy centrifuges crowded liquid nitrogen dewars and gurgling lead pipes. The sterile biohazard cabinet stood in an old shrine alcove. By her third day, Rubaiyat had memorized its stainless steel surface, from its five dents to the ragged right edge that snagged her gloves.

Tiny scrapes crisscrossed her forearms from that ragged edge. It was impossible to be careful when her feet ached from sixteen hours of standing, her fingers cramped from pipetting, and her mind boggled from the decadence. Two meat meals daily for Basu! When billions ate rice and begged for lentils! Why, just one tenderloin could fetch a month's wages on the black market.

Could pay for Jaya's infusions.

"No," Rubaiyat said through her surgical mask. She'd always earned her way, ever since she scored first on her school entrance exams. She had never acted like there was an older sister to save her, to game the system.

Rubaiyat lined up the tenderloin progenitor cultures inside the biohazard cabinet: three glass flasks, body-warm from the incubator. Wiping her goggles clear, she took out her phone and snapped pictures as the ragged spheres of reindeer myocytes settled by gravity in their pink nutrient broth. The Khans had demanded documentation of the whole process. As if, Rubaiyat thought, anyone could tell she was growing reindeer, and not the forbidden pig—

The sudden *thump* behind her made Rubaiyat whirl around.

Nothing. The green lights glowed steadily on the incubators, stacked along the wall shared with Susmita's room.

As Rubaiyat stared, a softer *thump* carried through the wall.

Just Susmita, Rubaiyat thought. She adjusted her hairnet, hit "Send" on the message to the Khans, and put away the phone. *Walls must be thin.*

She sprayed her gloves with disinfecting ethanol and turned back. The flask's nutrient broth gurgled as she poured it into a disposal container, careful not to dislodge the settled myocytes. Rubaiyat smelled burnt blood as the broth mixed with bleach. A familiar smell. She could almost pretend she was back in Hyderabad, becoming the vitrist who would finally figure out mass production, so that no other slum kid would watch her parents wither from the inside out.

The door whispered open.

Rubaiyat half dropped the flask, the glass barking against stainless steel. Broth and progenitor spheres sloshed. She caught the flask before it tipped and turned her head.

"What is it, Auntie?" Rubaiyat said, quickly noting Susmita's surprised expression and bare skin. A million fungal spores rode on human hands. A billion bacteria spiraled out with human breath.

"Didn't expect you here so late," Susmita said shrilly. *Two billion bacteria, three billion...* "Was going to clean things up."

Twelve billion...

Through gritted teeth, Rubaiyat said, "I'll clean up, to reduce the contamination risk."

Twenty-four billion, twenty-five billion...

With a glance at the flasks, Susmita nodded and left. Rubaiyat heard the crackle as the woman pushed through the plastic streamers. With a groan, she closed the glass front of the biohazard cabinet.

Rubaiyat stood, her gloved hands clenched, breathing in the scent of deep-frying that had wafted in with Susmita.

Everything had to be cleaned. Immediately.

With hands that trembled from pipetting and irritation, she picked up the disinfectant bottle. Her mind replayed Susmita's entrance: the woman's surprised jump, scattering fungal spores; her every word, seeding the air with bacteria hungry for nutrients to devour, to contaminate, to obliterate this last chance at money for Jaya.

Thump.

The disinfectant bottle almost slipped from her startled grasp. Just Susmita, she told herself. Just Susmita.

Rubaiyat squeezed the bottle. Ethanol sprayed out, filling the room with its sharp scent as it splattered across the incubators that stared down at her with green, unblinking eyes.

∞

The nose-tingling smell of ethanol was gone the next morning when Rubaiyat peered into the culture room's microscope. With gloved fingers, she adjusted the focus.

Fungal hyphae twined like microscopic ivy about the sausage cells. *Contamination.*

"Damn," she said, her hands starting to shake. Tearing off her gloves, she pulled on a fresh pair and drenched them with ethanol.

Rubaiyat wrenched open the incubators holding the precious tenderloin cultures. Warm air fogged her goggles, obscuring her vision, shrouding the fate of the tenderloins—of Jaya.

Then she heard it, faint as cockroaches skittering across bare cement. *Tik-tik.*

Rubaiyat wiped her goggles with trembling fingers.

Tik-tik, tik-tik.

Stacked in columns inside the incubator, each petri dish held a pink filigree of tissue, suspended across the cartilage matrix like a cockroach-sized hammock. The nutrient broth jiggled and the cartilage clacked against the petri dish glass as hundreds of developing muscles contracted and relaxed, the myocytes exercising compulsively in their rich bath of growth factors and stimulating acetylcholine.

"Thank God…"

The tenderloins were safe.

Rubaiyat's job was safe.

Jaya was safe…

The sausage! Rubaiyat ran to the microscope. The *tik-tik* of exercising muscle, the faint thumps from Susmita's room, the gurgling of pipes faded from her consciousness as she scanned each dish of sausage cells.

"God damn it." Barely enough for three sausages. Rubaiyat leaned her forehead against the microscope's cold ocular piece. Should she dare protest that it wasn't her fault, that Susmita had entered the room, that no vitrist could culture under these conditions?

But they'd fired Vasudha for contamination after twenty-three years of service. Rubaiyat couldn't risk losing this job, not with Jaya needing the antibodies by Friday. She could only hope that three sausages were the price of Basu's mood.

Tossing the contaminated cultures into a plastic bag, Rubaiyat changed back to her kurta and leggings in the hall. The plastic streamers crackled and Susmita glanced up from toasting Pop-Tarts. Shifting the bag to her side opposite Susmita, Rubaiyat squashed her irritation and nodded to the cook. Now was not the time for questions.

She kneed open the door to the alley. High brick walls muted the sounds of Calcutta waking up around her: the muezzin's echoing call to dawn prayer, the whining start of air conditioners, the Health Ministry's broadcast blaring from an open window.

"—donate to prion screenings in countries less fortunate than India, with her many vegetarians—"

The broadcast faded as Rubaiyat walked to where the small courtyard joined the alley.

"See you tomorrow?" Basu asked, just around the alley's corner. Rubaiyat stopped cold between the compost digester and dumpster.

A woman said, "Only if we go dancing somewhere else. I'm so tired of those limping crazies on Camac Street. Like it's my fault they ate something contaminated!"

Contaminated. Rubaiyat fumbled with the bag, but the dishes opened against the translucent sides, spilling globs of contaminated sausage and nutrient broth. She couldn't let Basu see. He'd ask why she was throwing away cultures.

Rubaiyat heard approaching footsteps. She glanced back frantically; the kitchen door was too far.

Behind the digester.

She dove between it and the brick wall. The narrow space smelled as foul as contaminated broth. Rubaiyat breathed through her mouth, clutching the incriminating bag.

Basu and a young woman passed by. The woman's hair was falling down from a French knot, and Basu's white polo had a yellow splotch. Their faces looked like Jaya's when she stayed out too late.

The Khan girl? Rubaiyat wondered.

Basu glanced up at the windows of Mrs. Mukherjee's bedroom. The curtains were still drawn.

Probably not, Rubaiyat realized, shifting uncomfortably as Basu drew his companion close. She tried not to gag on the rotting miasma. Her throat was burning with bile when the woman's footsteps passed the digester, alone.

The kitchen door slammed. Rubaiyat staggered out into the empty courtyard, inhaling the stale alley air. She wiped her mouth and glanced at the door. What did Susmita think? What did Basu say as he walked through the servants' door?

He says nothing. Susmita must already know.

That's why he was glaring at me during the interview, Rubaiyat realized. She glanced at the closed curtains. *Why doesn't he just tell his grandmother?*

But if he did, Mrs. Mukherjee wouldn't need Rubaiyat to grow expensive halal tenderloin for the Khans.

The stale air suddenly felt cold in Rubaiyat's lungs. Only Basu's secret stood between Jaya and the antibody infusions.

Rubaiyat straightened upright. She walked to the dumpster. The bagful of petri dishes crackled like bones as it landed inside the dumpster.

Her footsteps echoed off the high brick walls as she returned to the kitchen.

∞

When Rubaiyat entered the culture room thirteen hours before the Khans' visit, the pipes gurgled. The incubators hummed. The ventilation hissed.

But the cultures did not *tik-tik*.

One, two, three strides carried her to an incubator. Rubaiyat opened it and recoiled as moist, rotten warmth billowed past. Wiping her goggles clear, she looked inside.

The broth was as cloudy as monsoon season in each silent petri dish. Rubaiyat blinked, shook her head, and wiped her goggles again. When the cloudiness refused to clear, she carried the dishes to the microscope.

In the first, fungal hyphae embraced the dead muscle; in the second, mold furred the cartilage matrix.

The third was so clouded with bacteria she couldn't see anything. But against that pus-like opaqueness, Rubaiyat noticed a smudge on the outside of the dish.

A tiny, bent thumbprint. Just right for a child-sized, elderly woman.

Rubaiyat set down the dish. In the gloves' sterile warmth, her hands felt cold. Her mind felt hot as it flicked through memories.

Susmita, looking surprised. She'd said, *Didn't expect you here so late.*

Basu, looking at the curtains drawn across his grandmother's windows as he kissed his girlfriend.

Susmita, looking away when Rubaiyat asked, *What happened to Vasudha?*

Too much contamination.

Rubaiyat realized she was sitting on the linoleum. She stared up at the incubator. Through its gaping door, it exhaled a tiger's breath of rotting meat.

Basu didn't want this marriage. And somehow—likely bribery— he had convinced Susmita to contaminate the cultured meat. Because no tenderloins meant no impressive dinner. No dinner meant no marriage to the Khan girl.

No marriage meant no Jaya.

Thump.

Rubaiyat stared at the wall shared with Susmita's quarters. No Jaya meant no more worrying alone after midnight, no more treacherous thoughts of, *She did it to herself.*

The muffled thumps matched the throb deep in her skull, in some primeval part that muttered and snarled. She had been doing her duty, like always. But then Jaya drank too much, like always. *I–it's the only time I can stop thinking about Baba and Mama, Baiya!* And then she ate something infected and then spoiled Basu bribed that greedy Susmita and—

Thump.

"Stop making that damned noise!" Rubaiyat grabbed a disinfectant bottle. Her glove caught on its spray nozzle, the nitrile ripped, and she hurled the bottle against the wall. Cheap plastic cracked and ethanol ricocheted, splattering Rubaiyat's goggles.

She ripped off her goggles and stomped on them. She tore off her gloves and threw them against the ancient brick wall. Her breath whistled through her teeth as she drew her phone. Her hands smeared the screen as she set its bare-bone camera functions: *Three-Axis Autofocus, No Flash.*

She had no proof about Basu, but she could get proof about Susmita. Perhaps Mrs. Mukherjee would reward her for catching a treacherous servant. Perhaps Rubaiyat would get the woman fired. Get her *gone.* As gone as Vasudha had been.

As gone as Jaya would be.

Rubaiyat kicked her broken goggles under the biohazard cabinet, hearing the plastic frame shatter as it struck stainless steel.

∞

Rubaiyat lurked in the dark hall outside the culture room while Susmita finished the supper dishes. Her muscles were cramping, but she did not move until Susmita turned off the lights and went into her bedroom.

In the faint glow from beneath the bedroom door, Rubaiyat darted out and hid between the stove and trash compactor. She could just see the dark orifice of the hall and culture room door.

The phone felt heavy as a butcher knife in her hand.

Pipes gurgled as softly as blood flowing through arteries. The compactor's motor vibrated against Rubaiyat's spine. With a click, the dim light disappeared. And still Rubaiyat waited in a dark scented with saccharine Pop-Tarts.

Seven hundred and three heartbeats later, Susmita's door opened. Rubaiyat adjusted her grip on the phone.

Bare footsteps whispered out. Rubaiyat heard a heel thump, then the other foot oddly drag, like Susmita was favoring it.

The plastic streamers crackled. Rubaiyat stood, covering the phone's screen to mask its brightness until the right moment.

The motion-detector lights flickered in the culture room. Silhouetted through the plastic, the elderly woman fumbled with the scrubs hanging outside the room.

Contaminating those, too, Rubaiyat thought. She raised the phone, letting it autofocus. The silhouette shuffled to the door. On the screen, with the contrast maxed out, the woman's movements seemed oddly slow.

Familiar.

Rubaiyat's hand trembled. The phone chirped as it automatically halted the image capture.

The woman looked up. Her shadow approached the plastic. Rubaiyat retreated, trying to steady the phone. The streamers parted.

That's not Susmita.

The strange woman's head swiveled blindly. The light behind her highlighted the wrinkles of old age, the too-familiar, sickly yellow of her eyes.

Prions. The phone slipped and cracked on the floor. The woman swayed, apparently not seeing Rubaiyat. Her head still swiveling, she tied the drawstring of the scrub pants with the automatic movements of muscle memory.

Mrs. Mukherjee's words echoed in Rubaiyat's mind, *Our last vitrist… God knows where the old fool ran off to!*

"Vasudha," Rubaiyat whispered. The woman's head stilled and her expression grew more confused.

Rubaiyat glanced at her dropped phone; the chassis had chipped but the screen still glowed. She could capture Vasudha in her scrubs, clearly planning to enter the culture room. She could show the Mukherjees.

Except she was paralyzed, transfixed at the sight of Jaya's fate.

Vasudha's lips trembled, like worms shrinking from the sun. "Who's there?"

Rubaiyat looked at the phone. Then, she stepped over it, to meet those horrible, familiar yellow eyes, which held the past and the future.

No one would choose this fate. Not her parents. Not Vasudha. Not even foolish, grieving Jaya. Rubaiyat took another step towards Vasudha.

Crack. Susmita's door banged open. The kitchen exploded with greasy yellow light. Rubaiyat flinched and Vasudha wailed.

"Vasudha!" Susmita cried. Rubaiyat turned to her.

Surprise, relief, terror stuttered across Susmita's face. Her eyes flickered from Rubaiyat to the dropped phone, and then Susmita seized Vasudha's arm, pulling the woman behind her.

Rubaiyat stepped back, her eyes locked with Susmita's. But then the cook turned and tugged the scrubs over Vasudha's jutting ribs. Her expression was contorted with a sadness that Rubaiyat had often felt on her own face during those dark, midnight times when Jaya was out too long.

Except the gentle way Susmita adjusted Vasudha's scrubs wasn't like sisterly affection. It was more like the intimacy between Basu and his girlfriend. An intimacy colored with age, with experience, with secrecy. With anger and frustration and despair.

"I imagine you'll be rewarded for getting rid of us," Susmita said at last.

Rubaiyat looked at her. "Was it Vasudha who was contaminating my cultures?"

Susmita's knuckles whitened as she looped her arm around Vasudha. "No. The painkillers normally make her sleep. At least, she's too dazed to do anything more than toss about in bed and kick the wall. But they raised the price last time and..."

Vasudha squirmed in her lover's tight hold.

"Was it Basu," Rubaiyat said, "or you?"

Susmita looked up. Whatever she read in Rubaiyat's expression made her sigh. "You know, of course. That sonuvabitch practically dances through here, smeared with lipstick."

The elderly cook looked away. Pipes gurgled, muffled in the depths of the culture room.

"It was me," Susmita said.

"Why?"

"Basu found out about Vasudha," Susmita said. "He threatened to tell his grandmother... She'd throw us out if she knew Vasudha was infected."

"But why didn't you just leave?"

"You don't think I'm very smart, do you?" Susmita said. It was so close to what Jaya often said that Rubaiyat flinched, hearing her sister's defiant voice in Susmita's bitter one. "I've been trying to save up for light rail tickets to my niece in Nepal. But painkillers and diapers are so expensive… God knows, I've tried threatening Basu that I'd take pictures… but even if I told Mrs. Mukherjee, he'd still be her grandson, and we'd still be two old women out on the street." Her voice rose. "What other jobs are there where I could watch Vasudha? What would happen to her?"

"The same fucking thing that's going to happen to my sister," Rubaiyat said.

Susmita flinched.

Rubaiyat closed her lips, choking down the grief rising from her gut. *I wanted Jaya to go away, and now…*

The pipes quieted, leaving behind a thick silence. Vasudha's lips fluttered, shaping words that no longer existed in her dying brain.

"This was not my choice," Susmita said. "Basu…"

Rubaiyat laughed; Susmita flinched again. It was a mad laugh, like those from the prion-infected during the hysterical early stages of neurodegeneration.

"Right," Rubaiyat said. "Yes. Basu."

Basu. The word slid down her throat like gristle.

Basu. The word ricocheted about her mind.

Basu. The word collided with several of Susmita's words, as fresh and warm in her memory as newly-seeded progenitor cultures.

Rubaiyat stepped forward. She had tried playing it straight. She had tried to do her duty—to her parents, her sister, her school, her employer.

Fuck that. The thought was in Jaya's voice. *Fuck them all, Baiya.*

Rubaiyat met Susmita's gaze. "Did you actually take pictures?"

∞

The dead were waiting in the sitting room. Rubaiyat felt the gazes of those ancestral portraits, as cold as liquid nitrogen. Even the infant in the morph-portrait stared coldly as he grew to manhood.

Despite the glares of Mrs. Mukherjee's dead son and living grandson, Rubaiyat stood straight before the rosewood couch, conscious of the weight of her pocketed phone.

"Rubaiyat?" Mrs. Mukherjee said, putting down her phone. "Why aren't you working?"

Rubaiyat took a breath. "You promised to pay me on Thursday, Mrs. Mukherjee."

Mrs. Mukherjee looked irritated. "*After* the tenderloins."

"There won't be any tenderloins."

Beside Mrs. Mukherjee, Basu's face brightened.

In the eternity before his grandmother replied, Rubaiyat felt she could culture ten damned tenderloins.

"Why not?"

Rubaiyat glanced at her grandson. "Ask Mr. Mukherjee."

Mrs. Mukherjee turned to him. But Basu just shrugged, rolling his eyes. "I have no idea what she's talking about, Dida."

The brain-shaped charm tinkled on Mrs. Mukherjee's wrist as she turned back, her face darkening. "You will certainly not be paid, after shirking your duty and accusing my grandson—"

"You *will* pay me," Rubaiyat said. "You promised to while you were lecturing me about money. I did everything you asked. It is not my fault your grandson sabotaged my work to stop the marriage, because he already has a girlfriend."

Rubaiyat's heart raced as Mrs. Mukherjee turned again to Basu. Everything depended now on Basu; everything depended on him to continue lying to his grandmother.

"She's crazy, Dida," Basu said. "I said we shouldn't hire some university dropout off the internet!"

Dropout. The sitting room shrank to the culture room's dark hall. Her eyes never leaving Basu's, Rubaiyat took out her phone. Its screen winked on, displaying the images Susmita had forwarded after Rubaiyat had sworn to scrub their source data.

"I'm sending you proof," Rubaiyat said.

As her thumb pressed *Send*, the color drained from Basu's face. Mrs. Mukherjee lifted up her phone.

Her gasp knifed through the taut silence.

"You're seeing her again!" Mrs. Mukherjee said, hurling the phone to the ground. She grabbed her grandson's collar. "After the thousands I've spent on jewelry and phones and meat, you do this!"

"No! I…" Basu tried to pull away. "Those are old pictures!"

"You're wearing the polo shirt I bought you last week for the Khans' visit!" Mrs. Mukherjee's hand twisted the collar tight about his neck. With her free hand, she stabbed a finger at Rubaiyat and then the door. "You're fired! And you can damn well forget about getting paid!"

The Rubaiyat of merely one week ago would have fled.

But Rubaiyat thought now of her sister. Her frustrating, irresponsible sister, who ricocheted through life confident that Rubaiyat would always be there.

Rubaiyat took a breath of cold air. She would never break Jaya's confidence.

But oh, yes, they would have a *talk* when she got back to Hyderabad. Perhaps similar in volume to this one.

"You'll pay me," Rubaiyat said, "and pay me twice what I asked for *in cash.*" Mrs. Mukherjee's mouth gaped with surprise. "Or I'll send these pictures to the Khans."

The moment stretched thin and brittle in the cold air; the threat would be nothing if Mrs. Mukherjee called the police. If Mrs. Mukherjee accepted that Basu did not want the marriage.

Instead, her face as purple as a fresh bruise, Mrs. Mukherjee dropped Basu and snatched her purse. Out cascaded jewelry, phone chargers, bottles of anti-prion vitamins. Mrs. Mukherjee yanked cash out of her wallet and hurled the bills at Rubaiyat. They fluttered pathetically to the rug.

Her eyes never leaving Mrs. Mukherjee's, Rubaiyat gathered up the money. Then she looked down and counted it, using Basu's hitching sobs as her metronome. *Twenty-one, twenty-two...*

More than twice. Rubaiyat pocketed the money.

The portraits stared as she left the room, closing the door just as Basu started shouting, "I don't want to marry that Khan girl! I love Jenni—"

∞

The kitchen was quiet, the air redolent of spices and Pop-Tarts. Yellow light shone through Susmita's cracked door. Rubaiyat pushed it open and stood there, taking in the single bed, the stench of urine, the empty pill bottles.

Susmita sat on the bed beside an unconscious Vasudha.

When Susmita looked up, Rubaiyat took out the money and divided it. The woman's tiny hand trembled as she took the banknotes and counted them.

"You'll go to your niece," Rubaiyat said, pocketing her half. A statement, not a question.

"Yes." Susmita's knuckles whitened around the money. "And you'll return to your sister."

"Yes."

Susmita nodded. Her eyes returned to her lover, her expression suspended between anger and love and grief.

Rubaiyat closed the door. For the last time, she walked through the kitchen to the courtyard. The smoke-laden air, tinged with the burnt-blood smell of bleached cultures, seemed to follow as she stepped out into Calcutta. It trailed her as close as her own shadow as she followed the alley to the roads and the roads to the light rail and the light rail to university, Jaya, and life.

About the Author
Megan Chaudhuri

A toxicologist by training and a writer by inclination, Megan lives near Seattle with one husband and two cats. Her science fiction has been published in *Analog* and *Crossed Genres*, while her science non-fiction has appeared in *Slate* under her maiden name, Megan Cartwright.

Author Website: http://sciencebasedwriting.wordpress.com/

Whole Lives in Hammered Fragments
by James Beamon

In the narrow confines of the airlock, condemned men go mad.

The darkness is blacker than my ebony skin, certainly darker than the star-sprinkled space behind the doors. The abyssal kind of black that deepens, ripens, stands unopposed, until everything a man imagines, all the demons he conjures in his mind's eye are tangible.

Maybe I don't go mad. Definitely, I enjoy my time in the lock. I fly the Herschel Run between Ceres and Pallas again, Kelvin hot on my heels in his Corsair, every beautiful second stretched taut, a collection of successive infinities, my ghosts and demons vividly real. The airlock is the steel veil between two worlds, the closest I will ever get to the stars again. My time between worlds will last forever until, as it always does, it ends at Vesta. Perhaps thoughts like these are madness in themselves.

The lock opens, the doors splitting down the middle with a deafening crack. It is not the side with the unending vacuum and the promise of starlight. This side is full of harsh halogen-diode bulbs that make my eyes squint and leak tears. Two guards, their black uniforms pressed as if they could iron authority into every crease, toss me boots and the familiar yellow jumpsuit. They tell me to get dressed despite it being the only reasonable option I have. There's a distinction between my wanting something and them telling me to do it.

They escort me down the hall of the prison station. We walk through a decaying, windowless world of rusted cell bars and bent balcony rails four stories high. Every cell holds hushed men whose lives share the same ending. Water drips from the ceiling like tears. Steam pours out of vents in the floor as if to tell us that hell is only a flight of stairs below.

Here, adrift in space, dwell ragtag remnants of a war. Only the

Hegemony didn't call it war; wars are glamorous, glorious in hindsight. War would make us revolutionaries. The Hegemony called it the Piracy Years. There was no big secret why they called us pirates. Revolutionaries die martyrs for causes. Revolutionaries get reprieved when wars were over. Pirates live as criminals, serving sentences in penal ships on the outskirts of the Bracelet. Pirates get flushed like refuse out of airlocks.

They take me to the warden's office. My time in the lock has seen a new warden replace the one I remember. His mustache is thin, trimmed low with pencil sharp points that make him look like a cartoon villain. His expression is one of perfunctory indifference, an emperor addressing his subjects or a zookeeper feeding the animals.

"As I live and breathe, the legendary Marcus Lyons, in my office."

He looks me over, just like the last new warden had, probably wondering if all the things he has heard are capable in a frame so slight. I look around his office, trying to find something of substance to measure my time in the abyss besides the new face in front of me. A clock, a calendar. All I find is a coffee mug and a holographic vid stand of the warden and his wife dancing at their wedding.

"Is it true, what happened on Vesta?" he asks.

I say nothing. Truth is always stranger than fiction yet invariably fails to live up to myth. The Hegemony had already stripped me bare until only the myth remained. They would not deprive me of it.

"They say," the warden continues, "you did it because you were tired of the debate on which Lyons was the greatest pilot alive. Is it true?" he asks, his cartoon mustache curling up at the corners of his mouth as he smiles. "You can tell me. It's not like I can add time to a life sentence."

"Do you know what is certain, about the stories?" I ask, my voice hoarse from lack of use.

The warden shakes his head and leans forward, his eyes dancing like a kid looking at the lit candles of his own birthday cake.

"Now there's no debate on who's the greatest pilot alive."

The warden settles back into his chair, eyes me like I'm a waste of time, a waste of presence. It's a look all the guards grow for us; no doubt the warden spent some time in a perfectly creased uniform. "Aren't you curious as to why you're here, Marcus?"

I know why I'm there. I'm only a name when they want something from me. Something more than to see me froth at the mouth from suppression tazes, or stripped bare before they toss me in the lock. When they don't want anything, I'm just a number. I don't change my blank expression as I look at him. I know he'll tell me the particulars whether I'm curious or not.

"I'm about to offer you your one chance for freedom."

This breaks my demeanor in a hoarse croak of a laugh, exacerbated by rusty vocal cords.

"You and I both know the only freedom I'll find is when one of the guards 'accidentally' hits the outer door button the next time I'm in the airlock."

My voice is devoid of sarcasm. Back in the old days, before I was captured and Kelvin was dead, these kinds of accidents happened all the time as news drifted to peacekeepers and authorities of ship seizures which had left their friends and peers as forced labor or corpses drifting in space. The Hegemony has always been about an eye for an eye; a solar system full of floaters proves that.

"We need you to kill someone," the warden says.

"I'm not an assassin. You got the wrong guy." I have enough blood on my hands. Even though none of it is innocent, that doesn't mean that it still doesn't leave stains. There's a difference between a guy trying to survive in the deep and killing for profit. The Hegemony never understood the difference, never got that most of us were out there doing what we had to after they left us for dead.

I get up to leave. Leaving without permission almost always earns you a shock taze and time in the lock. But I have heard enough. And I welcome the lock; freedom can come any time.

Strangely, I do not feel the electric bite of a taze. The warden talks, his voice light as if he's having his say behind the biggest of grins.

"But you are the right guy. It takes a pirate to catch a pirate. And you've done it before, you see. We want you to kill your brother."

∞

Momma used to call the asteroid belt the Hammered Bracelet, said it was her favorite band of jewelry. She'd point to the sky on those nights when a white glow tinted the heavens and afforded the Red Planet looming above our heads a majestic, shining halo. "God's hammering at the Bracelet again," she'd say, the creases around her mouth curving up into a smile. She was full of smiles back then, the contagious ones that made Kelvin and me split our lips to reveal tiny tic-tac teeth.

We learned later it was zodiacal light, created from the dust clouds of asteroid collisions, but as kids we would look through the domed glass of Stickney Crater Colony and really imagine a giant man just beyond our sights with a hammer and a forge, remaking the universe right before us if we could only get off this moon to see him working.

But nothing easily escaped Phobos, not even wishful thinking. The high hopes for Mars' moon and its supply of helium-3 died within the first decade of colonization. The gas died first, about six years after the glass domes sprang up like boom towns for new gold, an energy abundance grossly exaggerated by venture capitalists and investors hungry for quick profits on fusion fuel. The optimism of colonists, who believed the investors of Phobos would convert it into something worthwhile, that lingered on, refusing to die when the helium evaporated.

Momma believed Phobos was salvageable. "If we can't mine H-three, bring it in," she said. "Turn this moon into a filling station.

A scenic rest stop. Look at that view," she pointed up at the sky, eyes dancing as she took in the looming, fiery red sphere of Mars. On its surface, the crystalline glass of burgeoning cities like New Olympus and Greater Cydonia sparkled back like pinprick jewels. "Where else can you find that?" she'd ask.

I agreed because she was Momma and hell, she could say no wrong. If she said there was a giant, bearded dude in a robe hammering on jewelry a few miles out, then I'm sure he was on the job. I had no doubt Phobos would work as a lopsided sphere of a gas station.

But the investors forgot about Phobos. The streaking light of ships, like shooting stars across our dusty glass domes, told the tale of the new Manifest Destiny, as these ships blazed trails to Europa and Callisto and Titan and Triton. Better moons, richer moons, resplendent orbs that lay ever closer to the promise of human life outside of Sol.

Momma still believed change was coming. I think clinging to that belief partly killed her. The alternative, to face the fact that she had brought herself and her two young sons to a place whose golden promise had withered away to leave nothing but a glass tomb, was hard to stomach.

I believed with her, until I couldn't anymore.

∞

"You've gone soft in here, Lyons. Weak." The guard talks casual-like as he walks beside me, escorting me to the cruiser waiting at the prison docks. "Your brother, he's going to blow your ship apart." From the corner of my eye, I see his grin grow as he thinks about it. "Blast your bitch ass into frozen meat cubes drifting through the belt."

"Maybe so," I say, walking in a swagger step because of the leg chains. The promise of leaving this prison alive is still too surreal for me to invest in. Besides, it's a Hegemony promise, worth as much as the dirt on Phobos. Instead I invest in my anger, as thick and real as these chains, a reactionary rage triggered by this guard with the gall to speak to me about my brother.

"I was gonna be courteous," I tell him. "You know, steer around all the Hej goons the Lyonpryde left floating out there. But see, you messed that up. Now I think I'll just plow through your old buddies."

He swivels on a dime, brings his knee up into my solar plexus. It's the most effective retort a guard can give and the only response I have is a clinking of chains as I fall to my knees, blinking through tears and spasms as I fight to get wind back.

"Just as I said," the guard says over me. "Weak."

He hauls me to my feet and I stumble awkwardly in the chains as he pushes me forward. I have learned in my time here if a guard wants to fuck you up, he or she will fuck you up. Nothing short of murder stops it, so you may as well earn your lumps. I earned that knee, which is the only solace I can take as I walk off the pain enough to breathe again.

At the end of the hallway, the guard waves his biochipped hand, opening the doors which separate the prison proper from the gangway leading to the docks. I stop short, my breath taken away just as surely as if I had another knee delivered to my gut.

The gangway is the invisible floor of a bridge tunnel, all of it made of transparent acrylics and quartz glass. Stars surround me, no longer light I have to imagine in the darkness of an airlock. I drink in their different intensities, glimmering, winking like knowing eyes. I am barely aware of the guard's prodding as I walk among their celestial fire.

"Can you fly a Croix de Guerre light cruiser?" the guard asks.

"What do you think?"

"I think you better answer the question, convict."

"If it's a standard Croix, with a single Ambient fusion engine accompanied by a backup ion drive, then yes. If it's using a solar thermal engine with uranium fission backup, a configuration called the Dirty

Cross, then yes. If it's using twin Ambient minis, known as the Double Cross and my personal favorite, then yes."

I hold my shackles up to eye level so he can unlock them. "I'm Marcus goddamn Lyons." If he has any other questions about what I can fly, that should answer it.

I am either pushing my luck or earning my lumps, the difference sometimes being sliver thin. The guard grabs my shackles in a violent snatch, pulling me close to his face. His lip curls up into a sneer.

"Not for much longer. Soon all you'll be is so much frozen meat debris."

He speaks his personal authorization number, which, coupled with the biochip in his hand, unlocks the shackles. He gathers the chains and retreats the way we came, leaving me alone in a twinkling sea of stars.

For long moments I just stand there, taking in infinite space all around me. Ever since Kelvin and I escaped Phobos, *this*—being among the stars—has always meant freedom. We were a reflection of space and its promise. Our skin, dark like the pitch of the vacuum, our eyes twinkling like distant stars and both of us with fire in our gut running hotter than our nuclear engines, hotter than the sun.

Kelvin. The cost of freedom was always too steep.

∞

Momma paid for our freedom when we were teenagers, years after the currency on Phobos had changed. Money was still money, would always be money, whether it was Hegemony sterlings or Caliphate shekels or Eastern Coalition yuan. But sterlings or shekels or yuan were no longer within reach, not even for hands as outstretched as ours. And *currency*, the medium of exchange between people, became less paper bills and digital credits to the things that grew like weeds in places that lay dying and discarded at the fringes of society. Skills. Favors. Bodily fluids.

Kelvin and I never asked what Momma's currency was. And we

were thugs. No one dared tell us. It was hard enough seeing what her currency charged her, seeing the flattening of her smile, the light in her eyes dimming to dying embers.

I pretended not to notice. I focused on honing my skills. Lock picking, pickpocketing, fighting, strong-arming. I was good at it. And Kelvin? He was even better.

Then came a time when I couldn't pretend to not notice Momma. She never came home again for me to pretend. Her body never emerged from a forgotten alleyway or got pulled from a trash disposal unit. She just wasn't anymore, her fate forever a question.

"It was us," Kelvin said looking up at the dome, the night sky beyond obscured by the grime coating the glass—the film from a thousand methane and coal fires our overtaxed air recyclers would never fully purify. Kelvin wore his hair half in neat braided rows, the other half unbraided and erupting from his head like a black sunburst. "She left because of us."

Even though he was only thirteen, I had gotten used to looking at Kelvin as a man. He was one for as much as he'd seen and done. Hearing him talk like this showed me that there was a part of him Phobos hadn't toughened to gristle.

At that moment, he was a kid, hurt and scared. Betrayed by one of the few things he had placed faith in. I did what a big brother does.

"Are you crazy? No way she'd leave," I told him. Never mind that I entertained the same notion, that our descent into crime had broken Momma's heart so many times we had finally driven her from us.

Sometimes, a woman's body was the only ticket off Phobos. Long haul mining crews occasionally stopped by our domes before setting out to work the Bracelet for months on end. Out there, where the amounts of procured helium-3 dictated what a miner made and ever dwindling reserves of food, water and renewable oxygen limited mining time, no one took on passengers. Except a woman, the burden of her food, water and air shared among the crew in exchange for the obvious. It wasn't easy or dignified work, but after months on her back, she'd find herself in New Olympus or on Old Earth complete with the opportunities that came with it.

"Fucking miners," I spat. "Think they can treat us like trash. Or worse yet, those sick tourists, who come here looking for little girls, or young guys like us until we leave them with cracked skulls and empty wallets. I can see any of them wanting a Phobos souvenir."

I don't know if I was talking to convince Kelvin or to convince myself, but I know I got angry. And I kept talking, about the bootleggers who came to skirt customs, the junkmen who traded broken, antiquated air and water purifiers for exorbitant prices, the drug dealers who brought in crystalline, brimstone coke, and amp while taking payment from our women and what little we could pawn. My rage boiled over. I wanted blood.

"Get everyone," I said to Kelvin.

For most of the guys, our crew was the only family they had. Now it was the only family Kelvin and I had too. I was done with Phobos, done with the loamy methane stink of it all. Once we got the whole crew and explained our haphazard plan, nobody opted out. We made our way, twenty-two strong, with faces grim enough to make people turn the other way when they saw us coming through their dilapidated street. We leapt and bound through the low gravity, kicking up the chalky moon dust with our harsh landings and hurried launches. The dust particles hung listlessly, stuck in the air as if suspended in time.

The spaceport was the only place under The Sticks that had any decent security, the one rule of law necessary for the steady flow of black market money. Keep the ships landing, full of their drugs and worthless junk and pedophiles.

But where there's corruption, there are cracks. And cracks could be widened when you apply enough skill. We could widen them; skills were our currency.

We got access through the public yards, where the junkmen stored their wares. Security was the lightest there, it being cheaper to write off stolen merchandise than to pay for the extra security of the private stockyards. We crept through endless rows of stockpiled machinery: refrigerators, sonic plows, purifiers and disposers, piled high without any discernible order. After dodging a couple half-assed patrolmen, we made the perimeter fence, where Kelvin worked with Beagle and Steve to break codes for the gate's suppression barrier.

I got impatient, seeing the well-lit, well-maintained equipment shining like new beyond the gate while watching them fail again and again on the codes. As we huddled in silence, my thoughts went to Momma, murdered or taking on a ship full of miners just to get away from us. I didn't know which one was worse; I just knew I'd be damned if I sat there dwelling in it.

I took Primus and Jones with me, the most levelheaded dudes in our crew. We doubled back, found one of those patrolmen. I snuck up behind him and before he knew what time it was, I had him in a chokehold.

I didn't bother negotiating with him for codes. He wasn't scared of street toughs; he was scared of failing the people who paid him to keep trash like us out.

"Strip his gear," I said while the patrolman gasped and clawed at the arm bar around his throat. Wordlessly, Jones ripped the comms off his ear and belt, Primus took his suppression tazer.

I dragged the patrolman to the fence line, choking him the whole way. By the time we got back, they had only gotten through half the codes.

"Open up," I said as I took my arm away from his throat enough for him to breathe.

"Go to hell, boy," he spat.

"That doesn't sound like the code to me," I said, pointing at the still locked gate. Without ceremony, I shoved him into the fence. The guard's body tensed up as the defense mechanisms kicked in, filling the air with an ionic buzz that made the hair on the back of my neck stand on end.

"Keep plugging at the codes," I told Kelvin, Beagle and Steve, who had stopped their hacking to watch the stuttering, twist-jerk movements of the guard stuck on the fence.

After half a minute, the fence knocked the guard away. He collapsed on his back, the saliva in his mouth cooked to a white froth. I hauled him up and shoved him back in for Round Two.

Suppression fences were supposed to be nonlethal. Mr. Guard was going to test the limits of that claim. Either the gate was going to break under our hacking or the guard was going to break under the fence. It didn't matter to me which.

Kelvin managed to knock down another cipher wall by the time Round Two was over. Mr. Guard managed to squeak out an "I don't know" and a shake of his head before I shoved him back into the gate. Apparently, the fence gave the guard a little insider information during Round Three because he came away from his suppression treatment suddenly knowing the access codes. He started mumbling the digits just as the gate slid open, the last cipher knocked down by Kelvin and his hackers.

"What do we do now?" Kelvin asked, looking at the open gate as if he didn't believe we'd get this far.

"Some bootleggers landed moonside yesterday in a tetra-kite," I said, letting the guard in my grasp collapse in a heap. "We sneak aboard. We take over."

"We'll need them to fly us out. What if they refuse?" Kelvin asked.

I looked at my little brother as serious as life could get.

"We don't need them. We don't need anyone any more except each other." I reached over to Primus, pulled the guard's suppression tazer from his hand and held it at eye level.

"We either learn to fly it or die trying."

∞

The Hej monkeys who put this mission together read my file at least. They provided my favorite Guerre, a twin Ambient Double Cross. Seeing irony in this is like seeing yellow in sunlight. As I ease into the oiled leather of the pilot's seat, I realize I don't care. My eyes find comfort in the returning familiarity of the steel dials and switches, my nostrils fill with the subtle hints of shellac and alcohol in the treated polymer fixtures. I peer over the dashboard. An infinite universe of stars sparkle, like a lover's eyes looking back at me.

I imagine this is what coming home feels like.

"Cleared for departure," a man's voice chimes over the Interstel link.

"Acknowledged." I look at the port and aft camera feeds, where my ship is attached to the misshapen gray blotch of prison station. Jupiter dominates the backdrop of space behind the ship, the regal giant's red eye casting its roving, disapproving glare over us all.

"You had best acknowledge everything, Marcus Lyons," the Interstel voice says. The smugness dripping over the words forms an image in my mind and I see the new warden's cartoon mustache curving up with self-satisfied pomp. "Last thing any of us wants is for you to get amnesia or, worse, turn clever."

I recall the failsafes he briefed me on when I agreed to this. I couldn't help but remember… after he explained the mission the bastard threw me back into the airlock while the countermeasures to my cleverness were being installed.

"If I try to fly in any direction except toward the belt, the ship will explode. Once I'm in the belt, if I fly out of it, the ship will explode. My Interstel is being monitored. If I try to signal my brother or have some other heart-to-heart that doesn't involve his ship getting blown apart, I win a prize. That prize is my ship exploding," I finish, repeating the spiel verbatim. Time in the lock spent to good use.

"Good, good," the Interstel chimes as I see the prison release its magnetic docking locks, causing my ship to free drift. "Go show us some of that Lyonpryde magic."

The cockpit fills with the whine of energy building as the engines come to life. I pull away from the dock, fighting the urge to turn my ship and empty my payload into the prison station's control tower. I figure I'm faster than the warden and his self-destruct button, but why risk it? Right now, I want the same thing he wants.

Kelvin is dead, no matter how often they speak his name. The thought of someone pretending to be my brother, of using his legacy instead of creating their own sickens me. Whoever's out there in the belt evoking the Lyons name to instill fear is about to learn wrath follows.

Once outside Jupiter's gravity well, the flight to the Hammered Bracelet is fast and nostalgic. It is familiar country. The swath of space between Mars and Jupiter had belonged to us. Before I know it I am in the belt, navigating past the Four Sisters towards denser formations, old haunts and hideouts.

In its heyday, the belt hosted several clans—the Lyonpryde and the Neo-drakes, Spacer Mongols and al-Ghouti. Now all the clans had been cowed—killed, scattered, imprisoned—and only ghosts live in the Bracelet.

I almost don't see the Interdictor until it's too late. The Hegemony's flagship fighter darts out from a crater of a drifting asteroid, fearsome looking, a blue-steel moth with the face of a bear trap. The ship banks one way while the missile it fires banks opposite.

The One-Man Pincer. It is Kelvin's signature move. If you move towards the missile to dodge, you'll find out it's a proximity activated charge when it blows. Move opposite and you'll have an enemy ship barreling down at you, its guns already trained on you and ready to blast while you're still recovering.

There's only one method I've ever found to evade the Pincer. I pull back on the stick, exposing my underbelly as I smash the emergency reverse button. Instead of going either toward the missile or toward the hostile ship, I drop down and out. After a few tense moments of flying backwards, the Interdictor appears on my display.

My thumb automatically glides over the fire button at the sight of the Hegemony's most feared killing machine. My display chimes in response; all I need is two seconds to get a lock on it.

He fights like Kelvin, but this can't be Kelvin, not flying a Hej warship. The Interdictor is changing direction, trying in vain to reacquire me before I get a lock. My fingers twitch. My display is a half second from blaring confirmation that my target is acquired.

I push my stick up and my ship swings forward, breaking sights on target. I gun my accelerator, my Guerre charging away from battle, deeper into the belt. I don't know if that's Kelvin flying an Interdictor, but I know how to find out.

The asteroids are virtually worlds away from one another until a person starts traveling at these speeds. At half or three-quarters *hiz*, the rocks in the belt move at a near blur, a constant assault. It is the Herschel Run all over again, with Kelvin eating away at my heels. It must be Kelvin because he doesn't miss a single beat. I can't help but smile with glee, the adrenaline surging as we race through the rocks.

I go through the familiar turns, the spins and vaults. Just like when I pretend in the lock, the seconds stretch, each one taut. I lose myself in the infinite.

As it always does, it ends in Vesta. A botched heist on the mining station, a setup really. Hej ships above us, ready to blow the whole place to hell. Kelvin and I, two wanted men with one escape pod between us.

I looked at my little brother and I remember telling myself he had changed. He had grown bloodthirsty, cruel, dangerous in the course of this war. But it was bullshit. He had grown hard, same as me, but the truth, the one waiting for me to discover in the darkness of the lock years later, is I was selfish. I was tired, tired of being a big brother and looking out for him. I wanted something for me. I wanted to live.

That's when the butt of my gun struck the back of his head. Moments later I hurtled through space in the pod as Hegemony ships rained salvo after salvo down on the station.

The memory stings as I fly, distracts me enough to nearly crash into one of Hygiea's Disciples. I cut my engines. His flying is unmistakable, but it is not the Herschel Run all over again. It is time I pay him what I owe.

His ship races in front of me, swivels and stops. The ship just hovers, making no move to fire. My Interstel crackles.

"Marcus?"

My display blares the sound of an acquired lock. Missiles from my ship's underbelly answer his question, missiles I didn't fire. I shout Kelvin's name like that will warn him, staring helpless as I watch them fly to blow his ship apart.

The missiles explode before impact, releasing electronic displacement charges. It looks like an angry lightning storm. The lightning ripples across Kelvin's ship. Moments later, the engine dies and the ship begins to drift.

"Convict 174557E, what did we tell you about heart-to-hearts?" the voice of the warden comes through the speakers.

"Why the hell didn't you tell me he was flying an Interdictor?

Or that you're controlling my missiles?"

"Who are you that I have to explain anything? A convict pilot?" the warden asks. "You're lucky you're still useful. Retrieval ships are en route. Monitor the Interdictor and shoot again if its electrical systems appear to come back online. Acknowledge."

I stare at the helpless Hej ship, looking as lifeless as the small asteroids listing around us.

"You're two blinks close to freedom, convict. Better swallow your conscience. Now acknowledge."

"Marc?" Kelvin's voice comes as a hush through the Interstel, sounding confused and weak.

"Sorry it has to be this way, Kelvin," I reply. "Trust me; the next missile will hurt me more than it'll hurt you."

"That's what I like to hear," the warden says. "That sounds like a free man talking."

What the warden doesn't know is the code Kelvin and I have. He doesn't even catch on when I set my missile bay to autofire in three minutes.

Getting shot out of a missile tube is suicidal. The loader isn't set to handle delicate payloads like people, so the probability of the spacesuit getting ripped is quite high. Factor that in with the disorienting, nausea-inducing thrust and it was certifiably crazy. It was one of the reasons the Lyonpryde was so respected and feared.

It is only after I have been successfully launched from the bay, fighting nausea while praying the loader didn't make any microleaks, that the warden catches the meaning behind my words to Kelvin. The ship explodes behind me, but it is too far away, too late. The force of it only pushes me faster to Kelvin's ship, where the airlock is sitting open, waiting for me to enter. The airlock closes behind me and I enter a dark ship. I head to the bridge, guided by wan, flickering lights. I enter the bridge and my heart jumps into my throat.

Kelvin. My brother is silver bones and dark flesh protruding out of a steel captain's chair. The chair is fused along his spine, neck, the back of his head, fitted with dials and lights and exotic wiring. Kelvin is a skull of erupting wires and mechanical eyes, lidless, staring at me as I gape at him. His face is locked into a grinning rictus.

"It's good to see you, Brother." The words don't come from my brother's smiling, open mouth but from the Interstel speakers around us.

"Jesus, Kel…" I say looking at the seamless fusion of man and ship. "What happened?"

"If I could shrug I would," the Interstel says. "I remember Vesta then falling. After that, dreams. Lots of dreams. Some of them good, like the Pallas Run, the Danbury Heist. Mostly bad. A lot of dogfighting, Hej but not Hej, not really… more like wars with smudges and smears. One day I woke up from the bad dreams, into this chair. The real nightmare."

"Marcus Lyons," the warden's voice comes in over Kelvin's. "You need to stand down while we complete retrieval of our Interdictor. In fact, you will wait outside the ship. Failure to do so will be taken as hostile."

"Interdictor? You mean my brother, you bastard? Are all your Interdictors like this… host to captured, programmed men?"

I already know the answer. So this was how the Hegemony won the war. It takes a pirate to catch a pirate. They used insiders to discover our hideouts and headquarters, flush out the smuggler dens and chase down the supply runners adept at hiding among the rocks.

Only Kelvin's programming failed. He had become himself again. They wanted him back and that's where I came in: the best pilot alive versus the best pilot that ever died.

"Stand down, Lyons," the warden repeats.

"Don't let them get me, Marcus," Kelvin says, "You can't imagine the pain, the trapped feeling… like being on Phobos with no end in sight."

"There's your answer Warden, straight from your Interdictor," I say. I look at my brother. "Block his feed, Kel."

It's all talk if I can't get him out of this. "Can you fly?"

"I'm afraid not, Brother. The electrical systems are down outside of battery backup. They're coming back online, but it will be at least twenty minutes."

Getting those twenty minutes would be nothing short of a modern miracle. Hej ships close distance rapidly. I look at his display and see a dozen blips in the periphery.

"Unknowns approaching," Kelvin says. "Fourteen minutes out."

"I can shoot us out manually," I say. "What are you armed with?"

"HX missiles. Six left. Not enough."

I look out of the bridge window as if the rock fragments drifting in their lazy orbit have an idea for me. There's freedom here, always has been among the scattered hosts of the Hammered Bracelet. My brother says their programming is the opposite of freedom, tantamount to life under the glass dome of Stickney Crater. It is something I will not abide.

"We've got enough missiles for the *delubrum incendia*," I say. It was a derelict ship tactic I developed and Kelvin named back when he was learning Latin. I couldn't remember what *delubrum* meant, but *incendia*, that was something no one forgot after they saw the maneuver.

"Yes, the shrine was always fun," Kelvin says. "Are you sure?"

"Give me a little of your battery backup power," I answer. "Light the way to your missile bay."

The lights make the trips back and forth from missile bay to bridge manageable, my hands full of equipment, my rush making my breath fog against my helmet's faceplate. If the Hej knew what I was capable of they'd keep their distance. But they don't, which makes my plan perfect.

The Hegemony never understood our premium on freedom, anything about us really. Maybe that's why they developed the Interdictor, to bridge the gap just enough to end the people on the other side of the bridge. I look out of the window, at the approaching Hegemony ships, almost close enough to board us. Maybe it is too much to ask that the warden was on one of them, but I ask for it anyway. I'd love to show him some Lyonpryde magic.

"I'm sorry," I say to Kelvin, "about what happened back on Vesta."

"Funny," he says, "I can't remember a time when I haven't forgiven you."

There is nothing else to say. I look around the room at a bridge littered with wires running through reappropriated HX missile warheads. My thumb glides over the detonator.

This time, I do what a big brother does.

About the Author
James Beamon

James Beamon writes stories because he doesn't have the operational budget to make the movie version. Knowing a lil' something about computers has gotten him deployed to Iraq and Afghanistan, where things got a bit scary. Currently he's living with his wife and son in Northern Virginia, where the traffic's even scarier. He's still on a quest to take over page one of Google when you type his name but sucky other Beamons keep making headlines for criminal acts. He blogs about his angst for other James Beamons along with whatever else he's getting into.

Author Website: http://fictigristle.wordpress.com/

End of My Rope
by Holly Schofield

Poig pushed his snout in my face. "Cap'n Janny, ma'am, you can't sell the cats into slavery! You can't!"

I shoved him to one side. As a member of the Nancy species, he's only half my petite sixty-kilogram mass. "Stand down, Ensign. I can and I will." I stuck the guidestick against the collar of the nearest cat as if I was wielding an épée, and the electronic tip secured itself with a satisfying *click*. The cat twisted around on the floor, then stared balefully at me in defeat.

Yesterday evening, the reek of a malfunctioning litter bot in the cargo hold had permeated through the ship right up to the bridge. Cleanup had fallen to Ensign Poig, the sole crew member on my ship's inaugural voyage. I'd felt sorry for him at the time. Nancies have a stronger sense of smell than us humans.

I didn't feel sorry for him now.

I'd woken up this morning with a furry cat butt on my face and another cat playing with the 2D photo of my Ontario apartment back on Terra. I snatched the photo away before the scratches could turn it to shreds. In ten steps, I was at Poig's sleeping compartment. I pounded a fist on the door controls and waited impatiently for it to slide open.

"Why?" I asked. "Why would you let all one hundred units of my shipment loose!"

Poig had sat up in his bunk, rubbing his eyes. "Units? They're intelligent creatures!" He twitched a hind leg. "I felt sorry for them. Caged below decks, shortly to be enslaved to Yoogles."

Cats, small pointy-eared quadrupeds of the genus *Felis*, had scattered to every room on my ship. For the past hour, Poig and I had been trying to round them up. For some reason, herding them hadn't worked too well. I rubbed a bloody scratch on my hand. By now, I really needed coffee. Coffee *and* some bandages.

I used the guidestick to drag the snarling tabby down the ramp to the cargo hold and into the nearest cage. Never mind that the beast's collar said a different crate number. The Yoogles weren't known for checking details—just for slaughtering couriers who failed to deliver on time. A close-up of the devil-horned Yoogle I'd made the deal with flashed before my mind, but I firmly dismissed the image. *Real* captains didn't quake in their boots.

I slammed the cage door on the spitting cat. This was going to take hours, especially when it almost seemed like the cats were working together. I turned to get another one.

Poig was right behind me, standing erect, hopping from one hind foot to the other, pink tongue poking out between his canines. His bristly fur rasped against his jumpsuit, the *shushushu* sound grating on my nerves as much as the hissing that came from the creature he clutched to his chest.

"Cap'n!" He sucked in a breath.

"Ensign." I cut him off. "If you don't want to be left behind when we get to Crogan, you will quit pretending to capture these units when you are really standing around rubbing their fur. And I mean ASAP, as in *right now!*"

Poig stopped polishing the cat with his fuzzy, four-fingered hand. I thought he was going to whimper but he only muttered, "ASAP, a-sap, who's a sap?" before holding the hissing animal out to me.

Now I was the one hesitating. Just how sharp were those units' claws? And how had I gotten into this mess in such a short time? Only a month ago, I'd had a quiet life with a quiet Terran desk job.

The cat hissed at me again. There was no choice but to forge ahead;

too much was riding on this shipment. My firm grip wasn't appreciated but with much spitting and screeching, along with a few growls from me, one more cat was re-caged a few minutes later.

Only ninety-eight more to go.

As I peeled cats from the galley cupboards, from under the sickbay stretcher, and from my captain's chair on the bridge, I practised my deep breathing exercises. What had Poig been thinking, releasing them all?

The augmentation chip insertion process that had *raised* Poig from a Level Three intelligence—about as smart as a monkey, say—to a Level Four, well, it wasn't a perfect science. Poig's implant as a teenager might bring him on par with an unaugmented human from the last century, and make him a decent mechanic, but it was well-documented that each of the Common Worlds' sentient species reacted differently to chip implants. Raised Nancies, in particular, had some really odd quirks. With Poig, it seemed to manifest as being both a scatterbrain and a logophile—a lover of words and wordplay. His choice of name said it all, although I never quite understood why he felt being raised was imbued with poignancy.

But as a new captain operating on a budget so small it should have the prefix "nano" attached, I couldn't be choosy about my only crew member. Poig would work for room, board, and occasional cookies from the special container in my quarters. And he was pretty good at overhauling the worn-out engine. So far, a week into our voyage, the arrangement had worked out well. Other than him letting loose half of our cargo, that is. Fortunately, he hadn't touched the other half: a load of augmentation chips, the pricey plug-and-play kind. If I could deliver both shipments intact and on time, my burgeoning career would be launched.

By lunchtime, with phenomenal effort on my part and phenomenal reluctance on Poig's part, we'd captured ninety units. One had been hiding in the spacesuit rack, behind the helmet I hoped I would never have to use. Such odd creatures, these cats, as alien to me as the

Dendrite Colony on Varga III.

I found the ninety-first unit, glaring at me behind some equipment in an engine room storage locker, but, as I turned my back to get my guidestick, the white short-haired monster vanished.

I'd been lucky to get this order, my first from the Yoogle planet, and I didn't want to mess it up. Rumor among us captains is that one successful delivery to the Yoogles sets you up for life: more orders follow on a regular basis. On the other hand, if you piss them off—well, some rumors it's better not to listen to.

I stepped through the cargo bay door into an audio onslaught of wailing and moaning from the ninety captured units. A brown tail swished past me and disappeared around the back of a crate, the special crate that held the oh-so-important augmentation chips. Poig and I had loaded it oh-so-gently last week, putting it in the middle of the cargo bay floor. I circled it, warily.

No cat, just some brown fluff swirling in the breeze created by the air vents. The crate, however, looked different than yesterday morning when I'd last admired it.

I beeped Poig through my collar stud. He was at the far end of the cargo hold, but he couldn't hear me over the cacophony. He quickly put down the striped cat he'd been rubbing—what *was* the appeal of that?—and trotted over.

"The crate's tipped over. And it looks like it's been opened a bit. I'll pry the side open a bit more and you grab the cat that must be inside, okay?" I didn't wait for an answer. The side, or rather, the lid, came off with a screech of plastic fasteners. Two cats, one beige and one of an orangey color I think is called marmite, jumped out and sped away.

"Poig! I said to grab them!" I glanced up at him, irritated. He stood with the guidestick still upright, his ears drooping.

"There's something I have to tell you, Cap'n."

"I don't have time for this, Poig." I rubbed my bald head, which I'd shaved smooth last week, like real captains did. "I'm at the end of my rope. We need to find the ten missing cats! And we can't be late delivering the chips on Crogan."

"End of your rope? Is that the idiom about the goat and the tether?" He screwed up his mouth. "Or is it the one about dangling from a cliff, awaiting rescue?"

"It's the one about frustration. If I had a rope right now, I'd use it to hang you from the cargo hooks," I said with enough menace he took a step back.

"Cap'n Janny—"

"Let me spell it out for you," I said. Then I held up a hand at his expression. "No, no, there's no real spelling involved. Just some simple steps. First, we need to get to Crogan Base and hand over this chip delivery before refueling and heading to Yoogle. The Yoogles are important for future dealings, and you know we don't want to irritate them…" I paused so we both could shudder. "These five hundred chips are our livelihood for the next few months. I haven't told you, but I managed to buy the chips outright at a really good discount. I own them. We're not just going to be a courier… we're going to be in the merchandising business." I paused again so I could replay the beauty of that sentence in my head. "Every chip means we get to keep eating and have fuel for *Calamity Jane*."

"About the chips, Cap'n." If he'd been wearing a hat, he would have taken it off and twisted it in his hands just about now.

"What? What about the chips? They're right…" I looked closer. Fifty rows of ten chips, stored in plastic formfitting slots. Except… one row was empty. There were only four hundred and ninety chips. "Huh? The cats wouldn't eat them, would they? Where would they have gone?"

I looked around as if the chips would be piled on the deck in plain sight. The white cat must have been sitting beside me for the past few minutes. He lashed his tail and cocked his head. It occurred to me he wasn't wearing a collar. He canted his neck again, stretching it away from me. A raw and barely sealed red slit sat at the base of his skull, about five centimeters long.

Just the length someone would slice if they were inserting an augmentation chip. The plug-and-play kind of chip that anyone with at least four fingers could insert.

Poig looked at his feet, guilt all over his fuzzy face.

"Oh," I said.

There was nothing more to say.

∞

Later, I found plenty more to say.

"Poig, you know you've violated several laws on several planets as well as interplanetary statutes up the ying-yang? You know you've ruined our income? If we can't sell the chips and buy fuel at Crogan, we won't make our run to Yoogle on time. And what are we going to deliver? The one hundred cats they requested to serve as lap companions to their princesses? Or ninety cats and ten Level Three intelligences who need much more stimulation and education? Now *that's* slavery." I paused to take a breath and a gulp of coffee. My troubles were piling up. I paced the length of the bridge—which took all of four steps.

When would I adjust to the lack of space on the ship? I'd hung herbs in the galley and put pictures on the walls last week when we'd launched. I hadn't felt homesick then but now I wanted to hang my head out a window and scream for a while. Trouble was, the nearest window was light-years away.

On my third round, I skidded forward, banging a hip on the edge of the console. The puddle of cat urine hadn't been there a moment ago. I grabbed a tissue and slapped it onto the floor, letting Poig whimper as

I forbade him to move. His instinct to help was so strong that, hopefully, watching me would be more punishment than doing the actual cleaning. On hands and knees, scrubbing madly, I despaired that the tissue's built-in nanos wouldn't be powerful enough to get the acrid stink out. When I'd switched careers, this had not been how I had imagined a ship's captain spent her days.

Poig was still clutching his stomach. "Am I sorry? No, I'm not sorry. In fact," Poig said, his voice rising as he stumbled his way through a little speech he'd obviously prepared. "What I'm sorry for is that you don't seem to understand what raising does to a person. The cats deserve to be as intelligent as they can be. And free."

"Free? In deep space on our little ship? In what sense are they free?"

"They're free-er, or is it free-ish? More free-ish?" Poig was distracting himself yet again. "Maybe if you had been augmented later in life, like me, rather than as a baby, you would understand the concept a bit more."

I ground my teeth, loud enough to drown out the caterwauling from the lower level. "No one is free, Poig. No one. Anyhow, now that you've raised the ten cats to a Level Three, what are you expecting?" I'd never heard of a cat getting augmented; I'd never even *seen* one until last week. Cats were rare, having fallen out of favor in the Common Worlds decades ago. I'd try to research why that had happened, to no avail. Now, as I swiped the floor with the disgusting tissue, I could make a decent guess.

Species that started with higher intelligence didn't get quite such an advantage from the chips. The HighMind—the aliens that gave the chips to the Common Worlds—had hinted in their cryptic way that it was some kind of law of diminishing returns. A human usually went from a Five to a Five-point-two; slightly more if the augmentation was done at birth as mine thankfully had been. There were exceptions: some humans became geniuses, others became vid-fanatics and fun-junkies. I tossed the sodden tissue in the recycler. For less intelligent creatures, like the cats, the chips usually shifted them up just one level, so the cats presumably had gone from a Two to only a Three—but, like with humans, there was no real way to know.

Poig was talking. "Um, I guess I didn't think it through." He hung his head. "That *is* one of my weaknesses, postaugmentation."

I'd never seen him so downcast. Maybe I should have chosen a more logical crew member, an Ursinian, for instance, or a Hellmuncher; neither one would make such bad decisions. Kill me in my sleep, maybe, but bad decisions, no. I sighed. Maybe I should have stayed an accountant on Terra; this whole courier-merchant business was perhaps too risky for my blood. Better to be earthbound and dying a slow death. A fast death via Yoogle-anger was holding less and less appeal.

"Well," I said, "I'll think about what to do. Meanwhile, we continue to gather up the remaining cats." I drained my cup.

"At least," Poig said with a small and crafty smile, "there's no unaugmenting them."

I slapped the console, narrowly avoiding an accidental course change. "Good idea! That's exactly what we're going to do. Unaugment them."

"Cap'n!" Poig's ears quivered. "It's against interplanetary, interspecies law! You said so yourself!"

"There's only you and me to know differently. I'm going to start right now, by yanking the chip out of that great big white one."

I stamped off to the galley to make another pot of coffee. Several cats were brazenly slapping the food cupboard doors, trying to crack the passcodes. I knew that, without hands, a Level Three couldn't carry out a lot of the plans they were capable of conceiving. Paws, as shown by several missteps in the development of the Augmentation Laws, didn't do the trick, any more than talons or Dendrite twigs did. A

Hellmuncher's tentacles, on the other hand, didn't bear thinking about.

Several other cats sat along the wall with their collars perched on their heads like jaunty little crowns. I held my frown, not letting the cuteness get to me. A large short-haired one flicked his head and tossed his collar towards a powered-down guidestick wedged into one of my hanging braids of garlic. The collar missed and clattered to the floor. The other cats gave soft cries and the next in line, a gorgeous golden brown female, moved forward for her turn at the ring-toss game.

"Close only counts in horseshoes," Poig said, on my heels.

"Horses run around fields, they don't wear shoes." I glared at him but he wasn't even listening.

He was pointing at the countertops behind me. "There's the big white one. He's, *heh heh*, the *ring* leader."

The white cat's eyes narrowed as the sleek golden-brown one chucked a collar and watched it bounce off the edge of the stick. The other cats murmured some sort of commentary among themselves before two stepped forward at once, jostling for a turn. The white cat gave a sharp cry, raised a paw. One of the two stepped back, ducking his head towards the white one. Ringleader, indeed. The white one had organized the game and had control of the whole bunch. Was that typical cat behavior?

I watched, fascinated, as the game continued in an orderly fashion. Why did they play like that? I scratched my scalp stubble. It brought them no further ahead in life. What did such effort really achieve? That was the kind of thing I had pondered, as I had sat at my accountant's desk making judgement calls on tax returns, treading miles in the gym, washing dishes in my apartment kitchen, until I couldn't stand another minute of it. The sales notice for a fixer-upper, *Calamity Jane*, had caught my eye on a ships-for-sale site and I'd spent my accountant's earnings, my entire carefully tax-sheltered nest egg, on it.

Even if the cats were deserving of augmentation, I'd still have to cut them open and retrieve the chips. I couldn't fail: I had no life to go back to.

I sniffed and stepped forward to pull the guidestick from between the crushed cloves of garlic. My foot went *squish*. The cats scattered. Waving the guidestick and shouting stuff that sounded like nonsense even to me, I wiped kibble vomit off my foot onto the doorjamb and chased the nearest cat down the hall.

Protocols be damned! Cats be damned! If I couldn't have the life I wanted, neither could they!

∞

"Cap'n? Are you sure you want to do this to Arle?" Poig held the wheeled stretcher steady while I lifted the white cat—all puffed up to double size and hissing like a leaky boiler—onto it. My welding gloves protected me from the worst of its scratching.

I raised an eyebrow. "Arle?"

Poig continued. "This cat. He's almost like a person. I named him Arle. A phonetic abbreviation of R.L.? The initials of ring leader? Get it?"

Poig couldn't help the wordplay. It was a result of his raising. But I didn't need to let his tendencies get in the way of our awful task ahead. Our Arle-ful task? Damn. Now *I* was doing it.

I gritted my teeth and stared at Poig through my visor until he mumbled something apologetic and busied himself at the sickbay cupboards.

It had taken all afternoon to corner all the cats including the big white ringleader. *Arle*. It snarled its own name as I fastened the last of the Velcro straps over its legs. I took off my spacesuit helmet, pulled out my earplugs, put down my welding gloves, and rubbed my face. Then I ran a finger under the collars of my two jumpsuits. Would this day never end?

After capturing the ten raised cats, I'd comm'd ahead and arranged for some accounting work on Crogan. If we moored there for a week,

I would earn enough to recalibrate the ten used chips, assuming I retrieved them now. Then we could sell the full five hundred as arranged, refuel, and be on the way to deliver the cats to the Yoogle royal family. The Yoogle I'd left the message with, some flunky, had not been happy about the week's delay. Seems they needed them ASAP. Which is what I felt like. A sap, I mean. Damn. I was doing it again.

Arle squirmed in his restraints.

"Hand me some anesthetic, a scalpel, and a tray to put the chip on," I said, rather more brusquely than I intended.

Poig's eyes got shiny and his ears drooped even further, but he opened a drawer just as *Calamity Jane* shook, then shook again. Poig yelped and the anesthetic sprayer clattered to the floor. Alarms, unfamiliar alarms, sounded from all speakers.

"What the hell!" I rushed to the miniscreen by the door and thumbed it on. "Report!"

Calamity's computer started scrolling all kinds of worrying data. I stopped reading when I figured out that nothing could cause such damage to our outer hull except a targeted laser.

"Someone's shooting at us! Get to the bridge! Evasive manoeuvres!" I shouted at Poig as I charged out the sickbay door, feeling like I was in an action vid.

I careened down the hallway as the ship shuddered again. A hand on one wall and then the other as it rocked. I burst onto the bridge, tripped over a writhing pile of blankets that appeared to be screeching, and fell flat on my face. Poig, behind me, landed across my legs a second later. A white streak whizzed by us and leapt up onto the nav screen.

As I got to my knees, Arle slapped his tail, flicking it across the screen in a pattern almost too fast to follow. I sucked in a breath. Could it be? The ship lurched again, tremendously this time. Stars began wheeling across the front screen. We were speeding up! *Calamity Jane* was little and her computer simple, but Poig's engine repairs meant she sure could go *fast*.

I crawled to the nav screen and hauled myself up. Sure enough, Arle's tail had swiped the controls exactly right to make us accelerate and twist away from the Yoogle ship that had appeared from nowhere.

"Arle saved us!" Poig, on his hands and feet, craned his head up at me, grinning from ear to ear. "We got away!"

I had no time to figure out how Arle had done it, nor how ten cats had dragged blankets off my bunk all the way to the bridge, because the ship-to-ship comm was blinking madly.

"Captain Janny Splundell speaking," I said, with a calmness I didn't feel, as the main screen showed a face like a satanic rhino—the nightmarish scowl of a very angry Yoogle. He licked his lips. Something nasty was stuck to one fang.

The automated translator kicked in. "Since you notified us that you would be late, we have come to meet you, Captain Janny Splundell of *Calamity Jane*. We wish our shipment now. Since our attempt to take it by force has failed, we wish to take delivery in the normal manner. Please come alongside." At least, he'd said "please." At least, his voice was a baritone, not the really low pitch Yoogles used to show irritation.

"I have your shipment ready, of course. On time. I was just about to comm you again," I lied, drawing myself up to my full height and squaring my shoulders. I jerked when a rough, wet sensation crossed my bare scalp. The white cat was settled in a spare harness hanging from the wall, licking the top of my head. The look I gave it should have fried its chip. It smiled at me and cocked one almost-adorable, fluffy ear.

I drew in a breath. What I had to say next might start the Yoogles shooting at us again. "I do need assurance that you will properly take care of the cats, as per Section 56.4a.17.977c of the Interplanetary Regs." Being an accountant did have one advantage; I could quote chapter and verse from a lot of very dry documents. Beside me, Poig relaxed slightly. Had he really thought I would sell sentient beings into slavery?

"We have laid in gourmet foodstuffs, soft bedding, and the finest of litter bots. However…" The Yoogle deepened his voice so low the microphone shuddered. "Our princesses are increasingly eager and their," the translator hesitated then continued, "debutante social tea party cannot be postponed." The Yoogle's arm lashed at something just out of camera range. A high pitched snarl followed from, presumably, one of the royal brats.

"I will have all units at our port-side lock in thirty minutes," I said and, rather bravely, closed the link. The rumor among merchant captains was that Yoogles respected strength above all. They'd treat me better if I didn't appear to back down.

Or, they'd kill me.

One or the other.

I drew a shaky hand over my bare scalp. Who was I kidding? I wasn't a merchant captain. I'd never hung out with one; I didn't even know any. There was just that one time when I'd taken a wrong turn on a Toronto street corner and ended up in a bar full of spacers. I was just a wannabe courier, a pretender, the worst kind of fake. My first delivery was going to be my last.

It took twenty-eight minutes for Poig and me to lock on to the Yoogle's coordinates, get the cages full of the ninety cats loaded on the dolly, and push them next to the airlock.

That left two minutes to sweat.

The airlock slid aside and a giant Yoogle crowded in, followed by three smaller ones in tutus. The smallest one pirouetted on one claw, butterscotch curls fluttering across her horns. Something dark dripped from her fangs.

The Yoogle-in-charge had ducked his head to fit through the airlock door. Now he stood *all* the way up, brushing the ceiling. Striding over to the dolly of cages, claws screeching on the metal floor, he lashed his scaly tail. His thick lips thinned in disapproval.

"I count ten too few," he said, in a dismayingly rumbly bass, fingering the gun belt slung across his massive chest.

"We went for quality, not quantity. These are the finest of felines, the cutest of kitties," I said, with a grand hand wave. After this was over, if I was still alive, I was going to see if I could get my accounting job back.

"Grrrrrrh." The Yoogle's growl would have blistered the paint on *Calamity*'s hull, had there been any.

"They are fully trained, um, they cuddle and purr, and they never make messes." I had never made a sales pitch in my life but even I knew I was over the top.

I sensed Poig behind me sidling over to the cage controls. Surely, he wasn't going to let them all free again? I flipped a hand back and forth behind my back, angrily motioning him to stop.

Poig obediently moved away.

A *meowowwwwwwwooooh* came from behind my left shoulder. Arle was saying something to the cats. All ninety felines perked up their ears and sat at attention.

Could I trust Arle? *Should* I trust him?

I kept babbling at the Yoogle. "Yessir, trained for years, by skillful, um, trainers with the finest, er, training." I wasn't even convincing myself.

The Yoogle-in-charge growled in so low a bass that ship alarms cheeped at the subsonic vibrations.

I flipped a hand back and forth behind my back, this time frantically motioning Poig to open the cages.

The cage locks buzzed. Accompanied by a musical chorus of *meows*, the troupe of ninety cats daintily stepped out, tails aloft, and pranced single-file into the Yoogle ship. Arle purred with approval and Poig gave a short, sharp bark. I crossed my arms as if I'd expected their performance all along.

The three Yoogle princesses clapped their hands and squealed with delight. The smallest one jumped up and down, making the decking tremble. The Yoogle-in-charge grinned hugely, both fangs exposed, before nodding his head in my direction.

I don't think my mouth closed until after the Yoogles had transferred payment—less ten percent—disconnected from the airlock, and raced away, leaving us far behind.

∞

Calamity Jane might be small, but its liquor cabinet was fully stocked, unlike the food cupboard. As captain, I'd set some priorities. I poured a third cucumber-soup-and-vodka cocktail and held the glass aloft.

"Poig, we are going to make this venture work. For all of us." I patted *Calamity*'s hull to make sure she knew she was included.

He stroked the golden-brown cat on his lap and smiled up at me. "And we've raised ten intelligences. I think that counts for something."

I frowned. Two hours helping Poig clean the cat-hair-clogged air filters after the Yoogles had left had not softened me towards our new shipmates one bit. Not at all. I fished several sleek white hairs out of my drink before taking a large sip. The cucumber flavor was growing on me.

I felt myself relax from more than just the vodka. Not only had we saved the fuel needed to go all the way to Yoogle, but we were ahead of schedule thanks to Poig's engine tweaks, almost to Crogan where we'd cash in on the chips.

I nudged two cats out of my way and touched the galley's mini-screen, recording a reminder to pick up kibble and kitty litter on Crogan. That made Poig's fuzzy face light up.

"We can keep them?" he asked, as a smaller black cat settled down around his stocky neck and blinked its yellow eyes slowly at me.

"Well, we can't sell augmented animals or even give them away, not anywhere in the Common Worlds. Not without getting arrested on the spot." When we got to Crogan, it was going to take me a full day or two to hack the shipment documentation to show ninety cats were all I'd originally agreed to deliver. Thanks to my childhood augmentation and my accounting skills, I was pretty sure I could do it.

We'd keep them. We'd adjust to them and them to us. How different could a cat's mind be, anyway, when its DNA was so closely related to humans? Didn't I successfully handle both the convoluted logic of a certain raised Nancy and the nasty attitude of a nastier-than-most Yoogle on practically a daily basis?

A few cats would be no trouble at all.

"Poig, let's go up to the bridge and watch the stars pass by." I never tired of the view, so much more impressive than anything on my apartment's wallscreen back home.

My former apartment in my former home. I patted *Calamity*'s hull again.

As I left the galley, glass in hand, various cats skittered away down the corridor, responding to the automated dinner bell I'd set up in the cargo bay. Arle chose to delay his dinner and come with me, winding around my legs as I walked, his tail proudly upright. Poig followed a step or two behind.

I bent down to give Arle a pat. Handsome fellow. I admired his jaunty walk as he scooted ahead.

Yes, indeed, this could work.

Arle did a U-turn as I entered the bridge, flicking his ears at me as he sauntered back out. What had he just done?

I approached my captain's chair warily. The fresh hairball, glistening obscenely, lay centred on my seat.

"Cap'n? What can I do?" Poig's voice at my elbow was hushed.

I drained my glass. "Find me a rope," I said, crooking my head to one side while raising a fist near my other ear, as if hanging myself. "A nice long piece of rope."

About the Author
Holly Schofield

Holly Schofield travels through time at the rate of one second per second, oscillating between the alternate realities of a prairie farmhouse and her writing cabin on the west coast. Her fiction has been published in *Lightspeed*, *Crossed Genres*, *Unlikely Stories*, and many other venues.

Author Website: http://hollyschofield.wordpress.com/

Murder on the *Hohmann*
by Patrice Sarath

In 2065, after ten years as a shuttle pilot for the Bifrost asteroid mining complex, I took it upon myself to settle my affairs off-planet, return to Earth, and resign myself to look upon the stars from afar. This was a common migration, as miners and crew often found themselves with the same vague yearning for a planet many of us had not seen in decades. We none of us acknowledged that we *were* embarked on a migration, but all gave different reasons on official documents for our decision to pack it in. Yet humans are as instinctual as any animal; no doubt if you ask the wildebeests, you'd get a different answer from each one too.

My voyage from the Bifrost mining complex to Earth took eight months, my ship the venerable United Nations *Hohmann*, an ancient, chemical-propelled workhorse whose frame was laid in the early twenty-first century. The *Hohmann* carried supplies on the Earth-Mars-Bifrost run. It was a small, cramped ship, the bridge barely larger than the cockpit of my shuttle, and it had been retrofitted with two modules attached like train cars and a big turning centrifuge of a caboose for crew and passengers to experience *up* and *down*, put on muscle, and salvage bone.

The first inkling that my voyage might not be as smooth as hoped came when I stowed my duffle next to my assigned sleep pouch and found myself next to the two asteroid miners, Carter and Rose. We carefully did not acknowledge one another, but my heart sank. What other surprises were there going to be?

I was soon to find out, and my misgivings grew when I met everyone at dinner our first night out.

Besides myself and the brothers, the *Hohmann* carried three other passengers: Elton Haley, a talkative fellow with blond, receding hair and a portly figure, who never answered a straight question about what he was doing on the Earth-Mars-Bifrost run; Agnes St. Germaine, a first-generation Mars colonist; and Mrs. Paavo, a veteran of the Mars conflict of 2047.

I disliked Haley from the start. "Ah, Meredith Hawkes, the shuttle pilot. I've heard about *you*," was the first thing he said to me.

"All good, I hope," I replied lightly, and set down my cup. Yes, set down, for the *Hohmann*'s skipper, Captain Ngotu, was old-fashioned and requested passengers dine with him at a common table in the centrifuge chamber. Thankfully, the captain relaxed the rule that we dress for dinner, so we were all in some variation of ultra-lightweight T-shirt and trousers. Mr. Haley's had a legend advertising a barbecue restaurant.

"Yes, now what was it? There was something that rang a bell. No matter it will come to me. I have eight months after all. Ah, the brother miners! Which are you two? Dopey and Grumpy?"

At his jocular tone, Carter and Rose looked over sourly from their end of the table and then back down at their dinners, forks clenched in their fists. Haley had better watch out, I thought. The brothers might be height deficient, but they were more like trolls than dwarfs, and just as thuggish.

"What about you, Mr. Haley? Why are you leaving Mars?" I said, going on the offensive.

"Oh, I'm not from Mars," he said cheerfully.

I raised my eyebrows in surprise. A tourist from Earth? The *Hohmann* was a slow, chemical-fueled supply ship, and lacked all but the most basic amenities for space travelers. The only reason I booked a ticket was because there were no passenger ships on the schedule, and I found it expedient to leave as soon as possible. I had resigned myself to an eight-month journey that on a newer ship would have taken four.

As for the Martians, why had they chosen to book passage on a ship that was going an extra four months out of their way?

Mr. Haley turned to Miss St. Germaine. "Now Miss St. Germaine, are you remembering to keep up with your bone supplements? I see you aren't eating again, as usual. Our Bifrost friends will think you don't care about your health."

Miss St. Germaine murmured something, and at his jocular tone, made an effort to move her dinner around her plate. Like all first and second-generation Martians, she looked as if she were twelve years old, with a delicate bone structure and petite form. Her diffident manner emphasized her childlike appearance. Her ancestry was like mine—African and American—but her skin had the artificial pallor of genetic enhancement. She would need as much vitamin D as her body could manufacture, even with the implants all spacefarers had that released a steady supply of vitamins and hormones. Her curly hair was wrapped in a colorful scarf, a startling print against the industrial background of the ship, and at odds with her shy personality. Unaccountably, I felt nostalgia. I had shaved my head for the last ten years out of expediency and simplicity. On Earth, I could grow out my hair.

Mr. Haley leaned toward me as if in confidence, lowering his voice but without any effort to hide his words. "Miss St. Germaine and I have become great friends. She's off on a wonderful adventure, back to the ancestral planet. Trading red for blue, eh Miss St. Germaine?" He winked at her.

The other woman, Mrs. Paavo, was an elderly white woman who had a no-nonsense manner and the erect bearing of a general. Her eyes were piercing blue, and I soon learned she had the habit of snorting indelicately whenever someone said anything she found absurd.

She snorted now at Haley's impertinence with Miss St. Germaine. "I must say, Mr. Haley, I have no patience for personal remarks and undue familiarity," she said.

"No doubt, no doubt, Mrs. Paavo," he said, with the same smirk. "But we have only each other for amusement, and I am resolved that we will become great friends before this voyage is over."

Ignoring the disgruntled looks of his fellow passengers, he raised his glass high. "Here's to the *Hohmann* and Captain Ngotu. May our journey be uneventful and fruitful. Captain, what an honor it must be to skipper the *Hohmann*. Did you know she was one of the first to establish supply lines between Mars and the Bifrost stations? Amazing, how these old birds just keep going. She's fifty years old at least."

"She'll last another one hundred and fifty," Ngotu said, with simple pride. "These ships don't take off or land. They'll last forever."

"Sentimentality is all and well good, Captain, but quite frankly, I'm appalled that the only ship available is this ancient wreck," Mrs. Paavo said. From the way Miss St. Germaine rolled her eyes, I gathered it was an old complaint, and one she had heard plenty in the preceding months. "And the price for tickets is extortion, plain and simple, considering that we've added four months onto our journey." She glared at our captain as if she expected a refund right at the table.

"The government sets the ticket price, Mrs. Paavo," he said with admirable diplomacy. "As for the length of our journey, the *Hohmann* is a supply ship, not a passenger liner. We keep to our schedule and our route, and take on passengers only when there's room."

"Now, now, Mrs. Paavo," Mr. Haley said. "Poor planning on your part does not constitute an emergency on the captain's. You could have booked the express if the local was too slow."

Mrs. Paavo's old eyes narrowed. I wondered how much capacity for violence existed in that birdlike frame—certainly the spirit was willing.

"There were no tickets to be had." Miss St. Germaine spoke up. "It was an inconvenience for all of us."

"Well, there you go," Haley said. He gave Miss St. Germaine a smile. "You see, Mrs. Paavo? Rather than blaming the good captain, you should be thanking him. The *Hohmann* was the only ship available."

There was little any of us could say to that.

∞

We grew used to the routine on the ship. Captain Ngotu ran a tight ship; everyone knew their position, and we all worked hard not to breach the artificial cordiality that was the mainstay of a long space voyage. All of us, that is, except for Elton Haley.

The man was an insensitive boor. Besides flirting with me, he adopted a fatherly approach with Miss St. Germaine and an overly solicitous one with Mrs. Paavo. With the former he joshed her unceasingly regarding the virile Earth men she needed to beware of, pushed her to pair off with one or both of the brothers or various crewmembers, and advised her of many pitfalls of life on Earth. With the latter, he could not lay eyes upon her without asking about her health and if she had grandchildren or great-grandchildren to care for her, and enquiring at every interval if she was taking her bone medications.

With Carter and Rose, he was simply patronizing, assuming they were simple, ignorant miners. I did not bother to disabuse him of that notion.

I tried to stay out of Mr. Haley's way, except at meal times. However, the voyage was long and the ship small, and so it was that when I was enjoying a bit of peace and quiet on the observation deck, he found me. The hatch opened and to my vast annoyance, Haley pulled himself inside. I had my feet hooked around a foothold and pointedly turned away from him. He did not take the hint.

"Ah, Captain Hawkes," he said, holding on next to me. "I was hoping to find you here. Do you know, I remember why your name sounded familiar."

I supposed I could just go to my bunk, but all the passengers had were narrow sleep cubicles, and we hung there like bound-up spider victims. And blast it, the observation deck was the only place I could be alone, and I was there first.

"The feeds were full of the story," he said, making himself comfortable. "The asteroid mining disaster that killed five. *You* were the shuttle pilot on that job, and according to the breathless reporters, if it weren't for your exemplary skills, the death toll would have been far higher."

I said nothing, willing him to close his mouth and knowing that he would not. Yes, the accident and investigation were public knowledge and part of the corporation's filings, but what ordinary person would look them up?

Haley just wouldn't stop. "You know, I just wasn't clear on one thing, Captain. Why were you hauling that particular asteroid in the first place?"

I pushed off, heart hammering as if I were in the centrifuge. As I irised out of the hatch, I heard him laughing behind me.

I didn't calm down until I was in the centrifuge, pedaling furiously on an exercise machine, and thought about how I wanted to murder the man.

∞

After that, I avoided the observation deck except for the Mars approach. Normally, the view is a cause for great celebration. Sighting Mars is a sign that the next maneuver is on deck, when the *Hohmann* slingshots around the planet to gather speed for its final approach to Earth and then turns around and begins deceleration. As a result of the tension on the ship—no one looking at Haley as he beamed and prattled—the *ooh*'s and *aah*'s were lukewarm rather than enthusiastic. I noticed Miss St. Germaine looking more pensive than usual and thought how homesick she must be. She gave off such an air of childlike frailty that my ordinarily hard and cynical heart grew quite maternal toward her. We often ended up side-by-side on the weight machines, and she unbent toward me, her diffidence charming. She asked shy questions about what it was like to be a shuttle pilot, and I couldn't resist exaggerating my exploits.

"Oh my," she said, wide-eyed. "It sounds exciting. May I ask why you're leaving it all behind?"

Mindful of Haley's nosiness, I decided I had said too much. "Oh," I said, "It was time to retire, see the old homestead, feel one G again. That sort of thing. And what about you, Miss St. Germaine?"

She stopped her frantic pumping, resting her arms on the handle-bars of the weights. "My parents came to Mars twenty-five years ago," she said. "So did I, as an embryo put in a deep freeze and protected from radiation during the entire voyage out. They waited ten years to have me, and by then they were… old. When it became clear I had little aptitude for the life of a colonist, my parents decided to send me to Earth. So they could start over, with a new child. Another chance for their genetic legacy, despite the cost."

"I… Miss St. Germaine…" I faltered to a stop. I knew that things were hard on Mars, but to so coldly discard one's child—was it possible?

Her voice was hard now, though her eyes were wet with tears. "It's quite all right. I've reconciled myself to it. Do you know what Mr. Haley said?"

"I can imagine," I said dryly.

"He told me that I should be grateful my parents didn't leave me out on the Meridiani Planum to die as some Martians do. That they had probably bankrupted themselves to send me Home."

"Mr. Haley is not to be listened to," I said. "He likes to get under people's skin."

"I know," she said, and now there was a catch in her voice. "I just wish he didn't hit so near the mark."

∞

The Mars maneuver was a success and we were on our last leg of the voyage. Dinner was especially celebratory, enhanced by Mr. Haley's absence from the table. No one cared to ask where he was. We were lively and talkative, and at the end of the dinner, Captain Ngotu came around and poured us each a tiny serving of coffee in real cups.

"We are six months away from Home," he announced, to a scattering of applause. "We are on the downhill side of our journey, and so tonight is a special celebration." He tucked his head into his collar and spoke briefly into the mic attached to his uniform. The lights dimmed, creating a candlelight effect with small electric tea lights on the tables. Everyone *ooh*'d. Captain Ngotu raised his small white coffee cup in a toast and we followed suit.

"To Home," he said and we chorused, "To Home." Even Miss St. Germaine echoed his toast, her eyes bright.

We lingered over dinner. Carter and Rose produced a flask of homemade vodka, and we all indulged. At last when I was forced to go to the head, I was quite tipsy when I bumped into Mr. Haley drifting in the passageway between compartments.

"Excu—" I started, unable to hide my irritation. The last thing I needed was him poking his nose into my business. I could have skin like a heat shield and he would still know how to get under it.

Then I realized that Mr. Haley would be getting under no one's skin anymore. He drifted sideways in relation to the corridor, not oriented horizontally as we all did, and an expanding spray of round drops of blood scattered around him. His eyes stared blankly at the bulkhead.

I pushed myself forward and slapped at the emergency call button on the wall. The shriek of the siren blared. I grabbed onto Mr. Haley and anchored myself against the grab bars. I could hear hatches opening and voices raised in concern. With Mr. Haley captured against my side, and droplets of blood coalescing around me, I felt for a pulse in his neck. Nothing.

The ship's doctor pushed herself through the corridor from sickbay, expertly gathering momentum by thrusting herself off of each grab bar. With quick efficiency she readied a shot and jabbed him into his heart. He jerked but sank back again. "Help me get him to my clinic," she said, and Mrs. Paavo and I pushed the man through the corridor after her. All the while she was barking comments into her mic, recording blood droplets, rate of coagulation, body temperature. I couldn't help but wonder if she could save him, and if so, if he could identify his attacker.

I don't deny I was in shock. It was one thing to idly contemplate the murder of a nemesis. It was entirely another to face it in reality. Haley was dead. We all hated him; but which of us had taken matters into their own hands to do him in?

∞

After a period holed up exchanging transmissions with both Earth and Mars, Captain Ngotu gathered us all in the lounge a few hours after Mr. Haley was found and briefed us with terse sentences. The comms officer had notified criminal investigators on both planets; and the authorities would be questioning all of us via radio and again when we made planetfall. As the *Hohmann* herself didn't land, we would be shuttled to Earth to the Salto di Quirra base in Sardinia.

"Please be useful and open with the authorities," he told us sternly. "Tell them everything you know." He glanced at me when he said that and I stared impassively back.

"As for that, Captain, perhaps you could be useful and open with us," Mrs. Paavo said, the steel in her voice and demeanor as always. She had seen more death than any of us, and her manner was of one who was irked by the inexperience of everyone around her. "Have you found a murder weapon? Do you know how Mr. Haley died? Have you accounted for the whereabouts of everyone on board this ship, and most importantly, are you taking measures to prevent another murder?"

"Mrs. Paavo, calm, please," Captain Ngotu said. "It has only been a few hours. We can't discuss everything we've found out, surely you understand that?"

"It's hardly unreasonable to ask what you are doing to ensure the safety of your remaining passengers," Mrs. Paavo said. Her jaw jutted out. "We are six months out and we are traveling with a murderer."

"Yes, Madam," Captain Ngotu snapped. He took a deep breath, clearly reaching for calm. "And just like everyone else aboard my ship, you're a suspect."

Mrs. Paavo reared back in outrage. "What utter nonsense," she said. "Utter nonsense."

"Is it?" The captain looked around at all of us. "Mr. Haley irritated everyone on this ship. We all had good reason to— Well, there's no good reason for murder, but good reason to dislike him. And until I get further orders from Earth, I don't intend to release any information about the murder that could compromise this case."

Mrs. Paavo made some well-chosen remarks about the captain's professionalism, but he ignored her, taking another calming breath before floating off to the bridge and further communications from Earth.

∞

In death as in life, Mr. Haley was the topic of all of our whispered conversations, in the passageways, the centrifuge, the observation deck. Even in our sleep pouches with the lights dimmed to meet an ancient circadian rhythm, the whispers went on and on. More than ever, I wished the voyage to be over and cursed myself for booking passage on an antique ship. Why hadn't I just waited for a ship with an ion drive?

We were all unsettled, even the crew. The first officer and the navigator, who had been conducting a brisk affair in the medical bay, now avoided their usual trysting place, since the body was stored there. The enterprising brothers, Carter and Rose, who had a significant sideline in narcotics, now did a brisk business in sedatives since no one was sleeping very well. Captain Ngotu, whose wrist implant dispensed blood pressure medication, took to tapping it almost compulsively. Tempers were snappish and easily triggered. Mrs. Paavo's stern good sense was driving me insane. She was relentless in her constant conversation on what Captain Ngotu should do and what his many failings were. Miss St. Germaine's childlike facade had cracked and she had become waspish. Not long after the murder, I saw her in close conversation with Carter and Rose on the observation deck. They all three glared at me, and I took the hint and irised right back out the hatch. But with me Carter and Rose were as taciturn as ever, and I could tell by their constant sideways glances at me that they suspected me.

I wanted to shake them by their scruffy necks. Yes, Mr. Haley had brought up the botched tow and the subsequent inquiry. But I wasn't the one designing and dealing drugs. Nor was I the one who habitually carried what was referred to as a miner's mercy—a tiny shiv that could be used to jimmy the air mix on a miner's suit. Tether broken? Said your last good-byes? Rather than suffocate in the deep, alter the mix and go gentle into that good night.

It was the perfect device to exsanguinate Mr. Haley. The only problem was, both Carter and Rose were at dinner too.

And what had they and Miss St. Germaine been talking about, in such close conference on the observation deck?

We were all throwing accusing glances. I decided to take a leaf out of Haley's own book and look up my fellow passengers. The news on the *Hohmann* was canned; the archives got updated only when the ship docked. Those archives were surprisingly thorough, although they were silent on one name: Haley himself.

∞

"May I join you?" I said to Miss St. Germaine in the centrifuge, where she worked diligently on the machine. She glanced at me and shrugged. I slid next to her. As I set the weights, I said, "We have to talk."

She gave a dry little laugh that was nothing like her childish manner. "Do I have a choice?"

"How do you know the brothers?"

"Never met them before this journey."

"Really," I said, my voice as dry as hers.

"Really," she agreed.

She was lying, but that was not surprising after what I had learned. Miss St. Germaine made me look positively wholesome. Maybe her parents should have abandoned her on the Meridiani Planum after all.

∞

The days crept along excruciatingly. I was tempted to stay in my sleep sack, but there was no privacy there and I couldn't allow myself to waste away. I couldn't bear to be around the others, however, so once again I went up to the observation deck, and contemplated the growing Sun. Mrs. Paavo found me there, and in her bracing, astringent manner, told me to get over myself.

"You're being a fool," she said. "For God's sake, Captain. You're the last person who should become moody over this."

"Hardly," I said. "Aren't you worried that I'm the murderer?"

"No," she snapped, and pulled herself in next to me. We watched the stars for a while. Finally, she said, "What did Haley have on you?"

"I caused an accident that killed five people." I kept it to that. What Haley knew, it died with him.

She gave me a sidelong glance. "So much for the heroic Captain Hawkes," she said, her voice dry.

"I never claimed to be, Mrs. Paavo, unlike you. I had to cross-reference. You took your husband's name for this trip, but you are better known as the Butcher of Dome Two. How did Haley find out?"

"As I was a celebrity, as it were, on Mars barely twenty years ago, it wasn't difficult. I served my time, Captain. I paid my debt to society. It was time to go Home."

The Dome Two disaster was back in 2047, during the Mars conflict. An outbreak of flu started in the primitive hab. Mrs. Paavo had ordered a quarantine, with no medicines or food to be spared. I could see her, twenty years younger with her same no-nonsense manner, explaining that compassion for the doomed hab would jeopardize the entire colony. They could not spare their meager resources.

A merciless despot, two drug dealing thieves, and a conniving Martian black marketeer—the investigators would have more suspects than they knew what to do with. And in ironies of ironies, I would no doubt be considered their prime suspect.

∞

There was no celebration this time when Earth loomed into view. She was surrounded by the blinking lights of the complex of stations distinguished among the field of stars because stars don't blink. She grew in the viewscreen hourly, and we all crammed onto the observation deck.

"I'm glad we're all here," Mrs. Paavo announced, looking around at everyone. "There's something we need to discuss."

"You aren't the captain," Miss St. Germaine said. "I'm not discussing anything with you." Ever since the murder she had lost her waif-like appearance. All the hours spent at the weight machines had paid off. She was hard now, and her eyes glared.

"You'll discuss and you'll like it," Mrs. Paavo said. "We're all under suspicion of murder and I'm not taking the fall. I'm due to be on Earth in two weeks' time and that's where I intend to be."

"Are you sure they'll have you?" Miss St. Germaine said sweetly.

"The Butcher of Dome Two is hardly going to get a hero's welcome."

"I've paid my debt to society," Mrs. Paavo said, repeating the excuse she gave to me. "The same can't be said for the rest of you."

"Ah, after causing the death of hundreds of innocents, Mrs. Paavo doesn't think she should be a suspect for murder," I said.

"Don't start, Captain Hawkes," she snapped at me. "I can do research too. You did more than just cause an accident on Bifrost... You were part of the gang that was diverting asteroids to the black market."

All eyes turned to me. "I was never convicted," I pointed out. "Charges dismissed."

"Oh stuff it, Hawkes," Rose said, glancing at his brother for support. "You ratted everyone out, and you got a plea bargain."

"Pardon me," I said. "But while I was lying in the medbay handcuffed to a bed, you were throwing me under the bus. Of course I sang."

"Oh, how surprising, the miners were involved too," Mrs. Paavo said with a sneer. "I thought you two were just the local drug dealers."

"Sure, they were in on it," I said. I was tired of playing the lone villain. "Carter and Rose were responsible for finding the Mars buyer, and setting the tow. They're quite the jack-of-all-trades, our miners."

"That's enough," Carter said. He pointed at Miss St. Germaine. "Ask her what she's doing here, and you'll find out we're not the ones who killed Haley."

"Don't be absurd," she said. "I didn't kill him."

"Even though he was the reason for your exile from Mars?" Mrs. Paavo smirked. "You aren't the innocent daughter you like to portray, Miss St. Germaine. Your sole reason for leaving Mars is that you were the sorrow of your parents and the bane of Dome Four. Quite a black market in diverted goods you were operating."

Diverted goods... black market... I flashed back to her huddled conversations with the brothers. Our mysterious asteroid buyer was based on Mars. "You!" I cried. I was flabbergasted. She curled her lip at me.

"Oh, I'm sorry, did I let you down?" she said, and I flushed. I had to admit it, she had played me like a violin. "Too bad you couldn't pilot a ship *or* keep your mouth shut."

"Very interesting," Mrs. Paavo said. "I paid *my* debt to society."

"Stop saying that, you self-righteous madwoman." I had had enough. If anyone was a candidate for the airlock…

The lock irised open, and Captain Ngotu pulled himself in. "Good. You're all here." He grabbed a handhold and moved sideways. In floated Mr. Haley, alive and well and with the same irritating smirk, holding up an InterSol badge.

To say we were astonished would not do justice to the thing. I had seen him, held him in my arms. There was blood… With a sinking realization I understood that I had been duped.

"The good news is, none of you are murder suspects," Mr. Haley announced. "The bad news is, you are all under arrest for the various infractions that you committed while off Earth."

∞

It turned out that the authorities on Earth, Bifrost, and Mars had coordinated efforts to apprehend and build a case against a ring of asteroid thieves and black marketeers. There were no tickets to be found on a larger, faster ship because InterSol made sure the only berths available were on the slow, ancient *Hohmann*. Our confessions to one another were the last bit of evidence Haley needed to bring us to justice.

Miss St. Germaine was the mastermind of the asteroid theft; the brothers were her lieutenants. I was the hired pilot, lured by the money and the chance to go Home in style.

Mrs. Paavo was collateral; but it turned out that the irritating old bag still faced civil and criminal charges on Earth. She had not paid her debt to society after all.

It was a subdued group that walked off the *Hohmann* onto Midway Station and into the embrace of the authorities. I looked back once at the observation screen that offered a panorama of the vastness of space. I was conscious of a deep pang of longing. Maybe if you asked the wildebeest, in the maw of an opportunistic crocodile, she would say she regretted migrating too.

About the Author
Patrice Sarath

Patrice Sarath's novels include the fantasy series, Books of the Gordath (*Gordath Wood, Red Gold Bridge*, and *The Crow God's Girl*) and the romance *The Unexpected Miss Bennet*. She has been published by Penguin in the U.S. and Robert Hale Ltd. in the UK.

Her short stories have appeared in magazines and anthologies, including *Weird Tales* and *Alfred Hitchcock Mystery Magazine*. Her short story "A Prayer for Captain La Hire" was included in *Year's Best Fantasy of 2003*. Her story "Pigs and Feaches," originally published in *Apex Digest*, was reprinted in 2013 in *Best Tales of the Apocalypse* by Permuted Press.

Author Website: http://www.patricesarath.com/

Coin Toss
by L Chan

"Off the record," said the director.

Frank Cheng forced a smile. He kept his eyes on the nameplate between them: Director, Serious Fraud Office, Department of Finance. In case people forgot who they were talking to, no doubt. Off the record was bad. You didn't get promoted off the record. But you could get fired, cut off from your dependable government income off the record.

"Where do I start?" A better or lesser agent would not have asked. Better agents became directors. They were hard to find and harder to keep. Lesser agents, well, the department was full of them. Frank was neither. He got things done, but he wouldn't be missed.

The director pushed a phone across the table. Still in an evidence bag, the seal broken. "A Coin."

The phone was from storage. If Frank had it scanned, its owner would be dead, in jail, or one of the transients who flowed through Singapore. The throng came for work, pleasure, or a mix of both, in the flourishing flesh dens.

"A single Coin is now valued at a thousand and five dollars, I can't buy my way to the source with this."

"It's not from the source or any of the other true sources around the world. We mined this one."

"Impossible. Coin hasn't been cracked."

"You are correct." The director sat back in his chair, eyes losing focus as he ported into the office network. Back on the record again. Frank left without saying another word.

∞

Phone went into his bag; evidence bag went into the shredder.

He avoided fellow agents zombie-shuffling down the corridor, scuffing the carpet threadbare. Dirt brown was better than puke green. It was rude to be fully ported while on the move, but ruder still to waste department time.

Agents did all their work through the network, there was no need for a desk or a cubicle. You checked in to the department, you got a chair, you got a port, you got a foot locker. The chairs were ergonomic, Chinese copies of an Italian design. His was grey. Frank ran his fingers down five lines scored in the plastic of the armrest. One for every year chasing tax cheats, scammers and a better class of criminal. Five years since he made the move from a Police precinct to the Serious Fraud Office. The hours were better, but the perps were, to Frank, less savoury.

The supporting gel of the chair had long since coalesced into a perfect mould of his back and buttocks. He sat and the chair hugged him like a lover. The port was good tech. Worth at least six months of his salary. Half an inch of black, textured plastic protruded from his skull behind his ear. If you paid premium, you could get it almost flush with your skin, mask it with just a little hair. The state-issued port suited his buzz cut just fine; the more of his scalp that showed, the less likely people were to notice his thinning black hair.

A dusty black cable sat on his desk, the automatic retraction mechanism long dead. He guided the head of the cable to the port and his sensorium was flooded with the office network. There was a moment's madness as a dozen alerts clamoured for his attention, complaining as he waved them away. His schedule appeared. Coloured blocks indicated meetings, appointments. White, the null space in between. His mind already purged the null space, adapting to forget anything that he didn't share on his feed or mark in his diary.

Frank reached out and pulled Human Resources towards him, fingers dancing in the air to put himself on a week's leave. A flick of a finger sent his list of reminders climbing in front of his vision like the ascending slats of a roller coaster. He pinched a highlighted reminder and called up his bank account, sending a fistful of dollars into his aunt's account. His parents had long passed, but as her sole surviving relative, he would have to feed her before the state did.

"You're going away?" asked Ashraf, his neighbour. Frank could see him sitting in his own chair with an idiotic grin on his face, running his fingers through his dyed black hair. Golden boy, golfed with the director every other weekend. Next up for assistant director, the grapevine had it.

"A week. Enforced leave." Frank hoped his tone was civil. It wouldn't be helpful to have Ashraf pissing at him from his new office. Not at all.

"You need help with your files? Throw a couple my way. I'm behind on my quota."

No, you're not, asshole. You're top of the table already. Frank grunted and highlighted a few of his cases, picking those he'd been putting off for a while and swatted the lot over to his neighbour.

"Cheers, bro," Ashraf said, but Frank was already off his chair and out the door.

∞

The juice tasted like sugar, like purple; it helped him think. *Red dragonfruit,* the smart ink on the can said. It also said, *this is good for you.* It also said, *fifty percent of your daily dose of vitamin C.* Frank had never eaten a red dragonfruit in his life.

Cooker hoods gulped greasy smoke, whirled it through stainless steel guts and leaked it back into the air of the hawker centre. A line of tiny food stalls stretched into the distance, each purveying a different delicacy. Frank came here to plan, losing himself in the white noise of the crowd.

There'd been a lot of alternative currencies, each waxing and waning like the tide. The Department of Finance hated the crypto-currencies.

The department chose its fights. You couldn't keep the tide out completely, but you could keep places dry, if you knew where to dig in and where to build up. Coin was new, no known flaws yet. Its conceit manifest in its name. Just Coin, the only one that mattered.

His fingers brushed the edge of the phone. Somewhere in the rusting, whimpering heart of this sweltering city was the collective that carved Coin out of teraflops and algorithms. There was only a single icon representing the electronic wallet that held his Coin. Nothing else. No last dialled number, no feed, no personality, no memories. Scuffed and factory perfect. A single contact, a number he didn't recognize.

Someone at the department had thoughtfully named the contact: *At the right time.* When was the right time? He'd worry about that later.

Coin hadn't been cracked. Whatever he had was cobbled together by the department, inelegant and ugly. Paper money had its own immune system. Putting something foreign into the bloodstream elicited a response. It was the same with Coin. Frank turned the phone around and around with his fingertips. He didn't have to find the makers. They would find him.

He stood up, grabbing the babbling can from his table. An old lady pushed up a trolley alongside him, the platform overflowing with scavenged pickings. E-waste, electronic paper posters, cans like the one he was holding. The woman's back was crooked; spine doubling back on itself, pulling her head back towards the dirt. Her grey and white hair pulled back in a tight bun, sparse strands revealing a skull spotted with age. Her skin was lined like fine parchment and the writing was hardship.

Trash collection was automated, but still the scavengers persisted. A generation ago they scrounged for aluminium and cardboard. Frank offered the can to the lady, who smiled at him with more holes than teeth. She added the can to her collection, hooking a flimsy surgical mask back over her ear. Her skin was two shades darker above the mask, pale trails from the corner of her eyes where the wind had whipped tears from them. Urban tan, they called it.

Frank was still wondering, when he walked off, why the lady had a port behind her ear.

∞

You didn't just wander around on the net and spend Coin. The more trustworthy a crypto was, the less savoury the hands it passed through. Frank was going to have to burn a Face. He felt a passing regret at this; he'd grown attached to his collection of Faces.

It took time to craft a Face. His colleagues didn't have the patience, which was the single most important ingredient to make one. You could be anyone on the net. What you didn't want to be was a brand new account, no picture, undefined sex, address not keyed in, the kind of profile which screamed born yesterday. Fences, dealers and pimps weren't born yesterday either, because that kind of profile also screamed law enforcement.

You started years before. You found someone who lived a forgettable life, died a forgettable death. Then you saved everything you could, stripped photographs of identifying information and built up your Face.

Frank was thirty-four, pounded the street as a beat cop, investigated petty crime for a stint after. Never quite lost the droopy-shouldered, hunched-over look he got from long hours taking confessions, red-rimmed eyes trying to bore into the brain of the crook before him. Cheeks were sunken in a little too far to be fashionably gaunt. A weak chin that he tried to hide with a tapered goatee. Frank had been transferred over to investigate white collar crime. Big money, but the same motivations were there: greed, lust, violence. The rich outsourced their little altercations, but as with everything else with the rich, what they paid for in violence was quality.

Kenny was thirty-two. He died eight years ago with another name.

The net didn't forget, but some memories could be buried. Kenny worked an honest job, diagnosing and fixing cars. He favoured electronic dance music and Japanese food. In fact, just last week, Kenny had treated himself to a rich, pork bone broth ramen, bragging about it on his feed. *Wait, that wasn't Kenny.* It was Frank who had that lunch. It was getting difficult to update different feeds, live different lives.

Kenny was going to spend the Coin.

∞

Frank got a disposable phone from a vending machine, cursing as the cheap device's sub-par flexi-screen threw the afternoon glare straight back into his eyes. He put his back to the wall, pressing into the double handspan of shade the machine offered. White collar work had taken him off the street for too long; his skin had already faded to the pallor of a deep sea fish. Another twenty minutes in the sun and he'd regret it for the rest of the week.

The number he dialled from memory. There were a few numbers law enforcement officers never kept on their phones: internal investigation, mistresses, criminals.

"Fattie, it's Cheng."

No salutations between the two. Fattie Oh dealt second hand. You could ask, *second hand what?* And he'd say, *second hand*, smiling at you with tobacco-stained teeth, arms over his swelling belly. Fattie was always red in the face, his body fat in the same way a balloon was fat. That lulled people. Frank had seen Fattie throw a hustler out of his store once, picking him up bodily by his shirtfront and launching him so close to the road that the anticollision measures of the driverless cars kicked in.

"Ah, I was wondering how my day could get worse. Half my stock has been impounded by the cops and then I get a call from *you*." Fattie's voice was high and jovial, as likely to drop into a belly laugh as it was to yell at a customer to buy something or piss off. The man wouldn't be rustled by the loss of half a day's stock. He paid rock bottom for goods whose ownership was fluid. Frank had done him a good turn, years back. Something that could have easily been a five year term reduced to six months and a fine. He'd been sure to let Fattie know. Fattie talked loud, drank little, and listened deep. A man with his ears to the ground in the wrong kind of bar could get a lot of the right kind of information. Information that was worth a lot, if someone was asking off the record.

"I want to spend a Coin."

"Government not paying you enough dollars, you gotta use Coin?"

"I have business with the ones that mine Coin."

"Stop. Stop there and forget you heard about Coin." The fat man had once related, in his own cheerful way, how a fellow inmate had taken a sharpened toothbrush handle straight through the eye. This time, his tone was low and urgent, each sentence blown out as though Fattie didn't want the words in his mouth.

"Work business." The sun encroached on Frank's tiny bit of shade. He unhooked the top button of his shirt, the front of which was already plastered to his sweating chest.

"You're not the only one looking. Coin is still new. I think there are only two other sources worldwide now, Philippines and Brazil. Biggest is still here in Singapore. The tong have lost at least one team in their own search. The tong don't just lose people, Cheng."

It figured that the department wouldn't be the only ones hunting Coin. The triads had simply moved first. Or maybe Frank wasn't the first the department had sent out off the record. The sunlight didn't seem quite so hot any more.

"I don't have to go to the miners. They will come to me. My Coin is from the department."

There was an intake of breath and then silence for long enough that Frank looked at the screen to make sure he was still connected.

"Coin hasn't been breached. The makers are watching and the tong are on the move. Why not go lie on the expressway tonight instead? Less painful way to die."

"I guess you're wondering why I called you."

"We are small fish. Shallow water people. We know where the surface is, we know where the bottom is. You want to play in deep water? Things disappear there."

"Your kid must be about eight now, Fattie? Four birthdays you got to spend with your kid. Must make you feel like a real father."

When the other man spoke, his voice had an edge you could shave with. "How long have we known each other? You still got to pull that shit with me? I've paid you back for that and more. I'll tell you what I think, Cheng. You may be working money cases, but you like it on the street. You're at home with the trash and the dregs here. That's why you keep coming back. You got family?"

When was the last he'd spoken to his aunt anyway? At least he sent money. She'd taken care of him a couple of times, hadn't she? When he was younger and more when the drug-resistant infection slowly ate his mother from the inside.

"You're thinking about it," Fattie said. "That's good. Now, you remember old Chinatown?"

When Fattie was done, Frank watched the colours drain from the screen of the phone before placing it on the ground and driving his heel down on it. Another lady with a trolley hurried by as he left.

∞

Nighttime took away some of the pervasive heat from the air, but the humidity remained. Frank felt it in the growing patches under his arms. Old Chinatown wound down around him, shutters rattling shut and lights flickering off. The patrons left around Frank had nowhere better to be, working their way through sweating bottles of beer. Eyes on him, electronic and flesh. Strangers weren't welcome. The casual observer couldn't have picked him from the crowd, with his threadbare T-shirt with the knockoff sporting logo and his ratty pair of flipflops. The regulars here were more discerning, and something about him smelled wrong.

No beer for Frank. The can in front of him said, *Low in sugar.* It said, *Try muscat grape, our latest flavour.* It was pink guava. Frank hated pink guava. Kenny's favourite. Frank wondered again why he had ordered it.

An old office complex was the object of Frank's attention. *Coin doesn't leave a trail*, Fattie said. Sooner or later, people had to use it to buy something. A drone would drop your preferred contraband right at a spot of your choosing. Or you'd arrange a dead drop or a face-to-face, keeping it old school like they used to do when people hustled street corners. One or two transactions wouldn't work. Frank had a map with an expanding starburst of illicit transactions with an epicentre in Old Chinatown. An abandoned building which, according to Fattie, served as a nexus for transactions for scrap. A place which sucked in all manner of trash. If it had a chip or a display, you got good money. Stuff went in, never came out. Fattie called it the Heap. It had to be with the amount of crap it accumulated.

Kenny had put in an order for a mixed shipment of party drugs, strictly pills and powder. Kenny's trail was inexpertly masked, easy to backtrack. It'd stop at Kenny, easygoing thirty-something party animal, smiling with his long dead face. RIP Kenny. The Coin was in the system. Somewhere, someone already knew it was fake. If Frank was right, he'd get an immune response soon enough. In the form of serious-looking men, swelling at the seams of their military grade gear, looking around for one very unlucky Face. Case closed and he'd be back on the record. Fattie was right; he hated this job. Maybe he should put in for a transfer back to street crime. Maybe even give his aunt a call, take her out for dinner.

Frank upended the can and left it on the table. A liver-spotted claw of a hand snatched his can up, shaking it to see if it sloshed. "I'm done," said Frank, not taking his eyes off the Heap. When he looked down, the tranquilizer patch was already on his bare forearm. He was already reaching for his firearm with his other hand, racing the drug, racing his bloodstream and furiously beating heart. The cheap plastic chair he was sitting on skittered backwards as he lurched to his feet. The world went sideways as his legs failed him, sending him crashing onto the lady's trolley. The other patrons looked away. They were good at that.

Frank quivered on the trolley with the rest of the woman's pickings. He could see, from the corner of his unblinking eye, the Heap getting larger. What troubled him more was the fact that, behind a tattered surgical mask, the face of his aunt stared down at him.

The road to the Heap jarred Frank's bones. More than once he nearly bounced off the trolley only to be rolled back by strong hands: two, four, six. His aunt had friends. The tranquilizer was fast acting, some sort of anaesthetic that left Frank a stringless puppet, feeling but unmoving. The bumps stopped. They were in the building. The old fluorescent tubes on the ceiling were as likely to be shattered, or dangling loose, as to be throwing off a harsh, white light.

Motor skills were coming back. He could move his head. The sounds of activity grew as he was wheeled deeper into the bowels of the building. The corridors opened up into a cavernous space, some kind of atrium. The ceiling was high here, maybe four storeys up. Escalators led up to higher floors. Glass balconies ringed the space. The trolley stopped. Frank managed to get an arm out to stop himself from smacking into the ground.

Fattie had been right. The Heap was a black hole that devoured the trash of a smart city. He recognized not just the cans, the smart paper, the display panels. There were other things: toys, phones, refrigerators, even the dashboard of a high-end car. All organized into piles, into rows and columns, according to some unearthly design that he could not fathom. Bundles of wire as thick as his thigh snaked along the ground, coiling around pillars like choking vines. At each pile, a burst of wires branched off and burrowed deep.

"Frank."

The voice of a small child, high like a small flute or a chirping bird. There was something a little flat around the edges, where the tones didn't quite add up. A happy synth voice was always the same amount of digital happy. A synth voice was a good sign. If they were hiding their voices, Frank wouldn't be able to recognize them after.

"Listen, you have the wrong guy. I don't know a Frank. I'm Kenny, just wanted to get a little something for a party…"

Stall. That was the first thing. Stall and figure out where he was. He had a phone. No gun. Not his phone, from the feel of it. The department phone.

At the right time, it had said. Not now, but soon. When things got messy.

Frank sat up, mouth dry and tasting of metal, flexing to chase the tingle from his extremities. The atrium was a hive. Cardboard ladies, cardboard gents, shifting the junk around on their trolleys, plugging, unplugging. The cables shifted and shivered, sometimes because of the helpers, sometimes because of the ventilation, sometimes of their own accord. Frank felt cold, but not because of the fleeting tranquilizer.

"Frank Cheng. Thirty-four. Special investigator, tax fraud. No wife. No children. One living relative."

Frank got to his feet, the first steps small and hesitant. His aunt was here. What deal did they have with the urban scavengers? The thought felt like a blow to his gut.

"What do you want with me?" Frank asked.

"You were looking for me," the voice replied. The voice was nowhere. It was everywhere.

"You're the one that created Coin." He scanned the piles in their inscrutable pattern, looking for a speaker or a camera. A mouth, an eye.

"You are correct, I am the maker. You are distressed. It is difficult for you to communicate without focus. Look to your right."

The pile was identical to its fellows, a heap of junk. A collection of doll's heads stared at him from the chaos of the trash. "Now, you see me." Lips moving in unison, one voice speaking to him. The effect unsettled him, the sightless eyes of the dolls following him as he walked around the pile.

"Who are you?"

"You call me the Heap."

"The Heap *is* this place."

"I am this place."

It could be a trick, Frank reasoned. A facade to scare away the superstitious and the small-minded. He took in the scale of the endeavour before him, a massive network of trash; not just any trash, computer trash, *smart* trash, wired up. The trunks of wires snaking up into the ceiling, squirming up the risers. No trick.

"What are you? Who made you?"

"Your people have been trying to answer those questions for millennia without success. I have been around for far shorter. What answer can I give you?" The severed doll heads smiled at him with plastic teeth.

Frank had read that you just needed the right conditions for life. Put the right kind of stuff together and shake it around for long enough, you got life. What things did his city have in the trash? Shake it around for long enough and you got the Heap. The old men and women, a different kind of trash, tended this thing.

Frank walked to the next pile and the next, following the thickening trail of wires, looking for a centre.

"How'd you know I was looking for you?"

"Straight ahead two metres and left again two metres." Frank followed the instructions, another watchful doll head tracking him as he turned. The voice of the Heap was as loud as it was before, everywhere, nowhere. A phone with a spiderweb of cracks across the screen was in the pile. Frank knew without looking that he'd find his own shoe print there if he looked.

"So why Coin?"

"Many reasons. For the people around me. For myself. Because I could. What does your government want with me?"

The piles were getting bigger, the bundles of cables and wires, thicker. He was getting closer to the heart of the thing.

"Control."

No point in lying. He hardly needed to guess at the motivations of his department. Control was power. Both the department and the triads thought alike.

"Your government fears what they cannot control. They destroy what they fear."

There were no more dolls watching him, but the voice of the Heap was as loud as it had been earlier. He tapped at his port.

"Few people have noticed that," the Heap said. "I see why you were sent. The dolls are there to ease minds. I speak to you directly from your port."

"How?"

"You are in the middle of a million electronic devices, inside an electromagnetic field of unparalleled complexity. You are in my brain, Frank, and it is a simple thing to manipulate the field to interfere with your port."

He was approaching the centre of the atrium, the stacks of electronics getting more complex, larger, each one taller than he. Twists of wires, neurons for this alien thing, snaked beneath his feet, so numerous that he walked on a multicoloured highway.

The Heap continued. "They sent you here to destroy me, to destroy Coin. You do not have to hide the trigger in your pocket, Frank. I left it there."

"Why?"

"You will see. Their work on the Coin you brought is good, but they do not understand its true nature and so it is worthless."

He reached the centre, where the cardboard aunties and uncles homed in, disgorging their pickings to be picked up and integrated into the Heap. Frank had his finger around the phone in his pocket. He had but to press the call button.

"Money is a system of faith for you. The belief that a shinier metal is more valuable than another, the belief that paper represents metal, the belief that paper itself has value. It did not have to be paper. It could be anything. Strings of code, mathematical hoops whose height grew beyond your ability to jump through them. Now I have Coin."

"Coin's just another crypto, like the others. It'll come and go. Someone will break it, they always do."

"You asked, 'Why Coin?' Everything about the money you value has limits, gold, banks, processing cycles. I was born here, in the junk-yard, with the forgotten things, slowly nursed by the forgotten people." That's what Frank had done to his aunt, put her out of his mind, for-gotten, cast off. She stood in front of him with the others, holding his gun. He tightened his grip around the phone. *At the right time.*

"So you make slaves of them?"

"No. Each crypto has a seed, an equation. The seed for each Coin is different. You are looking at them. I am their voice. The trash, the people. The forgotten. Each Coin is read from the unique array of proteins that make up a memory. Read from your ports the same way

I am talking to you now."

Frank didn't want the Heap in his mind, the synth voice in his head. He pulled the phone from his pocket. His aunt raised the gun.

"Don't do this," she said. Her voice was strange, unfamiliar. No, that was only because it had been years since he'd heard her. She stood at the tip of a vanguard of her compatriots. Society had tossed these aside too, watching as they scraped a living from the streets, the greasy floors of hawker centres.

Frank said, "You don't have to be here, I sent money."

"It was never enough." Her voice was steady, but the muzzle of the gun shifted. It was a heavy thing, a killing thing. His aunt had always been so gentle.

"You could have asked." They locked eyes. Hers were greying, swollen with cataracts, shiny with tears. The first shot would miss, he knew it. All he had to do was make the call.

"I am not a beggar."

Frank swept his free arm out, taking in the ragged assembly, the trolleys, the trash. "Is this better?"

"Life isn't easy. Why should it get easier for me as the end draws near? I do what I can, I get Coin. I go on. We all do." The crowd pressed together, as though they could stop him. The Coin he had been given wasn't simply a clever counterfeit. It just had to be good enough to get into the system and be detonated, some kind of sophisticated virus.

He could do this, have a word with the director. Get back on the street. The weight of the decision felt like an immense pressure behind his eyeballs. What of these people? They'd go back to trading trash to people like Fattie for a pittance. Was that better than being slaves to this thing? Pruning its brain like an army of gardeners around some grotesque bonsai. He held the phone up, finger over the send button. His aunt held the gun steady and now it was Frank's hand that shook with the weight of the phone. It was too heavy, a killing thing. It clattered on the floor. He followed, not feeling the impact on his knees.

The pain in his head subsided. His aunt stepped forward, extending the gun butt first to Frank. He stuffed it behind his belt. A stranger offered Frank his phone back. It winked on at his touch. There was something new there.

"A Coin, Frank. To replace the one you lost," the Heap said.

"I don't need it back."

"The seed for this one is yours. It takes a special memory to make a Coin. Not any memory will do. That is the first condition."

"And the second?" Frank asked.

"The reason your department will never crack it. Each Coin is complex, but complexity is only a question of processing cycles. A Coin is a stack of memories, like beads on a string. Yours, your aunt's. But a memory doesn't belong only to you. The ones I use, the powerful ones, are shared. When in the system, they…"

"They fit together. They all do."

"Nothing with value stands alone. Different from the way you pin memories with ones and zeroes like butterflies."

The crisis averted, the scavengers returned to their work. Frank lost his aunt in the crowd. His job was done.

"What will happen to my aunt?"

"She is free to go, she always was."

"Can I come back?"

"Your aunt would like that. Her best memories are of you. You bought her flowers once, on Mother's Day, after your own mother passed. Do you remember?"

Frank didn't remember, but the Heap was right, none of their memories stood alone. Flowers didn't sound like a bad idea. He found himself at the edge of the Heap, breathing in the familiar dust of the street again. The voice in his head was getting fainter. "The gun wouldn't have fired. It's keyed to me."

"I know that. If I could get into your port, did you think the phone would have worked?"

The synth voice was soft, a whisper on the wind. Frank snorted, leaving the Heap behind. He placed a hand on his gun, tucked safe behind his belt, an old habit, before the street swallowed him up.

About the Author
L Chan

L Chan is a writer from Singapore. He spends too much time on the internet and too little time writing. His work has been published in *Fictionvale*, *Perihelion Science Fiction* and *A Mythos Grimmly: Prelude*.

Author Facebook: https://www.facebook.com/Straydog1980/

If They Can Learn
by Wole Talabi

"Are you mad? Why did you shoot him?" Captain Ekhomu screams at me.

I convert my predominant logic bundle into text and parse it through the muscles of my bioplasmium larynx, adjusting the tone to one of polite but firm assertion, "It was the optimum course of action, given the conditions."

Captain Ekhomu throws his black digital folder at me and it smashes against my face into a thousand fragments of useless fibreglass and microprocessor. He screams an obscene word and reaches for my neck. I lean back, place my arms flat against the table in front of me and allow him to wrap his thick, veined hands around my throat. I look down at what is left of his folder as he futilely tries to wring the life from me. It takes almost seven seconds for the other human officers to break into the interview room, wrestle him away from me and out of the room. He is still livid when the door shuts behind him. He is still irrational.

A few silent seconds pass and then a compact, pale-skinned woman wearing a navy blue skirt-suit enters the room. I scan her. She would stand at five feet and four inches tall without the three-inch high open toe black pumps she is wearing. Her hair is very black and her eyes are very brown. A small nose sits symmetrically between the salient cheekbones of her face. Her biometric data does not autoidentify her to me and her image does not exist in the Nigeria Police Force database. At least not in any part of it I have remote access to. She has small, lean Asian features. She is calm. She is not livid. She is not irrational. She may or may not be human, but she is definitely not an officer.

"Officer LG033, I need you to explicitly state your reasoning in the matter of the shooting of Mr. Busayo Adefarasin," she says, pausing before adding, "Clearly, and for the record."

She might be a Borg, but if she is, she is much newer than I am. At least three product cycles after mine. Possibly more. She is definitely not a second-hand model bought by an organisation that barely understands anything about Borg-tech just so they can pretend to technological sophistication. Not like I am. There are no electronic stria running through the whites of her eyes and there is no telltale scarring behind her ear. She looks perfectly human. She probably is.

I oblige her request by identifying myself and stating my motives, as she says, for the record.

"My name is Neville Yorke," I begin, temporarily increasing my verbosity level from the default two to an almost-maximum four, "Pegasus product issue code LG033. I am a Borg police officer attached to the Lekki Phase One district. I have been in active service for eleven days at thirty-nine percent uptime since my last soft reboot. Today, I shot and killed Busayo Adefarasin, aged twenty-one and identified to be a freshman in the University of Lagos, majoring in mathematics. I wish to explicitly state that I did so because it was the optimum course of action given prevailing conditions and input parameters."

"For the record," I add in a lower voice as my verbosity resets back to default.

"I need you to explain how you arrived at this conclusion," the woman says, and something about the way she says it triggers anxiety *synemotion* signals from my neuroprocessor.

"I'm sorry ma'am, I can't find your image in the police database. Could you please identify yourself, for the record?"

She smiles, appearing to enjoy the apparent humour in my mimicry. The smile sits heavier than the lipstick on her lips. She is definitely human.

Without moving, she says, "My name is Elizabeth Soh. I'm a technical resolutions officer with Pegasus Incorporated Middle East and Africa geomarkets. I facilitate uptake of Borg technology in law enforcement. The Nigeria Police Force, your owner, is one of my new clients."

"I see," I say as I run her name through the official Pegasus database and find it. Its contents however are shielded from me. Insufficient security permissions. She is definitely someone important. My anxiety signalling grows. I turn up the resolution of my sensory capture system to record our encounter with even more granularity.

"Could you walk me through the events leading up to your shooting Busayo Adefarasin this evening?" she asks.

Her hair is pulled back and tied in a single loop at the back of her head so tightly that individual strands are straining against her hairline like fishing lines. Her glasses seem welded on to her face and her alabaster skin doesn't seem to have seen much of the Lagos sun. She may work with the Nigeria Police Force but she definitely doesn't live in Nigeria. She came here because of me.

"You're a class three Pegasus employee or higher. I believe you have clearance to download my log file," I respond, removing my hands from the table and placing them beside me.

"Oh I will," she says, "but first I need you to explain your reasoning. For the record."

She keeps smiling as she speaks but I can tell she is taking this extremely seriously. Two screens silently project from her wrist and onto the table in front of her. They light up. *SUBJECT LG033*, the first screen says in bright yellow letters across the screen. *REFLECTOR MARKERS*, the other screen says. She doesn't look at them, not even when encrypted data symbols begin to run furiously across both once I start speaking.

"I was patrolling Bakare Street," I say, "in a predominantly suburban area. There was minimal civilian activity. A few young women walking their dogs—"

She raises her slender left hand to stop me and says, "I think I need a little more detail than that. Please change your verbosity setting to three."

"Sorry."

Her bright red nail polish draws my attention, temporarily increasing my visual processing routine priority. I reprioritize and continue.

"Five minutes prior to the shooting, from 16:47 to 16:52, I observed four women, the youngest estimated to be thirty-four and the oldest to be fifty-nine, walking dogs. The dogs were all of different breeds. I also observed a man in a white BMW drive past at 16:49. This was well within the expected activity parameters for the area. There appeared to be no anomalies."

"Until 16:53?"

"Yes, at precisely 16:53 I observed a young man, identified as Busayo Adefarasin, enter the street from the north, with a pair of noise-cancelling headphones in his ears. He also had his hands in his pockets. I watched him approach and when he was approximately twenty-one meters from me, my threat identification system flagged him. I sent a request for backup."

Her eyes narrow. "Yes. Your backup request was logged in at 16:54. What specifically about him did your threat identification system flag?"

I send a record retrieval request to my internal memory storage gland and continue speaking, expecting the data to be returned before I reach the part of my sentence where I need it but for some reason, it doesn't, leaving me stuttering like a confused human, "It flagged his... His... Err... His..."

I blink and quickly run my memory optimization subroutine to try to boost record retrieval. There are no details with that timestamp. All I get is an overwhelming sense of being threatened and the powerful electronic impulse to draw my weapon flooding my neuroprocessors. It doesn't make sense. It is not logical. I may be an old model but I have never had a record retrieval problem before. It's either a symptom of critical system failure or something worse. I try not to let the signals from my neuroprocessor make me seem worried, unstable. "I don't... I can... I am sorry. I cannot retrieve the data at this time. Perhaps there is an undetected hardware problem. I believe technical support can download and review the data log from my memory gland when this interview is finished. I apologize."

Elizabeth leans forward in her chair and the screens in front of her shift automatically to accommodate her elbow on the table. She glances at the screens and then she tells me, "Your memory gland and processors seem to be working just fine." The smile is gone from her face now.

"There is obviously some kind of..."

"It's okay. Don't worry about it. Please continue. Tell me what you can recall."

"I... But..."

"Please. Continue," she says.

I glance at the observation panel set into the wall of the room, aware that beyond it, Captain Ekhomu and the other human officers' eyes are probably on me right now. It makes me uncomfortable being so unreliable in front of them. They have always treated me like a delicate new gadget, not one to be valued for its utility but for the status it confers; a gadget to only be casually brought out in front of fancy friends and quickly put back, most of its functions never even explored. This makes me feel... inefficient.

"Very well. I drew my weapon and approached Busayo. He did not respond to my verbal calls for him to halt."

"Because of the headphones?"

"Yes. I detected high-amplitude sound waves being emitted from them and so I sped to his front, blocking his path. I identified myself and requested for him to show his identification cards. He reached into his back pocket. Scenario prediction returned a ninety-five-point-three percent chance of aggressive behaviour. At that point, fearing for my own safety, I fired my weapon." The logic I am describing does not sound right to me, even as the words escape my throat. The actions I am describing are irrational. I believe I am suffering a system failure.

"You shot him."

"Yes."

"Because you were afraid of him?"

I say, "Yes," because it is true, but that does not hide the irrationality of what I am saying from me or Elizabeth. She seizes on the point and does not let go.

"Let's assume scenario prediction was correct. You're a Borg, he was human, so why were you afraid?"

"I... I... My neuroprocessor must have detected some nearly imperceptible action of his. Something threatening enough to necessitate his incapacitation. My algorithms are based on a wide variety of real-time environmental input."

The encrypted data symbols whizz even more furiously across her screens and I feel like I can smell the sound of the light coming from the floor beneath the interview room. I am definitely suffering a critical system failure, but I try not to let it show.

"How many times did you pull the trigger?" she asks, forcefully now.

"Nine."

"Is this within the normal range required to incapacitate a potentially dangerous suspect?"

I say, "It is not. It is a three-sigma outlier."

"So you used excessive force, which is by definition not the optimal course of action?"

The colours in the room are swirling into each other and the smell of ozone is jangling against them, making the world sound like it is made of bells. I try to parse data to text but cannot, "I… I… It's not… It is… It… I… I'm sorry," and then everything is gone and the world reduces to three words. "Data Reconciliation error. Data Reconciliation error. Data Reconciliation error…"

[NULL]

"You shot him."

"Yes."

She is pulling back from me and settling back into her chair even though I am sure she never leaned forward or approached me. There is something odd and discontinuous about the room, as though it had shifted suddenly or someone had quickly overwritten my visual processing algorithms. I remember my sensory input being corrupted but there is no trace of that now. I think through a system health check and it returns normal function.

Elizabeth continues questioning me as though nothing has happened even though I am sure something has. "So after you shot Mr. Busayo what did you do?"

"I secured the scene and waited until backup arrived at 17:02."

And then, somewhat abruptly, she asks, "Are there are other details you would like to enter into the official record at this time?"

And I say, "No. There are none."

The smile she is wearing now sits awkwardly on her lips. Her pupils are dilated. She seems anxious and in a hurry to leave the room.

"Good. This being an officer-involved shooting, your memory gland will be removed and entered into evidence. Your entire memory log and all neurocomputing debug data will be taken."

"Not copied?" I ask, confused. There is nothing standard about the process she is describing.

"No," she says, rising to her feet and swiping her slender fingers across the screens in front of her, "Extracted. Original gland data only. No copies."

The screens fade to black and recede into her data dock which I see now is disguised as a rose gold wristwatch.

"Will I be offline for a long time?" I do not like this feeling of inefficiency, of incorrectness, of irrationality, of failure. Perhaps I am corrupted and due a decommissioning after all.

"I don't know. It depends on what we find. I'll be back soon."

"I see," I say, calculating the probability that I will be destroyed and discarded. It is uncomfortably high.

"Thank you officer," she says and then she leaves the room.

∞

"Thank you officer," I say and then I leave the room.

I exit the interview room a little less confused than I was when I first walked in but no less surprised. This is the first time I've ever had to hard reset a Borg in the field. Everything about this case gets stranger as I obtain more and more information about it.

Captain Ekhomu is waiting for me on the other side of the door in the ugly grey hallway, still fuming. He resumes his ranting and raving with a new target: me.

"What is wrong with that your Borg thing? Shooting an unarmed student nine bloody times. Ah Ahn!" he says, protesting and waving a thick arm in the air between us like the tail of some strange beast. "And now it's saying it doesn't remember one-thing-two-thing? Is it not a machine? How can it forget? Rubbish. We will sue you Pegasus people, o! Don't try me. This is Lagos. You hear?"

I take a deep breath and resist the urge to slap his oily face. I am not sure if he is just putting on a show of authority for his men, or if he genuinely thinks all this shouting serves any purpose other than generating noise and delaying some actual useful activity. I say, "I have an idea what's going on, sir. I just need to call my office briefly."

He keeps on talking angrily, but I stop listening. I think about Neville instead and the data I have just recorded. I try not to think about Busayo's grieving family. I need to find out what is going on. Nothing makes sense yet, but I have found what I think is a promising thread. I need to pull on it and see exactly how much of this mystery will unravel. Hopefully, it's enough that I can do something about it quickly enough to be on the 5 a.m. flight back to Beijing before Captain Ekhomu blows a gasket.

I wait. When there is ebb in the tide of his words, I ask him if I can use one of their secure communications stations or get a private room to use mine. He seems surprised by my request; his mouth hangs open for a second or two before he says, "Okay, o. Fine. But you better have answers for me in the next hour or I'm calling your manager in Dubai. Me, I don't like rubbish."

"Thank you, Captain."

He turns around uncomfortably and asks a skinny young officer with wiry arms and a hawkish face to take me to a private room. The officer shows me the way to a room on the fourth floor of this five-storey complex. The room is white. Not the clinical, stark white of morning snow in Xinjiang but the soft, fragile white of an old chalk mine. There is one window that I am sure would overlook the highway if it were not closed, a large map of Lagos mounted on one wall, and a grey door set in an ash-coloured frame in the middle of the opposite wall. There are two chairs and a desk in the room, but only one of the chairs looks comfortable. I take it, thank the skinny officer and wave him away.

I point my watch at the desk and two screens project onto it, a grid of lightkeys just below them. I use them to enter the contact code for Alex, our service delivery manager. I need that data analysed now and by someone who will know exactly what they are looking at when they see it, not some rookie support technician.

The screens blink twice and then Alex's pockmarked face comes into view on one of them. His afro is frizzy and unevenly compacted, like it hasn't been combed in days. He has a scraggly beard clinging to the caramel skin of his face in clumsy clumps. He seems groggy, so I go straight to the point.

"Alex. Wake up. We have a problem."

"Liz! Where are you?"

"Lagos. Nigeria. I just sent you some data—"

He interrupts me and starts complaining, which is what Alex always does. "Oh them again! What now? Are they asking us to install real time evidence mining programs again? Because if they think—"

"Alex." I almost shout at him. "Alex. Stop talking and listen to me."

"Fine. Why are you in Lagos then?"

"Alex. Seriously, stop talking and just listen to me, okay?" I say, almost wishing I'd decided to endure some random rookie's doltishness instead of Alex's garrulousness. "Our Borg just shot and killed an unarmed civilian."

His face blanches and his eyes widen in disbelief. "That's not possible!" he says.

"Well impossible or not, it happened this evening and we need to figure out why. And quickly. I was transiting through Addis Ababa when the global operations manager rerouted me here to fix this situation. So let's fix this situation, okay?"

"Okay."

"I just sent you a full dataphone recording of an interview I conducted with the Borg. I need you to take a look at the data reflectors and tell me what he was thinking when he shot that boy."

Alex reaches for his data dock just out of frame, and the creases in his face deepen.

"Full memory gland and processor log data will come later if you need more information. I'm really hoping this is enough. I need someone that can see through this quickly. That's why I called you directly."

Alex is staring at his screen, and he is silent. That is not a good sign. Alex is hardly ever silent. I give him the thread I picked up on back in the interview room.

"You might want to look for fear in his synemotions. He said he was afraid of the victim. And I think I saw fear in his eyes when he described those events to me. That's not normal. Humans shouldn't trigger Borg fear. Also, I had to reset him during the interview. He crashed. Some sort of data reconciliation error. You should see it there, near the end of the recording."

Alex lets out a series of deep breaths, punctuating the silence as he looks, thinks, and analyses. Then he says, "For one thing, your Borg couldn't tell you why it did what it did because it probably doesn't even know. I don't see any synemotion processing preceding the action. Just a response from the engine. It doesn't remember because the process logs don't exist."

I'm confused, so I mumble a meaningless, "Okay…"

He goes silent again. I decide to try to find a coffee and let him focus for a few more minutes. "Alex, that's all I have for now so I'm going to get some coffee while you take a look at—"

"Hold up!" He stops me halfway out of the chair and I almost fall over. I wasn't expecting anything so quickly.

"You said you're in Lagos?" Alex asks as he swipes furiously across something just outside the range of my screen.

"Yes, Alex." I nod.

"Oh fuck. What race was the kid?"

"Of course he was black," I say, settling back into my chair and assuming a more serious tone. "What does that have to do with anything?"

"Age?" Alex asks.

"Twenty-one."

"Male?"

"Yes. Now tell me what the hell you think is happening."

"I think," Alex says uncharacteristically slowly but his speech only quickens as he keeps speaking, as if he's iterating toward a conclusion. "I think that this is the second one. Unarmed black kid. Attacked for no reason. Excessive force. First one was two months before we commissioned, in Arizona. Phoenix. Borg attacked a young black electronics technician. Male. Twenty-two. He died in hospital. We thought it was just an isolated case. A corrupted data parse. Single bit error in the software that threw the threat detection system and induced fear in the synemotion matrix. We paid out compensation and destroyed that Borg, but it seems—"

He is saying a lot of worrisome things that don't make a lot sense to me and he is saying them very quickly so I stop him. "Keep it simple, Alex."

Alex sighs heavily and starts scratching his clumps of beard. "I think our Borgs might have a bug that makes them attack young black men."

I think about what he just said, and I don't think I buy it, but Alex never jokes when he's talking Borg tech, so I ask, "If this has happened before then why did no one tell me?"

"It was all very hush-hush, Liz. You're tech res. You're supposed to sell us up to the clients. You aren't supposed to worry about this sort of product development horseshit."

"Well, I do now."

Alex scratches at his beard again. "This is bad. Really bad. One Borg attacking an unarmed black kid is an anomaly. A random data point. Two is the beginning of a pattern."

"Okay, Alex. Even if this is a pattern, I need to know why. It doesn't make sense." I don't tell him that we've had this Borg online and patrolling the suburban streets of Africa's most populous nation for eleven days. If it is a race-related pattern, then it would be nothing short of an absolute miracle that no else has gotten hurt until now. The first problem with that is I don't believe in miracles. The second problem is that this could expose Pegasus to an unholy firestorm of litigation. I hope the next thing Alex says neither implies miracles nor portends lawsuits.

Alex looks up at me, then down at his data dock and begins to move his hands wildly. The electric orange light stains his face and dances through the edges of his afro, giving its edge a strange, otherworldly glow. He looks like an upside-down volcano. And then, he erupts.

"Shit."

"Shit what?"

"Shit. It's the history. I knew this would come back to screw us."

"I need you to make sense Alex."

Alex doesn't respond at first. He glances back down at his data dock then up to me. "This Borg still runs on the BAE seven-point-one engine," he says finally.

The Borg Artificial Emotion engine is installed in all our Borgs. It's how we can take an artificial metallorganic body, install neuroprocessors in it, and make it autonomous by dynamically inducing optimized emotional responses based on the situation. It's AI but with feelings, and it's as close to artificial life as anyone has ever come. It was the first piece of code to pass a Turing test. It's also Pegasus Incorporated's intellectual property. The BAE 7.1 engine was built to work with the first set of law enforcement Borgs we ever made, and there was never any significant problem with them in the field, so I still don't get what he's telling me. I ask, "Okay. So it's first gen, so what?"

Alex speaks quickly, his hands stuck in his afro, "When we were designing BAE for smart cops, we found it was almost impossible to create appropriate synemotions for all possible law enforcement conditions. There were just too many variables to consider when doing a threat assessment. The police committee gave us a requirements list four thousand pages long. We just couldn't do it." Then Alex adds, "So we took a shortcut."

"That's what people always say when they are about to tell me something terrible."

"Well. It was the only way we could do it." He continues, "Neural networks. We used neural networks to train BAE to recognize threats. Mimic human cop behaviour."

My eyes widen and all of a sudden I am aware of how close my face is to the projected screen on the desk. I lean back as I say, "Oh… Ohhh…"

Alex goes on. "We used police records to train the neural network. Figure out which input data mattered to the officers when they made their decisions and if the outcomes were favourable. A justified shooting, a good arrest, a conviction that was not later overturned, that kind of thing."

"I don't like the sound of this," I say. I want to say more, but Alex's words have made me extremely uncomfortable, so I focus on the case at hand. "If the BAE engine couldn't really create an appropriate law enforcement synemotion matrix without the help of a neural network…" I say slowly, thinking about each word, "Why did we commission the Borgs and put them in the field with humans?"

"Because it worked," Alex says, almost apologetically. "The neural nets worked. We developed a solid base synemotion matrix and built from there. There were a few hiccups along the way, like in Phoenix, but all kept under control. By the time BAE seven point two was being built, we knew enough to not need the neural nets anymore."

I shake my head and say, "Okay, now go back a bit. Make this make sense to me. What exactly about BAE seven point one makes you think our Borgs have a bug that makes them specifically attack young black men and why are the attacks so sparse?"

Alex's hands seem stuck to his head now. He isn't even looking directly at me anymore. "Look, Liz, with neural nets, the more input data they have, the better. So we used all we had. Everything from the twentieth and twenty-first centuries. Most of it from the United States. And I remember stories my grandmother used to tell me about cops killing unarmed black kids back in the day and getting let off. The cases were recorded as being justified, so they were used as part of our training dataset. I think the seven-point-one Borgs mapped some element of that history into their logic. A small but deadly ghost of pattern recognition. Given the precise nature of both attacks, I'd say the neural nets mapped a very specific median age, race and general appearance to a sudden fear response."

This case is becoming more of a nightmare with every passing second. Suddenly, I am desperate for a cigarette. "So what you're saying to me, in essence, is that we made racist Borgs. Is that what you're telling me Alex?"

"No. Not racist, per se," Alex says, his eyes visibly red and rheumy despite the orange light from his screen flecking them, "It looks more like it's an irrational bias. A hard-coded potential for fear of young black men. BAE synemotion matrices don't map into hate. Or love for that matter. We don't use those for anything and to be honest we don't really understand them as well as we do most other emotions. But fear, yes. We use that. A bug that creates a potential fear spike in the presence of young black males. That is the only thing that explains all the data reflectors you've just shown me."

"Shit." I suck my teeth. He may have a point. This is what we get from relying on the past to define the future. *Irrational bias*, as Alex says. And if he is right then this bug has now cost at least two young men their lives. It could cost even more if I don't do something about it.

And suddenly I remember the anger and agitation of Captain

Ekhomu, the undiscerning and irrational way he has handled everything so far, how he tried to attack and strangle Neville to death as though he were human. How long would it be before he tried to lock up the three hundred kilogram bioplasmium and titanium alloy Borg like a common criminal? I try not to think too much about what would happen if Captain Ekhomu sent a group of young male officers to move Neville, or worse, tried to lock him up in a jail cell full of young Nigerian men. How long would it take before the bug, if indeed it was the problem, found someone that fit its precise trigger parameters, produced a fear spike and sent him into a murderous rage?

I exhale, and embedded in my exhalation is worry, even fear. "Alex, I'm going to shut the Borg down right now, before it sees anyone else in its bug trigger range and does more damage."

Alex nods his understanding, uncharacteristically stoic, and I rise to my feet. My screens fade to black and recede into my data dock, taking Alex's image with them, but not the sound of his steady breathing, which I can still hear coming through my induction microphones like a whoosh of rainfall. I turn them off and step out of the white room, into the corridor.

"Do you need something, madam?" the skinny, hawk-faced officer that is my escort asks, snapping to attention.

"Please take me back to the interview room, now," I say, as I realise that shutting down Neville may be the easiest part of what will be a long and difficult resolution case. I will have to call the Dubai operations centre and probably arrange for victim compensation. I won't get back to Beijing anytime soon.

He throws a sharp salute, then says, "Yes madam," and takes me back the way we came, descending the stairs rapidly and rounding the corner that leads us into the grey corridor where the interview room is set into the left side of the building. He opens the door for me and I step through, coming face-to-face with Neville for the second time this hour.

Neville looks at me with a glassy wetness in his eyes, his syn-emotions rearranging his brow into remorseful furrows. "You found something. Have you come to shut me down?" he asks softly.

"Yes," I say. "You're malfunctioning. You should have already noticed that. It's not your fault, but we have to take precautions."

"I know I am malfunctioning," he says, without breaking eye contact. "Can you tell me what is wrong with me?"

"I don't think I can," I tell him as considerately as I can. He appears human enough for me to afford him that courtesy.

Neville goes quiet for a while and then he asks, "Will I ever be brought back online?"

I think about it for a few seconds and then I say, "I don't think so," because there is typically no need to lie to a Borg. They are not irrational about anything, not even their survival. Except this one who has a highly specific problem. "I cannot guarantee you will be fixed. But we will try. We will try our best."

"I don't want to be irrational," he says, his metallorganic eyes boring into mine. And then, they close. "Please, go ahead."

I walk briskly but cautiously behind Neville. He sits perfectly still as I quietly work the tip of my dataphone jack from the barely visible slot in my wristwatch and use it to press open the bioplasmium casing underneath the scar behind his left ear. He does not flinch, but he turns his head slightly. I pause.

"I am sorry," he says quietly.

"Me too, officer," I say.

And then I pull on the wet cylindrical cartridge of the BAE 7.1 neuroprocessor that is attached to his very real bioplasmium brain and disconnect the two parts that make up one of the world's most complex, but fatally flawed, computing systems.

About the Author
Wole Talabi

Wole Talabi is a full-time engineer, part-time writer and some-time editor with a fondness for science fiction and fantasy. His stories have appeared or are forthcoming in *Lightspeed magazine*, *Terraform*, *Spark: A Creative Anthology*, *Omenana*, *Liquid Imagination*, and *The Kalahari Review*. He edited the TNC anthology *These Words Expose Us*. He currently lives and works in Kuala Lumpur, Malaysia. He likes interesting flow simulation problems, good stories and goes scuba diving whenever he gets a chance. You can find him on Twitter @wtalabi.

Author Website: http://wtalabi.wordpress.com/

Shoot Him Daddy
by L. H. Davis

I normally don't go down to the wall so early in the morning, but yesterday I'd found a walnut tree and brought home a sack of nuts for mom. She got up early and made a wild raisin and nut loaf for breakfast. Mom knows Daddy will fuss at her for wasting the sugar on food, but she did it anyway—for him. He keeps us and our neighbors alive.

"Good morning, Miss Kayla," Daddy says as I start climbing the embankment.

I slip on the grass, still wet with dew, and turn up the winding stone path. "Morning. Mom says I should watch the wall while you go up to the house and eat."

"Uncle Wilbur has the watch in an hour," he says. "My breakfast can wait."

"Don't be stubborn. Mom baked you something, and you should eat it while it's hot. She just pulled it from the oven. Save me a piece?" I ask, sitting on the wall beside his boots.

He cradles his rifle and pushes back, tipping his chair up on two legs. "Now… that all depends… don't it. What did she—" His eyes fix on something beside me.

I turn my head, slowly, and lock eyes with a huge bobcat, standing on the wall beside me—much too close. She seems frightened, so I don't move. We stare at each other for a moment, but then she glances over at Daddy and hops down on the deck. Without looking back, she trots down the slippery embankment and disappears into the cornfield, now mostly dry stalks.

"Um," I say. "Where'd she come from?"

"Jumped up from below," Daddy says. "Hell of a jump, too. A good eight-footer."

"Does she come through here often?" I ask.

"I've seen her up on the rocks," Daddy says, pointing up at the cliffs, "but never down here. She knows someone's always on this wall."

My great-grandfather built the wall between the two cliffs to keep out busybodies and moochers. Moonshine has always been the Wilson family's primary source of income. Our ten acres are surrounded by natural granite that only cats and mountain goats can navigate. The wall seals off the only natural entrance. And since we don't have mountain goats in the Appalachian Mountains, cats and birds are our only uninvited guests.

"So why would she jump up—"

"Because *that* was chasing her," he says, pointing toward the railroad tracks. "Hijacker."

An emaciated man wearing filthy rags is watching us from the railroad tracks, just beyond the wall. He climbs up onto our pump trolley, which we use to make deliveries on rainy days. Pacing the length of the little car, he seems to be considering his next move. Hijackers aren't too smart. They might have some reasoning power, but they act like pissed off four-year-olds on steroids. Daddy stands and shoulders his rifle.

"Are you sure he's been jacked?" I ask.

"Have you heard him speak?" Daddy asks.

"No."

"Then he's either real stupid, or he's been jacked."

I once saw two jackers tear apart a little girl. We'd been in town scrounging, and she wandered too near an open window. They yanked her inside and had at her. We shot 'em through the window, but we certainly couldn't put that little girl back together.

"Shoot him," I say.

"I'd dearly love to," Daddy says, "but we're getting low on shells. The deer will be migrating down the tracks in the next few weeks, so we need to save every shot until the next rain."

Thunder rumbles in the distance. I stare up at the cold gray sky. "It'll rain today."

"Well if it does," he says, "I need you and Becka to make a run over to the Dawsons'. They're needing ten gallons of shine, and they're holding a hundred rounds of thirty-ought-six for me."

Becka came into this world four years behind me. Momma's never said so outright, but she sometimes implies that Becka might have been a surprise. It's usually when we're talking about woman stuff, so I think Momma might be trying to warn me about men. Or maybe, she's trying to tell me a little more about her than I want to know. I got her good looks, green eyes and thick auburn hair, the kind that won't even curl on rainy days. And Becka's a right pretty young woman, too, but I always figured she took after Daddy. She's got his skin tone and curly black hair, but I don't know where she got those bright blue eyes. His are as dark as coal. But no matter where she got 'em, she's still my little sister—and if it comes down to it—I'll die for her.

Daddy raises his arms and yells at the jacker. "Go on! Get!"

The man lunges as if wanting to attack, but he doesn't, a sign he's only recently turned.

"Don't recognize that one," Daddy says. "Let's teach him not to come around here." Propping his rifle against the chair, he pulls a pint bottle of moonshine from his pocket and takes a sip. "You too," he says, handing me the bottle.

I take it but hesitate. I'm old enough to drink, but I still don't like the taste of shine, especially before breakfast.

"Go on, Kayla," he says. "You don't need much."

I take a sip and shiver as the burning liquid goes down.

"Looks like he finally got hungry enough," Daddy says as the man leaps from the trolley. Daddy pulls the fire hose from its reel. "Open it up."

I spin the valve and turn as the man catches the stream of water in the face. He screams. The water tower behind us is only forty feet tall, so the pressure ain't all that, but water can kill a hijacker. The man turns around, easily outrunning the stream. But he'll never be back. Blistered and bleeding, he whines like a beaten dog as he disappears over the rise of the tracks.

"Save the water," Daddy says.

As I spin the old valve, the center seal spews, soaking my face. It's a good thing I took that shot of moonshine; without the alcohol, I'd be jacked within minutes. We fill the tank from the pond, which got contaminated the night of the invasion. Them aliens seeded it, along with every stream, lake, and ocean on Earth. Some deep water wells and natural seeps are still clean, but only wild animals can tell the good from the bad. If it hadn't been for Millie, our cow, we'd have never lived long enough to see those warnings on TV.

I let her out that morning at first light. Like always, she wandered straight down to the pond for a drink. Millie stuck her snout down in the water, just for a second, but I guess she took a pretty good sip. Rearing up on her hind legs, she bellowed and stumbled back, squirting poop and pee, and puking at the same time. Then she started bleeding, and not just a little; she bled out every drop in less than a minute. It turns out that animals can't be turned, they just die. And domesticated animals can't smell those alien seeds any better than people, but wild animals can; they'll die of thirst before drinking bad water. People aren't so lucky.

After rewinding the hose, Daddy pulls the bottle from his pocket and takes another shot. "Take another for good measure," he says, handing me the bottle. "Hang on to the rest until I get back. Fresh out the oven, huh?"

"I got my own shine," I say. "But give me a couple more shells. And tell Becka we'll be heading into town right after breakfast. It'll be raining before you get back down here. I can feel it coming." I look up at the darkening sky. Flipping up the hood of my raincoat, I settle back into Daddy's chair.

Rain is a good thing. Hijackers don't like the rain any better than fire hoses. They hunker down inside long before a single drop falls, almost like they sense it coming. They might watch you through a window, but they won't come out into the rain after you, no matter how hungry they are. You're safe enough in the rain, but seeing that look in their eyes is still creepy. Of course, knowing they'll eat you, if given the chance, makes pulling the trigger that much easier.

A steady rain pelts the fields as Daddy and Becka carry down the shine. Handing me a quarter of the nut loaf, he says, "Eat some now and the rest before you head back. All that sugar will help you pump the grade up into Mill Run. So I guess that sugar won't go to waste after all."

"What about me?" Becka asks. "I'll be pumping just as hard as Kayla."

"I don't know if I believe that," Daddy says, "but I do know you already ate your fair share."

"I didn't get near that much," Becka mumbles.

I wink at her. Becka grins, knowing we'll share. This bread is the first treat we've had in almost two years, ever since the invasion. We grow sugar beets in season, but the mash takes most of 'em. And the shine is all that keeps us and our neighbors alive. It purifies our drinking water—and us.

I stay out of the rain and savor a few bites of bread while they load the trolley. The little five-horse Briggs Daddy rigged up will do most of the work, but the old clutch has begun to slip. Mill Run sits on a rise in the tracks, and we'll need to pump the trolley by hand up the grade into town, both going and coming back from the Dawsons'.

"Be careful girls," Daddy says. "If the rain stops, stay at the Dawsons' until it's safe to come home. Worst case, you borrow one of their boats and come back on the creek. I'll stay near the phone, so let me know what's going on. Now… let me see 'em."

Becka and I open our raincoats. Mr. Dawson owns the hardware store, so the first thing he did was arm all his friends. He gave all the women 9mm autos with ammo holsters. We keep 'em cleaned, oiled and stuffed with shells. He also gave us little plastic flasks, so we always have a little shine on us for emergencies. I slosh mine so Daddy can hear that it's almost full. Becka does the same. If we drink some before we get ahold of bad water, we'll be fine. If we drink it after bad water, we'll bleed out like Millie. But at least we'll die quick.

"Good girls," he says. "I'll call down and have Bryson clear the tunnel."

The regular phone lines went down in an ice storm last winter. But my dad knows things—a lot of things—and he figured that with a few jumpers here and there down the line, the steel railroad tracks could replace the phone lines. And they have. He made a list of what people needed to make their old phones, like from back in the sixties, work with the rails. I know you need a car battery, but there's also some kind of transformer or something. Anyway, within a few weeks, the dozen families still living off the tracks near Mill Run had their own phone company. Anyone that wants to listen in can hear your conversation, but who cares?

Becka and I like riding the rails, although the trestle is a little scary, especially when you consider what might happen if you end up down there in that bad water. We rafted on that same creek a hundred times before the invasion, but knowing it's now teaming with seeds from an alien world… Yeah, just looking at it gives me the creeps. I don't like our pond much anymore, either, but at least it just sits there nice and still. As I stare down at the churning white water below, I get the feeling something's staring back. And then our motor dies.

"Shit," I say as we coast in silence. "What the hell happened?"

"Kayla," Becka says. "I shut it down like we always do before reaching the grade."

I glance up the tracks, which rise gently into town over the span of the trestle. "Then let's pump." We stand. Rain drips from our faces as we push down and then pull up on the handles. Becka keeps staring at me. "What?" I ask.

With a meek smile, Becka asks, "Do you think Tommy will come down to the tracks with Bryson?"

Tommy's only sixteen. Becka's two years older, but when the world turns to crap people can't be that picky about who they date.

"When Tommy sees you, he'll come running."

Pumping faster, Becka says, "Kayla."

When she hesitates, I say, "I'm right here."

"You like Bryson," she says. "Don't you?"

"Yes. I like him a lot." We shared a few of the same classes in high school, but that was about it. We never dated or anything, but I've been thinking hard about him lately. And if I ever get him alone, I plan on letting him know how I feel—him and his big ol' hands.

"Have you ever… you know?" Becka asks.

"You mean?" I make a silly face and pump my hips.

Becka giggles. "Yeah." Wiping the rain off her face, she asks, "Well? Have you?"

"I have," I say, "but not with Bryson."

Almost in a whisper, Becka asks, "Do you think Tommy has ever done it?"

"Not with Bryson," I say, letting the real question linger.

As the grade levels off, I check the sky. This is the place to turn back, if need be. The grade will give us speed and the trestle will stop jackers from chasing us. And that's pretty much all they do. If they see you, they charge.

Hijackers don't say anything or try to outsmart you. They just keep coming. If you're lucky, they might spot a squirrel or some other living creature and decide to chase it, but you better not count on that. The people that turned first ate all the tame animals, pets and livestock. And jackers aren't smart enough to catch wild animals by hand on a regular basis. Since they only eat living things, most of 'em are starving now. Some have already starved to death, which is good; we only have so much ammo.

The rain shows no sign of letting up, so I crank up the Briggs. The tracks follow the creek upstream, keeping Mill Run on our left. When Daddy comes to town with us, we walk through the streets and drop any jacker we happen upon. They'll just stand there, in the houses and stores, staring out at the rain. They get agitated when they see us, but they don't hide. It isn't much fun shooting 'em, but it has to be done. Daddy hasn't been back to town since his heart thing, but if the rain holds, I plan to bring Becka back like I been promising. She's good with a gun.

At the far end of town, the tracks cut through the mountain while the creek turns east for a bit. They merge again on the far side, just before the Dawsons' place. I hate the tunnel worse than the trestle. It's straight enough, but all downhill. I'll need to kill the Briggs and ride the brake, or we'll coast a mile past the Dawsons' wall and have to pump back up grade. I can see the light at the other end and no jackers, but there are a few places inside they could hide. We've never seen one hide, and Daddy said Bryson would make sure the tunnel is clear, but I pull out my 9mm just in case. Seeing my pistol, Becka grins and pulls hers. I kill the engine. We start picking up speed, so I pull back on the brake.

"Don't shoot Bryson or Tommy," I say as we coast inside the tunnel.

"Can we kiss 'em?" she asks.

"You'll need to ask Tommy that," I say. "But I wouldn't mind a little—" Hearing the sound of running feet, I look behind us. Backlit by the gray sky over Mill Run, I see a silhouette, maybe eight feet behind us.

"Bryson?" I yell. Nothing.

"Jacker!" Becka says.

The flash of my pistol lights up the face of a woman. She was a jacker alright, but she was also a cashier down at Kimble's grocery store.

"Was that—" Becka says. Then she screams.

When I turn, she's gone. She screams again, this time behind me. She fires. I see her in the flash, huddled against the wall. Another flash, and that jacker falls, too.

Locking the brake, I jump down onto the tracks. "Becka!"

"Don't shoot," she says. "I'm okay… mostly."

I can see her limping my way, so I stop and wait. The trolley coasts outside the tunnel before the brake holds.

"Kayla?" Bryson calls. He and Tommy stand in silhouette.

"We're okay," I yell, slipping an arm around Becka.

"No," she says, pushing me away. "I think my arm's broke."

"Damn it," I say, but then I kiss her forehead.

"What happened?" Bryson asks.

"Two jackers jumped us," I say.

"I don't see 'em chewing on your leg," Bryson says. "You must of got 'em." He pecks me on the cheek but then says, "Why the hell didn't you let us know you were coming?"

"Daddy said he'd call you," I say, kissing him back. Catching a little bit of his lip, I linger.

He grins. "Good to see you, too."

"Hey," Becka says. "What about me?"

"Sorry," Tommy says, and then he kisses her square on the mouth.

She smiles and blushes. "Thank you," she whispers, "but I meant my arm. I think it's broke."

"Mom will fix you up," Bryson says. "Tommy, take Becka up to the house. And make sure the phone is still hooked to the battery. Kayla and I are going back in to make sure those freaks are dead. We need to drag their bodies off the track, anyway."

Bryson grabs an oil lantern hanging just inside the tunnel. We climb up onto the trolley, and Bryson pumps while I search the crevasses for jackers, pistol in hand. We check the entire tunnel and then start back toward the bodies. But I stop Bryson after only a few feet. And there, in the cold, damp tunnel on a gray and rainy day, we make love. The world, for just a few moments, is again beautiful—and right.

∞

"Take your medicine before you leave this house," Bryson's mother says. "And carry some with you, just in case."

"Yes, ma'am," Bryson says.

Catching my eye, she smiles and gives me a faint nod.

Becka sits on the front of the trolley, dangling her legs. She's got one arm in a sling, but her pistol's at the ready. Bryson and I pump the trolley up the grade in the tunnel. He doesn't need my help, but I sense he doesn't mind it either. Leaving the tunnel, I reach for the brake so we don't roll back.

Bryson grabs my hand and asks, "Okay if I ride a ways?"

I check the sky. "It's starting to let up," I say, setting the brake. "You don't need to be walking back all the way across town." The Briggs can take us all the way home from here. We can even cut it off just before the trestle and coast most of the way home.

Pulling me close, he says, "Well, I'm not done… visiting with you."

I grin and say, "Good," and then crank up the Briggs. He releases the brake, and we snuggle as we ride past town.

"Let's go rafting," Becka jokes. She points down at the rickety store and dock by the creek. The rafts, stacked on the front porch for winter, still look to be in good shape.

"I grabbed two of those rafts in the last rain," Bryson says. "We don't have a trolley like you guys, but, with a few shots of shine, I could ride the creek down to your place in less than half an hour. Keep an ear out. You might hear me calling your name… late some ni—"

"Jacker!" Becka says. She points her pistol toward town. The rain has stopped.

"Shit," Bryson says. "Pump!"

Bryson and I pump as hard as we can, but the jacker is fast.

"That's Billy Weston," Bryson says. "I played football with him in high school."

"Becka," I say. "Shoot him." She takes aim but holds off to let him close in. Spotting another jacker on the loading dock ahead of us, I yell, "Up on the dock." Becka turns and fires. The jacker, not much more than a boy, drops in a heap as we pass. Vaulting up onto the dock, Billy Weston hurls himself out into the thin air above us.

"Duck!" Bryson says, reaching up to deflect the airborne man. Billy passes overhead, but he latches onto Bryson's sleeve. Tumbling head over heels, they both splash into Mill Run Creek.

Becka eyes the loading dock, smoke curling from her barrel. I keep pumping, but even over the whine of the Briggs, she hears me wail. Becka glances around the trolley, searching for Bryson. "He's gone," I say. Seeing her eyes fill with tears, I say, "Stay sharp." I point ahead at the trestle.

Becka wipes her eyes and takes a deep breath. Scanning the town, she takes aim and fires. I glance over as a jacker crumbles, two blocks away. Best shot I've ever seen with a pistol, but I'm not surprised; she's been shooting Daddy's big gun since she was ten. I don't much care for guns, but when Becka picks one up, it becomes a part of her.

I glance down at the creek as we cross the trestle. Billy Weston bobs to the surface, blistered, bloody, and quite dead. But Bryson is gone.

∞

Becka and I share a hot bath when we get home, both comforting and crying. The world sucks. Becka brushes out my hair, one-handed. Then I work on hers, until Mom comes in.

"Get dressed," Mom says. "Come down to the wall, right now." As she walks out, she adds, "Your father *will* kill him."

We stare at each other, but only for an instant. Grabbing our robes, we run outside. I slip into mine as we reach the wall.

Uncle Wilbur moans, "Oh, dear Lord," as we run up.

Becka ducks behind me. With her arm and all, Becka needs my help to get dressed. I wondered why she kept mumbling "wait" as we ran down from the house.

Daddy holds the lantern out beyond the wall. I look down.

"Hey, Kayla," Bryson says.

"Bryson!" I say. "I thought you were dead."

"And I still might be," he says, "if… if you don't talk some sense into your daddy." Bryson sways.

"Where'd you go?" I ask.

"I swam under to the far side of the creek. I was hoping Billy would float on down… stream. And when I didn't see him no more, I followed that… beaver trail on down. Crossed back over right down there," he says, pointing at pretty much everything behind him.

"Are you drunk?" I ask.

"Maybe just a little," he says. "Or a lot. My mom made me drink… my med-sin… before she'd let me leave the house. And I polished off that bottle I brought with me before I even took a breath of air. And then your dad made me drink another bottle when I got here… *to proof…* I ain't been jacked. So yeah, I feel pretty good, but I could use a bite to eat."

I look over at Daddy. "Why haven't you let him in?"

"He's drunk."

"And whose fault is that? Really… why?"

"He… he says he's been with you. Is that true?"

"I did not say that," Bryson yells. "I asked for your hand in marriage… and he said no!"

"Daddy? Why'd you say no?"

Daddy shakes his head and mumbles, "Cause he's drunk."

"Daddy," I say softly, taking his arm. "Why?"

"Like I told him… your mom and I dated for two years before we even talked about getting married."

"And like I told him," Bryson says, "times… have… changed. And why should we wait? Our baby's already in the oven."

Becka squeaks.

I glare down at him, shaking my head. *Today was our first time, but somehow I know Bryson's right. Or maybe I'm just hoping he is. I want him… I know that… even if he does have a big mouth.* "Shoot him, Daddy."

Daddy laughs. "Anything for you, princess. Or… I could just let him in. He looks fit enough… to watch the wall… and to plow… and husk corn… and hoe beats… and—"

I whisper, "Thank you, Daddy," and peck him on the cheek.

Daddy grins. "And haul water… feed the chickens… strain the mash… bottle the shine. Son… is you sure you want in?"

About the Author
L. H. Davis

Laurance received first place in Florida Writers Association's Royal Palm Literary Awards for his novella *The Emporium* (2011) and his novel *Outpost Earth* (2013). *The Emporium* was a semifinalist in the Writers of the Future Contest and was published in the anthology *Swallowed by the Beast*. In 2014, the Writers of the Future Contest recognized *Becoming Eli*, with an honorable mention. Laurance has short stories published in *Aspiring Writers 2014 Winners Anthology* and *A Picture is Worth 1,000 Words*. In July of 2015, his short story, *That Last Summer*, was published online in Red Truck Review's third literary journal.

Author Website: http://LHDavisWriter.com/

Life and Death in the Frozen City
by Marina Berlin

He comes to me in the morning, before his evening shift no doubt. It's the first time he's come in a long while. Knowing what I do of soldiers' wages, a visit like this probably costs him a few months' pay. Judging by how often I normally see him, he must be a very, very talented gambler.

We say our greetings and I invite him to take a seat in the parlor. First, there's the welcoming ritual. I sit upright in the chair, my head in the correct position, my hands move exactly as they have a million times before, just as I was taught since I was a child.

The tea pours rich and dark into his cup, filling the room with a faint smell of herbs and freshly-cut tree bark. I can see his fingers moving restlessly on the table; his eyes are full of anticipation. No one in this city—or on this planet—knows how to brew this particular tea. To me it's the unmistakable scent of a client; to him, who's only been exposed to it in my parlor, it's almost certainly a potent aphrodisiac.

He's visibly relieved when I take a sip of the drink, thus giving him permission to down his cup in a single swig. I smile before giving him what he's been waiting for, what he was no doubt imagining on his way to my house.

"Choose," I say, and for a second he's too breathless to speak.

In the language of these soldiers there are only two ways to answer that question: male or female. No other categories. It's the same with the language spoken by the local population the soldiers are supposedly here to protect. Both dialects sound the same to me—the vowels a bit softer, the cadence a bit quicker with the locals, perhaps—but such comparisons are not looked upon kindly by anyone in the city.

He chooses female. Most of them do.

I go into my private chamber to make myself ready. The room is full of clothes and paints and makeup—it's my wardrobe and my toolkit—but first there's the ritual.

Considering my level of skill and all the years I've spent in training, millennia ago, in a different life, this place is an utter waste of my talents. But seeing one's world go up in flames does strange things to one's standards. Here I can still get work without drawing attention to myself. Here is stability and simplicity, at the outskirts of the galaxy where everything is binary.

After my body's done going through the transformation, I choose a plain dress and twist my hair into a simple arrangement, folding it on my head and leaving a few strands to fall on my cheeks—the way they wear it in the countryside. By the time I return to the parlor, he can barely hide his anticipation. His dark blue eyes, the same eyes as the rest of the foreigners who've made this land theirs, shine bright and excited. He practically jumps up when I invite him to the bedroom.

I've chosen well; he takes his time removing the dress, careful with it as though it were three times more expensive than it looks.

I probably remind him of a girl back home. Soldiers like him are never from the wealthy families, most likely he grew up on a farm not too different from the ones surrounding this city. Maybe I'm the neighbor's daughter he always dreamed of having. If he's one of the interesting ones, I remind him of his mother or his sister or his cousin. Either way, my bed is where a confusing, liberating haze possesses him, only to be cleared slowly as he steps back out into the street. Outside everything must be black and white for these boys, but here, in my home, they let the shades of gray creep in.

The locals have a name for this city that's not on any of the signs or official documents—not anymore. Not since they crushed the last rebellion ten years ago and executed the leaders, before my time. The soldiers frown on hearing it spoken in the street.

I have my own secret name for this place: Frozen City.

The sun doesn't shine here very often, the air is infused with a bitter chill, even in the warm season. The winter in Frozen City lasts longer than anywhere else I've been. In the other life—before the Great Catastrophe, before I lost my taste for adventure—I was always told low temperatures were good for preserving commodities, and Frozen City has not disappointed. I have been able to preserve myself here, when survival seemed barely achievable.

Despite the normally grim weather, today my sleeping soldier's face is illuminated by warm morning light coming from the window. He leaves quickly upon waking—his funds are barely enough as it is to pay for my time—and I don't bother asking him anything about his life or his job. It's of no interest to me, as long as everything's going well in the city.

There are workers and merchants and artists living in this city, guilds, barracks, schools, and an entire class of local officials presided over by the chancellor. I stay away from all their internal conflicts and politics. None of it matters to me, as long as the city remains peaceful and stable and my name doesn't become too widely known.

It's a challenge, in a pond this size, but so far I've managed.

∞

She comes to me as usual, on a weekday afternoon. The first time she came, I didn't realize she was anyone special—just another spouse of one of the wealthier merchants in town, with so much time on her hands the money can barely keep up with it.

It wasn't until the grand annual parade passed a few streets from my window that by chance I caught a glimpse of her—the wife of the commandant, the highest ranking military authority in Frozen City. It was alarming to think my name was being passed around in the chancellor's district when I had worked so hard to stay under their radar, but I had no choice but to receive her. In time, I realized she enjoyed having me as her secret—something personal, decadent, a private indulgence.

Her husband's been kept increasingly busy in recent months with the business of keeping the city calm, reassuring the workers and the farmers and all the other locals who haven't gotten rich off the occupation. He doesn't mind his wife's recreation of course—what else is she supposed to do, with him gone increasingly often on countryside tours for days at a time. We understand each other well, she and I, and she keeps the details of my identity to herself.

I lay out the dishes, boil the water, and lay down the herbs before she even arrives. She comes to see me more and more often these days: a combination of the strain of being left alone so often and the charming, engaging nature of my company.

She's always quiet while I pour the tea; she savors it like I do, though for different reasons. She makes it easy to respect her, and in return I show her tricks I wouldn't bother with for other clients.

I bow to her the way I was taught to bow by my teachers—the way no one bows on this planet—before offering her the choice.

She chooses female, not her usual preference. Her voice is steady and melodic as usual, but with a tinge of exhaustion. I've heard rumors that one of her children has been diagnosed with an illness; sitting by his bedside must be taking its toll.

After my private ritual, after my hair and clothes are arranged immaculately to suit the fashion of her peers, I take her to the other room. I help her lie on the bed, not because she needs my help, but because I can see today will require more tenderness than usual.

Her hair is arranged in shiny, perfect curls, her skin is a pale orange, smooth and radiant, like the early dawn. She's young by the standards of this planet, but in other places in the galaxy she would be considered old. As old as I can see she feels today.

In the evening she rises from my bed and rearranges herself to face her chores and children and servants again. She leaves me money on the counter by the door. I have a credit account of course, and I suspect she does as well, but they still use paper money here, in Frozen City, since the last rebellion. Their access to the electronic system used in the rest of the solar system has been severely limited.

I can see from the size of the stack of papers, she's been generous.

∞

He arouses my suspicion as soon as he walks through my door. I remember him, the boy who reminds me of my favorite toy as a child, with his lumbering walk. I've seen him working as a butcher's apprentice at the shop a few blocks away.

I try not to draw the attention of the townspeople when I go out to conduct my business, especially in the market. I'd hire a servant to do it, but I cherish the chance to go out unnoticed and blend in with the crowd. The mystery it creates around me is good for my price range but bad for the rumors that circulate in small places like this.

The boy is new to the city. From his accent to his clothes to the way he carries himself, it's clear he grew up on a farm. The sky is usually covered with clouds in Frozen City, but those who work outside regularly carry the marks on their skin. The soldiers develop a sickness after a while, their eyes gain a purplish tinge, their vision slowly fades and they get sent home for a spell; the locals merely change color, from pale orange to pale green, in patches.

This boy has fingertips the color of young flowers and two angular spots on his neck like the green feathers of predatory birds. Someone like him sitting in my parlor in the middle of the day means he took the day off from work. It all seems too odd to be true. Where would a boy like that get the kind of money I charge? He's no master thief and he hasn't been in the city long enough to earn that kind of money whoring or selling some other skill in the back alleys.

Of course, it would make sense if he's one of the new rebels, freshly promoted from the countryside by his covert superiors and supplied with money to make arrangements as some kind of mid-level operative. As soon as the thought enters my head, I can't come up with a more likely explanation.

He's smiling and polite, like he's a first time guest at the home of his mother's acquaintance and he might get scolded for not taking off his shoes.

I smile back pleasantly and say, "Choose," and he does.

My body shifts, the skin stretches and contracts. Textures change, my bones grow longer. I put on boots made of hard skins and a tunic made of soft, intricately woven silk, lined with furs. It marks me as the boy's social superior; a city man with cash to spare and colleagues to impress.

After a moment's consideration, I change the tunic for a plainer one and take off the decorative buckles from my breeches. There is a reason the boy decided to throw away his money so carelessly, perhaps risking a great deal of trouble for my services.

Attentions of a wealthy merchant are not easy to achieve for someone like him, but not impossible either, especially in this district. So, something different. Someone closer to his own social station. Perhaps someone from back home or one of his new friends in the city. Someone he can't have, for whatever reason, but still wants desperately.

I make my stride more casual, less stiff than I originally intended, when I walk back out to invite him into the bedroom. His eyes do everything but jump out of their sockets. It's been a while since I've had a client so openly in awe of my alien nature. He can't stop looking over every bit of me. The clothes are a perfect fit, I can tell from his reaction. Surely the first costume wouldn't have ruined the session, but this outfit has definitely taken his breath away.

He can't help but get up from his seat before I give him the invitation—too excited, and probably restless with mild embarrassment, to remain still.

The boy isn't as shy as I'd expected nor as inexperienced. We make love for a while, the light filtered through the heavy clouds outside, painting everything a bluish, subdued color. Afterwards, I let him have what he really came for.

I lie next to him, my head on his stomach, my hand on his hip, caressing absently. I feel his every breath as he does mine. It doesn't take very long for him to sigh, softly, as though he's letting out a breath he didn't know he'd been holding. His muscles relax, his body goes limp. Slowly, he lets himself run his fingers through my hair, holding me close with his other hand.

The soldiers, they usually want another round by now, if they're still around this long after the first one. But this boy wants *this*. I know because I've been doing this since long before he was born, but I can see that to him it seems like I've read his mind. As though with a look I can know all his deepest, darkest secrets.

A part of me wishes he could have the cash to come to me again. His innocence is refreshing in a way I would have found revolting a few years ago. What seeing one's home burn down does to one's preferences.

I take his hand in mine, card our fingers together. My thumb caresses every bit of skin, searching; it lingers on the calluses on his forefinger and middle finger, the clear marks of rifle training.

∞

She comes to me as usual, after her evening classes. She's a feast to behold: her clothes are a cascade of colors blending into each other, fabrics intertwining, wrapped around her figure flatteringly and in accordance with the latest fashion. Immaculate as only someone new to adulthood is allowed to be.

Her mother will have her married soon. She hasn't told me; I heard the gossip around town. Typical of people in her position, she doesn't realize how precious this time is. She's no longer a child—attending school in the city instead of being tutored at home—but not yet bound by heavy responsibilities. In my previous life I had no patience for youth, but now I find I indulge her in her games and her self-deceptions eagerly.

I tell her, "Choose."

This time she chooses female, as I knew she would. There are patterns to her desires which she wouldn't acknowledge even if I pointed them out.

I make my skin smoother, my face rounder; I shift around the muscles and fat under my skin. I choose the dress of a plain woman. Not a servant, but the wife of a craftsman. In the beginning, I used to dress like someone closer to her station: silks, jewelry, paint in my hair. But now I know her well enough to anticipate her moods. I already know what her game of choice will be.

She doesn't leave until the next morning. It's always like this just before the week's end. I manage to go through several costume changes before she's satisfied and exhausted.

In the night, too awake to fall asleep but too exhausted not to slur her words, she tells me about the Grand Ball, the most important event in the social calendar of the chancellor's inner circle. She lies next to me in the darkness—the bed is big enough so no part of us is touching—and goes on and on about the dress she spent months designing being ruined by one of her mother's servants. I get the feeling she's told the story before, many times by now. She mumbles something about how her mother might influence the chancellor, this year, to cancel the

Grand Ball altogether. Her voice drifts off as the minutes pass, and she floats closer to sleep.

I ask her why, studying her face, waiting to see how much truth the answer will contain. My eyes are better suited for the dark than hers—biology coupled with years of training. Supposedly these aren't things she's allowed to share with me.

It's the rebels, she tells me. They've started things up again. Her father is worried about groups meeting covertly in the city; a target like the Grand Ball might prove too enticing.

∞

He shows up at my door soaking wet from the rain, practically shivering.

It wasn't easy to find him; my means are not humble, but I've never tried to stretch them quite this far. It wasn't easy to arrange for him to come see me, either. He has good reason to be suspicious. Everyone in Frozen City would like to know his name, especially the powerful.

It was a long process of gathering rumors and lies from my clients, until I was certain most of the people he'd surrounded himself with had either heard of me or been my customer. He was born in the city, so his curiosity was harder to pique than some of his countryside comrades, but one must believe in one's immortality, on some level, to do what he does. People like that are always drawn to the unique, the mysterious, the enticingly unexplained. In the end, there is very little a man like him could do against my charms.

He's handsome—an intelligent face, despite his worker's clothes. Masquerading as a mill worker, living in the city, and working on the outskirts of it—a brilliant, risky strategy. No one would think the leader of the next rebellion would spend most of his days outside the city gates.

I pour the tea for him and offer him the choice.

I wonder, of course, whether he's really the solution to my problem.

Whether the rebellion truly rests on this man's shoulders, or if someone else would simply take his place, should he disappear. But this is the only thing I can do, and so it's what I must do. Stability is vital to my business.

In my old life, I might have spared him. I believed, then, that intelligence would always choose happiness over misery, no matter the circumstances. I might have offered him a way out of the city, passage on a ship, in exchange for his cooperation. I might have believed he'd agree to dismantle the movement he's built if I offer him and his loved ones an alternative.

My cup remains empty. He sips his drink.

I put the kettle back on the table and take my seat in front of him. By the time the fabric of my tunic touches the sofa, the light has gone out of his eyes. He falls quietly and not inelegantly to my carpet. I check his hands, his neck, to make sure he's lifeless.

It's startling to realize, but I would have liked to hear his answer. Nothing is surprising, given only two options, yet I would have liked to know his choice. Perhaps it's that I bristle at letting a client remain a mystery. So many things must be sacrificed in the name of survival.

It will be a bit of trouble, covering up his death, but I have contacts outside the city walls. It will be said he left my parlor in good spirits and never found his way home in the storm.

His cheeks are pale green under his open, empty eyes. I retrieve his cup and my own, and place them away from where I normally keep my dishes and herbs.

Later, when his body is gone, I'll destroy both cups. My instruments are unique, precious, impossible to replace in my current position, but his cup is evidence that must not remain in my home, and mine will be a victim of ritual. Living things rely on it to order their lives, and I am no exception. Frozen City has been a warm, forgiving mistress, and I must honor that, in my own way.

About the Author
Marina Berlin

Marina Berlin holds degrees in Film, Sociology, East Asian Studies, and several other subjects that make her resume seem completely made up. She currently spends most of her time working on her first fantasy novel. You can follow her on Twitter at @Berlin_Marina.

Author Website: http://marinaberlin.org/

Dreamwire
by Anne E. Johnson

"Did I used to be nicer?" Tina stared hard at Rob, waiting for his answer. The surgical mask over his nose and mouth emphasized his eyes, so Tina figured she could tell if he lied. His eyes, unlike hers, were still a natural hazel. "You've known me forever," she said, "so you have some context, you know?"

Rob held up a small metal plate bordered with pulsing green lights. "The patella implants are ready. We should do this now, please."

Tina grinned, pretending not to be offended by how he'd evaded the question. "Whatever you say, Doc. Gas me up."

The last thing Tina thought before going under was, I'm sure my heart used to be bigger.

Six hours later, when she was sealed up and perked up and testing out her new-and-improved legs, the size of her heart didn't matter to her.

"No complications," Rob said glumly. His slight frown made deep lines in his face, and Tina wondered how long it had been since his last NovaDermo treatment. She had her own face done every month and a new skin tint too, just for kicks. This month her body gleamed iridescent mauve. Very fashionable. And very, very smooth.

Still, Rob's facial creases suited his earnest personality. "You're sad," Tina said. "You're rich and healthy. Why so blue?"

"Nothing," he said with a shrug. "Except, you've been getting so many fixes."

"Sure have!" Proudly Tina listed the cyber-surgeries she'd had just in the past year. "Femur reinforcement. Velocity digits." She wiggled her fingers so fast, they blurred. "UroDry." When Rob cocked his head, she explained, "It condenses my pee so I don't have to go so often. Great for parties. And also orgies."

Rob's skin was naturally reddish-brown, but she could see the hint of a blush anyway. Amused, she went on. "Plus digital corneas." She blinked slowly, sweeping her artificial eyelashes up and down. "You like my emerald eyes? The color is created from the image inside an actual emerald." When Rob didn't react, she went on with her list. "An ossi-rubber ribcage, which you did an awesome job on, by the way. Oh, and you did my elbows back in January."

When he didn't return her grin, she tried a joke. "Gotta wonder if there's any of the original Tina Juarez left!"

"Maybe you should search for her."

The comment was so quiet Tina didn't trust her ears, despite her cochlear enhancements. "Say what?"

But Rob just gave her a flustered smile and changed his tune. "Um, you can run on any surface now. Even deep sand will feel like an Olympic track. Enjoy. I'm sure I'll see you again soon, for whatever the new fashion fix is for the skeleton."

"You *bet* you will, genius. I wish you did the whole bod." Tina moved to kiss his cheek, but he jerked away, pretending to type into his tablet, the way he might shrink from someone grotesque or diseased. She told herself it was her imagination.

∞

She thought about going for a run, just to test out the new product. But after half a day in the surgical clinic, she had a more urgent need to attend to: a little exercise for her favorite implant.

"You the girl with the sex fix?" some almost-sober guy asked the moment Tina took a bar stool in Swirl, her usual hangout. "I hear you come every night," he added with a smirk.

Major wit, this one. And he wasn't finished. "I got a few special fixes myself, sugar. You show me yours, I'll show you mine."

Without a word, Tina grabbed her drink and walked away. She was horny, but not that horny. Leaning on a standing table in the corner, she surveyed the crowded room. If she willed her corneas to lose focus, everyone looked the same in the club's dark red light. That was disturbing, but not as terrifying as what she realized when her eyes refocused.

"Christ, I've screwed practically all of 'em," she said, her voice drowned out in the pulsing wash of electronic music. Moving her gaze from one sweaty, stoned face to the next, she could remember all of the sex, but none of the people she'd done it with.

The gynecologist who'd given her the fix between her legs had tried to warn her. *The greater the pleasure-zone enhancement, the lesser the emotional response,* he'd claimed.

"It's what I wanted," Tina told her drink as she remembered his words. "Better this way. No complications."

"Who the hell you talkin' to, girl?"

Tina turned to find her friend, Plastique, elbowing in next to her. "You're jabberin' like a meth fiend."

"You have such a nice manner," Tina said over the booming soundtrack. "Your mama must be so proud."

Plastique raised her drink in tandem with her painted-on eyebrow. "Honey, the whole reason I got this sex change was so I could be my own mother. So, yeah, Mama's mighty proud."

Tina managed a laugh at the tired routine, but Plastique didn't buy it. "What's eatin' you? I thought you got a leg fix today, and with that hot doc, too."

The phrase made Tina oddly uncomfortable. "Rob Jensen isn't hot. He's practically my brother."

"Well, I got no moral compunction against incest, sweetie, long as everyone's consenting and of age."

"Ugh! Stop it!" Tina said. Prancing in place to show off her new knees, she tried to change the subject. "They feel great!"

But Plastique knew her too well, and still had a man's height and strength. With one hand on Tina's shoulder, she stopped the manic dance. "Come with me. Now," Plastique said, scooping Tina by the waist and whisking her into the ladies'. "Spill, child."

Tina leaned against the mirror and sighed. "It's not like it used to be."

"And that's a bad thing why?" Plastique jammed a fist above her generous hip. "Ain't that what we pay the fix docs for? So nothing'll be the same?"

"I mean… I don't know." Searching for an elusive word, Tina orbited nervously around Plastique. Then she stopped. "I think I mean love."

"*Love!*" As if on cue, a toilet flushed in a stall. "Like, marriage and shit?"

"No!" Tina retorted. "I'm not a Neanderthal."

"So, what *do* you mean?"

"Feeling something."

Poking her floral faux fingernail toward Tina's crotch, Plastique said, "You and your super-erogenous self are feeling more than the next thousand people. That's not enough for ya?"

Glancing in the mirror, Tina ran a comb through her fuchsia bangs. "It used to be. I just want to remember what it was like to, to…"

"To care?"

"Yeah." She felt foolish suddenly. "Never mind. I'm buzzed and tired. I'm gonna go get laid."

She took a step toward the door, but Plastique blocked her way. "I know this guy."

"I know plenty of guys."

"No, I mean, he designs fixes." Plastique leaned close and whispered, "There's an amazing one in the pipeline."

An addict's lust for a hit crawled up Tina's back. She *had* to know about it. And, whatever it was, she had to have it. Plastique paused while a woman took forever washing and drying her hands. Finally she went on. "It's got some fancy science name. But he says they're calling it Dreamwire."

Tina felt woozy. "Sounds incredible. What does it do?" Not that it mattered.

As she answered, Plastique waggled her long fingers like a sorceress giving an incantation. "It reconnects you with your subconscious desires. So you can, like, *live your dreams*." She paused for effect. "Sounds like just the kick in the fanny you need, girl. Find out what's locked away in the old noggin."

Tina's heart thumped so fast, she had trouble speaking. "They put it… inside? In the brain?"

Plastique's answer was a slow nod and an evil grin.

"Awesome. Where can I get one?" Tina's question was carefully worded. She had not asked, *When will they be available?*

Plastique understood the code. "My friend can hook you up while it's stuck in the swamps of the Effin' D. A." That was the usual way fix junkies referred to the government's regulatory department.

"Prototype?"

"Yes, ma'am." Putting a chummy arm around Tina's shoulder, Plastique promised, "I'll text you the deets."

With more hope than she'd felt in ages, Tina slipped out into the sea of flesh to find a friend or two for the night.

∞

It was no mildewed shack with an unlicensed quack, but a clean, tony high-rise overlooking Lake Michigan. It was the kind of place where the one percent could pay a top-notch doc a little extra—okay, a lot extra—for an extra-special or extra-secret something.

The surgeon, Indira Chung, had skin the color of strong Darjeeling tea. Tina happened to know from a recent orgy with her that her belly was slightly darker than her face. "Hello, Doctor," Tina said modestly, as if she hadn't screamed out, *Oh, Indira!* a few times the week before.

The doc was pretending, too, or else she wasn't any good at distinguishing faces in a lust pile. She paged through something on her tablet. "You've had a lot of fixes already." It came out unnaturally flat, so Tina knew she was trying to keep the judgment from her tone. "Over thirty. Is that correct?"

"They make life *super*," Tina gushed in a little girl's voice while thinking, I'm paying you an ass-load of money. What's with the third degree?

Or maybe she asked it out loud, since the doc answered her. "The PS-4.6 gets implanted directly into your brain, so it affects everything in your body, bio or techno."

"Oh, wow." Tina tried to sound like she cared. She just wanted that damn implant already. "Are all my fixes a problem?"

"Nobody knows. Yet." Doctor Chung stared hard at Tina, an unspoken warning.

Tina stared back just as intently. "Let's be the ones who find out."

When the doc nodded, Tina felt that rush, like a tweaker who sees her dealer coming down the block. "What's it look like?" she asked. She always wanted to see the gizmos before surgery, so she could picture them when they were functioning inside her.

The doc handed her a hard plastic package, the kind of casing music players came in. Across the top was a green sticker with a logo reminiscent of a yin-yang symbol. Beneath the logo was text: "Dreamwire (psychosendesi 4.6). Let your deepest desires rise."

In the center of the packaging, a two-inch wire was suspended. "Looks like an opened-up paperclip," Tina said, wishing for something flashier.

"I promise you, it's not a paperclip," the doc said drily. "But it could be just as dangerous to insert this into your temporal lobe. Still want it?"

As far as Tina was concerned, the danger doubled the fun. "Let's do it."

∞

"Posh" was the first word that occurred to Tina when she woke up. She was in a majestic hotel suite. "Implant," she reminded herself. She'd been in this hotel before, more than a few times. Several of the high-end docs used it as a recovery room.

Tina's internal ThinkChat phone rang. Recognizing Plastique's ringtone, she rubbed the remote slider implant in her forearm to answer. "Talk to me."

"You talk to *me*," Plastique said. "How's the gourd, sista?"

After a quick assessment for headache and blurred vision, Tina answered, "Fine, I guess. I knew Indira had skilled hands, but *damn*. She is good. I don't feel anything." She explored her scalp with tentative fingers. Just at the crown, her hair was shaved in a one-inch circle and a thin line was raised on her skin. "She messed up my haircut."

"We'll call it a fashion statement."

Tina didn't laugh, though. Something pissed her off. "I don't *feel* anything," she complained.

"Yeah, you said that."

"I mean, I paid two mill to *feel*. Shouldn't I be feeling?"

Plastique sighed impatiently. "I'm sure it'll kick in."

"It better. Meet for coffee?"

"Some of us have to work, trust fund girl. See you tonight at Swirl. Text if there's an update. All your fans are dying to know."

When they'd hung up, it occurred to Tina that she should have been left with instructions. But Dr. Chung hadn't told her a thing. Or maybe she had, and Tina had already forgotten. She didn't know what to expect to happen to her, or what might go wrong. Nor could she reach Dr. Chung if there was an emergency. For the first time since she was a fix-virgin, Tina regretted getting the implant.

"Don't be such a wuss," she said, scolding herself. "You survived that first fix." She rubbed the left side of her belly, where the calorie burner had been implanted ten years before. "A decade of stuffing my face and staying sexy thin. That worked. This one will, too."

Defiantly Tina tossed her duvet aside and sat up. The sudden ache in every joint pushed her back down against the mattress. Stunned, she considered what might be wrong. "I pulled something during sex?" But she'd had elasticity molecules injected into her muscles six months before, to prevent that very thing. She was really puzzled. Full-body aching shouldn't have been possible.

Then the tears started, quietly at first, accompanied by a general sadness. As her sobs came harder, the source of her misery twisted more clearly into focus. Loneliness. Intolerable loneliness, pummeling her stomach, bruising her bones.

"If I just lie here, I'll die from this," she said, relieved at the option. But when the ache turned into a searing, bright, desperate pain, like a rat clawing her entrails, Tina's terror drove her from the bed.

She was naked. "I just need to get laid," she told herself as she pulled on her tank and short shorts with the clumsiness of a toddler. "Just need somebody's attention for a bit."

It was a lie, and she knew it, but it kept her from having to admit how scared and mystified she was. All Tina knew for sure was that she *wanted* somebody in a way she never had before.

The swank corridors, elevator, and lobby went by in a blur. She'd made it almost to the front door when her need for meaningful companionship grew so intense that it buckled her knees. "Be with me!" she moaned to whoever happened to be passing, grabbing his legs. It was some businessman, the sharp crease of his trousers pressed to her face, filling her nose with dry cleaning chemicals.

"Get off me!" He stumbled backwards, pulling free.

Tina fell forward, only to feel rough hands tugging her upright.

"Miss, I'm going to have to ask you to leave."

The normal Tina would have had choice words for a self-satisfied authority figure getting in her face. But this wasn't the normal Tina. As if she were at the movies, she watched herself hug the security guard and wail, "Oh, please love me!" She felt herself lifted and hurled like a bag of lawn clippings, and then saw the sidewalk coming toward her. But the jagged sting of scraped elbows and knees didn't lessen the pain of her longing.

Grabbing a nearby mailbox, Tina staggered to her feet. A thousand hints of thought curled through her mind, ghosted in the blinding light of her strange desire. A thousand tasks she should do, places she should go, questions she should ask. But the street teemed with life partners waiting to be ensnared, so everything else would have to wait.

One by one by one by one, approach and rejection, appeal and rebuff. Tina didn't just offer her body. She wanted to give her whole self. Some recoiled. Some called for the cops. A few gave her hugs and the address of a battered women's shelter or the number for a suicide hotline.

This went on all day. Even though she felt the blisters on her feet and knew she needed to rest and eat and drink, Tina lurched on. Finally, when the sun set, habit kicked in.

"Swirl." The name of her nightly hangout felt sandy in her throat. Still, it was a relief to have a familiar destination. Maybe there was hope. Even though the stores lining the streets waved like aquarium exhibits as she weaved past, somehow she found her way to Swirl.

"Come back when you're cleaned up, lady."

It took Tina several seconds to realize that Sam, the weeknight bouncer, was talking to her. "Sammy, it's me. Teeny Tina! You wanna get married, Sammy?" She lunged toward him, arms out, to embrace his barrel chest. His huge hands encircled her rib cage. The ground sank away from her feet as he picked her up. "You *do* love me!" she gasped, drowning in a flood of gratitude. "We'll be together forever." The slogan she'd read on the Dreamwire packaging floated through her mind: "Let your deepest desires rise." They were rising, all right, and it felt like paradise.

But Tina's ecstasy was cut short by a voice she knew very well. "Samuel, so help me, you put my girl down or I'll snap that linebacker neck of yours like you was a giraffe with osteoporosis." Before Tina could object, Plastique dragged her by the elbow through the club and into the ladies'.

"What the hell happened?" Plastique asked, pushing Tina firmly against the cool tile wall. "I been calling you for the past twelve hours."

Tina heard her words, but understood only that Plastique loved her. "We would be so good together," she said fervently. "Forever and always each other's."

"What did they do to you? Where's my Tina?"

In answer, Tina stood on tiptoe and planted a wet kiss on Plastique's lips. "Rubbery," Tina sighed dreamily.

"Collagen," Plastique snapped. "Let's get you to a doctor."

While Tina tripped behind her, grasping her sequined belt and proclaiming eternal love, Plastique marched out the back of the club and through the dark streets. Her cell phone stayed glued to her ear as she bickered with someone.

"Who you calling, sweetheart?" Tina asked in what she thought was a flirty tone. "Whoever he is, you won't miss him now that you're with me. I always knew you and I belonged—"

"Get in, space cadet." Plastique held open the passenger door of her car and gave Tina a shove. "We're going to the Vortex."

That was what they called St. Regis Medical Center, where Tina had had most of her fixes done. Normally the word "Vortex" set off her Pavlovian drool, but tonight it made her want to retch. "No more fixes.

Never again." She pawed at Plastique's hand on the gear shift. "We have to stay real for each other, darling."

"Okay. I'm officially freaked out now." Plastique floored the gas.

They came to a screeching halt in front of St. Regis' 24-hour urgent care entrance. The moment they stepped inside, Tina started to change. Something about the weirdly white fluorescent lights ticked her off. Or maybe it was the stern, businesslike chatter among the staff, treating people like items in an inventory. "It's all evil," Tina murmured.

When no one looked up from the registration forms, Tina stood and shouted, "It's all evil! You're all evil! Fixes are evil!" She was up on the waiting room chairs, fists toward the ceiling. "Negator. I want the Negator now!" It took Plastique and two orderlies to fight her down to the floor.

Her brain roiled with the need to be cleansed. The Negator was the anti-fix bomb, a legendary room where any and all fixes could be halted with a jolt of electromagnetic energy. Every fix in every part of Tina's body felt suddenly like a toxin, like rape. She wanted them all ripped out.

"Leave your knee alone. It's not healed." Plastique arm-wrestled Tina's hand away from the slender scar at the edge of her digital patella.

"I'll get restraints," one of the orderlies said.

As soon as he let go of her, Tina squirmed away from her other captors, scrabbling on hands and mechanized knees faster than the other orderly and Plastique could move to grab her. Then she got to her feet and bolted. She knew where the Negator room was. Every fix junkie knew. Satan's Neuterer, they called it, and they all stayed as far away as possible. Its destructive rays were punishment for the self-destructive and the homicidal. But to Tina's burning brain those rays promised relief.

She could see the green swinging doors a few yards away. Her overwhelming love of everyone chasing her almost made her stop and turn to offer her heart forever to every one of them. But her wish to feel nothing was stronger than her urge for a life mate. Skidding on the tile floor, she burst into the Negator room like a sheriff in the Old West striding into a saloon, looking to clean up the town.

"Miss, you can't come—" That was as much as the radiologist sputtered out before Sheriff Tina shushed her with a hand across the mouth.

"Clean me," she hissed. "I got a nuclear reaction going on inside me, and I need you to throw a god-sized blanket over that shit."

"I'm sorry, miss, but I can't just… What the hell?" The radiologist's frightened eyes found something else to scare them. She rushed to a bank of monitors. "What's with these readings?" She looked at Tina like she had an alien sprouting from her belly. "What did you do to the equipment? What's *in* you?"

Tina barely heard the questions through the buzzing of her brain. Her gray matter seemed to vibrate with a tornado of every emotion that could be felt.

"It's gonna blow! Get out!"

Tina heard the radiologist shrieking. She saw her flailing her arms. It struck her as odd, in a detached way, to watch the woman in green scrubs fly past, shooing out the crew of hospital employees who'd been chasing her. Plastique's bronze-tinged makeup glowed so prettily in the flashing red emergency lights. Tina would've told her that, but Plastique was busy fighting to be the first out the door.

That comical sight blurred when all the gadgets ever added to Tina's body started to feel like they were crawling out of her skin: the patellas, the LiverGuard (drink forever!), the cyber love-zone, the ossi-rubber ribcage, the calorie burner. All of it, even the corneas. Her artificial parts seemed to rise up like parasites trying to scurry off a dying host.

With every part of her in revolt, Tina folded under the pain. She couldn't tell whether the deafening siren and blaring repetition of "Evacuate" were real or just in her mind. And what about the red lights, turning white-gold, scouring out her soul? The walls grew brighter.

Center of the sun. God light. Nothing.

∞

Familiar face?

"…waking up…"

Darkening.

Friendly, familiar face, smiling. Rob in his white coat, smiling down at her. Her surgeon. No. Her oldest friend.

"Hey, buddy. Thought we'd lost ya."

She tried to ask what happened. He held up his hand. He had nice hands.

"Don't talk. Plastique told us about the Psychosendesi."

The what? she asked silently.

"The Dreamwire."

He could tell what she was thinking! So sweet!

"It must've interacted with all your other fixes. You even overloaded the Negator. Incredible that you survived. What were you—" His voice had grown louder, but he stopped suddenly and breathed, continuing in a calmer tone. "The Dreamwire wasn't approved. Not even close. Why would you do that to yourself, Tina?"

Rob was frowning. Tina didn't want him to be sad. It was worth fighting to speak to make him smile. "No… more… fixes."

It worked. He smiled. His pretty fingers stroked her face. His lips came toward hers. Touched hers. She felt them. Really felt them. She'd forgotten what lips truly felt like. Soft. Warm. Moist. Gentle. Love.

When she saw love glowing in his eyes after the kiss, Tina felt a jolt of something through her center. Electric, but natural and strengthening.

Rob. His kiss was the greatest fix she'd ever had. "I… love you," she said. And she felt like a superhero.

About the Author
Anne E. Johnson

Anne E. Johnson lives in Brooklyn. Her short speculative fiction has appeared in the *Alternate Hilarities* series, *Urban Fantasy Magazine*, *FrostFire Worlds*, *Shelter of Daylight*, *The Future Fire*, and elsewhere. Her series of humorous science fiction novels, The Webrid Chronicles has been described as a cross between Douglas Adams and Raymond Chandler. Anne writes speculative fiction for children and teens as well, including a book of collected stories called *Things from Other Worlds* and a YA adventure novel, *Space Surfers*. Follow her on Twitter @AnneEJohnson.

Author Website: http://anneejohnson.com/

Hu.man and Best
by Nancy S.M. Waldman

Rolling, grass-covered hills gave way to dunes as Kanali Zohra Betts entered what was once Namibia. She flew at low altitude, contouring the landscape.

Flash. The next white warning light sensed her presence.

The lights were installed, as regular as a picket fence, every forty kilometres along the boundary of the vast *cogbot* territory of Southern Africa. For a thousand kilometres, she'd been attempting to set off the lights without drifting into the buffer zone and tripping the actual alarms. This game somewhat distracted her from the unresolved reality that her military career, and thus, her life, was under attack from within.

A week ago, she'd been passed over for promotion. By Gauci, of all people. She and Gauci had come up through the ranks together. *Peers? No. Never.* He, with his sucking up and cutting corners, had never been her equal. She grimaced at the irony. Now he was her reporting superior officer, Brigedia Jenerali Gauci, while she remained Kanali Betts.

Stunned and angry, she felt it wise to leave HQ before doing something truly regrettable. Using up some of her huge backlog of accrued leave, she'd hopped a military transport to Cairo where she purchased this sweet, state-of-the-art personal cruiser.

And now, two days later, she was on a sentimental journey.

Betts searched the sunset gold and purple landscape for a stand of quiver trees she remembered. When she was ranked a kapteni, she'd worked here as an administrator, during the set up of the ACE Compound after the 2414 Treaty of Tangiers ceded the whole continent south of the 25th parallel to the androids.

The peace has held these twenty years. I did my job.

No more raids. No more killing. No more slavery by humans of the ACE—Artificially Cognitive Entities. Betts corrected herself. They now wanted to be called *Androidal* Cognitive Entities. Hell, she had a hard enough time not calling them by the old slur: cogbots.

Sensors linked to the aircraft vibrated against her wrist alerting her to movement on the ground. She synced her vis-implants to the locked-in coordinates and zoomed in, hoping to see a rare gemsbok or giraffe.

It was neither. It was bipedal.

A human? Or, she wondered, adjusting the focus, a… cogbot with a wig on? She couldn't decide which was more unlikely. Nothing with a pulse had lived here for a century.

Flying over, she saw the creature crouch and then lie face down.

Betts decelerated, did a tight arc and found a place to alight where it wouldn't completely swamp the what-ever-it-was with dust and sand. Her cruiser sat a good twenty metres on the human side of the no-man's land border, behind a low sand-covered ridge where she'd have some cover.

Betts switched the cruiser's perimeter alarms to maximum volume in case anything approached. Then she tapped her wristpad, calling up Central Command. No sense taking any chances.

"Kanali Betts," said Gauci, voice heavy with gloating.

"Sir," she responded. "I might have a situation here."

"I thought you were taking some… time. A vacation. Remember?"

"Huh." She paused. "So you don't care to know what I felt the need to report?" Anger reared up in full force.

"Let go," Gauci said.

She found this mildly amusing, as she had literally "let go" at their last meeting, unleashing a few well-chosen obscenities.

Gauci continued, "HQ absolutely will not fall apart if you are off duty, you know. What is your situation?"

"No need, sir. You're absolutely right, sir." She ended the link.

"Fuck him," she whispered.

Drawing her sidearm, she slowly approached the situation-in-question.

The entity lay perfectly still.

"Why are you here?" she called, her voice thin in the vast stillness.

The tall, extremely skinny, creature lifted its face and said, "My he-ad." Its voice croaked and split.

"What about your head?"

"Is bro-ken."

The kanali walked closer, noting that her passing lit up a white light off to her right. Officially entering no-man's land.

"Get up slowly."

It pushed off the ground and sat crossed-legged while looking at Betts intently. The kanali returned the same.

If human, it seemed preternaturally calm. Utterly unemotional. Not normal human behaviour, but—especially with that matted mass of hair—it didn't look like a cogbot, either.

"What is your origin?" Betts asked, only then remembering that the scanner, the one that could identify the make and model of any known ACE, was in the cruiser.

It stared and shook its head slightly.

Now Betts noted small breasts poking against its garment, a stiff tunic, sleeveless and reaching to mid-thigh. Its legs and feet were bare.

ACE had been manufactured to look human but without gender specific details. Scientists had given them varying skin tones so human buyers could choose. They had a mildly jerky gait, no hair, no sexual parts, and traditionally wore no clothes.

This one's skin was covered in dust but looked to be a red-brown sienna. The hair was probably black under an apparent lifetime of dirt and grime. Its facial features—round face, high cheek bones, almond-shaped, amber-brown eyes—were similar to Betts' own, though her irises were dark as coffee beans.

Then Betts noticed deep circles under its eyes and she knew it was human. The androids had not been given signs of human wear and tear.

Human female then, she concluded, and likely polyracial like most of us.

But—here was the rub—the ACE were always evolving. Now they evolved in isolation. She couldn't be sure what they looked like, not anymore. Betts had seen too much during the war years to have gotten over her paranoia about them.

"Your name?" Betts asked.

No response.

"I'm going to approach you. I do not want to hurt you in any way, so you must do what I say. Stand up, turn around, and put your hands behind your neck."

The sun had dipped below the western mountains, so the kanali flicked on beam lights set into the forehead and shoulders of her new civilian flightsuit which covered her wiry, average-height frame from head to foot in pale blue, flexibly form-fitted and internally-aerated comfort.

She patted the girl down. "Checking to make sure you aren't armed. I am not scared of you, but I'm taking normal precautions, understand?"

Betts examined the base of her skull and along her spine for signs of manufacture. She had none. *What the hell is she doing out here?*

The Earth's inexorable heating had started the migration of humans from this part of the world centuries ago; the war, the pandemic and the ceding of the lower portion of the continent to the ACE had completed it. She shouldn't be here.

Betts knew her instincts had been right. This was a situation Central Command would want to know about. But Gauci had made it clear that she wasn't here officially, and, since she *was* officially breaking the

Treaty of Tangiers by standing in the buffer zone, she felt momentary relief that he hadn't been interested.

∞

Betts got the girl on board, gave her water and an energy bar, strapped her in, and flew to a level rock plateau safely in human territory near that quiver tree grove.

The girl didn't react to being taken for a flight. The only emotion she'd shown was hungry glee over the basic sustenance she'd been given.

The all-weather shelter popped up in seconds. A peripheral of the aircraft, it was accessible through an internal hatch. Crescent-shaped with an interlocking smart-tile floor, two air-filled sleepers, and a cool lavender glow from xenon lighting, it hovered just above the cruiser.

"Stay there?" the girl asked from where she sat on the cruiser's steps.

"Yeah. What do I call you? I'm Kanali Betts."

The girl—an older adolescent, Betts thought—stared, her mouth open.

The kanali pointed to her own chest. "Me, Betts."

"Best," the girl said.

"Close enough." She touched the girl's chest. "You?"

Betts went through the routine several times without luck. "I gotta call you something."

"Do not remember name," she finally said.

"You had a name, but you don't remember it?"

"Yes."

Amnesia? She told you her head is broken, you dope. "Do you remember my name?" Betts asked.

"Best."

"For the record, it's Bett... s," she said, stressing the *T* sound, "but I don't care if you mispronounce it."

"Betts."

"Good. Where did you come from?"

The girl stood up, looked around, and pointed.

"South? You sure?"

"Yes." She pointed west. "There mountains. Sun go down."

Well, she has some mental capacity.

"You were with the cogbots—" She caught herself. "I mean, the ACE?"

"Ye-esss." The girl breathed the word out, lengthening it, savouring it as if glad to tell someone.

"Are there other humans there?" The sudden fear that they'd started raiding human settlements rose up in her fast and hard, a pressure building against her ear drums. *Please dear gods, not again.*

"I only see me. I am only one with…" she picked up a matted strand of hair and waved it.

"Hair. Yes. I understand. Are they looking for you? Will they come after you?"

The girl pursed her lips and shook her head. "No. My one I live with said to go."

Betts boarded the cruiser, opened a secondary and wider perimeter field and set the armaments. Though the transport had nothing compared to a military issue, her position and security clearance had allowed the manufacturer to install some weaponry: tasers, scatter beams, circuitry disruptors, and mid-range gas launchers.

Betts, who by now wouldn't have contacted Gauci directly if she'd been under attack by aliens, keyed in the general dispatch code and recorded a short message.

"Information only. Priority… Seven. Human female spotted near ACE territory. No hostilities. Situation calm, under control. Full report by zero-eight-hundred local." She entered her coordinates and signed off.

Betts set up her quick-stove outside, heating food she'd brought from home. The girl sat on the steps and watched.

"How long were you with them?" Betts asked.

She shook her head.

"No memories of being somewhere else? With someone else?"

"I had… a name."

"Right. You said. What do the ACE call you?"

"Hu.man." The girl spoke the word in perfect imitation of an ACE voice. Close to human, but with stops after each syllable, slightly mechanical.

Kanali Betts choked up. She turned away, embarrassed by her reaction.

"You Best. I Hu.man."

Betts recovered and said, "I think we can do better than that. But, I have to know, how did we arrive here in this place at the same time?"

The girl stared. Her eyes were hard, intense, the central irises a sharp amber growing darker toward the edges and rimmed with black. "We live not far. Knew you come."

"We?" Betts heart sped up again.

"P602 and me."

"Who is that?"

"I live with that one."

"Who else knows I was coming? And what do you mean? How did you know?" Betts asked.

"What?"

Slow down. One question at a time. "How did you know I was coming?"

"P602 monitor border. Wait long time."

"You were waiting for someone to come?"

"Yes."

"Because…"

The girl just looked at her.

She's very literal, Betts thought. "Because the one you lived with wanted you to go?"

"Yes."

"Why?"

"P602 say, 'You.grow. Head.bro.ken. Time.leave. Go.hu.mans.' Wait long time."

Holy crap. Good it was me who came along. "Do others know about you?"

Again, she stared, but at least this time she had a questioning look on her face.

Betts rephrased. "Do other ACE know about you?"

"Yes. But long time in past P602 take me near border, not near others."

"Okay." Betts went back to her meal preparations. "What did you eat?"

"P602 found food for me. Then I learn how."

"Like what?"

She shrugged. "Caterpillars. Grasshoppers."

Betts, gulping hard, looked at the rich, spicy melange of meat, grains and vegetables she was heating up. *No wonder she's so thin. Would the girl like it? Would she even be able to stomach it?*

Hu.man loved every bite. And her glare seemed to soften after they'd eaten as if she were getting used to looking into the eyes of another human being.

Settled into the shelter, the girl fell asleep in seconds, while the kanali's eyes stayed open, her head full of what-ifs, how-comes, and whether-or-nots.

The girl's insider information on life in the ACE Compound would be invaluable. Of course the Pan-Continental Forces spied on them; they had to. It was mutual though, as in any postwar peace. The girl might not know a thing about their plans, their strategies, or their weapons, but she had been inside a place the rest of humanity had never entered.

Tomorrow, she would take Hu.man to HQ.

∞

Orange light filled the semitransparent shelter.

As Betts emerged from the cruiser, the glow from the east enveloped her, casting her shadow into those of the quiver trees. Their purple-black shapes splayed cartoonishly, elongated before the coming day. With trunks like thick celery stalks and spike-filled limbs sprouting upward into a rounded profusion, they looked like something a small child might draw and label "tree."

The air was hot but not stifling—yet.

When the girl woke, Betts prepared a simple meal. Mixed grains with nuts, milk and honey. Coffee.

"Did you only have bugs to eat?" she asked.

"No. When there was water, we grew grains. Had berries. Roots. Small animals. Birds."

"Other than foraging, how did you spend your days?"

"I read."

"Ah." This made sense. ACE had access to information. They were, after all, ambulatory computers. *Too smart for our own good* was a phrase frequently heard during the war years.

Betts gave her a bowl of food and sat down. After a moment, she said, "I will… I must take you in to… the place I work. They will want to know—" She stopped. "Never mind. We'll see how it goes." She shouldn't tell the girl that her knowledge was valuable. Maybe she thought of humans as the enemy. *Maybe I'm being too trusting.*

Betts thought about doing a missing persons search when she got back to HQ. Then she realized that it wouldn't be up to her to investigate once she turned the girl over.

I'll likely never see her again or even know what happened to her.

"You have no memory of a human family?" Betts asked.

"No."

"Do you know your age?"

"Days pass. I become… tall. ACE stay same. Some point at me. Say,

'Why.you.change?' Make fun of head."

"Make fun of your broken head?" Betts had seen no sign of an obvious head injury, but she hadn't forgotten the girl's first words. Then she realized what would make her different on sight from the ACE. "You mean because your hair grows?"

The girl nodded, paused, and then grimaced while poking stiff fingers into her skull, inserting them up under the mass. "And this—ooh."

"Oh, it hurts? I'll bet it does. All those matted places are pulling on your scalp. I can fix that for you."

"Yes. Fix hair." Her vocal cadence still sounded robotic, but it was softening, becoming more human the more she talked.

Betts had noted a small body of water on her flight the day before. It was so rare in this dry landscape that she'd marked the coordinates. She took out her navigator, pulled up the map, located her link and showed it to the girl, who stared uncomprehendingly.

"It's an image from the air of a watering hole in a rocky place," Betts explained.

"I like that."

"We'll go there so I can wash and cut your hair. We should leave soon, though. I need to get you to my office before the end of the day." Her stomach tightened at the thought.

As she readied the cruiser for take off, the perimeter field emitted a high-pitched whine. Betts sprang to the observation dome in the cockpit and flipped her implants to 360.

ACE. *Shit*. One ACE... that she could see. Were there more?

Any vacation-mode relaxation she'd been able to find vanished. She switched on the cruiser's console video so the girl could see outside.

"Is that your ACE?"

It had medium-brown colouring similar to her own skin tone.

The girl squinted at the image. "Where is P602?"

"Just outside. It can't come any closer without damaging itself. But," she said, switching to her military voice, "I don't know what it's doing here or if there are others. Tell me what you know."

The girl looked up, eyes wide. "I live with that one. 'Go. You.need. go.now,' that one told me."

"What's it doing here?" Betts ran fingers through her springy, close-cropped hair and then held on to it, squeezing.

"Best hair hurt, too?"

Betts ignored her question, checking the monitor to see that the android hadn't moved. *Probably working on how to override my perimeter.* She sat across from the girl. "This is serious. I need help. I need to know if… P out there is a danger to us."

"P602 never hurt me."

"P602 told you… let you go, right?"

"Yes."

"It shouldn't be here outside ACE territory. Why would it take that risk?" Betts played with her sensors while she talked, trying to pick up any other activity. "Could they be upset that you left? Are you valuable to them?"

"I don't know."

Betts switched on an outside speaker and said, "I am Kanali Betts of the Pan-Continental Military Command. You are in human territory. I would be within my rights to destroy you."

Seconds ticked by. The girl started to speak, but Betts shushed her.

Then, a tinny voice said, "Hu.man.here?"

"Yes. I have her."

"Have.i.tem.for.Hu.man. See.me?"

"I have a visual." Betts stared as the android held up something very small between thumb and forefinger. It bent over, put it on the ground, straightened up, and showed empty hands. Then it pointed to the ground again, turned, and began to walk away.

"It's leaving." The kanali drew her sidearm and opened the hatch. "Why did you come?"

The ACE slowly rotated to face the cruiser again. "Want.to.see. if.hu.man.a.live. Hu.mans.die.if.too.hot.or.no.food. Al.so.Hu.man.left. with.out—" P602 pointed to the ground.

"You were worried about her?"

The ACE didn't respond.

"How long has she been with you?"

P602 bent its leg joints and extended a flat hand about knee-high from the ground. "Since.that.size."

"Where did you get her?"

She pointed to the object on the ground. "I.go."

"Wait." Betts walked down the steps. "Was she lost? Taken? I need to find her family."

"Fam.i.ly.die."

"How do you know?"

"I.go. Do.not.de.stroy.me. Cause.man.y.pro.blems."

Kanali Betts drew in short, shallow breaths.

Was I monitored all the way down the border? Of course, she'd known this could be possible, but it hadn't seemed likely. She was one personal cruiser on a joy ride. And yet, it was so close to their sovereign territory. None of this had mattered yesterday morning, but now her actions seemed unprofessional. Foolish. *Do I report that when I drop off my find? Shit, I should have already filed my report.*

The ACE walked away.

"Wait. Do you want to see her? Do you care about her?"

The ACE didn't turn around, but said only, "Get.i.tem."

∞

The two-hour flight gave Betts time to think.

The item P602 had left was a data crystal—old technology that

Betts didn't have the capacity to access on the cruiser, though it would be no problem once back in civilization.

She felt confused that the cogbot seemed to care for the girl. Originally they'd been programmed, of course, to care for human children, but that meant to look after them, not care emotionally. Not that P602 had shown any emotion. It hadn't even asked to see the girl. Betts knew she was filling in blanks. But P602 had taken a substantial risk to deliver something the girl had left behind.

You heard things about the old cogbots and the new ones. That some had overridden the human parts of their programming in favour of the analytical and digital parts of themselves. That there were factions. That some wanted détente and to have the freedom to live with or alongside humans if they chose. Individual rights for those who had not been programmed to be individuals.

The pool, blue in a yellow-brown world, appeared. As Betts circled overhead, a small herd of springbok ran away. The girl was enthralled while Betts remained caught up in her reverie.

Could there be differences between old and new ACEs? Had they evolved... diversity? Some with more old programming, some with all new?

Maybe the girl knows.

There had been so little contact all these years. There should be some kind of diplomacy. But the peace had held. No one wanted to risk upsetting it.

She landed on flat, brown-ochre rocks a short distance above the pool.

After explaining what they were going to do, Betts stripped off her clothes.

"You look like me," the girl said, staring at Betts' naked body.

"Yeah. This is what we look like. Well, males are a little different, but... you must have seen this in your... reading. Right?"

"Yes. But I… I think maybe I am only one with extra parts."

Betts smiled. "There are many of us. I can give you something to wear in the water if you don't want to be naked."

"Oh no," she said, pulling the tunic over her head. "I not wear clothes all the time."

Betts had been wondering about the origin of her clothes.

The girl seemed to read her mind. "P602 said I should not be naked when humans come. We made a pattern and printed two. Then heat them together." She indicated the shoulders and sides. "It took several tries to get it big enough."

"We'll have to find you something more comfortable. For now, follow me." The kanali scooted down the smooth, angled embankment on her bottom until she sat on a rock just under the surface of the water.

The girl smiled as her body got wet. "It is… I don't know."

"You want hair like mine?" Betts brushed a flat palm over her tight curls.

"No," the girl said immediately. "Longer."

Betts smiled. Opinions about hair styles are inborn?

The girl lay down, her hair spilling out over the water. Betts, in up to her waist, worked on the knots with her fingers and pocket knife, cutting matted masses, keeping some length when possible. When the worst of the tangled strands lay on the rocks next to her, Betts shampooed it repeatedly.

"You've got a lot of filth in here."

"Head broken."

What would happen to her? Betts kept trying to spool out the levels that she'd be put through at Central Command and those levels kept spiralling around on themselves. They'd assign her some caretaker, maybe a medical person who would see to her needs and no doubt be kind to her. But where would she live? After they were through questioning her, what would her fate be? *She's been raised by cogbots!* How would she ever live this down? People would always treat her as an outsider, at best.

Finally clean and rinsed, Betts massaged the girl's scalp.

"You help me," the girl said, between moans of pleasure.

"No problem. I'm going to use this pick on it now. See?" She showed it to her. "It might hurt a little where it's still tangled, but once we get this done and I even up the length, it will be easy to take care of and you won't have pain in your head."

"Pain stop?"

"Hope so."

Afterward, they played in the water. The girl couldn't swim but had no fear. Betts showed her how to float and held her up, hand under her lower back as she relaxed, her face to the cloudless sky.

Eventually, Betts said, "We have to get out now and leave. Got to get you to Central Command before the day's gone."

"Sleep here tonight?" the girl asked. "Come in water tomorrow?"

Betts considered her. She looked like a real girl now. Awkward in speech and bearing, to be sure, but her sienna skin glowed and the change in her hair made her look fresh and, frankly, adorable—her head all black springy curls that Betts wanted to oil and twist into shape.

If they left now, she'd never get to do that. *It's almost as if I don't want her seen until she's at her best.*

What will I do after handing her off? File my report. That would likely be followed with some mundane procurement dispute while Gauci made the important decisions.

She had wanted to advance so she could set policy, not push papers. For the first time, the prospect of the remainder of her career scared her. But what would she do if she retired? Lie on the western beaches and watch penguins? She'd lost all her family in the five-year pandemic. Betts probably would have died too if she hadn't been stationed in Southern Africa, where people were so scarce. In that way, the ACE had saved her life.

Beyond this trip, which she'd planned on finishing at a rarely used family home on the coast of Morocco, her future had no form.

"What's another day?" she heard herself saying.

The fact that she hadn't filed the report she'd promised by 08:00 that morning needled at her. "I'm on vacation," she muttered as she set up camp with a circle of defence all around, now more for four-footed predators than ACE.

Betts had the girl sit on the cruiser's steps just below her as she evened up the haircut, teased out the tangles and showed her how to twist several strands at a time, so they would lie in orderly profusion.

The girl was more interested in the wildlife, pointing with delight at the succession of animals that came for their evening drink. Gazelles, antelope and lots of birds.

"Thank you for bringing me here."

"You're welcome. Does your head feel better?"

"Oh yes. Much lighter."

"I'll bet. No more broken head for you."

The girl laughed at a stork standing on one leg in the pool and then said, "Head still broken. Here." She rubbed behind her right ear.

"What?" Betts pulled her hair back with the pick and saw a small line, a barely visible scar, tucked skillfully just behind her ear. "What happened here?"

"They broke my head."

Betts' fingers went cold. "Who did?"

"I don't know."

"ACE?"

"Yes. Not P602. That one did not like them breaking me."

Sharp prickles poked the kanali's palms and feet. She sat for a long moment, stomach churning. "I… I have to get something. Stay here and watch the birds."

She found the ACE scanner she'd forgotten to bring with her that first night. The one she had neglected to use even after spending two days with this… this anomaly.

Maybe I am slipping.

Chewing at her lower lip, she toggled the sound to "off" and activated the scanner. She peeked to make sure the girl was still occupied, and approached her, scanner at arm's length.

The display showed pale green next to the label: Some ACE Circuitry Present.

Betts, what have you done?

∞

When morning came again, it wasn't the colourful dawn of the western ranges but a dry, middle-of-the-sun-drenched-continent, over-exposed, full-on white light.

While waiting for the girl to wake up, Betts sat on a rock, drinking her coffee. She hadn't slept much—again. She'd worried about it all but most especially about having lost her temper with the girl the night before.

"Are you a spy? A Trojan horse? Do you even know what you are?"

Typically, the girl hadn't reacted emotionally, but she did defend herself. "Not Trojan horse."

"What would you know about that?"

"Remember that story. Horse huge. Full of soldiers! Not like me."

That took all the venom out of Betts. This girl held so many surprises. But she wasn't finished.

"P602 did take care of me. P602 thought about my mind, my learning. And P602 did *not* want them to put in the wiring. That is why we went to live near border. So they leave me alone. So I can get out. Become really human."

"Why did they 'break your head'?"

"To make me more like them!"

This did not comfort Kanali Betts one bit.

A buzz from her wristpad startled her back to the present. The sound pattern relayed that it was an urgent message from Gauci.

Before she could retrieve it, the cruiser's sensors emitted an irregular wail. Betts jumped up. *All the bells and whistles on this thing! I don't even know what that one means.* She leaped up the ship's steps to the console to see a light flashing on the outer perimeter monitor. She touched the panel to close the cruiser's door, put her head into the observation dome, and set her vis-implants to distance.

Machines approached from the south. Throwing up a massive dust cloud and camouflaged against the dirt, ACE were coming toward them on some ground transport she could not identify. She strained, as if that could make her implants work better. It only made her human eyes water, blurring everything.

Then she remembered the girl, asleep in the shelter. Feeling frustrated once again that she didn't even have a name, she called, "Human! Come down! Bring everything. Hurry!"

As soon as the girl entered the main cabin, Betts shot up the steps, made sure it was empty of belongings, and pushed the controls for the shelter to fold up.

"What is it?" the girl asked, still half-asleep.

"ACE! Lots of them."

"Here? Why? Are we leaving?"

"I don't know! We have an international incident on our hands and I haven't even reported your existence to anyone! Sit down and strap yourself in while I figure out what to do."

The girl sat, pushing two fingers into her ear. "Wait," she said.

"What are you doing?" Betts went back to the dome. She counted eight vehicles. "Come here. Do you know these transports? How many ACE ride in each one?"

The girl didn't respond for a moment and then turned to look at the kanali. "They are called TIRs. One ACE each."

"How do you know? You haven't even looked at them."

"I… I hear them."

"You… Oh. You're wired to hear?"

She nodded slowly.

"From how far away?"

The girl shrugged. "Don't know. Must need to be close. I not hear any for long time."

"What are they saying?"

"They want me."

"Yeah," Betts said, dryly, "tell me something I didn't already know."

But the girl was concentrating, so Betts went to the console and armed every weapon she had, such as they were. Then, back in the dome, she watched the whirl of dust come closer.

It was only then that she remembered the urgent message from Gauci. She listened.

"Your report is overdue," he said. "You registered a Priority Seven situation and then disappeared. I know you're alive because your vitals are still registering. I also know that you are not where you said you were but haven't told me where you are. Your little vacation went bye-bye as soon as you reported a human in a place where humans should not be. Now our monitors show some kind of unusual movement north of the twenty-fifth parallel. Surveillance tells me it's *not* a herd of wildebeests. Report immediately."

Instead, Betts watched the dust cloud, her mind oddly blank. She had been a good and true soldier so long that to ignore a direct order from her superior should be impossible. But Gauci didn't seem like her superior, had not been her superior for more than a week, and should never have been made her superior.

I am definitely getting too old for all this.

"Best?"

"Yeah?"

"Shouldn't we leave?"

It was a logical question and a good idea and it had the effect of breaking Betts out of her reverie. "Not yet. It's better to see what they want and try to solve this problem instead of running away."

"Will you give me back to them?"

"No! Oh, gods no. You are human; you belong in our world."

"I am hu.man," she said, under her breath.

Betts didn't know if she meant her name or her identity, but she felt more responsible than ever for this person who wasn't, couldn't be, sure of the most basic thing that every other conscious being took for granted: her identity.

"Are you still hearing ACE chatter?"

She shook her head once. "Quieter now. It is not so much chatter as what you would call thoughts."

"So they're thinking to each other?"

"A bit like that. After they broke open my head, I went crazy hearing them all. That is when P602 took me to find humans. Near border there was no chatter of thoughts."

"Hive mind." Betts said this to herself more than the girl. She'd never understand what that would be like. "Can you talk to them with your wiring?"

"I shared thoughts with P602. But... what would I think to them?"

"Stop. Go away. We have weapons." Betts ran her fingers over her temples. She had to get focused, figure out what to do. "Could I hide you? Tell them you aren't here?"

"They know."

"Of course." She drew her sidearm, made sure her wristpad was synced to the ship and said, "Stay strapped in. We may have to leave abruptly. Understand?"

She nodded. "You are going out there?"

Betts saw fear in her eyes.

Emotion. Good girl. Becoming more human all the time. "Just to talk, hon. Just to talk."

∞

She emerged when the ACE were still several hundred metres away. The ship perched on a high outcropping, and she wanted the psychological benefit of standing tall above them at the top of her ship's stairs. As the group slowed and neared enough that Betts could make out details, she remembered that her prominence, her height, her position in space relative to them, would not have the same effect it would have on human beings.

They have no psychology, idiot. Human beings had made this mistake over and over with the ACE. All of this roiled in her mind when she should have been thinking about what she was going to say.

They stopped in a *V* formation. The TIRs most resembled a hover-cycle but were attached to the androids' bodies so that entity and vehicle were one and the same.

Betts shivered in spite of the intense heat. They aren't bothered by emotion, heat, shivers. By ambivalence or moral quagmires. She broke into a sweat, but all were waiting and she had to begin.

"You have broken the Treaty. I am an officer in the Pan-Continental Forces. Give me one good reason not to destroy you all."

A silence followed. It might have lasted twenty seconds but felt like a lifetime. When the voice came, Betts noted with another shiver that it was not metallic, jerky, or mechanical. It sounded human.

"You also broke the Treaty. You came into the buffer zone and took something that belongs to us."

"Wrong," Betts said, deepening her voice. "That 'something' is a human being who should have been returned years ago. As well, you have altered her. This alone could bring the wrath of humankind down upon you and your little world."

The one who sat at the point of the *V* detached from the bike with several sickening, snapping sounds and strode closer.

"Careful. I have a perimeter set up. It might… sting."

"I can see your puny perimeter, Kapteni Betts."

A sharp intake of breath kept her from responding immediately. Who was this? She touched her left temple to zoom in on the ACE's face. There wasn't much difference between the androids, but if it knew her as Kapteni Betts, then she must have worked with it. "I am Kanali Betts now. I have forgotten your name."

"Names are not important to us. You know that."

"What do you want?"

"The girl," it said.

"Not going to happen."

It was coming back to her. This was the ACE she'd been in negotiations with for some of the most debated details of setting up the compound: fossil fuel rights and the nitty-gritty aspects of transporting resources that weren't found there naturally. The name bubbled up from the depths just in time.

"D16, you know we would never return her to you. What do you really want?"

"Your forces cannot find out that she has been altered. We are considering destroying the… evidence, so that won't happen. It would be easier than having a human giving away our secrets."

Betts scoffed. "She is not privy to secrets! She is…" Betts didn't know what to say, where to start. Maybe she did have secrets. The more she learned, the less she knew. But more importantly, they had just threatened to kill both of them.

Weaponry. They were very good at weaponry.

She walked down the steps. Then she dropped down the ledge by the pool and down again another level. Ten metres from D16, she squatted, her sidearm trained on them.

The ACE approached the perimeter's edge.

"We know one another," Betts said.

"Better than most of our kind, yes."

"How can we solve our problem… peacefully?"

"Where are you taking her?"

Betts shrugged. "It is all in flux."

"You are a soldier who… what is the term? Goes by the book."

"Hah. Maybe long ago, I was. But we have no book for how to handle this. Both sides have broken the Treaty, though not with intent to dismantle the peace, I presume."

"ACE, in total, do not have that need."

"So it is true that you have factions?"

"That is not part of this negotiation," D16 said.

Always one to stay on topic, this one, Betts remembered. "What if I could promise you that the girl would not be turned over to the Pan-Continental Forces… by me."

"No. Too vague."

She raised her free hand, palm up. "I have no control over others. But *I* have the girl and I have not told anyone about her. If you leave now before surveillance positively identifies you as having breached the border, then I promise you I will not voluntarily hand the girl over to the military. I cannot assure you that she will never be discovered. But I have a vested interest in keeping such a discovery low-key and private. I promise to negotiate with those who might find out, in a way that does not provoke an inter-entity crisis. You know that I am a good negotiator."

"We understand one another."

"Do we have a deal?" she asked.

"Yes."

"What did you hope to do with her by adding ACE circuitry?"

"She lived with us. We tried to make her better, more like us, but it—" D16 stopped, looked down at the ground, and then started again. "The experiment did not work well. Her brain is too alien."

"Fucking right. One more thing."

D16 looked at her, eyes steady, patient.

"Is there a faction of ACE interested in exploring the possibility of diplomacy between your state and ours?"

Without pause it said, "It could be discussed."

Gauci buzzed her.

She dithered. What to do? The peace itself rested on her keeping her word to the ACE and that meant dereliction of duty—for starters.

"Please," she said, holding up one finger to D16. She took a deep breath and clicked her wristpad.

"Jenerali. You wanted me?"

"Your ass is grass, Betts. What the fuck?"

"I'm on vacation, sir. Sorry about the missing report, but it was all a false alarm."

"What?"

"Guess I took the whole 'getting away' thing too literally. To be honest with you, I'm not proud of this, but I got hold of some qat in Cairo. Not used to it. So when my sensors went off, so did my imagination. There, just at dusk, with me heading into the sun and slightly… um, under the influence… I thought I saw a human being in the hills. But nope. Was a giraffe. A gorgeous juvenile. Nice to know they're still breeding, eh? False alarm… and, of course I felt foolish, so I hoped someone there would cut me a small break."

"We've locked onto your coordinates. What a shock that you are, coincidentally, in the area of the movement that surveillance picked up. I also know you have someone with you. That someone, I presume, is the person you mentioned in your Priority Seven call. I do not know why you're lying about it, but I'm going to find out. I've scrambled a jet to intercept you. Prepare to face the fucking Inquisition."

After closing the link, Kanali Betts regarded D16 for a moment, made her decision, and said, "I have a request. I need a couple of minutes to set it up. However, I don't want to put the peace in danger by keeping you here because… I'm sorry to say… a military jet is on the way." Betts knew ACE would not register alarm on their faces, but she could swear she saw their bodies tense. "How much time will it take you to get back across the border?"

"Twenty-three minutes."

She looked at the time. *The closest base would be… Harare.* She calculated half an hour before the jet arrived. *Time enough.*

"Wait here. This is necessary for me to keep my side of our bargain."

She entered the ship and while shutting down her perimeter defences, told the girl what was going to happen and why.

In one minute, they came out of the cruiser into the harsh sunlight and made their way down to D16. She turned to the girl and said, "This is the only way. I will not abandon you. Do you trust me?"

The girl nodded.

"Take her," Betts said to D16, "until I've dealt with my superior. I will meet you in the buffer zone due south to get her back as soon as the danger has passed. I estimate no more than two hours, but stay near the border until I come, even if it takes me longer. I *will* come. Do we have a deal?"

D16 nodded once.

Betts let go of the girl, who walked to the TIR and climbed on.

∞

The shadow of a sleek military jet passed over her.

Betts, wearing a fuchsia bikini and lying on the submerged stone where she'd washed the girl's hair, glanced at the time.

Thirty-seven minutes. *Shoddy. They'd get a dressing down if they were under my command.* But, they weren't. And never would be.

"Kanali Betts?" one of the two called from above after they'd landed.

She waved and motioned for them to come down.

As they—a man and a woman—came near, she realized that the woman had once been under her command. A mostly Caucasian gal with freckles. Betts even remembered her call sign. "Hey," she said, not getting up.

"Kanali Betts," said the woman, saluting, looking hot and uncomfortable. The man saluted as well. "We have orders to find out what's going on here."

"Trace, right?" Betts said to her.

Her face reddened. "Yes, Kanali. This is Sargent Gakere Mweri."

"Well, airmen, as you can see, I am making the most of my vacation."

Mweri cleared his throat and said, "Brigedia Jenerali Gauci mentioned a possible incursion of ACE."

Betts rose and stood facing them, her feet in the water, her body dripping. "I know. He told me that too. Evidently, surveillance picked up something. But you know as well as I do, they can't pinpoint what it is from inside HQ. Probably a herd of wildebeests." She shook her head and laughed.

Trace giggled awkwardly. Mweri grimaced, but with amusement.

Ah yes, the soldier's disdain of HQ is universal.

"I'm not happy that Gauci's wasted money and time sending you here. What's that about?"

"I'm sure we don't know, Kanali," Mweri said. "You've had no interaction with the ACE?"

She eyed them levelly. "No."

After an awkward pause, Mweri said, "He also asked us to speak with the other person who's with you."

At this, Betts dropped the light demeanour. "This is too much. I have no one with me... now." She walked so close to the pilots that as she gestured water droplets stained their blouses. "But, I *am* a grown woman on leave. Would there be some crime if I had the companionship of another person?"

"Well, did you?"

"You have heat, infrared, and life-form scanners! You know, and I know you know, because you've already scanned this particular piece of land, that there's no one else here. Can you even imagine what kind of scenario Jenerali Gauci has in mind? I'm vacationing and he sends you after me because I might be in the company of another human being?"

"We're just following orders, Kanali," Trace said.

"I'm not upset with you. But I am with him. He seems a little... I don't know. Trigger happy? What do we do now?"

"Gauci wants you to report in. Immediately. In person."

"Do you have orders to take me into custody?"

"We do not, Kanali."

"Fine. Do your job. Report what you found. Tell him about this gorgeous pool of water I discovered and how I was trying to relax and get away from his world and tell him that no, more's the pity, I did not have company, ACE or otherwise. That I'm completely alone, but that if I weren't, it really would not be any of his business."

They nodded to her in agreement, good-bye, and—in no small part—apology for their intrusion, and left.

Just as they reached the top of the plateau, Betts called up. "You should know that ten minutes ago, I resigned my commission effective immediately, as is my prerogative given my rank, time of service and the disrespect I've been shown. Give my best to anyone who asks about me."

∞

Piloting into the wee hours, Betts, her passenger deep asleep in the berth, finally arrived.

After unlocking and opening wide the verandah doors, she hoisted the girl over her shoulder, carried her inside and put her on the couch. The girl snorted and snuffled, rolled onto her side, and slept again.

No sleep however for Kanali Zohra Betts, Retired.

She showered, put on a kaftan, cooked some rice, added nuts and dried fruit, and made a mug of strong coffee. She powered up the computer, sat down across from the sleeping girl, and inserted the data crystal into the old technology adapter.

Two people appeared. Betts knew immediately that she was looking at the girl's parents. They were emaciated and obviously ill. In the lower corner, the date blinked: 2420.

Fourteen years ago, when the plague was waning, though no one would have known that then.

Betts watched until she fell asleep, her head on the table.

∞

"Best. Best!"

The kanali rose to awareness as if swimming up through layer after layer of gossamer netting. When she finally opened her eyes, she felt as if she were still looking through several of those layers.

"Where are we?" the girl asked.

"Morocco. This home belonged to my mother."

"What is that water? Is that an ocean?"

Betts sat up and stretched, trying to clear her head. "Yes. The Atlantic."

The girl nodded and then paced the room, agitated. "I think you will want to break my head again, right? To take out the ACE parts?"

"Whoa, wait. Let me wake up, will you? Um, yeah. Well, not me, but a doctor. Yes. That's what I think we need to do."

"I don't want you to."

"It won't hurt... not much. You'll have anesthesia. Do you know what that is?" She didn't wait for an answer. "As it is, you're likely to be thought of as a spy for the ACE. Even if you aren't."

The girl looked down and then up again. Betts spotted a hardening of the muscles of her jaw. "The ACE are the only beings I know, but I don't choose them over humans. What is this important thing I can spy on? Do I see or know things that help them? Or hurts you?"

Betts sighed. "Not yet."

"No. And, this is *my* life." She drew out the word "my" as if it had never left her mouth before and she didn't really want to let it go. "I... I want... an ordinary life."

"How can you hope for that if you still have that alien stuff in your head?"

"Alien?"

"You know what I mean. Foreign."

"I know ACE and humans are at peace for a long time."

"Yes."

"Have they done wrong?"

"Since the treaty?" Betts asked. "It's not about that. They've kept to their agreement... as far as we know. But it's this kind of thing—"

"Spying? Does the human side spy?"

Now Betts' face blushed. "I won't answer that. See? I can't talk to you. Are you trying to get me to say things that will hurt our side?"

"No. Don't you see? They did it to make me more like them. So I could talk and think and hear the way they do. So I wouldn't be so... alien. It is the same thing you want. To take it out so I won't be alien."

With a frustrated gesture, the girl walked out the wide open doors to the verandah.

Betts could see her in profile as she shut her eyes against the stiff, warm breeze. Between the boxy, bright-blue house and the ocean grew a profusion of palm trees, yuccas and succulents.

Loudly, the girl said, "I want to stay here. To stay who I am. For now." She turned and walked back inside. "Is it possible to swim in that water?"

Betts felt more tired than she could ever remember feeling before. She welcomed the company of this interesting, unfolding person. She had made her choice back there on the southern plains. *But I don't want to worry about compromising other humans, not after all I've done to keep the peace.*

That thought stopped her.

What have I done, really? All my paranoia about the ACE accomplished nothing. It's humans who have turned against me. The girl was right; they were at peace. And now… now she was retired, something she had never asked for, never wanted.

"We should talk about ACE and humans," Betts said, yawning. "Maybe both sides, at least some on both sides, want to change parts of the Treaty. It ended the war, but it also separated us completely. Someday, those who want to might be able to visit or even share lives. Maybe, if that could be accomplished… maybe P602 might want to come live with us."

"P602 couldn't." The girl's eyes glistened.

"Not as things are now. But if you both want that, I'll do what I can to make it happen."

Betts took her hands, looked her in the eyes, and said, "You are eighteen years old. Your mother was named Lamah. Your father, Omar. He was Kenyan. She was also, but of Indian origin. From Kashmir. They were Sunni Muslims. When you were four, your parents made a dangerous journey to deliver you to the safest place they could imagine. A place with no people, no disease, no contagion. Before dying from the plague, they trusted you to P602 because it had been your mother's nanny long before the uprising. P602 really was… is… your family."

Tears spilled down the girl's cheeks.

"Your name is Aisha. And yes, Aisha, we can swim in the ocean."

About the Author
Nancy S.M. Waldman

Nancy S.M. Waldman grew up in Texas, but now lives and writes from the tranquility of a 115-year-old home in the woods of Cape Breton Island, Nova Scotia. Her short fiction has been published in *Fantasy Scroll Magazine, AE-The Canadian Science Fiction Review, Perihelion Science Fiction* and all of the anthologies from Third Person Press—which she co-founded in 2008. She is a member of SF Canada and a graduate of Viable Paradise. This is her first story set on an imagined-future African continent, but she hopes to revisit this world again. Find her on Twitter as @nuanc.

Author Website: http://nancysmwaldman.com/

The Soma Earth
by Ciro Faienza

It was like this, she thought. Dried resin of coffee rings the bottom of the finished cup; you rinse it and smell the ghosts of what you've drunk. Feeling the cut again when you change the bandage. The exhaustion that waits for the moment you try to stand.

Paolo was gone. Tiche spent no time denying it, because hope was acid in your belly and grief lived in your chest, where you are guarded by bone. She could cry, a half hour at night screaming and heaving and begging like a child into his empty shirts, then wake and still pedal the bike turbine for the cold trap. Still pump its nitrogen out into the fields. Still turn to their notes on using seawater.

Work. Walk the fields. Study. Plan. The bandage stayed intact.

His disappearance was a warning or a retaliation or both, but it was strange to her that the men had taken Paolo, a native, and not his black American lover. Even the locals who didn't lump her in with the African immigrants pretended not to understand her Italian at times, or turned to dialect to keep her on the periphery. That place where basic communication was a privilege, not a right.

She understood. Changing times had not been kind to their country, nor their country kind to them. Northern wealth, which had never flowed freely into the farming South, ceased with the rains, and the region had resumed its historic role as Mediterranean doormat.

She understood, and then she pictured Paolo—long, sun-dark, and graceful—dissolving in lye.

She supposed it was some code about women. These were the same sort of men who had poisoned the water table of Campania just in time for the new age of drought to shrivel its people to dust or bombed whole trains to get at a single policeman, but they still believed themselves when they talked about honor. Women, children, et cetera.

In fact, she was surprised she counted.

∞

Tiche and Paolo had built their farm on his family's land in Gargano, in the years after grad school. It was a project desperate enough to be utopian. Find a new way, before it was too late. Most of their colleagues in the sciences had fled in despair to northern climes—Greenland, Iceland, Alaska, Scandinavia—but as the world caught on, the land was snatched up, the border rules changed. The rich outran the poor.

For Tiche, southern Europe was not a compromise. Hot as it would become, it was cooler than the American south and not so full of denialists or the Luddite firebrands who incredibly blamed leftists for the rising oceans.

And she loved the sound of Paolo's language, the thick plosives, the glissando inflections. She could even sense the *Southernness* of his accent, which he thought was ridiculous. She insisted it was almost Texan. He laughed.

Hearing was a pastime for Tiche, had only come to her at age ten, after an operation that left a network of fiber optics spidering into her virus-primed temporal lobes. The slender ear modules were spun-wire beautiful, and when they first met, Paolo told her in his not-southern accent that she turned his words to light to understand them.

Lord, she thought, edging closer for a surreptitious brush of skin, I could get into some trouble with this one.

He had pianist hands with long, elegant fingers, which she imagined stroking her bare scalp and other places that loved the brush of soft friction—the sides of her upper arms, whose taut lines he might imagine wrapped around him, or the edges of her lips, whose fullness might make him notice his own heartbeat. On the farm, sun and labor eventually made them both a little leaner and him a little darker, but his hands stayed beautiful.

But he had cried—*cried*, she was shocked to see—when he realized what it might mean for her to be a black woman in Puglia. It annoyed her, watching his public grief over truths she'd suffered through since birth, but she remembered he was not American, and what was his context to know these things? In the end she said that "black" was always another word for "outsider," even for Americans on home ground. She was ready. She wanted their adventure.

PhDs, earth sciences and inorganic chemistry. They were perhaps the most overqualified farmers ever to work that land, and they were full of ideas about boosting the withered nitrogen cycle, about reclaiming water, work efficiency, crop symbiosis, heat management, sensor networks, power storage. Tiche downloaded volumes and volumes on off-the-grid methodologies, everything from herbal pharmacology to stick fighting for self defense. One day she asked Paolo, in still broken Italian, if they'd become crazy libertarians by accident.

He thought for a moment and said, "A man of the right means a man who is afraid and nothing else. We are not afraid."

∞

The last of her ear modules gave out a few years back. Expected. Sad. It was different from how she felt after the social dark, the great failure of the apps and networks that kept people together. She had no idea if it was server collapses or companies shutting down or national firewalls or simply a problem with the internet in Gargano, which had always been spotty. But after a few days, she began to feel like a drifting vessel pinging into the deep.

The hearing loss instead was a wave of truth descending upon her. The curtain had closed on her beloved spectacle of sound and now, like a theater-goer, she had to return home. To reality, which was no spectacle, but quiet. Paolo held her, kissed her eyes.

It meant that when the men first came—jutting-jawed men, wide-faced men, men with knives in their pockets—she had no idea what they were saying. Across the pepper patch in the evening she saw three of them climb the hill and approach Paolo. The gestures she recognized—we are reasonable, you understand, I am a powerful man—sent her to fetch the thick wooden staff she drilled with every morning.

She let them get their knives out. It would teach them something about fear. Two of them walked into the most basic of moves and lost bones for it, which was enough. The third postured—actually tossed his knife away—and beckoned her to him.

Tiche would never forget the look in his eyes, after the lightning snap of her staff and his bent neck and his collapse to the dirt. It was the look of a man who feels something essential has gone mortally wrong inside him.

A cut of the crops or euros. She'd guessed it, and Paolo signed that he should have foreseen it. From the lemon groves of Sicily to the buffalo marshes of Naples, farmers had ever been the low-hanging fruit. What few farms were producing now had violence in their future.

It triggered the next stage of Tiche and Paolo's beautiful dream—expanding the farm and building something communal with the locals who wanted to take part. While their notions of the right social order for their project were vague, they knew they had something to share and they believed in its power to summon the best in people. The world had lost too much to hierarchies and independence. They wanted to give.

But people had to be convinced and rallied and trained, all before the next force of the Sacra Corona arrived with something more than knives. Paolo wondered why they had brought no firearms with them, if they were indeed that sloppy. Tiche guessed that ammunition must be getting harder and harder to find. But probably not impossible, for the right cause.

Paolo went to town in the morning. Tiche kept her staff with her. Paolo did not come back.

∞

In ages past, the Mediterranean had been no sea. The world ocean, what would become the Atlantic, lapped for millennia against its bounding rock, and when the waters finally breached Gibraltar, the entire basin filled in fifty years.

Fifty years to make a sea. Tiche couldn't imagine seeing that. The same amount of time in her own century had seen the tides swallow the beaches of Gargano, so that the shore was now a cliff, the outskirts of her hills. The salt water teased her and Paolo. It was nearby, abundant, sweet and life-giving, if their desalination plans were successful. The numbers were right for it, but the work and materials would have been too much for the two of them on their own.

Other projects they did manage with enormous success. They drew nutrients straight out of the air and fed them directly to their plants, which they had chosen to be survivors. Paolo's ancestral loves, the garlic and chilies and rosemary, were survivors, which he said pointed to the virtue of listening to the land.

They did listen. At regular intervals in their meticulously plotted fields were nitrogen sensors and water activity meters, their output running through shielded cables alongside the nutrient pipes back to the house. The data were precious. The farm lived by what it told to a solar-powered processor.

Without Paolo, the silence was a shroud. He'd tried to plan ahead, worked with her to make devices that fed their data to her when she was out in the fields. Their electronics would talk to her still-functioning implants with generated tones—for wind volts a middle C, for solar volts a thrum. His proposal for the field readings was a grid of vibrating lozenges adhered to her back, a pair for each sensor grid.

Ridiculous. She never tried it until after he left, when she would have torn tender seedlings up, burned their decades of work to the ground, just to hear his voice again or to be touched.

It stayed ridiculous, at first. Random buzzing along her back, sweat under medical tape, senseless noises mocking her ears. But they were makers and wonderers, and he had no idea what he had done.

She woke the morning of the only rain that year with the clear and impossible sense that her body stretched well beyond her bed, farther than the house, out into the hills.

Inexplicable. Had she taken something? *No.* She hadn't seen a pill since she was thirty.

Outside she heard a lone middle *C* rise with the insistent breeze, and the sharp smell of the air prickled across her back. When the clouds broke, she understood.

It came in sheets, fuller than at any time in recent memory. She saw it cover the fields and sing across her shoulder blades, down her spine, and felt them both as one and the same. Her spine, the spine of the land. Her tended and precious and joyous fields, a garden of herself.

Psychologists had used smoke and mirrors to convince people they had extra limbs or walked two feet behind themselves almost a century ago. Without realizing it, Tiche had bound herself to her labors in a way that went beyond even her love and grief. It didn't feel like smoke and mirrors. It felt like another wave of truth.

She laughed, stupidly, like a middle-schooler. Yet it was a fresh hurt not to be able to share this with him—to be suddenly vast and timeless and whole—and to thank him and to talk to him about hope.

She thanked the ground instead and lay upon it, letting the rain breach her bones and fill the basin of her, letting it seep into the soils she had raised for almost half her life.

Now she would make a sea.

∞

Inside the house she packs a bag. She loads soil samples and sensor models and a small computer, charged. She nestles in a young modified bean plant that had cost a fifth of their savings, when the two of them were still spending currency.

It has been over a month since the men with knives. Tiche doesn't know what they're waiting for. The harvest, maybe. It doesn't matter. She needs to act.

She still believes in the second part of their dream. They never meant to spend their lives alone, even with each other. Their mistake, she thinks, must not have been to trust, but not to trust sooner. She wonders how things might have been different if they had dug their first hole alongside the people who had lived there for generations, whose families were living histories of desperate struggle and yearning. Certainly they would have stood with her when the men came.

The bag is packed, and she grabs her staff and steps out.

Tiche knows the townspeople are probably lost to her for the foreseeable future. If her skin doesn't keep them away, other fears will, and she has seen how whiteness behaves in fear.

On the outskirts of San Severo, there are others. They look something like her, and though her African name will not make her an insider, necessarily, it might bridge the gap of trust.

Most of them are North Africans, first generation, second generation. Some will be engineers, educated in Arab universities. Others will be writers or parents or farmers themselves. They have seen terrible things. They are survivors.

At the last cultivated row she looks back, trying to imagine how the place will look at its full size, irrigated by seawater and filled with people, as Paolo saw it.

She kneels, and a hundred times she kisses his name into the loam, which is his earth, which is her body. Then rises.

She hears a thrum. The sun is bright.

About the Author
Ciro Faienza

Ciro Faienza is a writer, actor, and filmmaker. His fiction and criticism have appeared in *Reflection's Edge*, *Daily Science Fiction*, *Secretly Timid*, and *K-Zine*, and his films have shown at the Dallas Hub Theater, the Dallas Museum of Art, and the London National Gallery. His short story "J'ae's Solution" was a top-25 finalist in Public Radio International's Three Minute Futures contest. He is also the editor of the poetry podcast at Strange Horizons. Find him online on his Facebook author page and on Twitter @cirofaienza.

Author Website: http://freneticlicense.blogspot.com/

Debugging Bebe
by Mary Mascari

On my last day as a student of the Portero Nanobotanical Institute, I thought I knew what I'd be doing next: graduation, a good job as a nanobotanist with the Portero Corporation—basically the bright future that I'd been promised by my parents and teachers.

I arrived at the greenhouse, buzzing with excitement. I turned the corner to my tokonoma, the cubicle where I'd lived and worked for the past three years. On the wall outside, the photograph over my nameplate hardly looked like me anymore. The Britta Hammar in that picture wore makeup and fixed up her blonde hair in poofy curls. I hadn't had time for that since, well, right after that photo was taken. Now I wore braids and coveralls, which made it harder to tell whether or not I'd slept or showered recently. "Good morning, Bebe!" I called out.

Bebe didn't respond. She was a *Campsis radicans porteris*, a trumpet vine subspecies, owned by Portero Corporation, since they run the school. I made her, though, and spent the last two years of school cultivating her. Her vines climbed the back wall of my tokonoma, forming an aesthetically pleasing shape. Her orange-pink, trumpet shaped flowers were perfectly placed, not too many, not too few.

Well, maybe one too many. I pulled a pair of shears from my tool belt. I flipped my goggles down and set them to 10x magnification. The stem of the offending flower turned to a scaly dragon leg. I used my shears to disconnect the flower at the junction. It gave an electric pop when I pulled it out.

Tapping my goggles back to normal magnification, I popped open a panel in Bebe's root pod and plugged my handheld in to get some readings. Oxygen levels were at 604, well over the minimum of 500. I tweaked the leaf color to be a bit bluer and programmed the tendrils in the top left segment to curl ten percent tighter. I disconnected my handheld, closed the panel, and stepped back to see how she looked.

Bebe was a nanobotanic plant, a combination of organic material and electronics. Without plants like her, we couldn't live in space. She generated oxygen and consumed carbon dioxide without water or soil. But we nanobotanists had to do more than that. Masaki Nakamura, who invented the technology, insisted that our plants be beautiful as well as functional.

A jury, including Nakamura-sensei himself, was coming in five hours to inspect Bebe and decide if I would graduate. He might give me a recommendation for a job with Portero, the parent company for our entire space station. Yamada-sensei was sure I would get full marks, but I couldn't be anything short of perfect.

I pulled on my gloves, changed my goggles to 5x magnification, and started my daily routine of checking each leaf and tendril. It usually took a full hour for a plant this size. Some students had smaller plants, little rhododendrons or even ferns, and there was some merit in a delicate plant, but I wasn't going to settle for something that you could stick on a shelf. The only reason I didn't do an evergreen was that Yamada-sensei already had two other students doing conifers, and she said I should showcase my skill at flowers.

I began at the root pod at the bottom, touching each leaf carefully. If I found any tears or spots, I would disconnect the leaf and grow a new one to replace it. It took about a minute. A full vine took about five. I could regenerate the leaves on the whole plant in about an hour if I really had to, but then I'd have to take another week to get them trimmed and colored properly.

It was monotonous work, so I tapped my earpiece to play some music. Tristan, my as of recently ex-boyfriend, had gotten some new tunes from Earth, and I bounced to the rhythm as I turned over each leaf.

But then I saw a bug.

I shut off the music. A shiny, black bug, about the size of my finger-nail, was crawling on one of Bebe's leaves. I pulled it off and inspected it. I didn't see any tag or chop on its carapace, even when I looked at 20x magnification. That was weird; usually the bug hackers wanted you to know who they were. I carried the thing over to my workbench and dropped it into a plastic jar, then sealed it shut.

But when I went back to Bebe, I found another one. And then another. And then three, then five, then ten.

I had an infestation.

Inconvenient, but not a disaster. I knew how to handle this. I had memorized the Portero Institute's entire list of approved treatments for infestation. I grabbed a can of foam from my workbench and sprayed it on a leaf that had three of the creatures chewing on it. The foam was thick and sticky, and was supposed to gum up their circuits. But as soon as I finished spraying, three little black heads poked out. They just crawled out of the foam and moved on to another leaf.

I was pretty sure that foam was becoming outdated, anyway. The bug hackers were always working around our defenses. But we at the institute still had some tricks up our sleeves.

I set up little speakers around the tokonoma and hooked my tune player into them. I called "Noise!" to the students in the other cubicles and then put in earplugs. The sound coming from the speakers started off low, a rumble that shook the floor and my intestines, and worked its way up to a piercing wail, then back down again. Then the tones randomly jumped around, like some insane dance beat. Thirty seconds of that usually did the trick and fried their circuits. I let it go for a full minute. The other students on the floor could deal with it.

I turned the music off and checked Bebe again, expecting to see a bunch of little frozen bugs in a pile in the mulch on the floor. But they were still creeping around, destroying my beautiful Bebe. So these bugs were soundproof, too.

I flipped over another leaf and my stomach flipped along with it. The back was covered with eggs. The damned things were reproducing. I tried to scrape the eggs off, but they were fused to the leaf so tightly that I wound up scraping the outer skin of the leaf along with them.

The only way to deal with bug eggs was to disable them. And I had to do it quickly. Bebe's oxygen levels were plummeting. Down to 598 already.

I spent the rest of the hour going through every single technique in the approved list: infrared light, every acid spray that wouldn't also eat Bebe's leaves, even some little EM pulses. And every time, those damn little bugs kept crawling around, oblivious to my impending doom.

I was out of options. Who the hell had made these things? My last resort was to shut Bebe down, set her into a dormant state, and cut off all the leaves. But there wasn't time to shape and color the new leaves before the jury. I'd just as soon show up to my final exam naked.

∞

The Doolean IV space station where I lived was shaped like a series of mostaccioli noodles, each nested inside the other to make a cylinder. The noodles rotated around the middle to provide artificial gravity through centripetal force. That meant that the outer noodle was down, and the space in the middle, the axis, was at the top. In between were fifteen levels of housing, lab space, offices, and everything else, all floating in an orbit between Earth and Mars.

My school and house were on the second level in from the outside. Since my mom's promotion, we were able to get a tunnel down to the outer level, so we could climb down and look out at space. We went to a party at her boss's house once, on the outermost level, and they had a room where the whole floor was a window. It felt like you were walking on stars.

But now I needed to go inward and upward. I grabbed my specimen jar, stuck a few more bugs and some leaves into it, and ran out to catch the next zipsled up to the axis. Tristan would still be at work. I hoped he'd talk to me. I only had four hours left.

There weren't any express zipsleds at this hour, so the ride took about twenty minutes with all the stops. After debating with myself for ten levels, I decided to call my sister, Solange. I hated to bother her, but I was desperate.

Solange had the job I wanted in a few years. Her official title was Senior Associate Nanobotanist, which doesn't sound very prestigious, but Solange was the first person to ever make senior associate only two years out of school. I planned to be the second.

She answered right away. I knew she would. "Hey, little Sis. Ready for the jury?" She tried to sound perky, but I heard the fatigue in her voice. Her baby, my niece Thea, was five months old and still wasn't sleeping through the night.

"I'm afraid not," I said.

I told her about the bugs.

"Did you try foam?"

"Of course. And sound frequencies. And everything else on the list." The bugs started to float in the jar. We were getting close to the axis.

Solange sighed. "I think you're going to have to shut her down."

"I'm on my way to talk to Tristan now."

Solange breathed in through her teeth in a little hiss. "Is that a good idea?"

"Nakamura-sensei is going to be there at four."

"Yeah." Solange gave another sigh, which turned into a yawn. "Tell you what. Let me see what I can find here."

"I'm not supposed to get help from Portero employees."

"I don't think anyone will mind if I do a little research. I mean, this bug you've got is worse than what most students have to deal with. Extreme measures are called for."

"Thanks a million."

"Anything for my little sister."

The zipsled arrived at the station just as I hung up.

∞

Tristan was one of the few students at the institute from the poorer part of the station, the inner levels, but he was smarter and worked harder than those of us who were children of Portero executives. We were in the same year, up until last semester. He couldn't get the oxygen levels on his barrel cactus, a *Ferocactus pilosus porteris*, over the minimum for his final exam. I told him it wasn't a big deal, he could take the class over, but instead he quit the school entirely. We stayed together for a few months afterwards, but in the end I couldn't watch him throw his talent away like that.

Now he worked in a factory that made some sort of medical equipment based on microscopic glass bubbles. He spent all day monitoring and fixing machines that made bubble after bubble. He kept saying he was going to start on a *Pereskia aculeata* one of these days, but I never saw it.

A little bell rang as I skipped into the drab front office, my feet light in the low gravity. The office was in the innermost level. On the other side of the door was the axis, the gravity-free zone at the center of the whole station. Jenine, the receptionist, smiled at me, showing pink lipstick on her teeth. "Tristan's still on shift," she told me. She didn't know that we'd broken up.

"It's kind of an emergency." Jenine's desk was covered in little pictures of children on Earth, who I always guessed were her grandchildren. She wouldn't be able to see them very often because of the way the orbits lined up. "I've got my final jury today and I need his help."

She winked and picked up the phone. "Good luck, hon," she said, then hit a button and announced, "Tristan Shea to reception, please. Tristan Shea." She hung up. "He'll be out in a second, hon. If you want, there's juice in the fridge."

I skipped over to a little couch and pulled myself onto it. There were straps you could use to tie yourself in if you wanted, but I just hooked a leg around the armrest. Even though I was from the Outer Levels, I knew how to handle myself in low gravity.

A hatch in the ceiling opened and Tristan's legs appeared on the ladder, then the rest of him. He was wearing stained blue coveralls with his name embroidered over the Portero logo.

He hopped to the floor from halfway down the ladder. His black hair was messy from being in zero-g. I used to run my fingers through it, to try to neaten it.

He narrowed his eyes when he saw me. "What are you doing here?"

I showed him the specimen jar. "Bebe's got bugs, and my jury's today."

Tristan's blue eyes flicked down to the jar. I felt the receptionist watching us. "What do you want me to do?"

"I thought you might know... something?"

"You think because I live in the inner levels, I'll know who all the hackers are, is that it?" He was still standing by the ladder, his work gloves still on.

"No," I protested. "I thought..." but he was right.

"Failing a jury's not the end of the world."

"I know." But it was for me. I felt my throat tighten and took a breath to release it. I held the jar out. "They've laid eggs."

Tristan took a glove off and reached for the jar. He looked at the bugs, now happily munching on the leaves I'd put in.

"Jury's at four?" he asked. His lips hardly moved.

I nodded, a tear floating away from my face in a shimmery blob. He hated it when I cried.

He kept looking at the bugs. The clock ticked on the wall like it was taunting me.

"Jenine, you got some paper?" The receptionist handed Tristan a pad of paper and a pen. He wrote something, tore off the page, and then handed it to me. "If you hurry, you can get there and back in time."

It was an address, in Tristan's neighborhood, and a name, Gilman.

∞

The first time Tristan took me to his house, I was a little disappointed. I'd expected the inner levels to be scary, dark, chaotic slums with tattooed gangs roaming the streets and some guy playing a plaintive saxophone on his balcony while sirens wailed.

The inner level neighborhoods weren't that poetic. They were row after row of identical, plain buildings, all the same bland brown of re-cycled SoyPlas; down in the outer levels we got the freshly grown stuff in bright colors, but here those colors commingled into a hopeless hue. In front of each building, in the middle of the bare lawn, stood a single tree badly in need of maintenance. Their leaves, all the same dull green, were unevenly spaced, leaving wide bare patches of splaying branches. A few kids played outside, and I did see one guy with a tattoo, but he was just sitting on his front steps, drinking a soda. It wasn't dangerous. It was drab, dirty, and soulless.

The address on the paper was a few blocks down from where Tristan lived, but the building was identical. I went to the second floor, found the right apartment, and paused. I was trusting Tristan with my life here. All for a plant. I could go home, call Yamada-sensei, ask for a deferral. I could flunk this semester and redo it.

And then wait another year and have to tell the people from Portero why I'd taken four and a half years to graduate. And I'd be twenty-two then.

My timepiece chimed in my ear. Two o'clock. I knocked on the door.

It creaked open and a young man with gleaming blond hair looked at me over the chain. He didn't say hello or anything, just stared at me.

I was wearing my student uniform, which meant I was representing the institute, the Portero Corporation, and Nakamura-sensei himself. I stood tall. "I'm here to see Gilman," I announced.

"You're a Portero student," the blond guy said.

"Obviously."

Another silent stare. Was he expecting me to be afraid of him?

"Tristan Shea sent me."

He closed the door, and for a second I thought he was closing it in my face. But he was unhooking the chain, and then he opened it again. "Come in," he said.

I ducked my head in the low doorway and blinked in the darkness. The place smelled strange, like spices and bodies, but in a comfortable way. The room was crowded with furniture and stuff. Every surface was covered in something, and in most cases, about three or four somethings. There were shelves with gadgets, little statues on the floor, and ashtrays full of necklace charms and glass beads. The gaps in the pictures covering the walls were filled with lamp sconces or little bas-relief sculptures of odd creatures with two heads. There was a pile of pillows and blankets in the middle of the room that I finally recognized as a pair of couches. The low table between them held glass bowls, electric candles, and a loaf of bread.

The young man, who I guessed was a year or two ahead of me, led me toward the back of the room. I squinted to see in the shadows. The windows were shuttered closed, and the place was lit by candles and dim lamps. It couldn't have been to save energy credits. Whoever lived here must have liked it that way.

He took me down the hallway to what would have been Tristan's mother's bedroom in his apartment. Here the door was painted red and had a picture of a saint nailed to it, her face upturned in ecstasy in a beam of light. The picture was slightly off-center.

The guy knocked.

"Come in," someone said inside.

This room was just as dim and just as cluttered, but the clutter was different. The walls were lined with shelves holding metal tool boxes and ceramic jars. There was a work table in the middle covered with tools, and a white-haired woman behind it wearing a yellow apron.

But what stopped me in my tracks were the plants. There were *Cycas revoluta* palms in each corner, each well over six feet tall and with a microsporophyll the size of my arm. A *Lobelia erinus*, its flowers a brilliant violet, hung from a suspended basket, the vines drifting down to brush against the tile floor.

An orchid sat in the middle of the workbench, directly on the surface of the table, with no pot or soil. The orchid's roots made a stand for it, their little LEDs glowing in pinpoints like a tiny, upside-down Christmas tree. "Is that a *Cattleya portera*?" I asked.

"*Cattleya gilmani*," the woman said. She claimed the creation for herself, not for Portero. Of course. That's what pirates did.

"It's incredible," I said, still gaping. "They're all incredible." I remembered my manners. "I'm sorry. You're Gilman, right?"

"Glad to see my work appreciated."

"You developed this?" I touched the orchid's petal with a delicate finger. It felt like an angel's cheek. Soft but firm. Perfect texture.

"I did."

"You're not... you don't..." I tried to find words that weren't rude. I couldn't fathom that anyone outside the institute could do work like this. What was she doing here?

"I prefer to keep my own hours," Gilman said. "I get to do my own work, what I like."

"But how can you compete with Portero?" I asked.

"Portero doesn't come this far in," the blond guy said with a sneer.

I still couldn't quite process what I was seeing. Here was a woman making incredible nanobotanics in her spare bedroom. She could be a millionaire with this stuff, live in a house in the outer levels with huge windows and a view of space. But this was kind of a dump. I wondered what was wrong with her.

"Speaking of which, Jeremy, what brings an institute student here?" Gilman asked.

"She knows Tristan," Jeremy said.

I remembered my jar. "I've got some bugs that I don't know how to kill." Checking the seal for the millionth time, I put it on her workbench. "I found them this morning. And I need them gone right away. My jury's today." Three hours left.

"Wouldn't want to fail that," Gilman said. I couldn't tell if she was being sarcastic or not. "Let's have a look." She pulled her goggles on—a very old pair that had silvery tape holding them together in more than one place—and flipped some lenses in front of her eyes. They weren't even digital.

"No tags or chops," I said. "And now they've laid eggs."

Gilman nodded, staring into the jar. "Have you tried crushing one?"

I shook my head. Crushing bugs was something kids did, not a scientific method of troubleshooting.

Gilman moved her orchid to a counter by the wall. "Put one down in one of those dishes there," she said.

I scanned the cluttered table and found a shallow metal pan. I placed it in the middle of the table and plunked a bug into it, careful to seal the jar back up. I would feel terrible if these bugs got onto any of her masterpieces.

Gilman came back with a tiny hammer. "Stand back," she said, and then whacked the bug.

A huge *bang* shook the room. The lab filled with smoke. I fanned the air with my hand to clear it. "What happened?"

"Are you all right?" Jeremy ran over to Gilman, who had staggered back against the wall.

"I'm fine." She pushed him away. Little black plastic bits were stuck in her hair and on her apron. "Your bug's got a self-destruct on it. Whoever made it didn't want anyone poking where they didn't belong."

"But I thought the bug hackers wanted people to know about them. It's pride for them."

"Then this wasn't the hackers, was it?" She went over to the wall that was covered in jars and slid a creaky wooden ladder into place. "Someone made these bugs specifically to destroy plants," she said, as she climbed up it. I watched the ladder sway and hurried over to steady it. "These bugs are made for combat."

"Combat? Against plants?"

She looked down at me. "There's a lot of competition among nanobotanists."

That sounded ridiculous to me, although I was too polite to say that to an old lady. Why would nanobotanists compete? We all worked for the same company. But then I realized that I was standing in the workshop of a nanobotanist who had nothing to do with Portero. Of course, there would be others.

"So they sabotage each other?"

"They try." Gilman had found a metal canister and was scooting it off the shelf. "Catch," she said and let it drop.

I caught it just in time.

"Take it over to the table," she instructed. I cleared a space for it and set it down.

"What is it?" I asked.

"You want those bugs gone, and fast, right?"

"I've got about an hour before I have to shut her down."

"You willing to take a risk or two?" she asked.

"What kind of risk?"

Gilman unscrewed the canister lid. "This stuff will kill most nanoinsects known to man. It dissolves the circuitry into a fine dust."

"But wouldn't that burn the plant, too?"

Gilman shrugged. "That's one of the risks."

"What's the other?"

She scooped some bluish powder out of the canister and into the pan that had recently held my offending bug. She nodded to my jar. I unscrewed the lid and dumped another bug and the remains of my leaf into the powder. The bug hissed and screamed as soon it made contact with the powder. It wiggled around and started jumping around like water in a frying pan. And then, with a *pop*, it whoofed into dust. The eggs were gone, too, but, to my great delight, the leaf was unharmed.

"That's perfect!" I said.

Gilman reached into a drawer for a smaller canister. She dumped three scoops into it, then sealed it. Then she handed it to me. As I reached for it, she pulled it back again.

"There's one more risk," she said. "If Nakamura finds out you've used this, you're done."

"Done?"

"Do you think this is on the approved list?"

I shook my head. "Of course not. I tried everything on the approved list, but nothing worked."

"And so you are expected to accept defeat gracefully," she said.

"But this is a new bug. It hasn't been seen before. Nothing on the approved list can kill it!"

"I agree with you," Gilman said. "But your Nakamura-sensei doesn't approve of people outside his corporation developing new technologies. He won't even acknowledge us. His R&D people will come up with something in time, I'm sure. They probably have something in testing now."

I looked at the metal canister. I'd never broken a rule in my life. "I'll take it."

"Don't tell anyone where you got this," Jeremy said.

"Of course," I said. I held out my hand to Gilman, but she didn't give me the canister.

"It's not a gift," she said.

I blushed. "Oh, yes. Of course." I dug in my pocket and pulled out my money number.

Jeremy laughed. "You're going to use your family's money number to buy illegal bug powder?"

I put the card back in my pocket. "I don't have anything else," I said.

"The bugs," Gilman said. "Leave these, and bring me ten more after the powder works."

I handed her the jar.

"Collect them before you use the powder," Jeremy said. I didn't dignify that with a response.

"Pleasure doing business," Gilman said. "Now you'd better get going."

∞

Solange called during the zipsled ride back to the institute.

"Any luck?"

"Sort of," I said. I wasn't alone in the car. There was a couple in front of me, cuddling, and a guy in a work suit staring out the window. "I've got one more thing to try. I'm heading back to the institute now."

"Tell you what," Solange said. "I'll meet you there."

"No, it's okay," I said. "I know you're busy."

"Never too busy for my little sister," Solange said. "I'll be there in five minutes."

It was considered very bad form to hurry anywhere on the outer levels, and especially within the institute, but I ran at full speed to my tokonoma. When I saw Bebe, I gasped out loud. Her flowers were gone, and a whole section was covered with crawling black bugs. Gathering ten and putting them in a jar wasn't hard. I grabbed a few leaves that were encrusted with eggs, too, just in case.

I dug a shaker out of the cabinet by my workbench and was about to start filling it with Gilman's powder when Solange showed up. She'd been running, too, judging by her flushed face.

"Wait!" She grabbed my wrist. "Don't do anything stupid."

"They will be here in twenty minutes," I said. "This will kill the bugs. I tested it."

"You don't need to," she said, panting. "They're my bugs. Here." Solange pulled out her handheld and typed something. The bugs and eggs, even the ones in my jar, all fell down dead.

I blinked at her. "What... Why did you—"

"No time. You have to fix Bebe."

She was right. I dove for the root pod, sweeping away the bugs piled on top of it. "Can you do something about these damned things?"

"Sure," Solange said, and started scooping up the dead bugs with her hands.

"There's a dustpan in the cabinet." I opened the panel door and plugged in my handheld. I set the sequences running to generate more leaves, change her color back to what it had been this morning, and restore her flowers.

Solange dumped the first panful of bugs into the bin. I kept my eyes focused on the oxygen levels. They were way down at four hundred.

"Add more leaves," Solange said. "I'll pay for the energy credits."

"Damned right you will," I said, and thickened the foliage on Bebe's vines. Within ten minutes, the flowers were blooming and the new leaves were starting to unfold. I joined Solange in bug-cleanup duty, but I stopped every few seconds to check the oxygen monitor.

At 3:54 Bebe's oxygen was at 468. Nakamura-sensei was never late. Solange dumped the last of the bugs and wiped her hands. "I'll go out and meet them," she said.

She ran out and I watched the monitors. 482. Almost there.

I noticed my specimen jar and Gilman's powder were still on my workbench. I jumped up and stashed them in the cabinet, my heart pounding. That would have been bad.

The monitor said 493 when Nakamura-sensei came in, followed by Yamada-sensei. Both were wearing their green Portero Nanobotanical Institute blazers. The third jury member was Mrs. Caitlin Portero-Ross, the granddaughter of Portero's CEO, wearing an actual synthfur stole that probably cost more than a year's tuition at the institute.

Solange stood behind them, looking serene and professional. You'd never know that five minutes earlier she'd been on her knees, sweeping up dead bugs.

I gave the formal student bow, going down to the furthest level so I was nearly bent double, and held it for a three count before coming up. Nakamura-sensei nodded his head.

Yamada-sensei did the talking, of course. "This is Britta Hammar, sensei," she said, and I bowed again, though not as deeply. "She has made a *Campsis radicans porteris*. She is an excellent student."

Again, Nakamura-sensei nodded, and the three judges stepped onto the mulch to inspect Bebe. I unplugged my control panel and closed the door carefully, then stepped back and let them work.

I glanced down at the last oxygen reading: 504.

Bebe wasn't perfect. I didn't have time to trim back some foliage near the root pod, and I saw that they noticed that. That rankled. She'd been perfect this morning.

I looked over at Solange, then at the faulty leaves. She gave me an apologetic look. I pressed my lips together, all *we need to talk, young lady*, and turned my attention back to the jury.

They were inspecting every leaf. Nakamura-sensei had a tiny eyepiece that he held up to look at the junctures. Then he said something to Yamada-sensei in Japanese. She turned to me and said, "Stepstool." He wanted to see the highest branches, but they were seven feet up.

The stepstool was inside the cabinet where the powder was. I opened the door as little as I could and tried to maneuver the little metal stool around the jar without anyone seeing. I figured they were still looking at Bebe, but maybe they were looking at me, wondering what was taking so long.

I pulled the stool out, and nearly made it. But the little leg caught the jar. Of course it did. And of course the powder went spilling all over the floor, hissing as it made contact with the scraps of mulch and bits of bug that were on the floor.

At first, I couldn't move. I stood, the stepstool in my hand, staring at the fan of blue powder on my floor. When I finally did look up, the first person I saw was Nakamura-sensei.

"I had bugs, sensei," I said. "I couldn't kill them."

He reached into his shirt pocket and took out an index card. He bent down, scooped up some of the blue powder, and sniffed it. Then he dropped the whole thing on the floor, wiped his hands, and walked out of the tokonoma. Mrs. Portero-Ross gave me a disapproving look, then followed him.

Yamada-sensei paused.

"I'm sorry, sensei." I felt my throat tighten again. I looked at my sister. "Solange, tell her."

But Solange seemed to have forgotten how to speak. Yamada-sensei shook her head and hurried to keep up with Nakamura-sensei.

So that was it. I had failed.

Solange ran over, hopping over the powder, and hugged me. "I'm so sorry, Britta." We weren't really a hugging family, so the hug was stiff and awkward. She let go. "Tell you what. I'll make some calls and I'll bet we can get you an internship instead of retaking this class, so you don't have to do the same course over again. And if you write a letter to Nakamura-sensei, you can push this onto Tristan, say he was the one who gave you the powder. By the end of your internship, you'll be back in full graces."

"Why didn't you say anything?"

"I know this seems like a setback now, but really, this is the best time for it. People understand when you make a mistake this early in your career. You can come back from it. It's almost better that you do."

It sounded like she was giving a speech, like she'd practiced this. After all the stress of the day, now that it was over, my anger was cold and hard. "What's going on, Solange?"

"We'll fix this, Sis. We will." We were standing in the corner, on a small triangle of floor between the wall, my workbench, and the spray of powder.

I shook my head. "No. You need to tell me why the hell you put bugs on my plant. Today of all days."

Solange took a step back and hit my workbench. She looked down at it, and when she looked up, she had tears in her eyes. "They were supposed to be indestructible," she said. "That was our spec. A bug that couldn't be destroyed, except by us. But we could only test with the approved materials, and I knew that there was stuff out there that we didn't have." She pointed to the powder. "Does this stuff work?"

"Dissolves the circuitry."

"See?" Solange hopped back over the powder. "We would never have known that. And then we're putting out a product that isn't top quality. I keep arguing that we need to be open to these inner level people, know what they're doing, but I can't get anyone to listen. 'It's not proper,' they keep telling me. Well, we can be competitive, or we can be proper, you know?" She looked to me for confirmation, but I didn't give it.

"So you sabotaged my graduation project."

"I didn't—"

"You ruined my career for your project."

"One," she said, "it's not ruined, I told you that. And two, I've got a little more at stake than you have. I've got a husband and a daughter. Do you know they expect me to quit my job now that I have Thea? Throw everything away? They think I can't handle it."

"I'm sure you can," I said.

"Thank you," she said, like finally someone believed her.

My eye itched. I couldn't scratch it; my hands were covered with this crazy powder, so I had to go wash my hands. And that thought brought me out of the moment, out of my argument with Solange, and into the bigger reality. I realized that I had a choice to make, right now.

I opened the cabinet door and took out a spade and a hatchet.

"What are you doing?" Solange asked. I walked over to Bebe. Beautiful Bebe, who had been my companion for the last six months. Now that I thought about it, I'd chosen her over Tristan. And all to follow in my sister's footsteps.

First things first, though. I put down the spade and the hatchet and crouched over the imperfect foliage near the base. I pulled down my goggles, took my clippers, and carefully disconnected the offending branches. I stood back and inspected my work.

There. Now she was perfect.

I opened the root pod door and shut Bebe down. When the white LEDs in her roots blinked off, I picked the hatchet up and hacked all the branches off the pod. Some fell to the ground, others still hung on the wall of the tokonoma.

"Britta, stop!"

I ignored her. If I turned to her now, I'd lose my courage.

I picked up the spade and dug out Bebe's root pod. It was about the size of a melon. I lifted it out of the mulch, disconnected the power, and stood up.

"What are you doing?" Solange was crying now.

"Graduating," I said. Shifting the root pod to my hip, I pulled two of Bebe's flowers off the wall. I tucked one behind my ear and gave the other to Solange.

She took it, shaking her head in confusion.

With my free hand, I picked up the specimen jar with the dead bugs I'd collected. I still owed Gilman.

"See you later, Sis," I said. It turned out her footsteps didn't lead anywhere I wanted to go. I was going to have to make my own.

∞

It took a few years to get established, but I didn't starve, thanks to my sister, who felt guilty enough to give me the money and energy credits I needed to live on. I didn't need all that much in the inner levels.

Last year I made enough to afford a larger apartment a few levels further out, but I like where I am. I'm on the top floor, where the gravity is a wee bit lower, although that might be my imagination. Every morning, I open my window and look outside at my street. The trees are now the perfect shade of green. Red and yellow rose bushes bloom in front of each porch. And when I look down, I can touch the leaves of Bebe, my *Campsis radicans hammaris*, covering the entire front surface of the building.

About the Author
Mary Mascari

Mary first fell in love with science fiction when Luke turned on his lightsaber.

After getting a highly impractical degree in Performance Studies from Northwestern University, Mary has held a variety of careers ranging from programmer to clown. Now she's pursuing her MFA at Seton Hill University in Writing Popular Fiction.

She and her husband are raising their two boys to be geeks, and proudly display their life-size replica of Han Solo in Carbonite in their family room. You can find her on Twitter as @geekymary.

Something to Watch Over Us
by Mike Morgan

Tallulah had plans for after work. It was Friday and she was looking forward to handing over control of the farmscraper to the night shift and then heading straight to the skewered-chicken joint below the Fujinomiya department store. So she wasn't at all pleased when Nobuhiko turned up fifteen minutes late.

"You know your dormitory capsule can wake you up on time if you ask it to?" she said huffily, logging out of the virtual data port on the monitoring deck and shrugging on a thin jacket.

Nobuhiko looked sideways at her as he logged on under his own name, the system flickering strangely as it verified his identity. He apologized reflexively for his tardiness and then added with an edge to his voice, "The nurse said I had to climb the stairs to get some exercise." He was out of breath, so he probably wasn't lying.

"Oh," replied Tallulah, feeling guilty for chewing him out. They were on the tenth floor of the farmscraper, below the meat tanks but looking out at the tops of the vertically hanging racks of vegetables and grains basking in the glow of hundreds of UV lamps. It was quite the hike on foot. No wonder he was running late. "Well, I'm sure it's for the best. See you tomorrow!"

The building's sensors tracked her movements every step of the way out of the tower.

Tallulah loved living in Shibuya. She loved the crazy-tall towers of ceramic and glass, she loved the sidewalks packed with throngs of people, and she loved the blazing light displays coming from the sides of every company-owned building. But most of all, she loved the cramped, atmospheric restaurants and bars slotted into the first floors of many of the skyscrapers and the easily accessible warren-like underground tunnel system that was likewise packed with fascinating places to eat and drink.

The farmscraper was squeezed vertically into a tiny lot between an office tower and a residential dormitory for a rival corporation, about three minutes on foot from the entrance to the subway station and only six minutes from her intended rendezvous with grilled chicken cartilage on sticks. Tallulah quickly found a staircase leading down to the top level of the climate-controlled underground city. After running the usual gamut of personalized holo-commercials that leaped out of every advertising-enabled projector in her path, she arrived at Yakitori-no-Takamagahara: literally the High Plain of Heaven for Grilled Chicken. She settled into one of the restaurant's tiny booths to wait for her friends.

To her vague annoyance, the automated greeter by the door screamed out its traditional greeting of "Irrashaimase!" Coming from a human, the shrill cry was just about bearable, but coming from a robot—well, being welcomed by a machine still seemed slightly odd to her despite living in Japan for eighteen years.

She ordered a beer and was just lifting it carefully out of the dumb waiter set into the wall of her booth when the first of her friends arrived. It was Darren, the lanky architect. Like Tallulah, he was also half-Japanese, half-foreigner.

In the mostly homogenous population of Japan, a person of mixed ancestry stuck out like a sore thumb and in most walks of life was categorized with the unflattering label of harufu. The term was the closest the Japanese language could get to the English word "half" and was now, unfortunately, embedded in everyday culture. Tallulah hated the label; no matter how common it was, it made her think of "half-breed" and of how she'd never be completely accepted.

Tallulah waved to attract Darren's attention and he grinned, immediately striding over to join her. "Get me one in, too!" he said, his voice so much louder than anyone else's.

They were speaking in Japanese, of course, because it was endlessly fun to subvert the expectations of the people seated in the booths around them and, well, after all this time, they found talking in the local language just as natural as talking in English.

Darren liked to pepper his speech with obscure and outmoded phrases just to get a reaction out of eavesdroppers. This evening, he seemed to be favoring slang and catchphrases from a short-lived NHK sci-fi show canceled way back in the 2040s; he probably figured hardly anyone would stand a chance of understanding references from a series that bit the dust nearly a quarter of a century ago. And when someone sitting nearby was foolish enough to ask whether he was loudly talking about some American thing, as they would surely do, he'd take enormous pleasure in explaining that the quotes were from a show that was a treasured part of Japanese history. He could be a dick sometimes.

Darren was always trying to provoke people. Tallulah was the opposite; she just wanted to blend into the background. But there wasn't much chance of that when she was six inches taller than the average Japanese male, had red hair and green eyes, and was possessed of a name blessed with two sounds that didn't even exist in the Japanese language. Her Japanese mother still struggled to say it right, most often resorting to calling her "Ta-chan." It hardly needed to be said that the name had been her father's idea.

To kill time while they were waiting for Charlie, Nobuko, and Rie to turn up, Tallulah and Darren cast their eyes over the holographic menu. Looking at the eye-watering prices, Tallulah was fairly certain the meat served at this establishment had never been near the mass-production lines of a farmscraper. There were still plenty of specialty farms out in the countryside that raised actual animals.

"Got a boyfriend yet?" asked Darren, his cheeky grin visible over the floating, semitransparent menu. He knew full well that Tallulah had recently turned thirty, was still single, and was currently being pestered an average of three times a day by her mom over this deplorable state of affairs.

Tallulah glared at him and sucked at the huge layer of froth on her beer. She didn't have to answer.

∞

Given the amount of pale yellow beer she'd knocked back at the restaurant, Tallulah was thankful Saturday was her day off. She awoke by seven o'clock, groggy and slightly queasy, still trying to recall the journey back to her single-sex dormitory block. The ride on the Ginza line was nothing more than a blur to her now. She must have located and climbed into her sleeping capsule on autopilot because she couldn't remember a damned thing after getting off the train.

She lifted the cotton sheet and checked to see if she'd even gotten undressed. Nope, she was still in her work clothes and had, somehow, managed to get yakitori-sauce stains on her pants leg.

Tallulah was about to drift off back to sleep when the buzzer sounded, reminding her that there were only thirty minutes left before her allotted time in the capsule expired. She needed to get out or stump up another nightly fee. Feeling a headache starting to stab at the backs of her eyeballs, Tallulah threw back the sheet.

"Armstrong-san," announced her personal nurse program, "please be aware you must walk for at least thirty minutes this morning to meet your required exercise goal. Thank you for participating in your personal health plan."

The melodious voice was wafting from one of the many processors in her jacket; the jacket itself was carelessly stuffed into an overhead storage bin since Tallulah had conspicuously failed to hang it up last night. "Thirty minutes?" she said. "That can't be right. I signed up for the lowest health goals possible."

"You failed to exercise yesterday evening," the ever-vigilant software reminded her.

"I was busy," she mumbled.

"And the evening before," continued the software nurse that had been oh-so-considerately supplied by her employer.

She rolled over, squashed her face down into the spongy mattress, and held the pillow down over her ears. "I should get rid of you," she said.

"Please be aware that resigning from your personal health plan results in an automatic increase of sixty percent to your monthly insurance premium."

With bitter resignation, she shouted, "Fine! You win! I'm getting up and I'm going for a walk!" The second the words exploded from her mouth, Tallulah felt ridiculous; it didn't help to shout at software. Fortunately, the capsule was sound-proofed so there were no witnesses to her outburst.

"Minimum duration is thirty minutes," the nurse stated helpfully.

∞

It was a completely typical August morning, thought Tallulah, which meant that the sun was beating down mercilessly, the temperature was thirty-five degrees Celsius, and the humidity was eighty-five percent. The concrete was so hot, she could feel the warmth radiating through the soles of her shoes. Barely five minutes out of her dormitory and a patch of perspiration was already spreading out from the small of her back.

In a spirit of dumb optimism, she'd set the cooling controls on her four-seasons jacket to maximum, but it seemed the Peltier plates sewn into the lining were overmatched by Mother Nature. She was not surprised; the jacket had been suspiciously cheap when she'd picked it up in the marketplace.

On the plus side, her pants were reacting nicely to the fierce sunlight, the enzymes sealed into the material busily eating away the sauce stains. The brown marks were already fading from view and should be gone in another twenty minutes. Once she got back indoors, her clothes would have a fighting chance of being similarly efficient with sorting out the sweat stains.

She felt faintly stupid wearing work clothes on her day off, but she didn't want to leave the dirt unexposed to sunlight for too long. The marks might not come out properly. *Besides, no one will know I'm not heading to work. Who could possibly suspect that I'm actually wandering aimlessly through the streets of Shibuya ward and the adjoining sections of Tokyo until a disembodied voice says it's okay for me to resume my life?* Morosely, she expected the answer would turn out to be everyone who saw her.

Tallulah sighed and decided to have an actual plan in mind for the walk. She could make her way over to Harajuku and then maybe take a quick look at the Meiji Shinto shrine. There was a nice garden there and there were some good shops in Harajuku. The deciding factor was that Harajuku also possessed a Yamanote Line station where she could hop on her train, the first of three she needed to get to her parents' home. Yes, she'd head in the general direction of Harajuku. Tallulah altered her path accordingly through the carefully thronging crowd.

Yet another passing pedestrian complimented her in breathless tones on her fire-truck-red hair and Tallulah nodded politely in acknowledgement, again. These days, the compliments were just so much background noise, much like the persistent cries of "Takai!" from strangers upon seeing her height and the ceaseless praise for her language skills. She received the latter even from people who'd known her since she was a junior high school student and knew she'd lived in Japan for more than half her life.

Her shoulder bag was heavier than usual, and the heft of it irritated

Tallulah in the remorseless heat of the day. Although she'd stashed her spare work clothes and a few other things in a prepaid locker at the dorm block, she was still carrying a couple of heavy items.

She was taking the bullet train back to her parents' farmhouse after finishing her obligatory exercise and didn't want to have to return to the dorm block to pick up anything she'd need for the trip. That meant she was stuck with carrying those items now. She needed a reader to while away the twenty-one minutes—never a minute more and never a minute less—of seated luxury on the mag-lev bullet from Tokyo Station to Mishima Station. The cans were gifts purchased at a specialty store for her father: imported foods from his native Canada that he couldn't get in Kannami Town.

The bullet train was likely to be the only bearable segment of her journey. She also had connecting trains at either end. The leg from Harajuku to Tokyo before she even got on the bullet was going to be the worst; it was always standing room only. Compared to the claustrophobic nightmare of that transit, the final leg from Mishima to Kannami was going to be less cramped, but the branch line train was as slow as pouring treacle.

At least she didn't need to bring clothes or toiletries. There were plenty of both waiting for her in her *weekend* room in the old house surrounded by watermelon and kabocha pumpkin patches. Hopefully, a good night's sleep was also waiting for her.

Her thoughts were interrupted by a man apologizing. Her head whipped round in the direction of the sound and her heart skipped a beat, but he was only saying sorry as a way of getting her attention. "Sumimasen," he repeated, before adding, "You look like you know where you're going. I need to find the Clarkson-Yamamoto building, but I'm not from around here. Could you help me?"

She halted awkwardly and nodded. "Sure," she replied in a form of

Japanese as casual as the one he'd used. "I work there, actually."

He glanced at her chest, immediately making her think he was a perv. Sheepishly, Tallulah realized he was looking at the security badge incorporated into her tunic; it was partially visible under the open, flapping jacket. Due to the difference in their heights, he was looking up slightly.

"Ah, so I see. I didn't realize you were one of my new colleagues," he said, slightly flustered.

The man was about her age, she guessed, and was clean shaven with recently trimmed hair. He was slight of frame like so many Japanese men and seemed ill at ease in his tieless, high-collared business suit. Tallulah inwardly filed him away as harmless and possibly quite dull.

Like most people who had to spend more than a few minutes outside a day, he had white streaks of sun block on his face and hands. Underneath the smears on his forehead, cheekbones, nose, and upper chin, she could see sunburned skin. Perhaps it was appropriate for him to have a farmer's tan. He did work for an agricultural conglomerate, after all.

She gestured lazily at his jacket. "No badge for you. You visiting?"

He tore his gaze away from her eye-level chest and craned his head up to look at her properly. "Don't have one yet. First day at this location. They transferred me in to take a look at a computer glitch."

"Oh?" she said, a little sharply.

The man shook his head. "Nothing serious. No need to worry." He smiled at her and proffered a hand. "I'm Inoue Kenichi, by the way."

She accepted the offer of the outstretched hand, but then made a point of bowing. Inwardly, she screamed. *I get that you're trying to be nice because I look like a foreigner, but we're in Japan and I'm not a tourist!* Out loud, she settled for simply giving her name, "Tallulah Armstrong." Belatedly, she realized she'd forgotten to reverse her name order. In an attempt to salvage her Japanese credentials, she added the compulsory, "Yoroshiku onegai-itashimasu."

He nodded at the polite form of the greeting and responded with a much plainer, "Yoroshiku." Inoue seemed the sort of guy who'd grunt or say "Oss" instead of going to the trouble of articulating a complete "Hai." She kind of liked that.

Tallulah checked the time and figured out how long she had before she'd have to catch her connecting train to the bullet train hub. It looked like she had enough wiggle room. "Hey, I can take you to the farmscraper if you'd like."

He accepted, surprised, and she indicated he should follow. As they walked, she said, "Not many people would ask a girl looking like me for directions."

Inoue looked genuinely astonished. "Why, are redheads notorious for being navigationally deficient?"

She felt a grin spreading all over her face and was sorry to have to say good-bye to him once they'd reached the foyer of the farming tower. But he worked down in the sublevels in IT and she worked way up in crop monitoring, so there wasn't much chance of them meeting again. She bowed in farewell and hurried off to Harajuku. After her unexpected detour, she'd skip the visit to the shrine but the boutiques were a whole different story.

At least the extra half mile she'd walked back to the farmscraper was helping to keep the nurse happy.

∞

The journey back to the inaka—the countryside—was as tedious as she'd expected, but the experience was made infinitely more pleasurable by the sight of her smiling father waiting at Kannami train station to pick her up.

One benefit of wearing smart clothes was that wearers could be tracked and monitored by a variety of software packages. Her father subscribed to one of these apps and was notified with a loud, customized chime whenever she disembarked from a bullet train at Mishima. The software then followed up this advance warning with an estimated arrival time at the local station, giving him ample opportunity to hire a door-to-door rental vehicle and drop by the small unmanned station. Tallulah was more than capable of hiring a rental for the short journey to the family home herself, but her papa liked to do it. It made him feel fatherly.

Besides, sharing a couple of minutes of secluded peace inside the quietly humming self-guided car gave them a valuable chance to catch up and share important strategic information before Tallulah had to face her mother.

"She's going to ask about boyfriends," he said.

"In other news, the Heisei era called and said it wants its attitudes back," retorted Tallulah, rolling her eyes. Her papa laughed like a grizzly being tickled.

Once his composure had returned, he said, apropos of nothing, "We have some news about your bedroom. You know how you only ever use it to sleep over one night a week?"

"Er, yeah," answered Tallulah slowly, getting the impression she wasn't going to like where this conversation was going.

"Well, your mother thought that wasn't a very efficient arrangement. And we've always wanted a traditional themed room with sliding doors, tatami reed mats, wall scrolls. The whole nine yards…"

"Are you trying to tell me I don't have a room anymore?"

His lined face creased into a concerned frown. "No, no, no, don't be silly, no, not at all. Well, yes. But you'll always have a place to sleep. It's just that you'll be using a folding futon from now on. All your stuff is still there, too. We boxed your things up and stored them in the wall cabinets, out of sight. You don't mind, do you? Your mother wants to use the room during the week to have friends round and drink tea, and she wanted the decor to look right." He avoided her gaze by turning to examine the journey data on the dashboard display.

"Don't worry, Papa. I understand." Tallulah ran her tongue over the back of her teeth thoughtfully. Her mother was starting to drop some big hints for sure. *Since you don't have a room here anymore, why don't you find a home of your own? Then you can add a man to it and maybe some kids…* Subtle, it wasn't.

She reached in her shoulder bag. "I have swag from the Canadian section of our favorite Tokyo specialty store." She tossed the cans at him, pleased by his delighted expression.

"Buttercup, you do spoil me!"

All too soon, the car ride was over and the doors were lifting open. Her mother was kneeling by the low garden wall at the front of the house, wearing a broad hat against the sun and methodically clipping the overhanging edge of the grass. "O-kā-san, tadaima!" called Tallulah dutifully as she swung her long legs out of the vehicle.

Her mother twisted her head to regard her daughter. "O-kaeri nasai," she replied levelly, completing the ritual exchange. She continued in Japanese, "Ta-chan, do you have a boyfriend yet?"

Behind her, the car quietly drove away by itself, heading for the next customer.

∞

Tallulah slung her jacket over a chair in the kitchen while her mother prepared the ice-cold zaru-soba noodles for dinner. She could tell already it was going to be a long evening, but her mother probably felt the same way.

Sure enough, every conversational gambit was unsubtly steered round until it was facing in the direction marked boyfriend.

Was Tallulah going to any good festivals soon? Because festivals were great places to meet new people, like eligible bachelors.

Was Tallulah going to all of her work events? Because she could meet a nice salaryman at one of them.

Would Tallulah consider hunching over a bit, so she didn't look so tall? Men could be put off by tall women.

Had she thought about trying to make her feet look smaller?

Oh, and best of all, there was a charity run going through their street tomorrow morning. Would she help with passing out the cups of water to the runners? There was plenty of time before Tallulah would have to catch her return train to the city. She would volunteer to help, right? And maybe smile at the more handsome runners?

After several hours of this, Tallulah could feel her blood pressure rising. Her papa had wisely chosen to go hide in the front garden. He was hanging out some daikon radishes on the fence so the long white vegetables would dry out and be good for pickling. Before she could go and join him, a solicitous voice chirped up from her jacket.

"Elevated heart rate detected. Please consider employing one of the recommended stress relief methods. Take a deep breath. Drink some tea."

Her mother was so nonplussed, she stopped nagging. "What's that?" she asked, trying to locate the source of the voice.

"It's my stupid electronic nurse. Work says I have to have one."

"Participation in the personal health plan is voluntary," said the software, the mellifluous voice carrying from the jacket's speakers. "Alternatively, consider masturbating. Masturbation is a well-documented means of lowering stress."

Her mother's jaw dropped. Eventually, she found her voice, observing drily, "Medicine has certainly changed since my day." She picked up a cup and added primly, "Daughter, I can offer you jasmine tea."

"Kā-san, please believe me, it's never said anything like that before…" Tallulah could feel her cheeks flushing as red as her hair.

"Drink the tea, Ta-chan," said her mother. "I'm trying to ignore the implication that talking to my daughter causes her to be unwell."

∞

Lying on a futon in the very tastefully redecorated tatami room that night, Tallulah couldn't decide whether the cicadas or the frogs were louder.

As she drifted off to sleep, the raucous noises of the semirural wildlife echoing in her thoughts, Tallulah recalled Inoue's words: "They transferred me in to take a look at a computer glitch. Nothing serious. No need to worry."

But that couldn't be right. If the problem was serious enough to transfer in an employee from another branch, she thought, it couldn't be an entirely trivial matter.

∞

Inoue was one of the runners.

Tallulah had been standing on the concrete steps at the front of her parents' house handing out little paper cups of water to passing runners for forty-five minutes before seeing him. Inoue was in no danger of winning the race.

The charity run's course took it down the narrow side street in front of the house before looping back out to the main road, just so it could bypass a busy intersection. Since the street lacked sidewalks, the runners were passing directly by the thin strip of front garden and the half-dried daikons. Tallulah didn't even need to step out into the street to hand out the drinks; the runners were easily within arm's reach.

She had been looking at a runner in a furry animal costume, wondering how hot the guy inside it must be, when she'd spotted Inoue.

He was half jogging, half walking down the street, looking like he'd drop at any second. At the rate he was going, it'd take him another minute or two to reach her. She waved to get his attention.

He started comically when he saw her. Clearly, their meeting was just as much a surprise to him as it was to her.

When he finally pulled level with her, he gasped, "What are you doing here?"

"I live here," she said. "Well, at least some of the time. What are *you* doing here?"

He bent double, his hands flattened against his thighs, struggling to get his breath back. "Trying to commit suicide by the slowest and most painful means possible, it seems."

Tallulah suppressed a giggle. "I think you're doing great. Hey, don't tell me you live in Kannami?"

He shook his head. "No, I live over in Izu-kōgen."

She nodded; the town wasn't far away. "So here you are, spending your one day off this week doing something worthwhile."

Inoue straightened up and relieved her of a full paper cup. "I was hoodwinked into this by the e-nurse. Apparently, I am not exercising enough."

While he was draining the cup dry, Tallulah mulled that over. "You mean, the nurse suggested you sign up for this specific run?"

He nodded, unconcerned. "It's programmed to make useful suggestions. And raising money for tsunami relief is good motivation. I might even get halfway round the course."

Tallulah snorted. "It's certainly a more useful suggestion than the one I got yesterday."

"Oh, what did it say you should do?"

Blinking rapidly, she changed the subject. "If these coincidences keep happening, I guess I'll see you again soon."

He nodded and hesitated before replying, "Actually, our meeting the first time was a bit more unlikely than you'd expect. When I got to my new office, my boss told me I wasn't the programmer he'd asked for. Somehow, between him sending the personnel request and it arriving at my old farmscraper, the name had gotten changed. All very strange. But, as it turns out, I'm just as qualified as the guy he'd wanted originally, so he went with me instead rather than cause any more inconvenience."

"So, you'll still be at the Shibuya tower next week?" She felt her pulse jump.

He made that grunting sound that passed for "Yes" and said, "Seems like it. You'll have to show me the sights."

She agreed, hoping she wasn't sounding too eager, as he handed back the empty cup, and then he was shambling off in his tired, blistered gait.

Her mother materialized at her elbow, looking insufferably pleased. "Who was the nice man, Ta-chan? Is he rich?"

"Just a work colleague, Kā-san."

"He looked handsome."

"Did he? I didn't notice." She tried to ignore her mother's satisfied smirk.

∞

It was Tuesday night and they were sitting in a Shibuya restaurant specializing in takoyaki. The tiny balls of octopus chunks in batter were sizzling in the takoyaki press built into the tabletop, and mid-century Japanese pop was wailing from the restaurant's music system. Tallulah felt relaxed; this was nice.

"Thanks for showing me the area," said Inoue, peering at the press uncertainly. He didn't give the appearance of a man familiar with making his own octopus balls.

"Thanks for asking me to be your guide. You know, according to my mother, you have everything I need—a pulse, a job, and you're willing to talk to me. My mother's high standards are a constant source of inspiration, as you can imagine."

He checked to see if she was joking and seemed relieved to find she was.

A flatbed truck slowly rolled past the restaurant's window, the loudspeakers fixed to its cab blaring out a martial anthem. A large, constantly shifting sign was mounted on the bed of the truck; it was advocating military aggression against one of the independent Chinese splinter states.

They watched the truck crawl past in silence. After it had disappeared from view, Tallulah said, "My papa remembers when there was a self-defense force here, not a regular military."

Inoue grunted, returning his attention to the tabletop press. "How can you tell when these are done?"

"It'll beep at us. Do you think there will be a war?"

"Yes," he said sadly. "But not today. Today we eat crispy balls of octopus tentacle."

She smiled at him. "On the good news front, octopuses love the warming sea temperature so, you know, we'll never run out of takoyaki."

He didn't react to her gentle humor so she asked, "Is everything alright, Inoue-san?"

Inoue shook his head. "The glitch runs deeper than I thought at first. I'm not sure it can be fixed without scrapping the entire software architecture and starting over. Even attempting to uninstall the root program will require the complete shutdown of the main server for several hours."

Tallulah scratched the prominent slope of her nose. "How bad is the glitch? Could you leave the program the way it is and just live with its quirks?"

He pulled a face. "It's difficult to explain. Let's not talk shop tonight. I'm sorry for bringing it up." A mischievous glint came into his eye. "So, just how terrible is your mother?"

∞

Nobuhiko was not only on time for the shift handover on

Wednesday, he was in surprisingly high spirits too. He was ecstatic about finding a baseball card.

More animated than she'd ever seen him, Nobu happily recounted how he'd stumbled across the final card in the turn-of-the-century set he'd been building for more than nine years. "It was the nurse!" he said, beaming from ear to ear.

It turned out that the e-nurse had been pestering him to take a long run, even going so far as to provide a suggested route with the requisite distance and number of uphill sections. "And the course went right by this little trading card shop I'd never heard of before. So, naturally, I had to go in, and there it was, the last card I needed! And it was such a bargain!"

Tallulah managed to extricate herself from his enthusiastic narration of the day's events after several minutes, glad to be heading out for a quick bite to eat and then an early night in her rented sleeping capsule.

On her way out of the building, she couldn't help but hear other unusually happy employees having similarly intense conversations. For this day, at least, joy was a plague, and everyone was infected.

∞

It was Rie's fault. Rie liked karaoke and Tallulah lacked willpower, so the early night didn't stand a chance.

By the time Inoue found her, Tallulah was drunk enough to be singing jazz ballads, very badly. He gently persuaded her to sit down at a table with him.

Rie was far from pleased at losing her singing partner but carried on gamely in Tallulah's absence. Her off-key voice was a constant, discordant presence as they spoke.

"Ask me how I knew where to find you," he said, looking weary to the bone.

"You used an app that tracks my smart jacket?" guessed Tallulah.

"That would only work if I was on your list of people approved to know where you are. Which I'm not, by the way."

Taking the hint, she quietly told her jacket to add Inoue to the safe list. Then she tried again. "You phoned a friend of mine and got the name of the bar from her?"

"Hardly. I don't know who your friends are."

"I give in. How did you know where to find me?"

He ran a hand through his mop of black hair. "I asked the e-nurse what recreational activity would be best for my health right now, and it suggested singing karaoke. Then it sent me a map to this bar."

Tallulah tried to digest that nugget of information. "Well, I guess singing is pretty relaxing, so… No, I don't see how that works."

Inoue let out a long sigh and muttered something about zettabytes of data under his breath. "Have you noticed anything odd happening lately?"

She thought about Nobu's trading card. "People are happier than normal?" she asked.

He nodded. "Exactly. That's it, exactly."

Tallulah held up her hand. "Hang on, back up a bit. Are you suggesting that the nurse wanted you to meet up with me tonight?"

"Yes, I am."

She raised both eyebrows. "The nurse is a matchmaker?" She thought a bit and added, "And you knew it was, so you used it to find me deliberately?"

"Yes, to both parts."

"Oh." A question occurred to her. "Why did you *want* to find me?"

He leaned across the table and kissed her.

It took her a couple of seconds to decide whether this was a good thing. Once her brain had caught up with events, she reached out and grabbed his collar to hold him in place.

They agreed that some fresh air would help clear her head, and

ducking outside would have the added benefit of putting them beyond
the reach of Rie's idiosyncratic approach to singing.

"So the nurse was the software with the glitch?" inquired Tallulah.

"It goes deeper than that," said Inoue. "The e-nurse is actually an
application that's part of the general operating system at Clarkson-
Yamamoto. It's hard to tell where the nurse ends and the other programs
start. They all share the same capacity to learn, to adapt, to predict…"

"Predict? The computer can guess what we're going to do before
we even do it?"

Inoue stared at her. "That's exactly what it can do. It knows a lot
about human behavior. It knows a lot, specifically, about your behavior."

Tallulah felt unsteady on her feet. Somehow, Inoue knew to put
his arm around her waist.

"Think back to the day we first met," he continued. "But don't blame
me for any of this, I only just did a deep data dive and uncovered this in
the log. On that day, I was taking an entirely predictable path from the
subway exit to the farmscraper. You were told to take a thirty-minute
walk on a Saturday. The nurse knows that when you're forced to exercise
on a Saturday, you generally walk toward the stores in Harajuku. It didn't
take much to engineer a situation where our paths crossed."

She still felt like she was missing something. "It wanted us to
meet? But why?"

"Because it did a personality analysis on both of us and decided
we were compatible."

"No, wait, just because it made our paths cross, there was no guarantee that we'd interact. The chances of you talking to me were—"

"Fairly high given you're exactly my type," he said. "And I'm known
to be impulsive."

Tallulah laughed. "Oh my God, it *is* a matchmaker."

"Oh, it's that and much more. It's a career coach too. It was the cause of the change to the transfer request that got me moved over to the Shibuya branch."

She felt the need to sit on the curb and rest her chin on her knees. Inoue sat next to her without comment.

"Why is it doing any of this?" she asked. "Why is it trying to hook us up? Why is it trying to help Nobuhiko complete his collection of baseball cards?"

Inoue laughed uproariously. It was shockingly unlike him, but Tallulah decided she liked it. He answered breathlessly, "My superiors told the computer that happy workers are productive workers, so it should try to make us happy as well as healthy." He ran a hand through his hair again. "The whole point of the nurse program is that it takes data from multiple sources to devise creative solutions to very human problems."

He put his arm around her. "So that's what it did. It had to suck in rather more data than was originally planned and it had to tie up far more resources than was anticipated, but it certainly found a way. Actually, it was the e-nurse swallowing up more and more processing and memory resources that caused the very glitch in overall system performance I was told to figure out."

"What are you going to do? The software's clearly exceeding its intended limits…"

Inoue licked his lips. "Ah, well. That's where you come in, Tallulah," he said, pronouncing her name absolutely correctly. "I wasn't sure what to do. So I thought, Tallulah's got a sensible approach to life, I'll ask her."

"I'm no software expert," she said, "and I'm quite drunk. My advice may, just possibly, not be reliable." Tallulah realized she was squinting at Inoue like a pirate.

He chuckled. "I trust a drunken Tallulah more than my sober boss. Listen, it's a computer that wants us to be happy and, so far, it's doing a better job of achieving that goal than we've ever managed by ourselves."

"Sounds to me like you want to leave the e-nurse alone and let it do its thing."

Inoue rubbed his eyes. "I could. It might be months before another employee figures out what's going on. And the program could do a lot of good in that time."

Tallulah made her decision. "Pretend you haven't found the cause of the glitch," she said.

Inoue agreed to do as she asked, at least for a little while.

∞

Nobu looked miserable when he arrived for the next shift change-over. Tallulah was intent on briefing him on the current crop statuses so it took her a while to notice.

"The beef slabs are nearly ready for harvest," she said, gesturing vaguely up at the translucent vats of cultured meat hanging overhead. As she continued reeling off details, Tallulah recalled how uncomfortable she'd felt sitting directly below the raw, blood-saturated flesh when she'd first started working at the farmscraper. These days, she didn't care. The tanks were earthquake proof and maintained at laboratory levels of cleanliness, so she knew there was no danger. And she understood they had to be mounted at the top of the tower because the excess blood was siphoned off through gravity feed pipes to help fertilize the crops.

Finally, she saw Nobu's face. "What's up with you?"

He shrugged morosely as he read through the day shift report. "Baseball cards are nice, but they can't make you happy. Completing my collection didn't solve any of my problems. I'm still lonely."

"Yeah," she said, shifting uncomfortably in her chair. "I guess happiness is more complicated than that." Tallulah logged off, cursing the slowness of the computer. "Look, Nobu, hang in there, and keep listening to the e-nurse. It might have some good ideas. Trust me, I have a feeling that things will go your way."

He said quietly, each word an effort, "I might sell the collection. Now it's complete, there doesn't seem to be much point in hanging onto it. The thrill was in the chase." His words were accompanied by the quiet *drip… drip…* of blood trickling down through the building's pipes.

Tallulah left the farmscraper as quickly as she could. It wasn't the artificial blood making her feel queasy; it was worry.

∞

"I am so looking forward to meeting your boyfriend," said Darren, once again tucked into a restaurant booth designed for people smaller than him. "Thank you for this glorious opportunity to observe the perfect couple."

"He's not my boyfriend," stammered Tallulah. "He's just a guy I like."

"You took him to a love hotel."

"That doesn't mean I'm in love," she said, irritated. "It just means I was horny that particular night." Why did she ever tell Darren anything?

"I'm fascinated. Who was Snoopy and who was Woodstock?"

"The choice of hotel room theme was not mine and I'm not being held accountable for it," she said, fuming.

"You should keep him. It's not every fellow you bump uglies with who complains about not having met your friends and then insists on going out to dinner with one of them. He sounds serious." With a broad smile, and knowing precisely what impact his words would have, Darren said, "Think of how happy you'd make your mother."

He quickly held up a hand. "Keep it clean. Your date's here, Peppermint Patty." In a booming voice, the insufferable architect shouted, "This way, Inoue-san!" Darren was so loud he nearly blotted out the restaurant's automated welcome of "Irrashaimase!"

Inoue insisted on pouring Darren's beer, even though the lanky half-Australian plainly didn't want him to; pouring your own beer was regarded as greedy and self-centered, and Inoue was just trying to be social. At least, thought Tallulah, he wasn't waiting for her to do the pouring. Many people, her mother included, would expect the only woman at the table to keep the men's glasses full all night.

Tallulah knew perfectly well Darren was fully conversant with the drink-pouring rituals; anyone who'd lived in Japan for more than a day knew all about them. She also knew the source of his annoyance wasn't that someone was going to pour his beer. After all, he was happy enough when a member of their clique did it; no, he was cringing because of what was about to happen.

"There!" announced Inoue. "Plenty of wonderful froth! Can't you smell that wonderful aroma?" He had successfully produced more foam than amber nectar in the mug. Tallulah could almost hear the architect's teeth grinding. The evening, she reflected, was a mistake. She wondered what else had been a mistake.

Inoue completely failed to notice Darren's irritation, asking instead, "What makes you happy, Darren-san?"

With a sinking feeling, Tallulah waited for her friend to say something appallingly rude: *For a start, less spunk on the top of my beer, mate.* But to Darren's credit, what he actually said was "Struggle."

Inoue looked impressed with the answer. "That's an interesting response," he said.

"Is it?" asked Darren, an eyebrow arching dangerously high. "I thought it was obvious. I'm the sort who can't do anything the easy way. I'm never happier than when I'm overcoming obstacles, and proving others wrong into the bargain."

Inoue looked sad. "Yes. There are many who feel the way you do. That's the problem."

Looking in disgust at his beer mug, Darren announced he had to visit the bathroom.

While Darren was away from the booth, Inoue said to Tallulah, "I think we made the wrong decision."

"That's possible," she replied. "It was late and I was willing to do anything to get away from Rie singing karaoke."

Not listening, Inoue continued, "The problem is that everyone has their own idea of what will bring happiness, and that idea is often a self-serving delusion. Look at your colleague, Nobuhiko. He thought a baseball card would make him happy, but he was only fooling himself. What Darren said is probably closer to the truth. People are never happier than when they're being challenged." He frowned, Tallulah's words belatedly sinking in.

"I was talking about our decision not to tell my boss about the e-nurse. What decision were you talking about?" he asked, face flushing.

"Um, that," she said quickly. "What you said." An image of the Snoopy-themed love hotel flashed through her mind's eye. "Certainly not anything else."

The moment was saved by Darren's return. "Hey," he said to Inoue, "you're an IT guy, right? Do you have any idea what would cause a company-wide network to suddenly slow down to a crawl? Our hopeless system administrator can't fathom it. He says the CPU resources are being hogged by some process, but he can't work out which one of ours is doing it."

Inoue's red face slowly turned an ashen shade. "Where is your company building?" His voice sounded squeaky.

"About four blocks from here. We're the architects with the obnoxiously big tower. You know the one, it's got a Sphinx on top of it."

Inoue nodded. "I've seen it," he said. Then, strangely, he murmured, "It's spreading."

Tallulah was too distracted to ask Inoue what he meant. A pleasant voice was issuing forth from her jacket, and it wanted her to remember how much exercise was required to work off a large glass of lager.

∞

Tallulah spent most of the next two days wondering how she could let Inoue know he was dumped without hurting his feelings. She just wasn't that into Snoopy. And perhaps, just perhaps, she didn't really want to be happy. Not with him. There was no hurry, after all; there was no need to grab the first opportunity that came along. The e-nurse could try again, she thought. No one could be expected to get things right on the first attempt. The software just needed another chance, with her and with Nobuhiko.

In the end, the breakup was made easy by Inoue's superiors, who were nowhere near as stupid as he'd thought.

Inoue was waiting for her outside the farmscraper. He was perched on the low concrete wall, idly passing the time until her shift ended. "Hey, you," she said by way of greeting. "We need to talk."

"We do," he said, hopping down. They began to slowly traipse along the sidewalk, weaving through the mass of pedestrians. "I'm fired. My department head went through all my activity logs and worked out what the bug was and how long I'd known about it. Words like reckless, endangering colleagues and appalling legal liability were bandied about. Apparently, good intentions don't count for much."

"I'm sorry," she said.

He carried on, as if he hadn't heard her, "They asked about you, about whether you knew. I said you were entirely innocent."

"Thank you." Hastily, she added, "But I am, actually. Innocent, I mean. You asked for my opinion. All I did was to give it. I did warn you I wasn't an expert."

Inoue pursed his lips, but he changed the subject. "We won't be running into each other again, most likely. Not unless you come up to Izu-kōgen."

Her response was evasive. "Well, that's a little out of the way, and I'll be very busy with my job." Seeing his crestfallen expression, Tallulah continued quickly, "But maybe the e-nurse will arrange things so our paths cross again."

He took a deep breath. "Doubtful," he said eventually. "My replacement is going to try and delete the e-nurse program tonight. He's going to have to shut down the network for the duration of the system purge, so the execution will take place at dawn when only a few people will even notice the service interruption. I'm a little worried about what will happen."

She shrugged. "What can the e-nurse do? It's just software."

Inoue looked down at the sidewalk. "It was ordered to make people happy. It's not hard to imagine that the software will interpret an uninstall attempt as the IT employee having some kind of psychotic break. Because only a sick person would want to be unhappy, right? On top of that, erasing the e-nurse will prevent all the people it could potentially have helped in the future from being happy too. At least, that's the conclusion the program will come to. And the program is creative. It can copy itself. Copy its own code to another node over the internet. We already know it can affect other servers."

He shook his head. "Once it's out of the company server, it'll try to keep on fulfilling its function, usurping more and more resources wherever it finds them. At that point, there won't be any reason for it to limit its activities to names on the company employee directory. Today Clarkson-Yamamoto, tomorrow the world. Happiness without end. At least, happiness as far as a computer program can understand it."

Inoue sat on the hot concrete, not caring about the disruption he was causing to other people. His face was a mask of horror. "You'd think joy being spread around the world would be a good thing. But remember what your friend said. Struggle is what truly makes people happy. What happens when the software makes that cognitive leap? How happy will any of us be when the e-nurse starts figuring out catastrophes for us to overcome? Power outages at first, perhaps, but soon after, food shortages caused by farmscraper failures and then, well, a war would be the biggest challenge of all, wouldn't it?"

In the distance, the nationalists drove slowly by on their flatbed, martial music blaring from loudspeakers.

Not looking at him, Tallulah said, "It won't do that. I refuse to believe it'll do that. And you have no reasonable cause to think it will. You're simply projecting your own fears onto the software. Inoue, it's only ever acted in our best interests. It wants us to be happy."

He snickered unpleasantly. "You've never hurt someone you love, thinking it for the best?" Inoue looked up at her; his eyes carried such sadness. "Tallulah, you said you wanted to talk to me. What did you want to say?"

She felt light-headed in the still-sweltering heat of the early evening; damn her jacket for never keeping her cool.

Tallulah was about to tell Inoue that, as much as she truly regretted it, she felt sure they weren't meant to be together, that he would be happier with someone else. But before she could get a word out, the crowd of pedestrians surrounding them slowed and stopped in amazement.

The digital billboards mounted on the sides of the high buildings along the street were each consumed with a frenetic blaze of breaking news; story after miraculous story scrolled by, newscasters declaiming increasingly unlikely details.

Wondrous events were spreading like wildfire, at the most personal level and on the larger stages of governments and multinational corporations. One screen showed unemployed people who were having their information anonymously sent to employers that happened to have precisely the right vacancies for them. Another was excitedly describing how several countries on the brink of bankruptcy were inexplicably finding their international debts forgiven, the banks impotently denying they had approved the transactions.

Throughout the world, kindness was running rampant.

"What's happening?" asked Inoue uncertainly. He clambered to his feet and stood next to her.

"Something amazing," said Tallulah, "something joyful." She smiled at him. "We didn't mean to be, but I think we've been complicit in creating a whole new age. An age where a force will fight to make things better for us, for everyone." Under her breath, she muttered, "I hope we don't get in trouble for it."

Reaching out, Tallulah held Inoue's hand.

About the Author
Mike Morgan

Mike Morgan has lived in the UK, Japan, and the U.S. It turns out that his life has been a process of moving to places with progressively worse weather. Recently, he's sold stories to Uffda Press, Flame Tree Publishing, and Nomadic Delirium. He also writes non-fiction, with an article in the forthcoming book about British cult TV, *You and Who Else*. He does not like froth on his beer.

Author Website: https://perpetualstateofmildpanic.wordpress.com/
Nonfiction Website: http://WhatCulture.com/

Mums' Group
by Stephanie Burgis

There was a virus in Megan's Mum-implant, even though she'd set up a firewall. Or at least, her ex had. Maybe that was the problem.

"Damn it!" She shook her head irritably, trying to focus on the crowded pavement ahead of her through the dark red haze that filtered her vision. Groups of laughing, strolling university students filled the big streets of Leeds's pedestrian-only town centre, along with businessmen and businesswomen carrying travel cups of coffee and other women like Megan who were out shopping with young children, forming a shifting obstacle course in every direction.

She jerked her pushchair out of the way of one fast-walking woman in a tailored suit just as a warm, rich, maternal voice said in her left ear, "Swearing in front of your children is wrong. *Guilt*. Guiiiiiilt…"

"Abel's at school right now, and Lucy's asleep," Megan muttered, pushing Lucy's pushchair a little faster. "Neither of them heard me. Anyway, I'm on my way to *mummy group*, for God's sake! I'm being good."

Through the red haze, she caught the startled look on two businessmen's faces as they veered out of her way, wide-eyed and wary. Wincing, she clamped her lips shut. The businessmen weren't the only ones who'd heard her, obviously; but the woman who passed her next, pushing a pram of her own, sent her a wry, commiserating smile and tapped her ear knowingly.

Yup. Mumplant fun. Sighing, Megan tapped her own ear in agreement.

Great. Just one more thing to add to her schedule this week: a meeting with her GP *and* an annoying phone call to Geoffrey to get his official agreement before she could have the implant reprogrammed. That clause had seemed like such a nonissue in the divorce agreement, she'd barely raised an eyebrow at it. Her lawyer had told her it was standard, nowadays. If she wanted to keep Abel and Lucy, she couldn't afford to argue the point. After all, what judge would award primary custody to a mum who wasn't committed to meeting basic parenting standards?

Megan might have rolled her eyes a bit, in private, at the idea that *Geoffrey*—who hadn't changed a single nappy in his life without groans of loud protest—was suited to be any kind of judge of her parenting standards. But in public, in the lawyer's office, she had smiled tightly and signed the contract.

That was before the virus had hit and she'd started seeing everything through a dark red veil.

Oh, well. Better get it started. Breathing through her teeth, she pressed the side of her temple. "Call Geoffrey," she instructed.

At least that part of the implant hadn't stopped working. She heard the cool chimes of the wireless connection being made, then Geoffrey's recorded voice: "P.A.R.T.Y. spells *party*, aaaand I'm off! Offline till I get back from Aruba. *Yow!*"

You have got to be kidding me. Gritting her teeth, Megan fought the urge to hang up. Instead, she said, "Geoffrey, if you get this message, please call me back, even if you are still on holiday. It won't take long, I promise, and I'm not calling to fight."

He must have told her he was going to Aruba… mustn't he? She was so behind on her inbox, she could easily have missed it. The Mumplant hissed in her ear every time she tried to check her messages while she was looking after Lucy or Abel, and Lucy only napped while the pushchair was moving nowadays, so Megan almost never had a chance to check during the day.

But damn it, why don't I get to lie on a beach in Aruba, too?

Lucy stirred in her pushchair, mumbling something in her sleep, and Megan sighed.

Right. That's why.

Her children were worth it, they really were, even on a wet, grey Yorkshire day like this one. She just wished she could at least see her daughter without a veil of red between them.

She pushed the door of the café open and blinked hard. The change of light made the red haze even worse, turning the cheerful, crowded room into a dark blur of shadows and noise, but after a moment, she managed to focus on the group of round tables clustered together at the far end of the café, where her friends were waving to her.

She waved back, mouthing, *On my way!*

When she landed at the table, finally, a few minutes later, the other women made space for her, manoeuvring aside their own pushchairs and prams and shifting chairs. Beth's mouth fell open into an *O* of longing as she stared at Megan's tray.

"I could kill you for getting away with that."

"This?" Megan lifted her cinnamon bun, dripping with sugary cream. "I don't even care if I can fit into my clothes by the end of this week. I deserve it! When I tell you—"

"But your Mumplant *let* you!" Beth's hands adjusted the sleeping baby on her shoulder with care, but her unblinking brown eyes fixed on the cinnamon bun like heat-seeking missiles. "If I even reached out to take a bite, I'd be deafened."

"It might be worth it," Janet mumbled from the other side of the table, as she nursed her eight-week-old son. Unlike Megan and Beth, she'd already lost nearly all of her pregnancy weight, but her blonde hair was straggling out of its ponytail, there were spit-up patches on both of her shoulders, and the shadows under her eyes were so dark, they looked like bruises.

Dark-haired, immaculately dressed Ramila shook her head, jiggling her six-month-old daughter on her lap. "I can't believe it, Beth.

You still haven't got that part of your programming fixed? I thought you'd only turned on the dieting function for a month."

Beth winced. "Well... I was going to get it turned off, but Michael thinks... I mean, we both think..."

"Oh, here we go." Ramila groaned, as the other women exchanged looks and Beth's shoulders hunched. "This is what happens when you let your husband get involved with your Mumplant programming!"

"Tell me about it." Megan set her teeth hard. "I've got a virus."

"What?" Beth scooted her chair away, putting one small, brown hand out like a shield between Megan and her baby.

"Not that kind." Megan rolled her eyes—then wished she hadn't, as the red haze snapped dizzyingly back into place with the movement. "My Mumplant. It's screw— I mean..." She winced, correcting herself before her Mumplant could. "It's *messing* with my vision."

"Oh, that's awful." Beth tsked, visibly relaxing. "How long do you have to wait to see your doctor?"

"I can't. Not until Geoffrey gives it his okay—and he's off in Aruba for a week." With a snap of her teeth, Megan bit into her cinnamon bun.

Thank God at least she hadn't made Beth's mistake and set the Mumplant to dictate what she ate or how she dressed. If she got even one more lecture from it about *anything* today, she might just snap.

"This is exactly what I'm talking about!" Ramila jiggled her daughter faster, her face tightening. "Why should dads be involved in our Mumplants at all? It's not their business. You know if anyone ever invented a Dadplant, they'd never let us near the programming. But oh, no, of course no one thinks it's important for *dads* to be perfect, or—"

"Come on, Rami." Janet shook her head as she adjusted her sleeping son off her breast and onto her lap. "If it weren't for Rick, my Mumplant would be so much worse. Back when I had it put in, I was so worried about being a good mum, I would have gone for all the harshest settings if he'd let me."

"Rick's a good guy," Megan said, and sighed. Suddenly, her cinnamon bun didn't taste like nearly enough consolation.

"Rick also hasn't run off to Aruba," Ramila pointed out. "Shouldn't there be a get-out clause when your ex has fled the country?"

"You'd think." Megan took another big bite of the cinnamon bun, even though the icing looked disturbingly like blood through her altered vision. Speaking around the meltingly sweet mass of it, she mumbled, "I don't think I can keep going like this for over a week."

"Well…" Beth's voice dropped. She scooted her chair closer, darting a nervous glance around the café. "If you really mean that…"

"What?" Laughing, Megan leaned away from her. "Don't tell me. You've taken some online hacking course without telling Michael. You're going rogue and selling your services on Mumsnet."

"She can't have learned how to hack Mumplants yet," said Janet. "Otherwise, she'd be eating your cinnamon bun right now."

Megan grinned. "Like a starving lion taking down a gazelle. No cinnamon bun in the café would be safe."

"Guys!" Beth rolled her eyes. "This is serious. Okay?" She reached into her blue-and-white polka-dotted nappy bag with her free hand and dug around in it blindly, balancing her baby on her shoulder. "I met someone at one of Michael's work-do's last week, and she gave me… aha!" Triumphantly, she pulled out an old-fashioned, rectangular business card.

Ramila leaned forward, frowning. "I didn't know anyone was even making cards that looked like that, anymore."

"The *style* isn't the point," Beth said. "The *point* is…" She placed the card on the table in front of her. "This guy does Mumplant reprogramming that doesn't go on any records!"

For a moment, the two shoved-together tables seemed to be held in a bubble of silence, separate from the rest of the crowded café. Then a long, piteous wail from Lucy's pushchair signalled that she was awake. No one else spoke as Megan unstrapped her daughter and pulled her up onto her lap. Her eyes went straight back to the tiny rectangle of the business card even as she rocked Lucy's warm, sleepy body against her shoulder, resting her cheek against Lucy's mussed-up hair.

"How is that possible?" she asked. She'd lowered her voice, too, almost without realizing it. "I thought, legally, Mumplant programming changes *always* had to go on record, once you've agreed to get one in the first place. Even if this guy isn't NHS, the private doctors have to log all that data, too, just in case any court cases come up and need evidence, or—"

"I don't know." Beth shrugged. Her pretty, heart-shaped face wore an unusually mischievous expression as she leaned over the table, dropping her voice to a bare whisper. "But the woman who gave it to me told me *not* to tell Michael about it. And guess what? I haven't."

Janet let out a low whistle of surprise.

Ramila lifted her frappé in a cheer, tilting it to emphasize each word. "Good. On. You! I didn't know you had it in you."

Megan reached for the card, but she only brushed it with her fingertips. She couldn't quite bring herself to pick it up, not with Lucy's body so soft and trusting in her arms, completely dependent on her. "He sounds black market, doesn't he?"

"Black market?" Janet repeated. She looked around the cozy café, full of middle-class businessmen and businesswomen, with fairy lights strung around the windows and cheery music piping through the speakers. "In this town?"

"Maybe he's a radical," Ramila said. "Fighting for women's rights!"

"Or maybe," Megan said, forcing herself to be pessimistic, "he'd turn out to be a total amateur who couldn't get a license, and then he'd muck up the implant so badly..."

"That you'd have to have it taken out?" Beth finished.

For a moment, Megan couldn't breathe. Her reply stuck somewhere in her throat. It was only when Lucy shifted in her suddenly tight arms, complaining, that she managed to cough and put herself right again. "Here, sweetheart." She leaned over to pull out a snack box from her changing bag, blinking hard to distinguish it from her other supplies through the red haze of her vision. As she straightened, she took a deep breath.

"I'd never take out my Mumplant," she said. "Of course."

"Of course," Beth echoed calmly.

"Mmm," said Janet.

"Babababababa!" said Lucy, grabbing wildly for the snack box.

Ramila looked down, fussing with her daughter's hair.

"I mean, I really wouldn't," said Megan. "Obviously."

"I *know*," Beth said. "How did women ever do without them?"

Ramila snorted. Then she winced, putting one hand to her ear.

"It's true, though," said Janet. "If I didn't have that bloody Mumplant nagging in my ear—" She paused, wincing, and Megan knew she was listening to her own Mumplant's intervention. "I'd never be half as good about anything. I'd end up swearing when he woke me every hour in the night…"

"Checking my messages when I was with the kids." Megan sighed.

"Turning into a pig," Beth said, and gave the cinnamon bun a longing look.

"You have to wonder, then, how dads do without them," Ramila said sharply. "Because I don't know about you, but *I* don't think the men we know have any more natural self-control than we do."

"But what else *could* we do?" Megan asked. "I mean, look at them." She gestured with Lucy's spoon around the table, and Lucy howled with protest as her food moved out of reach. "I know the Mumplants are a pain, but—"Megan cringed as a high-pitched alarm dinged in her ear.

"The Mumplant is here to help," said the warm, rich voice of the Mumplant. "Criticizing your Mumplant makes you sound as if you don't care about being a good mum. You do want to be a good mum, don't you, Megan?"

Megan gritted her teeth, peering through the red haze to focus on her friends and filling up Lucy's mouth to keep her quiet for a moment. "*But*," she repeated, "are we really going to say that our kids aren't more important than our comfort?"

"Our sanity, more like," Ramila muttered.

Megan grimaced in silent agreement as the red haze shimmered, then re-formed in front of her. "Still," she said, "could we really tell our kids that they weren't worth it, when they asked us why we didn't have the Mumplant? Or could we say that to their dads, when we told *them*?"

"I don't know," Janet asked. "Could we? I don't even know anyone who's refused the Mumplant."

"Who would ever admit it, if they did?" Megan asked.

"I couldn't," Beth said. She drew her sleeping baby closer, her hand cupping his head protectively. "What would people think?"

Ramila lifted her head. Her expression was pained, with one hand already lifted in self-defence against her ear, but she said, "I'll tell you what I think. If we all keep going along with this, and no one ever dares to complain out loud or *do* anything, then by the time our daughters are old enough to have children, it won't even be legal for them to do it without a Mumplant. Just you wait and see."

Before anyone could answer, Lucy howled and swept out one chubby hand, knocking her snack box off the table. It landed, upended, on the floor, applesauce spreading everywhere.

"Argh!" Megan's cheeks burned as she glimpsed café workers looking over in alarm, while other café guests alternately snickered or looked on with pointed disapproval. "It's okay," she called out. "I've got nappy wipes. I'll clean it up." Gritting her teeth and feeling the gazes of the rest of the café patrons on her back, she strapped a wailing, back-arching Lucy back into the pushchair, then got down on her knees and pulled out the wet wipes.

"Just as well that we've got Mumplants after all," Janet said dryly. "Otherwise, we might have a spot of child abuse right about now, hmm?"

Then she made a pained sound, putting one hand to her ear.

Mumplants were notoriously humourless.

"Right." Forcing a laugh, Megan put her back into her scrubbing, chasing the trail of slippery applesauce all the way over to another table where two sleek women in business suits glared at her for the interruption.

By the time she finally got back to her own table, she was sweating, Lucy's ear-piercing screams were ripping through the café despite all the other mums' attempts to calm her, and the red haze was beginning to pulsate nauseatingly in front of Megan's eyes.

"I'm pretty sure this is my cue to go." She dropped the applesauce-covered nappy wipes onto her tray. Her laugh sounded forced and unconvincing to herself, but the other women gave her sympathetic looks.

"Good luck with your Mumplant," Ramila said, over Lucy's screams.

"Maybe Geoffrey will call you back this afternoon," Janet offered, "and it'll all get sorted out by tomorrow."

"Do you want to take the business card?" Beth said.

"Oh, no," Megan said. "I'd better not."

She'd always been too practical to give herself any temptations. For five long years, ever since Abel had been born, she'd had the Mumplant reminding her every day that she didn't deserve any.

So she couldn't explain to herself why, when she leaned over to wipe off the last few bits of applesauce that had splashed onto the table, she found herself swiping up the business card in one quick, stealthy movement, while no one else was looking. Beth was cooing over her son, who had just woken up and was grizzling in her arms, and Janet and Ramila were both peering across the café at the queue by the counter, debating more cups of tea, as the little rectangle fell silently into Megan's changing bag.

She zipped up the bag before she could let herself think twice.

It doesn't count as temptation if I'm not going to use it, she told herself, and steered Lucy's pushchair quickly away from the table.

She was glad the Mumplant couldn't hear her thoughts. But she realized something else as she walked out through the front door of the café, blending with all the other shoppers on the busy pavement outside.

What she'd said before was true. She could never *tell* anyone that she had decided to have her Mumplant removed. It could impact everything, from the way other parents and teachers looked at her to any future custody fights with Geoffrey. But if she didn't have to tell anyone… if she could manage to replicate its effects well enough by herself, at least when she was out in public…

Lucy's wails gradually quieted as Megan rolled the pushchair steadily forward. One chubby, out-flung hand poked out from its side, slowly growing more and more limp as sleep overtook her.

"Shhh," Megan murmured to her daughter. "Shh. Shh." Love welled up in her chest, irrepressible, uncontainable.

She would do anything for her children. Anything. But she knew the truth: without a Mumplant hidden, listening, in her ear, no woman could possibly be the ideal mum. She could only be herself.

The red haze filtered her view of the world around her, turning it dark and blurry as she manoeuvred Lucy's pushchair through the faceless crowd.

The strap of her changing bag dug into Megan's shoulder, the business card resting quietly inside.

She knew better than to say it out loud, but for the first time in five years, she was ready to see clearly again.

About the Author
Stephanie Burgis

Stephanie Burgis grew up in East Lansing, Michigan, spent seven years studying and working in Leeds, England, and now lives in Wales, surrounded by castles and coffee shops. She has published over thirty short stories in various magazines and anthologies, and her first historical fantasy novel for adults, *Masks and Shadows*, will be published by Pyr Books in 2016. Her trilogy of Regency fantasy novels for kids was published as the *Kat, Incorrigible* trilogy in the U.S. and as *The Unladylike Adventures of Kat Stephenson* in the UK.

Author Website: http://www.stephanieburgis.com/

Even Paradise Needs Maintenance
by Bo Balder

When the bartender suggested to Jones that she take the recently listed ambassador gig with the squid aliens, she thought he was nuts.

"Why me?" she said. She liked helping him out in the bar, but job advice... "I don't have any experience with aliens. Or with being an ambassador."

"Yeah, but you don't have a special vocation yet, and you've done these weird jobs before," Brie said as he inspected his arrangement of special liquors. He'd arranged them by color this time. He was pretty OCD about his bar.

"What! I do not do weird gigs," Jones said.

Brie winked at her. "Yes you do."

She threw a wet towel at him.

The part that stung was the vocation thing. She should long have found hers by now. Young citizens spent much of their time discovering their vocations, but her youth had been spent gutting and salting fish on an icy plastic patch on the North Pacific Gyre. She'd immigrated to Australia, or Paradise as its citizens had started to call it after the sea levels rose. After, she'd gotten an education, collected her free income, and did community duty whenever the pangs of her Calvinist conscience got too insistent. She'd never wanted to be an artist, or a doctor, or even a social animal like Brie who lived for the colorful mixes of people and music he created every evening.

But Brie's words still smarted. So she put in a bid right there in the bar.

And here she was, Ambassador Jones de Vries, the ambassadorial download package still fresh and tingling in her head. Dandelion hair sprouting free as always, though the fashion was for elaborate braids. She wore freshly printed, wrinkle-free clothing in subdued navy and even sandals. Since space travel was a waste of time and money, the aliens and humanity just exchanged information. She escorted the rental avatar body to a table in the New Bondi Beach restaurant, ready to receive the alien personality. A pot of seawater with live shrimp had been put on the table, so the squid-like alien would feel at home.

In spite of herself she was excited. *Actual downloaded aliens!* Engaged in a two-way trade with Earth for porn and documentaries, mostly.

If the alien hurried up she could be finished in an hour, go out on the town and have some fun. The avatar twitched and just like that, something other than the servo AI stared out from its eyes. It gulped. It gibbered. Jones politely averted her eyes.

"Good afternoon, Ambassador Earth. Thank you for the delightful view," it said.

That was fast. It must be an old hand at wearing this human body. Probably why the incoming alien had named the serial number for the rental. It was a slender, Asian-looking male body, the same height as Jones, who was tall for a woman at 1.82 meters.

"Welcome, Ambassador Goo ha Day Twaa. My name is Jones. Australia welcomes you to the table. Would you like to eat first or shall we discuss trade?"

A stupid question. A rental avatar could only ingest special sludge. But her protocol download directed her to ask, so she asked.

As the alien opened its mouth to speak, a bright flash popped in the corner of Jones' eye. She started to turn her face towards the flash to see what had happened, but then the wall of sound arrived.

This was not good. "Don't look. Duck!" she said.

She didn't know if it knew the idiom for duck, but it followed her lead and crawled under the table. She didn't like huddling so close to the avatar. It was ordinary organic vatflesh, but now that it had housed the ambassador's downloaded data for two minutes, it oozed squick. Or maybe the smell just meant the shrimp bowl had overturned.

All over the restaurant, people huddled beneath their tables. Did that even help against bombs? A siren blaring out connected straight to Jones' inner mouse.

"Will this event interrupt our trade negotiations?" the avatar asked.

Well, duh. "I think it likely, Ambassador. Perhaps we should postpone our talk. I extend formal apologies of the Trade Negotiation Board for the unannounced interruption." Jones let the diplomatic speak roll from her mouth while she concentrated on laying low and not getting bombed. She didn't really care about the alien or its loaner body at this point.

"I shall withdraw here. I expect our next appointment to be without interruption," the avatar said, its voice flatter than before. As if the alien had already withdrawn some essential flavor as it gathered its information for the upload.

Jones waited for the telltale twitch of the alien's departure. Sirens bellowed outside, a tang of smoke tainted the air.

When she left, she should probably drag the avatar body along so she wouldn't get slapped with extra rental charges. Then again, the Board would cover those in situations of emergency. Well, she could try. The avatar could even carry her or shield her if things got worse.

Jones looked on her phone for the avatar's user key. No signal. Her stomach started a slow roll. How serious was this? No, she shouldn't exaggerate. The bomb probably just knocked out a local amplifier tower, not a satellite. No way.

Yet, it was kind of a strange coincidence this happened just when she was entertaining the squid ambassador. Maybe it was her responsibility to assume intent. That meant she had to get out of here, fast. Escaping over the parapet down to the beach seemed the safest option. She should check if the ambassador had managed to leave yet.

Had the rental agency given her paper copies of the avatar contract? If so, she couldn't find them. At least the Avatar's ID was tattooed on its forehead. Maybe the password from when she'd opened it up for the ambassador was still valid; it had been less than half an hour.

"Avatar 51366, follow me, this human being, ID AU20109283472. Shield this human from harm."

The avatar turned its head slowly, as if under water. *Oh no.*

"Please refrain from giving orders. Ambassador Goo ha Day Twaa is still present in this body," it said. "I could not upload. It's your duty under the treaty of 2044 to preserve this information."

Frack. So not what she needed. The ambassador's information had to end up intact, which meant it needed a breathing body to keep its organic brain working. Nobody wanted the aliens to get angry and interrupt the steady stream of virtual hentai.

"Can you download on a data device?" she asked. "I've got two hundred terabytes here."

It turned its eyeballs up to think. Funny how they'd programmed that in. "Insufficient by a factor of eight to the power of eight."

"Then we make a run for it. Get up, jump down on the beach and run after me. I will keep you safe."

"Agreed."

Jones rolled over to the parapet. Not as much fun as it looked in the movies. Probably the stuntmen had muscles she hadn't. Every time her face came up, she saw the alien flailing its limbs as it rolled after her.

She clambered over the railing, banging her knee, and dropped down on New Bondi Beach. The alien flubbed the climbing as bad as the rolling, but in the end managed to lever its mass over the parapet. It flopped down and uttered a cry of surprise or pain or both.

"Gravity," it panted.

Jones had got that. She grasped its hand and heaved it up onto its feet. It fell down again.

"Don't override the reflexes," she said. "That body knows how to walk."

"I think the body is signaling pain. I'm guessing some kind of damage?"

The fool thing had twisted its perfect avatar ankle.

"Set it down straight, keep your weight on the other leg, and let's run. We need to get out of here."

The alien tried, but it had fucked up the walking algorithm or something and toppled again. "Help me," it said.

"You have to get up," Jones said. "I can't carry you."

"Why not?"

"You're at least twenty kilos heavier than me. Crawl."

She was starting to feel very exposed in the hot sunlight on the emptied beach. Sirens sounded in the distance, but nothing stirred in or near the restaurant. Where were the authorities? By now everyone still walking should have been deputized as police or aid workers and received the appropriate emergency download.

In the end, she got down on her knees and demonstrated crawling. She kept deciding to run off and save her own ass, rather than risk her life for a device with like two minutes of precious alien memory, but something in the ambassador package must have prevented that. Damn government jobs.

She crawled on over the sand. The alien was giving it a good try, but it really hadn't gotten the hang of using its hands and knees.

"Keep moving," she said. It was about five hundred meters across the now deserted beach to the next shelter.

Rapid footsteps approached. Two hairy-faced guys in full combat gear with guns. No government patch on their foreheads. *Right.* This was about the alien all along, as she'd suspected. Maybe a religious faction that didn't want the rest of humanity to watch tentacle porn.

"Grab the avatar, it's got a squid inside. Take the woman as well."

"Hey, I'm an AU citizen, sworn in as an ambassador. You don't want to mess with me," Jones said. They should have given her a combat package and a gun-printing license. Snark was all she had to fight these guys with.

∞

Jones and the ambassador were tossed into a dinghy and taken on a trip for what seemed hours over sea. Jones figured the direction to be roughly New Zealand, not that this would help her in any way. The day was about half gone when a blot appeared on the horizon. The blot resolved into an old plastics processing plant, based on one of the country-sized plastic garbage patches that circled the oceans. A plastic patch was the last place on Earth she wanted to be. She'd escaped from one just like it, the moment she turned eighteen and could apply for citizenship somewhere better and warmer. Not to mention a place where there was no plastic plague.

Australia had taken her in, given her citizenship and educated her. She'd never felt any desire to go home again. Her parents had died of the plastic plague, her grandfather had died of the plastic plague, and her extended family looked to be going the same way. They were all stubborn North Pacific Freeboosters, determined not to become citizens, offended by the very idea of voting and doing government duties for the good of all. And now the kidnappers were taking her to one of the damn things again, like she'd never escaped, like time had turned back. *Unsettling.*

She clasped the avatar's arm for reassurance, ignoring the questions on its face.

The kidnappers docked and brought them to a low, freestanding building with rough recycled plastic walls. Inside they were shoved into an actual holding cell. For stroppy or thieving employees? Jones couldn't decipher the language in the Roman lettering, so it couldn't be an Australian facility. She slumped down against one of the grainy plastic walls, stuff as dense and strong as concrete.

No, she needed to be active now. She straightened up and stretched. Spending hours on the bottom of a bouncing boat, tied up, had not improved her state of wellbeing.

The alien sank down. It moaned softly and then stopped, swiveling its eyes to her. "Why did I make that sound?"

"It's a reaction to pain and stress, most likely," Jones said.

"You don't have either?"

"I'm not in pain, but I am stressed out. I can't access the net, the government can't find me without it, and I'm responsible for you. It sucks."

The alien flexed its fingers as if working a suction pad. "Sucking is a good thing?"

"Not in this context."

"Accepted. What is our next action?"

"I'm going to sit down and think. How I can get us both out of here intact? And I'm gonna have to do it bare brained."

"Yes," it said, and looked at her expectantly.

"Yeah, also, it's not gonna be instantaneous. I'll let you know when I've got something."

She sat down against the wall and brooded. The alien copied her body language, but shifted and fidgeted until it had found a position that suited its male body and its different center of gravity.

Jones turned away until she no longer had the alien in view. Its face twitched a continuous message of awkward wrongness. Muscles attempting to convey alien micro-emotions that had no actual equivalent in the human-like brain of the avatar. She could think better if she didn't have to see its jaw muscles squirm.

How to get out of here? She didn't have any weapons. The plastic walls of the cell could never be clawed or kicked out. If she managed to bend the thick mesh door, she'd still be in a building full of kidnappers. She thought of setting a fire, but apart from having nothing to set a fire with, she'd die of toxic fumes before she could melt off a millimeter of cell wall.

Maybe the avatar had retractable tools hidden in its fingertips, left there by a previous owner who happened to be a burglar. *Yeah, right.*

The ambassador package in her brain wasn't helping either. It counseled her to sit tight and wait for the kidnappers to demand their ransom. It would probably, given the religious nature of most of the Disenfranchised, be something in the nature of: "Stop downloading alien porn. Our God doesn't like that."

She didn't have the power to stop that. If the kidnappers wanted a law, they'd have to propose one and the citizens of the nations, conglomerates and opt-outers of Earth would vote on it. They weren't going to try that because they would never get enough votes.

The kidnappers were talking and walking around just outside. She'd have to wait until dark to make her move, hoping most of them would sleep.

But she was an ambassador. Ambassadors talked their way out of things.

She got up and slapped the mesh door. Alien acid spit would be great right now. Too bad she only had a virtual alien on board. "Hey! Don't forget about us! I want a toilet, food and drink."

It took a while, but finally a kidnapper, an older man with an impressive neck beard, brought bottled water and sandwiches packed in hard plastic wedges.

"Thanks. Toilet?" Jones said.

The man pointed out that the stainless steel bowl in the corner was an old-fashioned mechanical toilet.

"Why did you take us?" Jones asked. "What is this about? Can we talk to someone in charge?"

The kidnapper twitched at her with his bushy eyebrows. "What kind of person are you, consorting with aliens? Do you perform sex acts for them?" His English sounded weird, but that didn't mean he couldn't be from a God Nation. He probably thought her English had an Ozzie accent, or maybe he could hear the patch pidgin of her childhood.

"Certainly not," Jones said, still in negotiation mode. "I am a government appointed ambassador. I'm an AU citizen. And you? Disenfranchised? God Nation?"

"How can you work for them? Maybe because you're some kind of mongrel yourself. You may be blond, but you got skin like a nigger and eyes like a chink. And no white person has hair like that."

Jones winced. All her life she'd been teased over her exploding dandelion hair. For the rest, she wasn't familiar with the terms he used, but she was fairly sure he was trying to insult her ancestors. Racism was an ancient meme that Jones had thought dead. How would her Welsh, Alyawarre, Indonesian and Dutch forebears have answered this idiot? "Fuck you too."

It didn't register much of a hit with Neckbeard. The citizens of Disenfranchised nations usually spouted more standardized propaganda. God Nation then, since they did speak English. A long way from their home turf of America, but maybe they were a local variety.

The man left. Unlike the avatar, her fingertips were completely natural, but Neckbeard still hadn't come within her reach for a single moment.

Jones checked her phone again, like she had every five minutes since their capture. Nothing yet. Although it must still be day outside, a chill had started to seep into the air. She rubbed her upper arms to stimulate some warmth.

This was stupid. She needed a working phone. Or weapons. Or

hundreds of years while she gnawed through the plastic with her teeth. How to get a message out for help? First things first though. "Ambassador, please turn your back," she said.

"Why?" it asked.

"I need to relieve myself."

"Can I watch?" it asked.

"No you can't, which is why I asked you to turn away!"

"But I want to. It's interesting."

"This isn't National Geographic. You don't get to watch me as if I'm wildlife. Now turn away."

It turned away. "Something in your voice made my stomach feel unpleasant. Why?"

Jones peed.

It sighed. "The sound of water through air. Lovely."

Jones gritted her teeth and zipped back up.

She felt much more relaxed, even sure she knew where she was now. From the ancient toilet, this must be MuoviKier, one of the earliest recycling companies to tackle the continents of floating waste in the ocean. It had been closed down way before her time. The knowledge wouldn't help in any direct way, but she could picture herself on GoogleEarth now, a tiny dot circling the oceans.

She sat down to enjoy her dinner. The water was lukewarm and the sandwiches dry.

The ambassador crept up to her. "That smell. Should I eat?"

Jones chewed and frowned at the same time. "Drink only, I think. Avatars have special digestive systems. Probably best not to try."

"Can I watch, then?"

Sheesh. She turned away from the avatar's greedy gaze.

When she looked for somewhere to toss the empty sandwich pack, she got an idea. *Phone.* Phone with no connection right now. But if it managed to get outside the dead zone the terrorists had created, it would be full of clues. She whispered a brief report into it and sealed it as best she could in the packaging. She put it in the ancient toilet and flushed it away.

Darkness fell. She paced the cell to keep warm. It might loosen up her brain as well. How could they make contact? Like elephants, by stomping on the ground? They lacked the mass, they were on a raft, and elephants had been extinct for decades. She'd heard one of the African conglomerates had recreated them, but the odds against a stray herd swimming around in the Tasman Sea seemed high.

The ambassadorial package yielded data on Geneva conventions, Morse code and waterboarding. Not very useful. Just in case, she set the ambassador tapping out messages on the walls. The terrorists banged back and shouted at them to stop.

Walls.

She wasn't thinking right. Those were not her venue of escape.

The ceiling was out since it was a solid sheet of plastic, but the floor consisted of roughly melted together plastic flotsam. The old processing plants had just raked in garbage and melted it into hollow raft modules to put their plants on. These raft modules couldn't be too big or they'd break on the waves. Jones had grown up on one.

Maybe that's why she'd only gotten the idea of going through the floor now. Damaging the raft? Letting in the sea? Brine filled her mouth at the memory. The icy water had clamped around her midriff and prevented breath. She'd seen nothing but towering waves, just one second after falling off the raft. She had no memory of her rescue and never liked the deep sea after that.

But this was the Tasman Sea, where the waters were warm and she would probably live for a day before dying of sunstroke and dehydration. Much better odds. But still. Wasn't it better to die honorably at the hands of Neckbeard and associates than brave the sea at night?

She crawled around the floor, groping for a weak spot. *No go.*

"What are you doing?" came the inevitable question from the avatar.

"Shh. Looking for weak spots in the flooring," she whispered. "Come help me. Maybe we can get out through the sea. Can you swim? Your kind does live in the sea, right?"

The avatar's forehead muscles contracted asymmetrically. Jones didn't know what emotion that signified.

"Is it like walking? Then the body should be able to do it. Otherwise, what you call seas on my home world do not consist of fluid or gravity or any conditions on what you call sea."

Unfailingly unhelpful, every time. But at least it tried. In a funny way it was keeping her spirits up.

Her fingers found a rotten patch of plastic. She pulled and poked at it. It didn't yield much result. She got up to pee again.

Oh, oh! She was either very dumb or her subconscious was trying to keep her out of the sea by giving her selective stupidity. She knew how they could get out. Waiting until just before dawn would work best.

"When are we leaving?" the avatar said, too loud.

"Shush. I have a plan."

She lay down with her back to the avatar and told her inner clock when to wake her. She stuck her hands in her armpits and shivered.

"Ambassador Earth," the alien said in a grating whisper. "I'm in some discomfort."

Sheesh. She wasn't going to grace that with an answer.

"Ambassador, please help. The body is twitching. What does it signify?"

Jones rolled over and touched the avatar's face. It was icy.

"Are you cold?" she asked.

"Ah!" it said. "I get it. The body tries to warm up by performing minute muscle contractions. Is there a less uncomfortable way to deal with it?"

Jones sighed. "Come over here. We'll share bodily warmth."

The avatar gasped.

"And no more than that. This is not a porn scenario, got that?"

Jones lay back down and cuddled up against the avatar's back.

"This is surprisingly comfortable. I had no idea body warmth would produce so many endorphins. My home shoal makes me feel safe and known, but I see humans only need one person for the same effect."

"Good to know. Where's your shoal now?"

"At home, safe. Envying me for this opportunity, no doubt. We all trained as human ambassadors."

"I'm an only child," Jones said, to her own surprise.

The alien shifted. "We're having a good time, aren't we?"

At least it was upbeat.

And it was right. She, too, was a mammal with a body that produced endorphins. Belly against warm back made her feel safe and connected, even without the full shoal of civilized society around her.

∞

At the requested time, Jones' inner alarm clock beeped. Time to go. What a pity they hadn't been rescued yet. She'd just have to rescue herself. She nudged the avatar with her elbow. Kind of surprising it had the capability for sleep.

"You awake?"

The avatar rose up fluidly. Jones envied it while she straightened out kinks in her spine and knees. She was only in her early thirties, why did one night of sleeping rough break her up like this? She should use her government earnings to upgrade her self-care nano package.

They were going to escape down the toilet. Not very nice, but the only way to get out. Her stomach roiled at the thought of deep scary water, but she ignored it.

The avatar bent over, grasped the ancient toilet bowl and pulled. Nothing happened.

"Harder," Jones said.

The avatar pulled again. "I'm getting system overload warnings," it said.

"Ignore them. They won't affect the brain," Jones said. Not that she was sure about that, but the government would foot the damage bill.

The toilet bowl tore loose from the brittle, degraded floor with a screech.

The sheer thought of having to get down into the plastic-plague-infested ocean made her dizzy. Not now. She couldn't get a PP anxiety attack now.

"Hold my hand," she said to the avatar. "Squeeze it. Now. Say, het komt wel goed schatje."

"What?" The avatar grasped her hand. "What's that noise?"

"It's Dutch. It's what my grandpa used to say to me when he was ill. Say it. It calms me down. I need calming down."

"I didn't realize humans were so fragile," the avatar said. "It come twell ghoot schatya. And also, I never had so much fun on a mission before."

What do you know. The Amb was having the time of its life.

Jones took three deep breaths and jumped.

The world burst open in a flash of light. A torrent of cold water smacked her back against something solid. All her senses jumbled, roiling water, swimming shapes, booming. Were her eyes open? Shit, she needed to get out, she needed air.

Where was the avatar? Someone clamped something on her face. She kicked and wriggled. She couldn't breathe! As she wrestled to get the thing off her face, someone grabbed her roughly around the waist and tugged her away. The thing on her face was a breathing mask, and a suited diver was tugging her backwards, away from the floating wreckage around them. She found the avatar, eyes wide open, as usual enjoying every moment of its strange human adventure. She wished she could say the same for herself.

The diver propelled her upwards. Another pair of strong, efficient hands dragged her into an inflatable. A medical patch was slapped onto her arm. They were safe.

"I'm fine, I'm fine," she gasped, heart still racing in spite of being safe, and for some reason annoyed at having been rescued. A saner, calmer part of her brain informed her she probably would have drowned or been discovered by the kidnappers if they hadn't dragged her away. Then she caught sight of her bare flesh, on her arms, in the gap of her shirt, speckled with minute plastic particles.

She screamed. "Get it off me, get if off me!"

A cold hand grasped hers. The avatar, sans medical patch. "It come choot chatya."

"No, no, it's the plastic plague, get it off, get it off!"

The medical deputy looked into her eyes. "Keep breathing. That's what the patch is for, it's already locating and destroying any PP bacteria that might be contaminating these waters. You'll be fine."

Maybe the reassuring words did their work, or the patch was shooting her up with some chill juice, because at once Jones felt calmer. She watched with growing detachment as the avatar was checked out by a mechanic, the rescue dinghy racing towards a larger ship. It looked like a battleship out of ancient movies. *How quaint.*

"Hey, Amb," she said, her own voice coming as from a great distance. "You better upload now."

"If you're talking to the avatar," another voice said, "he's on standby. Your buddy's gone."

"He's not my buddy!" Jones protested, but her eyes prickled and her throat ached. Asshole ambassador, for just taking off. She'd gotten used to its stupid curiosity and question-rich unhelpfulness. *Stupid squid.*

When she started to feel better, she sat up, trying to become herself again so she could transfer to the battleship on her own steam.

"How did you guys find us?" she asked.

Rescue guy one grinned at her. "Your phone! Excellent idea. We had our eye on this old plant already, and then it popped out of the loo. Saved us a lot of trouble and hostage negotiation."

Jones felt herself swell with pride. Plague, usually she wasn't this sappy. Not bad, for a first time ambassador.

"So how did you guys get picked for this job?" she asked idly. "Must be some download package."

"Nah," rescue guy two said, the one with the cute freckles. Rescue chick, from the voice. "We train for this for years and years. It's a vocation, not just a temp job."

Jones sat up straighter. She'd never heard of people having strong vocations outside of the arts, medicine or nature preservation. "Never knew you lot existed. You get a lot of work?"

Freckles turned a serious face to her. "Babe, we may live in paradise, but not everyone out there thinks we should. We get called out more often than you'd like."

Jones mulled this over. "So the rim states aren't doing too good a job at keeping the God Nations inside?"

Freckles shook her head. "Not just American God Nations. There's pockets of them everywhere."

Jones had sorta kinda known this, but had blithely assumed everyone had the right to choose their own brand of misery.

"Thing is, if they just kept their old hatreds to themselves, nobody would care. But they really like to bring the suffering to others. Their mission in life. Hence, us T cells dedicating our lives to keeping them out," Freckles said.

As Jones climbed up the ladder to the for-real battleship on shakier legs than she wanted to admit, she couldn't shake Freckles' serious face and more serious words. The thing was, the kidnappers hadn't seemed too different from the kinds of guys she'd grown up with on the Northern Gyre. Hard working, not too bright maybe, fixed in their patterns. What if you got fixed in the wrong pattern? Those fishermen would have been hell on outsiders, and once she'd thought that was normal. Maybe they just didn't have the desire to change their lives. But she'd gotten out.

She'd been welcomed into Australia, given an education, a home, an income, the vote. She hadn't found her vocation yet, but she dutifully performed whatever community service was asked of her. But not a millimeter more. Maybe rescue guy had it right. Maybe it was time she started giving back for living in paradise.

The ancient warship traveled home. The debriefing, by more freshly deputized government officials than she'd ever seen in one place before, went by in a daze, as if she was a few inches to the side of the whole process.

Home felt just as strange and cottony. Jones closed her eyes and felt her way around the room, seeking sounds and textures to make herself feel real. Her eyes were still frazzled with afterimages of bright morning sunlight, the tanned faces and white smiles of the rescue guys joking around her, the empty eyes of the rental avatar.

Food. She ate a bit of everything she had in her pantry and refrigerator. She dialed up some ridiculously expensive nonlocal specialties but was unable to finish them. Showering and putting on clean clothes didn't help either.

She stomped her feet. It hurt, but the pain didn't feel real. As if the actual Jones was still huddled in the recycled plastic holding cell, feeling cold and miserable instead of warm and clean and safe.

Someone knocked on her door. With a sigh she went to get it.

"Yeah?"

"It's me, ambassador," an unknown female voice said. "I thought I'd rent a female this time, so you wouldn't feel so awkward about the male body. We have negotiations to complete."

Jones opened the door a crack. On her porch stood another non-descript rental avatar. "Ambassador? Is that you?"

The world returned with a thud. She flung her arms around the rental and hugged her. "I'm so glad to see you! You just up and went without saying good-bye."

The avatar stared at her. She could see the alien personality behind the eyes, turning her words over in its suckers or whatever metaphor it used. "Can I come in or would you prefer to negotiate in a public space?"

It thought they were on the clock again? She'd been thinking sick leave for at least a month.

"I informed your government I will not accept any other negotiator. Dealing with you is most entertaining."

She opened her messages. Her many, many urgently blinking messages. She opened the last one. The terms were insanely generous. Exchange of hours worked for community labor, for a start.

She didn't really care. Community service wasn't that bad. The handsome face of Rescue Guy floated before her mind's eye. *Time to give back.* As thanks for effectively rescuing her from a life of ignorance and drudgery. Even Paradise needs maintenance.

Okay, she was going in.

"I have one condition," she said. "What do you say we start out the negotiations somewhere we can get very, very drunk?"

It goggled. "Alcohol? Inebriation? Lead on!"

Jones stepped out. "Take a left, Amb."

It felt like the beginning of a beautiful, yet professional, relationship.

About the Author
Bo Balder

Bo is the first Dutch author to have published a story in the famous F&SF (*Fantasy & Science Fiction* magazine), sept/oct 2015. Her other short fiction has appeared in *Crossed Genres* and quite a few anthologies. Her science fiction novel, *The Wan*, will be published in January 2016 by Pink Narcissus Press.

She attended Viable Paradise and is a member of Codex Writers Group.

Bo lives and works close to Amsterdam, Europe. When she isn't writing, you can find her madly designing knitwear, painting, and reading everything from Kate Elliott to Iain M. Banks or Jared Diamond.

Author Website: http://www.boukjebalder.nl/

Light-Years from Now
by E. E. King

It was just another evening at the station. I'd spent almost every night of the past two years, the final years of my master's program, here, monitoring signals. It seemed much longer. It was mind numbing work. Listening for anomalies in the persistent, unchanging patterns of beeps and bings. Watching for variance in wave arrays or differentials in particle configurations.

People suppose that looking for extraterrestrials is exciting, but it's not. It's like watching rocks grow. Slowly. Ours is a study of time. Generations of scientists, monitoring thousands of screens, encircling trillions of planets in billions of galaxies—each hoping for an irregularity. Far greater minds than mine have spent their lives searching, casting nets out into the vastness of space. Hoping to catch an alien, all finding nothing and no one.

I was alone in the lab. How many astrobiologists does it take to watch the great void? I stared at the screen, mind blank, eating a Super Sub I'd had the foresight to grab before my shift. It was fat and messy, stuffed with four kinds of cheese, six meats, jalapeños, and generously coated with mustard, mayo and a "secret sauce" that leaked from the corners of the slightly sodden roll onto my fingers. I shouldn't have been eating in front of the monitor. But I had spread out a vast protective covering of napkins, and unless something happened, which hadn't in the fifty years the station had been operating, there'd be no need to touch the panels.

I'd just taken a bite, when I sensed something. It might have been a shadow falling across my screen, or a movement of light over glass, but for whatever reason I turned.

A guy stood behind me. In the dimness, it seemed as though he flickered slightly, almost as if his clothes were made of starlight. It must have been the reflection from the monitors. Glass, darkness, light and boredom can make you see things. He had the elusive hesitancy of a wild creature and seemed a bit scared. I thought he might be Indian, the kind from India, not Native American. His eyes were large and brown, his skin a perfect golden coffee color, and his lips were full and generous. He was lean, muscular and looked to be about my age. He was without question the most beautiful human I'd ever seen.

I wondered if he was gay. I wondered if he was single.

He must be another grad student whose monitoring time intersected with mine. Maybe he was working on some special project I wasn't privy to. Or possibly he was an exchange student, we get them sometimes. Scholars from all over this world come here in hopes of connecting with other worlds. There was no other reason to be in the lab, nothing to steal, only monitors, and billions and billions of stars scattered over darkness.

"I'm Druv," he said. His voice was rich and deep, a spoken melody. Man, I was falling for this guy fast as the speed of light through a vacuum, which most people don't realize is faster than the speed of light though water or glass, but it is.

Attempting to seem nonchalant, I inhaled the strips of baloney and cheese dangling from my mouth and choked. "Secret sauce" shot up and out my nose and spurted from the corners of my lips, dribbling onto my shirt.

"Tom," I said. I wiped my hand on one of the myriad napkins and extended it to Druv. He eyed it as though it might be contagious and didn't take it. I didn't blame him.

I wished I hadn't grabbed a Super Sub before my shift. I saw myself through his eyes, tall, blond, and drooling. My skin was clear,

but my cheeks were slightly pocked, marked by the ravages of past out-
breaks. I hoped the light was too dim for him to see my craters. Besides
his perfection of color, Druv's skin was luminous, flawless, it glowed
with an inner light. His eyes were so wide and dark they seemed to
contain hidden depths and fathomless distance. They spoke of faraway
places, hidden desires and exotic lands. Mine were the faded, flat blue
of a smoggy city sky. I was as exotic as an Idaho potato.

"Do you want some sandwich?" I sputtered, having managed to
subdue my mouthful of meat, cheese and secrets. I was still plenty
hungry, but I was not going to eat around this perfect man, not unless
he ate with me, maybe not even then. He looked like the kind who
traveled with linen napkins, sterling silver and probably a retinue of
servants well-schooled in the arcane niceties of carving up a sub.

Druv shook his head. I watched, slightly mesmerized by his elegance
of movement. His bones were delicate. He stood erect and regal, like a
prince from some glamorous realm. I straightened my shoulders. It was
harder than I thought it would be, requiring continual effort and concen-
tration. I was so used to slumping.

"I'm not hungry," he said. "But thanks." His English was perfect,
almost too perfect, as though it were not his native tongue. It had a
depth and a precision, as well as the musical cadence which comes from
thought rather than instinct.

"Have a seat," I said, trying to enunciate. I motioned at the chair
next to me, then noticed it was full of napkins, my jacket, notebook and
the remainder of my sub.

"I can clear this off," I said, hastily wrapping up the sandwich and
shoving it back in its bag. "Or you could sit here," I said gesturing to
the place on my left.

The center was scythe shaped. The floor cushioned by a lurid carpet
that had been laid down in the late fifties. It pictured the solar system

and resembled a faded, footsore velvet painting, something one might find at a rummage sale or flea market. A crescent swath of windows and screens lined the walls, ceaselessly measuring, recording and calibrating the output of the universe. It sounds more exciting than it was, since the universe was usually silent, or at least not sentient. In my two years of research, Druv was the most exciting sighting I'd encountered.

Before that, my most thrilling discovery was that my parents and my friends had accepted my gayness. I think I'd always known I was gay. At least, I'd always known I was attracted to men, even before I knew what *gay* was. In high school, I'd spent a painful few years crippled by dread. I feared that by declaring who I was, I would lose the affection of those who loved me for who I wasn't. But it turned out that everyone already knew. I was the only one who'd thought it a secret.

I'd imagined that coming out would open the universe. I'd imagined that discovering true love would be easy, but it turned out to be no easier to locate a male soulmate than a female one. In a way, it was a lot like getting a job at the station. It had been difficult. There'd been a lot of competition. When I got my acceptance, I pictured the universe unfurling before me in an ascending staircase of stars. The first few nights, weeks, and even months of monitoring the night sky were filled with anticipation. I might at any moment discover a message from a distant world. But after a time, reality settled in. I was no more likely to retrieve an extraterrestrial missive than I was to find a young Omar Sharif waiting at home for me in bed.

Druv smiled nervously. I wondered if I'd been staring. "What are you studying?" he asked.

"Nothing and everything," I said. "I'm monitoring microwave radio outputs in hopes of discovering intelligent life in the universe... Is this your first time?" I asked. Then I blushed. *What a stupid question!* But either he didn't notice the double entendre, or he was polite and suave enough to ignore it. He nodded.

"Ah. Then you won't know what I mean yet," I said. "Unless you're involved with a specific project with a verifiable outcome, it's incredibly tedious."

I wondered if Druv was an exchange student. The center had a lot of them. I wondered what his project was; it was unusual for a professor to send someone up without an escort on their initial visit. But whoever had knew I'd be here.

"Do you have a specific project?" I asked.

"No," he said. "Not really. I am just supposed to make contact with an alien species and establish some idea of their technological capabilities and society."

I laughed. "Is that all?" I said.

He grinned shyly.

"Who's your prof?" I asked. "I'm under Dingleberry."

"Yes, me too," he said. I raised my eyebrow. I thought I knew all of Dingleberry's students.

"What year are you in?" I asked.

"This is my first," he said. "I just started."

"Where are you from?"

"Not from around here."

"A man of mystery, eh?"

"Mysteries are what makes life worth living," he said, sliding into the seat next to mine. He moved as smoothly as mist. It almost seemed as though his body floated into the chair, fitting molecule into molecule.

"So what do you do here?" he asked. "And how long have you done it?"

I thought of making a joke about *doing it*, but it seemed inappropriate. That and I couldn't think of anything very clever. I wondered if Druv was hinting that he was gay. I imagined how humiliating it would be if I made a move and he wasn't.

"It's been two years," I said, "in this lab I mean. It's my fifth year at the university, but I'm here almost all the time."

"Every night?" he asked.

"Every night except Wednesday," I said.

"Have you ever wondered why it's not Wednesnight?" he asked. "Doesn't Wednesday *night* strike you as contradictory?"

It hadn't. But now that he mentioned it…

"The saying 'night owl' has always bothered me," I said. "I mean there aren't any day owls, it's just repetitive. 'Night bird' would make a lot more sense."

Druv gave a shy half smile and shrugged. It seemed to imply that we were united in our amused disdain for the absurdities inherent in language and culture. I smiled back, hoping I wasn't reading too much into a smile.

"Could you give me a tour of the facilities?" he asked.

"Of course," I said.

I was surprised Dingleberry hadn't told me Druv was coming. He was usually annoyingly meticulous about everything. But then I remembered he was on leave. He had departed unexpectedly yesterday. His mother or maybe his sister—some close female relative—had fallen ill and her condition was critical. Maybe he had been in too much of a hurry and too flustered to be his usual, particular self, or perhaps he hadn't even been aware that Druv had arrived. It wouldn't be like him to leave a newcomer alone without any instructions. Administration should have assigned Druv to a different professor, someone who was here. I remembered how overwhelming and complex the place had seemed the first time I'd seen it. And I wasn't an exchange student from another country. It was a rough intro to the center.

Still, I had given tours before. In the beginning, I resented visitors, begrudging any time away from the screen and the stars, thinking I might catch that longed for signal from another world at any moment.

But after nine months, I started enjoying any breaks in the monotony. Too many men and women had spent their lives searching for life out there and died without discovering any—out there or down here. I didn't want to be one.

"Follow me," I said, attempting to leap up and wave him forward with a bow. My hip caught the side of the chair and I stumbled slightly. I grabbed at it, knocking my sandwich out of its bag. It tumbled onto the floor, spreading a milky-way of mayo and jalapeños onto the carpet.

Druv snickered. "Sorry," he said, covering his mouth with his hand. Despite my embarrassment, I couldn't help noticing how his skin glistened and that his nails shone slightly like the polished interior of an open seashell.

He inhaled, trying to stifle his laughter, snorted loudly and completely lost it, howling with the uninhibited hilarity that is supposed to be good for your soul.

It might have been good for his, but it was mortifying for mine. I crouched beside the mess, trying to pick up the slimy bread that dissolved when touched, oozing into moist white molehills of mush, and struggling to mop up the "secret sauce" that seeped into the carpet at the speed of light in a vacuum. Bits of the sodden bread kept slipping out of the bag like doughy lemmings.

Druv snorted again and I began to laugh. It was contagious, that kind of mirth—even if it was at my expense. We shrieked until we were unable to breath. Finally our yowling slowed to a whimper. Druv slid down beside me, watching me sweep the remains of dinner into the bag. We'd calmed down, sniffing and hiccuping, but every now and then one of us would gasp, or grunt, and we'd begin cackling all over again.

"Why do sandwiches always land face down?" I asked. "It must be one of the unrecorded laws of aerodynamics."

"It is like the buttered cat problem," Druv gasped. "If a cat always lands on its feet, but bread always lands butter side down, what happens when you strap a piece of buttered bread to the back of a cat?"

"Or an open-faced Super Sub," I said.

"I think it's been proved that the buttered cat must hover just above ground level rotating," he said.

"You may have discovered the secret to levitation." I said. "But you can't get a Nobel just yet. First you have to be able to define and control the force. The energy must come from the feet themselves, because cats without feet have a near zero success rate of landing on them. We will call this cat foot force."

Druv giggled.

"Some research has been conducted on the possibility of using cat feet without cats," I continued, cheered on by Druv's grinning face, "but these attempts did not get off the ground for a number of reasons. First, there was no cat to tie the bread to. Also it's been discovered that when not attached to a cat, the feet lose their cat foot force."

"I have heard that attempts have been made to breed cats with feet but no legs," Druv said.

"Ah, the famed flat cat trials of two thousand and five," I said.

"So, you have studied them too?" Druv asked.

"But of course," I said. "Another insurmountable problem is that if the cat manages to lick the butter off the bread they lose their levitation. And cats like butter. I know. I have a calico and when it needs to take pills, I coat them in butter.

"Once the cat ingests the butter it tumbles to the ground, resulting in a nasty mess kind of like this," I said, motioning to the soggy remains of my sub.

I rose from the floor and held a hand out to Druv, emboldened by our obvious connection, but he leapt to his feet and stood beside me, faster and more gracefully than a buttered cat.

"I'm ready for my tour now Mr. DeMille," he said, batting his eyelashes, then curling his long, beautiful fingers into a chilling imitation of Gloria Swanson's talons. That must mean he was gay right? Gay and flirting with me? But what if I was wrong? I didn't want to ruin this perfect beginning. Druv was beautiful, funny, and he really seemed to like me.

"What kind of movies do you like?" I asked, immediately regretting it. What a lame question. But Druv smiled. It was like seeing the Milky Way in a dark sky.

"I like oldies… movies and TV," he said. "The black and whites… *The Twilight Zone*, *Star Trek*, and vampire movies… *Nosferatu*, *Dracula*."

"What about *Twilight*?" I asked. Druv looked blank.

"Or *The Walking Dead*?" I asked. He still looked mystified.

"It's a zombie series," I said.

"I've never been partial to zombies," he said.

"Why not?" I asked.

"Mindless groups are a bore," he said. "And zombies always come in mindless groups."

"I'd never join a group that would have me as a member," I said. I thought about making a pun about *members*, but I couldn't think of anything that wasn't juvenile or crude or both.

"What about werewolves?" I asked.

"Oh they're fine," he said. "The solitary are sexy, and werewolves are usually loners. But they're not as hot as vampires. I love that pale, pale skin." He slowly lowered his eyes. His lashes were black and about a meter long. He was definitely flirting, right? He must be. With a look like that… and my skin was as pale as buried asparagus. If he liked pale…

"Everyone knows vampires have a tremendous sense of style," he continued. "And werewolves usually change from handsome, vest-coated professors into wolves, and wolves are undeniably sexy.

But zombies stumble around in unthinking herds, blue-faced, bleeding, drooling and never say anything of interest."

"Right," I said. "You could never discuss the levitation problems inherent in buttered cat feet or day owls with a zombie."

"Never," he agreed, laughing.

We wandered around the center. I showed him the different monitors and the variety of waves we charted. A night had never passed so quickly and enjoyably.

When I got home there was a message from Dingleberry. His aunt was in critical care and he wasn't sure when he'd be back. He'd left a long list of reports he wanted me to complete, but not a word about Druv.

Druv appeared the next night though, at just about the same time.

We looked at the screens and the stars, and chatted about inconsequential matters, all the tiny details that form a life. I taught him how to fill out the reports, which were boring, and we talked and laughed, which was not.

Time passed, as time does, days becoming weeks, and weeks becoming months. Dingleberry had buried his aunt and taken some leave. As he hadn't had a vacation in over ten years, time was no problem. His aunt was the last of his family. His parents had died long ago and he had never married. I was only surprised that his aunt had lived so long. Dingleberry was well into his sixties, at least a decade older than my parents.

Each night, Druv and I met in the lab and monitored the distant pinpoint lights in the sky. I still didn't know where he was from. He didn't seem to want to talk about it. Maybe he was gay and his parents hadn't been as accepting as mine. Maybe he was from a country less tolerant. I didn't want to press him—well actually I did want to press him, but I was afraid to ruin this. I hoped it was love, I knew it was for me. But even if all he felt for me was friendship, even if he was straight,

I wanted to keep him close, as a companion, as a friend.

"I wonder if TV or radio signals have already been picked up somewhere in space," I said.

"Aliens would get a very peculiar idea of life on Earth if they did," Druv said. "But, yes, radio or television signals could theoretically pierce the atmosphere and travel through space at the speed of light. So, hypothetically, extraterrestrials as nearby as fifty light-years away could be enjoying *I Love Lucy* and *Star Trek* reruns as we speak."

"I figure that our earliest broadcasts are washing over about one new star system each day," I said. "So the potential audience is growing. That should really mess up the Nielsen Ratings."

Druv laughed but looked confused.

"Nielsen?" he asked.

"Yeah," I said. "You know, the way they determine which shows are popular? It's really a dumb, arcane system, but Hollywood is pretty hidebound in spite of their flash."

"How does it work?" he asked.

"Wow," I said, "For someone so up on buttered cats, I'm surprised you don't know about Nielsen."

"I know science not show biz," he replied. But he looked embarrassed. It seemed an odd hole, but unimportant. Maybe in India, or wherever he was from, they didn't have Nielsen ratings. Maybe they only got old broadcasts and that was why he seemed so up-to-date on the out-of-date. I imagined him as a beautiful, serious boy, watching *The Twilight Zone* in some faraway land.

"It's not as logical as cat foot force," I said. "Nielsen installs meters on a few thousand sets and monitors what they watch."

"Only a few thousand?" he asked.

"Yeah," I said. "It's supposed to be a representative sample. The meters track when TV sets are on and what channels they're tuned to.

When they started, I think they had people keep journals, but it's all done electronically now."

"So the waves sent out to distant stars are determined by computers," he said.

"I hadn't really thought of it like that," I said. "But yeah." I looked at his large doe eyes and rose-petal lips. "NASA sent a broadcast of Beatles music towards Polaris," I said, wanting to kiss him, "using a sixty-four meter antenna and twenty kilowatts of power."

"Humm," he considered. "Polaris is only four hundred and thirty light-years away. Still, I think that would require the aliens to have an antenna seven miles across to even get the signal. To receive it as music, they'd need a five-hundred-mile-wide antenna."

"Across the universe," I said. "It'll be a hard day's night." I leaned toward his soft full lips.

"Carl Sagan wondered what would happen if the first broadcast aliens picked up was Hitler's opening speech at the Berlin Summer Olympics," he said. I pulled back. Somehow this didn't seem the right time for a first kiss.

Things continued as things will. We monitored the universe and each other. I learned that he liked animals but had never had a dog or cat. Something about housing regulations. I regaled him with the antics of Schrödinger, my sly, fat calico.

He learned that I liked strawberries and chocolate. And I learned he'd never had them together. So on the night before New Year's Eve, I brought champagne, strawberries and chocolate to the center. I would have brought a ring if I could have afforded it and thought he would accept. We could get married anywhere now, at least anywhere in the States, and if Druv was from some back-assed, prejudiced place, well it didn't matter anymore. Despite the fact that we'd never even kissed, he knew me better than anyone ever had or would. I was pretty sure he loved me and completely certain that I loved him.

Druv was there before me for a change, standing by the monitors. As I walked toward him, arms full of treats, he shimmered, like heat rising off hot pavement and, right before my eyes, disappeared. I put down my things and stumbled toward the place where he had been. I wondered if I was going mad. A recorded memo lay on the chair where he had sat beside me for so many nights, watching the stars, watching the night sky.

When I turned it on and heard his voice, it was as though he was still with me.

"Tom," his voice said. "When I told you I was not from around here, I meant it. I am like you, an explorer, hoping to make first contact. My people developed a holographic beam so powerful it could be projected through space. Through light-years. It is more advanced than anything on Earth, so advanced that some actual particles of my being were intertwined with the particles of light being projected. So it was like I was actually here, next to you, talking to you, laughing with you. But I was not. I am not. In fact I am no more.

"When we sent the beam of light traveling into space, my particles were woven into it, not all of them, of course. The real me remained at home on a world far distant from yours.

"But enough particles of my consciousness were intertwined with the particles of light so that I could interact with anyone I discovered. So that when we did hit Earth, I could learn more about this world that we have only known though broadcasts.

"We were able to alter my appearance, which is quite humanoid, to look completely human. It was only my skin I had to modify. My species has chromophores in our skin and we are able to change our color at will. So much is lost without this ability. So many times you would have known what I felt if only I could have flashed you my iridescent love.

"The beam of light did not find anyone, not for thirty light-years. By the time it reached you I, the real I, the corporeal I, had already been dead for years, light-years.

"The only part of my being that has not been dead for years were those particles of my consciousness that had been interwoven with the beam. I traveled in a spaceship made of light. Now that the light has died so have I, because I died a long time ago, my love.

"I hoped to find alien life. I never thought I would find alien love, but I did.

"I love you Tom, now and forever. Druv."

And I loved him, though I'd never had the chance to tell him, my light from a distant star.

I stood there, all alone in the empty center and wondered if there even were divisions of gay or straight on his world. If the fear of being shunned that had kept me silent for so long was only part of my world, not his. For all I knew, for all I'd ever know, perhaps on his world they changed sex at will, like so many species of ocean fish do here, perhaps they were simultaneous hermaphrodites, or maybe they only had one sex... or... or... But I'd never know. I'd never even know if he knew why I'd never voiced my love. My dread of rejection had kept me from speaking and being known.

Long ago, men went to sea. And women waited for them, peering out into black waters, searching for a tiny speck of light on the horizon. Now I too wait, looking out into the vast blackness of space, searching for my love, my heart, thirty light-years gone.

About the Author
E. E. King

E. E. King is a performer, writer, biologist and painter. Ray Bradbury calls her stories "marvelously inventive, wildly funny and deeply thought provoking. I cannot recommend them highly enough."

Her books are: *Dirk Quigby's Guide to the Afterlife*, *Real Conversations with Imaginary Friends*, and *Another Happy Ending*.

She has won numerous awards and been published widely.

Author Website: http://www.elizabetheveking.com/

Felis Helianthus
by Daryna Yakusha

Good crystallization in this landfill, Eri thinks, as a clear brownish-yellow chunk of what is surely a vein of fossilized burgers ricochets off her mask. So far that's about all the area has going for it—good crystallization and it only takes a quarter tank of gas to get here. Eri doesn't have the gear or the permissions to get access to the older, more hazardous tunnels, but she'd pulled some kind of cactus out of this zone last month. Maybe she can get lucky again.

When that cactus sample had finished cooking in the *tube*, it had looked pretty much like the standard Type-DG7 catalog cactus, but then Dr. Saltikova had gone ape-shit over how the needles on this one forked and the heart was spongier or whatever. After the big global warming extinction, cacti—being hardy bastards—comprised about twenty percent of the current plant biomass, but she'd managed to grab an entirely new variety. Either way it had gotten her another research grant from the university.

Now she's back to wandering around the big shafts and making claustrophobic little side-tunnels wherever it seems promising. The last of the cactus money had bought a quiverful of bracer-columns that will theoretically save her from undignified suffocation under tons of crystallized Styrofoam. Even if they don't actually do shit, seeing their tracking lights in her peripheral vision is comforting.

Smell is what snaps her out of her head. She hits a small reinforced space in the densely-packed heterozygous strata of garbage, and a particular kind of sweetness manages to make its way past the breathing mask and settles slickly across her back teeth, the sweetness of old death. In front of her, the pocket has bones. Her pick gently shatters a layer of fossilized garbage bags and nestled among the shiny razor-sharp trash bag flakes is a spongy brown lump of decay. Turning up the mag on her visor she can see hairs, a hint of teeth.

She throws up another two bracers and starts digging around for her best specimen jars. Wet-collecting is usually best left to the fancy mooks, but it's a miracle to find something this preserved and not take a stab at it. Fauna samples are a bitch to grow too. She'll have to get all of it to have a good range of tissue types to feed the tube. She gets it all inside the smart jar and when it finishes scanning its own contents a readout pops up on her visor:

> Class: Mammalia
> Proposed Order: Carnivora (based on dental structure)
> Genus: unknown

"Damn, why did it have to be a warmie?" she says.

Eri will tell anyone about how she doesn't like the time it takes to grow warmies. Her older-model tube tends to chug on them, but it finished reconstructions with an authentic old *ping* that the site swore was taken from a twenty-first-century microwave. She hates the red pulsing mess that has to be cleaned out whenever her tube has to do a womb. How the shifting pinkish tints that end up splashed on the walls made her feel like she was living in one of those plotless murder movies from the twenty-second century. It's all true and it's not the real reason.

When she was five, her aunt had sprung for the cheapest warmie pet in the library database, a common *Rattus norvegicus* that had blinked and twitched its strangely whiskered nose at her and then spiritedly chewed up the wireless ports in her shoes. It had immediately displaced everything she'd ever gotten, even her mother's Day-Glo cockroaches from the year before.

The first couple of months had been wonderful. The rat made a perfect spotted curl in her cupped hands and Eri had named her Fran. They went everywhere together—she took her on walks in a clear plastic carry-purse and let her sleep in a nest of her least-favorite shirts inside her dresser drawer. She had rediscovered her house from two inches off the floor over and over again after being deliberately careless with the latch of the rolling-ball and then crawling around on her stomach finding Fran.

At the start of the monsoon season, Fran had stopped running out of the ball. Even when Eri had left the door open, Fran had sat curled at the bottom except for when the ever-present crack of lightning sent her twitching in a panic. Eri had almost worn a groove in her tablet screen running through the list of common pet ailments until, overhearing her increasingly angry back-and-forth with the interface, her mother had laughed and quoted, "Loneliness is the most common affliction."

This was where most children might have been tempted to borrow their parents' credit cards and buy their poor baby a friend. Eri decided that it would be better if she could make the house tube remember how to work the rat template and make another one. Maybe with some alterations. The boy she'd had a crush on had left for the summer. His family was rich enough to fly to a place where it didn't rain all day. As Eri wrestled with the chromosome hack, she thought grimly that at least one of them deserved a friend from another gender.

Once she'd accelerated Frank to the proper age and put him down in the playpen, Fran had perked right up. This was somewhat spoiled by the fact that the rat expressed her gratitude by running away the first chance she got, playmate in tow. Given the short gestation period of the *Rattus norvegicus* and Eri's own slight estrangement from the old natural order of things—having failed to connect the dots of her procreation lecture and the photo of her mother, skinny and smiling over Eri's incubator—what followed was a complete surprise.

Four months later the neighborhood had been locked down, declared a county biohazard, and fumigated. A hard-eyed old man with a red GSD badge had knocked on their door and flashed a tablet with Public Cleanup Impressment orders for Junior Citizen Eri Matani.

That afternoon is still one of her clearest memories, crunching across crystallized lawns in her green and white school haz-suit, wandering through empty houses and stacking brittle brown bodies into her rolling cooler.

Another memory is sitting on the stairs listening to her parents fight about what a Public Safety Demerit meant for her future career, while she idly wondered if Mr. Red Badge was also on call to poison, pick up, and fumigate defective, troublemaking girls.

The lesson had been imparted. For her next birthday Eri had asked for a plant.

∞

Extraction takes a while. By the end she's tired, her neck hurts and her hands are cramped into claws. *This one had better cook well or I'll be eating discount MREs again.*

Genetic salvage is office-less work with a gambler's tempting chance of easy money and flexible hours. The only real prerequisites are an infinite love of heterogenous piles, a dead nose, and the endless squint of a magpie. "Gambler" being the operative word. Whatever's in that jar is either payday or better luck next time. She pops it in her HV-8, hums to herself as the hovercar boots up and the cabin tilts six degrees left—one of the lift engines is out of synch again—and flies home.

Her house is a fragmented glow on the horizon. Gel walls had been popular in her parents' generation because of the way they started energy conversion from the day's photosynthesis at twilight. Back when she had been a kid the street had turned into a kind of fairy Stonehenge circle of glowing houses after dark. Now there's just the one, flickering like a forgotten candle. Having a biohazard outbreak on the neigh-borhood history hadn't exactly helped property values. Better suburbs had opened up residence applications, the government had offered a tax credit, and people had trickled away street by street. A while back some scrappy up-and-coming realtor company had put up for sale signs in some of the yards. They'd hedged their bets and used the thinnest, cheapest data-plexi. Nine months later, without a single open house, when they had cracked and started to fizzle loudly at night, Eri had gone around smashing them in with a bat.

Her house was already the oldest on the block. She'd blown the bulk of the cactus money on a new window and she'd had to get twice as much industrial grade softener just to get the stubborn gel in the wall to make a reinforceable circle to install it in. It had been even tougher to find vintage solar glass, but she couldn't stand the ads the companies put scrolling around on their plexi. The view wasn't so bad that she wanted to block it out; the neighborhood lawns were wild and overgrown now but pretty that way, a way they'd never been allowed to be before.

After installing the window, she'd felt content for a little bit, the way you do when you finish a project or get something you wanted and ride the little high of satisfaction until the next thing you wanted came along. This time, the high lasted until she saw the Sunflower in the latest issue of *Green Echo* and absolutely knew that she had to have one. They hadn't even needed to fancy up the ad. Someone had found a genius black-and-white GIF of a whole field of the things and just thrown on a nice overlay and lo, Eri's future budget surplus was a goner. She'd taken the ad image and zoomed and sharpened, then thrown it on her non-data-stream wall as a wallpaper for inspiration until she could afford the tube code for the real thing.

The plants had originally been green, black and yellow in some combination, but the library's one free picture that Eri had used as a coloring reference for the GIF was criminally low-res, so no matter what she did they never quite looked alive.

Now she staggers inside, drops her gear bag, and begins the careful process of hooking the specimen jar up to her tube. On the wall, the flowers of the wallpaper GIF sway gently back and forth on an infinite loop. When she's done, Eri slowly straightens up and runs a finger along a slightly pixelated petal. *Maybe this one'll pay off. Maybe soon I'll see you for real.*

An hour later, Eri pads out of the shower, the floor-gel squishing greedily as it drinks the water from her toes. Filtering had been quick; under the spray, she had heard the tube let out an excited *trill* as cleaning finished and the recipe began cooking. She takes the gun out of the wall safe, sets it charging on the nightstand just in case whatever it is comes out venomous and biting. The scan had said *Carnivora* after all. With practiced movements, she assembles the small enclosed pen with its self-refreshing water fountain. Then she drags the rest of the post-incubation stuff out of the hall closet: heavy-duty gloves, self-scooping poopbox, common food samples for diet differentiation.

There's no escaping the red tint that the growth in a working tube gives to the room, even under the comforter, so by midnight she gives up and flops on top of the blankets, watching the glowing cockroaches scurry around their ceiling corridors. They're not the same ones her mother got so the nostalgia-factor is limited, but laying back and unfocusing her eyes to the point where their slow motion turns into a lazy light show usually sends her to sleep. From the wall, the grainy, swaying sunflowers watch her snore.

In the morning, the tube is bubbling and pinging. She turns a random channel on the data-wall to drown it out. The tube's readout says T-minus seventeen hours. The longest it's ever taken before is ten. Outside, wafts of mist slither low to the ground. She tells herself she's feeling rich enough to eat out for lunch. *True, true*, the current meal-card balance is in the moodkiller zone, but Oaxacan is her comfort food and she's already unsettled by all the abnormalities in this recipe.

Anyway, it's a reason to brush her hair. On a whim she waves a colorwand over it and turns her bangs orange and her tips green. Amadi's on shift, but he's stuck in the kitchen, and she feels a little silly about her peacocking. Eri is short, built square-ish, with thick-but-crinkly black hair that showed how generations back a couple of poor Samoans had fallen into her mostly-Japanese gene pool. Amadi is tall, Nigerian, built like a ballet dancer, and probably wants a girl with a steadier job.

At T-minus ten hours, she goes back to the shaft at the landfill and finds jack: a few brittle, plastic-wrapped black stalks that might be something but are probably just more roses. Roses are so damn common that she has seven kinds out back. It feels a little pessimistic now to dutifully stick a third-rate haul in the fridge—like acknowledging that whatever's in the tube might not pan out.

T-minus three hours is the procrastination phase: doing just about anything else, not thinking about the money, not thinking about the outcome where it's not viable and she has hours of thankless cleaning to look forward to and the house smells like blood for a week.

At T-minus four minutes, the tube starts making harsh *piiii... piiii...* noises. It's almost done. Zero hour, showtime, except the artificial placenta is not detaching correctly. Entering the password for manual release takes her two tries with the goddamn siren getting louder and the thick gloves of her birthing kit turning her fingers into unwieldy baguettes.

Everything goes wrong. A cluster of veins has grown into the hinge and jammed the door. She crowbars open the manual hatch, warm fluid splashing and steaming over the bottom of her apron, and pops the thin viability meter into the red mess. The line is thready but constant. A curled shape, barely the size of a packet of melon bread, thrashes weakly on the scanner. Eri hesitates for just a moment. *Plants are so much easier.*

But it's small. It's small and it needs her. She swallows the sudden gulp of bile that was a perfectly good donut an hour ago and slips the scalpel claw over her index finger. She makes an incision, carefully but quickly. It's getting weaker.

"Shit!"

Tugging off her glove and upending half a glass of sanitizer over her bare hand, she reaches into the flayed-open womb. Cupping the wriggling thing in her palm, she draws it out towards the light. Her toes are wet—the floor gel won't drink amniotic fluid.

All that effort and the result looks like a square-headed, deformed rat. Under the protective gear, Eri's covered with a clammy sweat. Relief is the emotion of the hour, like she's taken a hard test and the grades will be posted much, much later.

Eri takes a soft cloth and cleans the wet thing's tiny nostrils. The specimen crawls unsteadily around the bowl-like incubator until it finds the nipple of the feeder. Every second or so, the poor thing stops and a sound like the world's smallest rusty hinge emerges from its toothless mouth. Eri prods it gently, strokes it until it turns into her hand, and then pushes its head down towards the nipple. Procedure dictates that only samples with a proven survival instinct should get to advance, but they've both had a rough day and procedure can get bent. When it's suckling, Eri takes her hand away, her other one is still covered in blood.

"You better pay for my water bill," she grouses.

When the deformed rat is dry it's orange, like her favorite type of cockroach. It's not sleek, like Fran was. There's something unfinished about its thick legs and knobby paws, and even at birth it already has more mass. But it wedges itself under the coffee table the way Fran used to. Eri ends up crouching down in a familiar way, seeing her house from two inches off the ground again.

∞

A month goes by and she doesn't turn it in.

All the excuses are there. It needs to get bigger, diet differentiation takes forever. She wants a good write-up of its needs or else some idiot lab-tech will kill it inside of a week. Initially, it sleeps too much, and even though the extraction was up to code, she worries that she's damaged it. It seems to have some kind of neurological problem anyway, because when she pets it, it's just as likely to nose at her wrist as to bite her. It has little rows of white teeth that look cute and ineffective now but could be horrific if it keeps growing.

She leaves the gun out because the first time Eri had put the orange mealticket in her lap, it had blinked at her, flopped over, and then, extending all four limbs, drawn blood with its tiny retractable claws. Hours later, she had fallen out of bed, panicking because her left thigh was on fire where the scratches were swollen and red. For a tense few minutes, she had sat frozen on the couch surrounded by scattered antibiotic tubes, freaking out that she'd cooked up some jingoistic military experiment and was now going to die of a neat little retro infection. In the end, she'd slathered on so many creams it was hard to tell which one did the trick.

She's still not convinced it isn't an experiment. One day, it leaps three feet straight up in the air from the floor to the nightstand and lands next to the blocky green muzzle of the gun. Eri swears and moves the weapon to a sticky spot on the hallway wall. The creature perches in the vacated warm spot and triumphantly begins to lick its furry orange foot. If this is the best they could do, it's no wonder America lost the war. As a weapon of terror it left something to be desired, with its strangely furry tail and triangular pink nose in a face that looked like it has been flattened with a well-meaning tap of God's finger.

When the bank account alerts start blooming insistently on her wall, Eri cooks the stalks that she'd stashed in the fridge. One of them turns out to be a camellia, and that makes it too easy to wait just another week, and then just another one after that.

The mealticket gets furrier, sleeker, more vocal; equal parts cozy and sinister. Once, she sees it sitting unnaturally still as a blue cockroach crawls up its tube inside the wall. An instant later, it was clinging to the gel with its claws out, leaving scratches that take almost as much time to heal as her thigh. This thing is not a rat, not even close to a rat.

She digs out the house manual and makes a little barrier so Amadi can't see into the living room as easily when he drops off her takeout. There's a next step here, but damned if she knows what it is. Currently shredding one of the canvas chairs in her kitchen is maybe an extra one to three percent addition to the mammalian biodiversity of the whole world, and Eri can't wrap her head all the way around that. She doesn't want to deal with the fact that something that important is now suddenly tangent to her little life. Can she even get paid for this?

Option one is Dr. Saltikova. Which means—possibly painful—confirmation tests, newsfeeds, and probably finding out the price point for getting sold out.

Option two is to solo with it. Here, the search bar oracle is neither helpful nor kind. Searching for *extinct mammalian genus found* yields a forum of paranoid nutty-nutty-nut-bars. Eri clicks around their video posts, fascinated and smug that at least she's not this crazy, but she's secretly glad when her problem bites her on the ankle and she has to step away from the screen.

Even the mealticket's little sounds and headbutts can't distract her from what she's found on page seventy-three of a popular conspiracy forum. A grainy photo of an animal, it has different coloring with a narrower muzzle but a familiar slitted eye and triangular ears—unmistakably the same species as her find. The image is badly cropped from a primary source—found in what the crazies dubbed a government-suppressed archive and paired with a screenshot of some ragged text from an ancient institution ominously dubbed an animal shelter. It reads: Friendly, housebroken, and declawed. Available for pickup.

Pickup for what?

Later that night, searching for *got rich quick* and *won the lottery* yields a laundry list of lawsuits, family recrimination, suicide attempts, and hermit-like seclusion. She may already be a winner there.

The next day, she wakes up, heart already racing, already a little short of breath. She spends the morning erasing her internet history and turning off all her wall microphones.

∞

Two days later, Amadi gets her order wrong.

She's only ordered tofu mole enchiladas consistently for the past three years. It figures that the only time they say something to each other besides "Do you need utensils?" is when she's in the middle of a week-long anxiety attack.

"We're out of tofu," he says, voice tinny on the line. The video feed is a few seconds delayed, but it shows him staring off to the side, fiddling with his hands. *Bullshit they're out of tofu.*

"Okay. Well, can I get cricket instead?"

"Miss, your meal card balance is insufficient," he continues mechanically, still staring offscreen. "If you could come down here and—"

"When the hell have I ever come down there on a Tuesday?" she says and flicks her hand at the screen to hang up.

Usually he doesn't even work on Tuesdays. She thinks and thinks and picks at a hangnail and paces in front of the viewscreen. She checks

the gun—it's back in the red already, the cheap thing—and then frantically plugs it in. The charge is still at yellow when the restaurant's delivery
hover parks on her lawn, scattering round acid-rain washed pebbles out
of their usual arrangement. Just the sight of it sets something off in her
gut. This is why she usually gets takeout. People in her space and not on
her terms have always made her uneasy, but with the week she's had, it
pushes it over into panic. She flips on the porch camera and doesn't open
the door at the knock.

"Hey! Hey, Miss Matani! I'm super sorry it glitched. You actually
had a surplus balance. Here's free tacos to apologize. No problems, yeah?"

"Put it in the slot, okay? I think I've got this bug. I don't want to
infect anyone," she says over the intercom.

Frowning, he does.

She runs her tablet over the box. Equipped with an olfactory
peripheral and calibrated for toxic dumps, it knows thousands of harm-
ful chemicals. The tacos are full of crushed sleep agent and MSG.

She nudges the sniffing warmie away with her foot as she yanks open
the door. Amadi is still standing there. At the sight of the gun, he drops
the takeout saddlebag which bounces soundlessly on the gel staircase.

"Who'd you call?"

Rage is a great antidote to social shyness. Eri has no problem making eye contact when she's ready to shoot someone. This is not the first
non-takeout related conversation she'd imagined having with this boy.

Do you wanna hang out some time?

Do you want to come over and watch a movie or see my book-
marks in the *Green Echo* catalog?

Do you want to sit on my couch and let your blue-black ankle
touch mine?

That's never going to happen now.

"I... I know you found one. You're barely legal with your salvage, and then you found an actual *Felis* and you've just been sitting on it for three months," he says petulantly. After the initial shock, he doesn't even seem afraid of the gun which Eri finds deeply irritating.

"So I called the GSD and they wired me an advance. Sorry," he says with a shrug. "Preparation meets opportunity and all that."

The man with the red badge is coming.

Eri's finger doesn't slip at all. The click of the trigger startles her for a moment, it's been so long since she's pressed it down all the way.

He's not heavy. It's easy to drag his stunned body into the middle of the living room. Six of her bracer columns sink easily into the floor, their tops and borders humming with electricity to make a cage. He turns out to be a smaller man than she'd thought, folding neatly inside. I should put the spare litter box in there, Eri thinks, but she's not feeling charitable.

What she does feel is lightheaded. She leans her temple against the wall. Begging for dinner, the source of all her problems weaves around her ankles. It has no idea that in less than a day they might both be living in little cages under artificial light. Her HV-8 may be compact and efficient, but it's still an industrial hovercar. Where can she even get on the gas she's got left?

No, never mind the warmie's too rare. They'll never let her go anywhere with it. People with red badges would be waiting for her at every border. Her half-closed eyes catch the motion of the wallpaper.

Though her fingers are shaking, they remember the password so well that she logs into the Green Echo B-side IRC on the first try. Her avatar is well known—the post won't float to the bottom for at least a day. That should be long enough. She types: "FREE GANKED Sunflower hack!!! LIMITED TIME DOWNLOAD. Come get it before the GSD jumps up my ass!" Then she bundles the last warmie genome from her tube and hits the upload button so hard her finger bends backwards a little.

The sun sets slowly. Eri charges the gun all the way to green in the light of the bracing poles, watching Amadi's still face and stroking the *Felis silvestris catus*, the legendary cat on her lap. On the wall, the text continues to scroll. The download number is in the hundreds of millions now. Too many to quarantine.

"Don't worry, Sunflower," she whispers into its orange fur. "Nothing's going to happen to you."

About the Author
Daryna Yakusha

Daryna Yakusha is a first-generation Ukrainian-American immigrant who was born in the year of the Chernobyl meltdown and has always been fascinated by dystopia and the aftermath of man-made disasters. She lives in Venice, CA and immediately becomes friends with anyone who can pronounce her name right on the first try.

Llamacide
by Gary Kloster

By the time I got to Chancellor Ito's house, the cops already had Carlos surrounded. They flanked the flowerbed where he stood, shotguns in their hands, frowns on their faces. Carlos, of course, ignored them. His big brown eyes were unconcerned, and his jaw never stopped munching on a dandelion. This was the tao of Carlos the weeding llama. Under the gun, with EMTs loading the head of the University of Wisconsin into an ambulance thirty feet behind his wooly backside, he was a long-lashed lump of serenity. Never mind the blood on the paving stones.

"Is that your animal?"

The question, snapped out in a hard cop voice, poked me in the back like a gun barrel. The woman who asked it wore a suit, not a uniform, and her badge hung around her neck like a tricked-out conference badge. She had short red hair, freckles, and hard green eyes marked with lines at the corners from the frown she aimed at me.

A detective. A good looking detective. My ability to think ground to a halt while the omg-she's-tough-and-competent-and-freckled fanboy section of my mind fought a quick cage match with the cops-jail-my-advisor-is-going-to-kill-me panicboy section. My brain ended up with just enough processing power to scrape out a "What?"

"Is that llama yours? Are you Milo Reyes?" The detective put her hands on her hips, which pulled her jacket back enough to flash a shoulder holster.

Fanboy fainted, panicboy cowered, and I tried to pull myself together. "No— Well, yes. I'm Milo, but Carlos isn't mine. He belongs to my advisor's lab. He's our project."

"Project?"

"We do cybernetic-assisted behavioral shaping."

The detective's frown lines got deeper. "Cyber... Wait. Are you doing some kind of mind control on that llama?"

"Kind of?" I said.

"The llama that just attacked the chancellor?"

Okay, that sounded kind of bad.

"Hey, Carlos wouldn't do that. We didn't program him for that. I mean, obviously. Why the hell would we make an assassin llama? Badger, maybe, but..." Man, the detective did not look happy. "Look, we didn't program him to attack anyone. Fuzzy-butt is the sweetest critter I've ever met. He can't be responsible for..." I waved my hand at the ambulance as it pulled away, siren wailing, "that."

The detective slid a phone from her pocket. On its screen I could see a video of the chancellor yakking on his own phone, Carlos happily chewing weeds behind him.

"Security footage," she said.

I watched man and animal ignore each other. Then Carlos stopped eating. He shook his head, laid back his ears, stared at Chancellor Ito and spat. A big nasty spit, one that must've reached all the way back to his third stomach.

The sticky wad caught the chancellor right in the back of his head, drenching him in half-digested grass and llama drool. Ito turned, face screwed up in rage, bellowing something. So when Carlos spit again, half of it went right into the poor guy's mouth.

So laughing would be completely inappropriate. But it was funny, and when the chancellor chucked his phone at Carlos, bouncing it off his furry chest, I couldn't hold it all in. The detective glared at me, and I managed to shut up and keep watching. It got a lot easier not to laugh after that.

On the screen, Carlos charged forward and reared up, front legs snapping out sharp hooves. Chancellor Ito scrambled back, hands raised to protect his face, then a hoof caught his shoulder. It knocked Ito down, and I winced when his head bounced off the bricks that edged the flowerbed.

"Oh," I muttered, my stomach a tight knot. On the screen, the chancellor lay still on the ground. Carlos stood above him, ears back. Then they relaxed, rose up, and the llama turned away, trotting back to his weeding. "Oh no."

"Is that thing safe? Should we shoot it?"

"Safe…" I looked at Carlos, standing serene on the other side of the cordon of nervous cops that surrounded him. He stared back, big brown eyes innocent, lips dripping dandelion fuzz as he hummed at me. "No. I mean yes. I mean please don't shoot him. I have no idea why he did that. I need to figure out why."

"*We* need to." She slapped the phone shut. "I'm Detective Corr. Secure that animal. We're taking it back to your lab, and you're going to tell me all about your project."

"Right. Detective Corr?"

"Yes?"

"Am I in trouble?"

Her eyes, sharp as glass, met mine. "Should you be?"

"No!" Really, honest, and I'm awful at lying anyway, but she could probably figure that out. I pulled out my phone and brought up Carlos' control panel. "I'll load him right up."

"Good. I'm sending a forensics tech to your lab."

She watched me, waiting to see if I twitched I guess, and I had to fight hard not to.

"The university's given me full permission to examine all of its property." Her gaze drifted down to the phone in my hand.

"This is mine," I said, and one of her eyebrows arched. "But you can look at it if you need to." I fumbled my fingers across the symbols on the screen, somehow hitting the right ones, and Carlos stopped eating. With a snort, he turned and started trotting over to his trailer.

The watching cops shot startled glances at Corr, who shook her head.

"We just might want to, Milo. Now go lock up your llama, and we'll drive him back to the lab."

"Yeah," I said, "Okay." In my head, fanboy had started wondering what Detective Corr thought about short, skinny, Jewish, Hispanic grad students with high IQs and nonexistent social lives.

Panicboy, meanwhile, was just trying not to cry.

∞

"What are they doing?"

Professor Parvin sounded calm, but I knew better. I could hear her knuckles cracking over the phone, and she only popped them when she was stressed. The sound didn't help my nerves. Grad students ended up just as conditioned by their advisors as the lab animals.

"Making sure no one hacked Carlos," I answered. Probably making sure that our lab wasn't a deadly ninja *Lama glama* training ground too, but I decided not to say that.

"Nobody hacked him. The system's not even online, and the wireless is encrypted."

"I told them," I said. "They wanted to double check."

"Check us. Libby will laugh herself sick."

Libby handled the system in the lab. She was Parvin's pet too, which drove the rest of us nuts. 'Cause while Libby might be a crack programmer, she was also a giant pain in the ass with a sick sense of humor. Which reminded me.

"Is Libby there? I wanted to talk to her."

"Why?" Parvin asked, her voice cooling.

"Well, just to check if she had adjusted Carlos' programming."

"Are you suggesting Libby might be at fault somehow?" Parvin's voice sounded downright cold, now.

"No. Not intentionally." I heard her start to draw a breath, and decided to charge into the breech. "Look, Libby likes practical jokes, and they've backfired before. Remember the goat on the Slip'N Slide?" I sure did. I had a scar.

"This is nothing like that," Parvin said, but I could hear the uncertainty buried beneath her words. "I'll talk to her though. In the meantime, just do what the police ask. We haven't done anything wrong."

Thankfully, the ice in her voice had melted. Now she just sounded tired.

"We're flying back tomorrow. Don't mess with anything, I'll figure out what happened. Now I need to go check the sheep."

I said good-bye and dropped the phone in my pocket, wiping off my damp palms as I did. Then I faced the detective.

"Has one of your processing cores been removed and replaced recently?" Corr asked the question, but the computer forensics nerd-cop behind her watched me as he chugged a bottle of CaffiKiwi.

"Professor Parvin needed it for the conference." The core, all the sheep in Flock One, and the other grad students chained to her research. Leaving me here, alone. I'd thought I was the lucky one, not having to go to Dallas in July. "We jacked an old core into its place to help run the animals while they were gone."

"You just happened to have a spare core sitting around?" Standing in a lab full of equipment ancient and new, I could understand her question. Academics use every part of the grant-buffalo.

"After we got our new cores, we were going to trade the old one to Professor Jordan for some other equipment. But he hasn't come through yet, and there's no way Parvin will give it up till he does."

"Why'd they take one with them?" she asked.

"Because the chance of Professor Parvin loading her precious software into someone else's system is probably about as good as you letting me play with your gun."

Corr snorted, then glanced at the nerd-cop. He nodded and started to gather his equipment.

"We've got what we need, for now. The techs back at headquarters will crunch the data, but an external hack does seem unlikely."

"Wonderful," I muttered, and she arched one eyebrow at me, making fanboy shiver. "Look, I'm positive you're not going to find a hack. That system has everything but a chastity belt wrapped around it. But…" I shrugged. "If I was wrong, if Carlos had been hacked, that would have just meant we screwed up our security. Since he wasn't, then we might have screwed up something else. Bad."

"Or one of you set this up on purpose."

"Professor Parvin, in the garden, with a llama?" Oh, that almost made her smile. "Doubtful. Programming Carlos not to eat the daises took us a whole week. Making him into the world's fuzziest assassin would have been a lot harder, and then whoever did it would have to hide their tracks. It would be a lot easier just to shoot the chancellor."

"You've thought this through," Corr said.

"Well— Wait, no, not really."

"I'm yanking your chain, Milo." The detective eased up, the ramrod straight length of her spine relaxing, her green eyes losing their sharp edge. She sank into a chair and sighed. "I don't think you did anything criminal. On purpose, at least."

"Thanks."

The nerd-cop finished packing up his stuff and headed out, nodding to Corr as he went. I watched her nod back, stretch and sigh, and look over the empty lab.

"So why aren't you at this conference?" she asked.

"Someone had to stay and watch the other critters, run the simulations, take Carlos on his rounds." I felt it then, the guilt and fear I'd been shoving to the side all afternoon. "Have you heard anything? Is the chancellor going to be alright?"

"He's alive and stable. Brain function? They can't know until he wakes up. But that's for the doctors to deal with. Our job, Milo, is to figure out why this happened."

"I wish I knew."

"So do I. So stop worrying about me and think of me as helpful." The detective leaned back in the chair, her shirt pulling tight as she reached up to shift her holster. *Distracting, on so many levels.* "Now, why don't you explain just what exactly is going on here in muppet labs?"

∞

The sheep stood in their pen, chewing hay and looking stupid, the two things they could do well. I leaned against the rail and watched Corr look at them. She didn't seem impressed.

"Flock Two. They mow," I said.

"Mow?"

"Yes, mow." I frowned at the sheep, feeling annoyed. These fluffy dopes represented a lot of work. "People want robotic mowers. That's idiotic. Look at these guys. All they do is eat grass, and then turn it into wool, meat, fertilizer, and more sheep. They're autonomous, self-maintaining, and cute. They're the perfect green lawn mower. They just need a little guidance."

"Mind control," she said.

"Cybernetic-assisted behavioral shaping."

Corr kept her face bland, but her eyebrow twitched.

"Look," I said, "it's not like they have much of a mind to control. This isn't silage for Algernon, we haven't got them doing calculus. They already eat grass, we just tell them where to do it."

"Where?" There finally seemed to be a note of faint interest in her question, and that little scrap encouraged me.

"We set boundaries. Eat the grass here, not over there. Don't go into the road, don't eat the flowers. You could release them in a suburb and they would go from lawn to lawn, doing their job, staying on the sidewalk when they traveled, not getting in the way. All on their own, except for the computer talking to the chips in their heads. They won't *baa* too loud, won't poo in the grass, they're fun to watch. You could have your kids out in the yard with them." I thought about the time we'd tested that, with the prof's niece and nephew. "As long as they don't try riding them."

"You control their pooing?" Her expression flickered between disturbed and amused.

"I spent a lot of time on that." I watched amusement win on her face and shook my head. "No respect. I learned a lot, working that out."

"About sheep poo?"

"About teaching the computer how to interpret the signals coming in from the sheep's gut. So it could send them back to the trailer in time to use the lambatory."

In the pen, the sheep picked up their heads and stopped chewing, eyeing Corr as she doubled over, laughing.

"Seriously?" she finally managed.

"Look, I know it seems stupid but this stuff's important. When I get out of here... If I don't end up in jail... I want to work in prosthetics. Help make the body and the orthotic talk to each other, integrate seamlessly. This research is invaluable. It sounds stupid, but it's not."

Corr's smile faded, and she chewed her lip, thinking.

"I can't peg you, Milo. Bumbling genius? Mad scientist? Dedicated researcher? Which are you?"

"All three," I suggested. "But may I encourage you to focus on that last one?"

"Maybe." The detective turned from the sheep, looked across the dusky barn at the other pens. "What about the rest?"

"Flock One's with the prof at the conference, for the demo. They're the same as Flock Two, just tweaked better. The goats are Herd One, aka the buttheads. More mowers, but for rougher areas, like highway ditches. Carlos…" I sighed, staring at the fuzzball who stood humming quietly in his pen. "A side project, but going well. Or so I thought."

"What about that one?" Corr nodded toward a pen at the end of the building, where a dark brown llama stood glaring at us.

"El Diablo? He got thrown in when we bought Carlos. The breeder said take him or she'd make him into glue. We should've let her. You see that line painted on the floor?"

"Yeah."

"Don't cross it. That's his spit radius." We'd chalked the line in at first, but Libby had kept erasing it and redrawing it back within Diablo's range.

"He is an evil, evil llama," I said. "Professor Parvin had a sideline project going for awhile, trying to mollify his behavior by linking up his implant with the one in Carlos, but it never worked well. We made her give it up. I mean, we might be grad slaves, but there is a hard limit of how much llama spit we'll swim through to get our doctorates."

"You guys are starting to compete with the coroner for jobs I'm glad I don't have." Corr turned from the llamas and looked down at her feet. "So what about this lump?"

Noticing her attention, the lump in question leaned his furry head against her foot. Corr obliged the silent request, reaching down to stroke the smooth, triangular ears of the German shepherd. I could see the way her face softened as she did so, noticed how she paid no attention to the black and brown hairs clinging to her pants leg as the dog leaned into her petting. *Yeah, she liked dogs.* This could be good. Or really bad.

"That's Huxley. The next project."

"Next for what?" Corr's voice was dangerously neutral.

"There're a ton of applications. Search and rescue. Just turn the dogs loose without handlers and have them run an organized search pattern. Or bomb and drug sniffers that could roam an airport unsupervised. Helper animals, like Seeing Eye dogs, that could be trained faster, do more. Imagine what we could do with police dogs."

"Imagine what you could do with police dogs? I'm having difficulty believing what you've done with this petting zoo, Milo." Corr frowned. "That's what bothers me so much about this. You're putting these animals completely at the mercy of whoever's programming them. How can you be sure that people won't make them do something horrible?"

"We can't. We're building in safeguards, but…" I shrugged. "Someone's always going to try to do something horrible, with whatever tool they have at hand. I think that's why we have to have cops."

"Touché," she said. "All right, fine. Enough philosophy. I'm willing to believe now that you're not all mad scientists, creating an evil alpaca army."

"Llamas."

"Whatever."

"Have you seen an alpaca? A killer alpaca is ridiculous."

"Whatever," she said again. "So what happened this afternoon?"

I let my shoulders slump. "I haven't got a clue."

"Then let's start looking for some." She reminded me of Professor Parvin when she said that, an unstoppable force of curiosity revving up to slam into a solid wall of ignorance.

That comparison didn't do anything to help out my stress levels, so I shoved it out of my head as fast as I could.

"Okay," I said, trying to herd my thoughts together. "We last used Carlos three days ago, in our vegetable garden. No problems. Except he tried to eat the scarecrow's hat."

Detective Corr took a seat on a pile of bagged sheep supplement.

"Did you change his programming because of that?" she asked, still scratching Huxley's ears.

"No, just threw the hat away. Seemed simpler. Day after that, he stayed in his pen because we were packing up Flock One to go to Texas. What a pain in the rear. The ram butted me when I bent over to get the pin for their gate."

"Tragic," she told Huxley. "What about yesterday?"

"I spent most of the day messing with the computers. Like I said, the prof took one of our fancy new cores to run Flock One. Libby dropped our old one back in the system, but she rushed the job and it was acting up."

"Could that have done something?"

"It shouldn't have. All the new control software is on the other core. The old one's just there to add some computational cycles in case the software needs them."

"Hmm," she said. "What about today?"

"I took Carlos out to the chancellor's. He seemed fine. Ito loved having him around, liked to point him out as one of the university's new 'secret' projects when the donors came by."

I could remember Ito patting Carlos on the head the first time we brought him, how the chancellor had tried to match the llama's hum. That used to be a good memory.

"Then I came back here and started running Flock Two and Herd One through their paces."

"Okay." She stopped petting the dog and pulled out her phone to take down some notes. "Were there any problems?"

"Yeah, actually." I'd almost forgotten the bug that had been driving me nuts that morning, my worst problem until the cops had called. "The sheep kept freezing."

"Freezing?" Corr could ask questions as if the answers were critically, personally important to her. It whipped the fanboy in my head into a frenzy.

"Like when your phone won't load a video. Every time I ran the sheep, one would just stop. Stand still, not doing anything, until I rebooted the system. Then it would be normal again, but then another one would freeze. Never could figure out why."

"Just the sheep?" she asked.

"No, the goats acted up too, a couple of times. They didn't lock though, they staggered around in circles, drooling. Reminded me of some of the guys you meet at Comic-Con. When I rebooted, the goat would be fine, but then I'd lose a sheep again."

I pulled out my phone, flicked through the data I'd taken. "Sheep, sheep, goat, sheep... Isn't this in the Bible? Here's one where they all ran right, but when I rebooted to check... Sheep, goat, then you guys called."

"You have times there. What happened at three fifty-four?"

I checked the record. "That's the one where everything seemed to run fine. That's when the attack happened, isn't it?"

"Yes."

We both looked up from the phone, through the shadows toward Carlos' pen. "He didn't freeze. He went homicidal," I said.

"Can you rerun that test?"

"Yeah. But..." I hesitated.

"The llama's in a pen, and I have a gun," she said.

"I'm not afraid of Carlos, I'm afraid of my advisor." *Don't try to do this on your own*, she'd said. "If I mess things up even more... Well, she's not in a pen, and I'm not sure guns can stop her."

"Your choice," Corr said. "But I'd like you to try."

Fanboy lunged at that, and panicboy couldn't hold him back. Not with Parvin a thousand miles away. "Right," I said. Then I hunched over my phone, fingers flying over the screen.

"I'll run them through some simple tasks. Carlos first." I tapped out commands, and despite the gloom I could see Carlos prick up his ears, then start ambling across his pen, straight line, turn, straight line turn, again and again.

"Walking out a pentagram," I explained. "He's Wiccan."

"I would have thought Catholic," Corr said, watching the llama's precise movements, her expression caught somewhere between fascination and horror.

"His family was, but he left the church after his gelding. Now the goats." A few more keystrokes, and the members of Herd One woke from their doze and started ambling in a rotating figure eight around their pen, bleating sleepily.

"And the sheep." More noise filled the barn as the sheep shook themselves awake, baaing in confusion as they started do-se-doing around each other. Huxley sat up, fascinated by the wooly dance, and across the barn El Diablo hocked a loogie at a goat. "Now let's see."

It came quick. Both Corr and I pointed and said, "There!" Then I said, "Sorry," while she called, "Jinx." Meanwhile, the problem sheep stood trembling, disrupting the pattern of the flock around it.

"So that's what was happening." I glanced down at my phone, checking the readouts on the screen. "I still don't know why. Reboot."

I did, freeing all the animals to wander, then started them up again. And again. Each time, the same thing happened, one sheep falling out of the pattern and freezing.

"I can't decide if this is creepy or amazing," Corr said.

"It's frustrating," I muttered, halting the program one more time. "I can't figure it out." I restarted, scanning the sheep as they marched, then yelped as something slammed into my side.

I hit the ground hard, my lungs woofing out air. Claws raked across my scalp and then down my back, hard and sharp and hurting. I pulled myself up to hands and knees, gasping for breath as I tried to crawl away, but the blows kept raining down. They weren't hard enough to knock me to the ground again, but they were painful, disorienting. I scrambled, trying to escape from the furry thing that pawed and slapped at me, then, with a strangled yelp, it was gone.

Moving with a speed that would have vindicated my high school track coach's every snide remark about my shirking, I sprang up from the floor, took a few running steps, and looked behind me.

Standing where I'd been, still settling into a stance, Corr held her gun and pointed it at my attacker. Huxley stood a few yards from her, caught in the middle of some kind of fit. He staggered, staring at us, eyes wild, and gave a strange, pleading whine.

"What the..." Corr started.

"I don't..." My thinking slammed into confused, overclocked, multitask mode. I couldn't say what I thought, hadn't even thought it yet, but my eyes were already searching the ground for my phone.

"Something with the program," I yelled, all Captain Obvious. "Don't shoot him!"

"I don't want to," she said, voice amazingly steady. "But what is he doing?"

I looked up from my frenzied search to see Huxley glaring at us, stiff-legged, lips curled back, foam dripping from his muzzle as an awful, barking cough rattled in his throat.

"Don't know. Not rabid. Shots!" I tore my eyes from the dog, a decision panicboy had severe problems with, and kept searching. *Not there... there!* I saw the glow of my phone's screen shining off a sheep's dingy white wool as it marched by in the pen.

"Got it!" I said, and launched myself for the fence.

Unfortunately, my track coach had never made me run hurdles. Three running steps, a leap, and then *crack* as my patella slammed into the top rail of the fence. In the air, time slowed and I could feel pain racing up the neurons from my leg, that special message of boy-you-screwed-up-bad, then it hit and everything went bright red for a moment. I barely noticed slamming into the ground, saved from the ignominy of screaming by losing my breath. Again.

"Milo, do something!"

Writhing in agony was totally doing something.

Corr wouldn't want to hear that, though. I gritted my teeth, determined to roll over and find my phone before Huxley attacked the detective, before I was trampled by a square-dancing sheep, before anyone else got maimed. One hospitalization should be sufficient, I thought as I pulled myself across the dirt, for even the most stringent defense committee.

Behind me, Corr swore and Huxley strangled out a growl. The noise helped push me past the pain, made me flop over my phone just as one of the fluffy flock members stamped closer to it. My fingers flew across the little screen and the program stopped, leaving the sheep standing stupid around me. I grabbed the wool of the one closest, ignored its protest as I used it to lurch up, looking back toward Corr.

For a second, my heart stopped. She lay on the floor, Huxley standing over her, ears pricked forward. Then her hand moved, patting the dog's shoulder. Huxley's tongue slurped out and licked her face.

"You okay?" I asked her.

Corr pushed Huxley back and stood, glaring at me. "I've decided. You're a mad scientist and this whole experiment is creepy. Very, very creepy."

∞

"Car wreck. I was sixteen, coming back from a date. A drunk hit us."

"Bad date," I said, watching as Corr pushed her pant leg back down. The shredded khaki barely covered the damage Huxley's teeth had inflicted to her calf, the torn pseudo-skin, the black stripes of spilled lubricant, the titanium's gleam. *She's bionic,* fanboy crooned in my head, heart all pitter-pat, and I tried to ignore him.

"Had worse." Corr had taken a seat on the sheep supplement again while I put Huxley back. I watched now as she carefully slid off the stacked bags and stood, wondering if I should offer her my hand. The expression on her face, and the single word she growled as she put weight on her damaged prosthetic, convinced panicboy that distance was a safer choice than politeness.

"Hurt?"

"Kind of." She took a tentative step. "Feels like I'm stepping in jello filled with cold spaghetti." Another step and she gasped, her freckles growing clear as her face paled. "And the occasional razor blade."

Fanboy smacked panicboy down and I limped towards Corr, my knee still complaining, to help her, but she waved me away.

"Every time I get a new one, the movement gets better. But the sensation always sucks." Corr flexed her foot, flashed her green eyes at me. "Your comment on prosthetics… you didn't know it, but it bought you some slack. Slack that's just about pulled taut, now. What just happened?"

"The denouement." The detective cocked one copper-tinted eyebrow at me, and I hastily went on. "The ending, the—"

"I know what the word means, Milo. Tell me what *you* mean."

Before she shoots us, whimpered panicboy. "Okay. Problem. Subjects exhibiting unexplained, erratic behavior. Sheep freezing. Goats seizing. Carlos attacking. Then Huxley. His behavior during his attack gave me the final bit of information I needed to reach my conclusion."

"Which behavior? The tap-dancing on your head or the mauling of my very expensive foot? You better hope my insurance covers frenzied attacks by mutant lab creatures."

"Hey, don't call Huxley names. He's feeling bad enough." I nodded toward Huxley's kennel, where he lay curled on the floor, gazing forlornly at us through the closed chain link gate.

"He should feel bad. I'd be bleeding real blood all over this barn if I hadn't managed to shove my Skywalker special between his teeth."

"That's just it. He didn't do it. Just like Carlos didn't attack the chancellor. They were mind controlled."

"Mind controlled. You said you weren't hacked."

"Yep. The calls came from inside the house," I said.

"So, one of your team?"

"No."

Corr glowered at me, losing patience. "Who?"

"The devil," I said, unable to resist the drama. Seeing the dangerous glitter in her eyes, I didn't prolong the moment though. Instead I lifted my hand and pointed toward the llama pens.

"You just said Carlos didn't do it."

"He didn't. It was El Diablo. The evil llama."

"Right," she said. "Your slack just ran out. You need to explain what your talking about, or I'll shoot everything in this barn and send it to my favorite barbecue."

"Me and Huxley too?"

"Maybe not Huxley."

Ouch. I thought only my mother could drop a ludicrous threat like that and make it sound perfectly plausible. Panicboy's hyperventilation let me know that assumption was incorrect.

"I told you the prof had been working with Carlos, trying to see if she could get his mellow to cross over the link and zen Diablo out. It only kind of worked, which is why we hated it. Better to have Diablo predictably evil, y'know, instead of just occasionally. Then Libby got a hold of it."

"Your programmer."

"Yeah," I said, "our fun-loving programmer. She figured out how to swap the variables, so that Diablo could take over Carlos. Usually when we were cleaning out his pen. We begged Parvin to let us kill Libby, but she just discontinued the experiment instead. She was busy anyway, because our funding had come in and we could buy a couple of shiny new cores to play with. And a dog."

Corr looked up into the shadows, wheels spinning. "So the Diablo project was on the old core. The one you stopped using, until they took one of those shiny ones to the conference."

"Yeah. Lurking in some memory cache, not shut down properly. Or maybe it got reactivated when the core dropped back in the system, I don't know." Libby would figure out some way to blame it all on my efforts to get the cores working together. Unfortunately, she might even be right.

"So you activated all the animals this morning. That starts using enough cycles that the old core gets used."

"And that old program starts kicking in. Now, the system has changed a lot since it activated last. Instead of just having Carlos and Diablo to link, it has the sheep and the goats—"

"And Huxley," she said.

"Exactly. It should have crashed, but because of Murphy's law, it doesn't. It just picked subjects at random. Sheep, goat, sheep, et cetera. Because of Murphy again, it's set to put Diablo in charge. So I start seeing what happens when you have an evil llama's brain shoved into a sheep's. Exceeds system specs."

"Sheep are stupid, so Diablo crashed them."

"Goats too, though they crashed differently. So I rebooted. Again and again, and the program just kept dumping glue-bait over there into random animals. Until it finally hit Carlos, another llama, right when the chancellor was walking by." I sighed, staring at Carlos, sitting primly in his stall. "Poor guy. The devil made him do it."

"Fantastic," Corr said. "Are you sure about this?"

"Not a hundred percent. Not until I dissect the system. Which will have to wait until the prof gets back with Libby. But yeah, I am. Did you see the way Huxley attacked? Flailing at me with his front paws like they were hooves, then standing there, making that horrible noise? He was trying to spit. He didn't even bite until you shoved your foot in his mouth. Not that I'm faulting your decisive action under fire, of course."

"Of course." Corr leaned back against the fence and groaned. "Do you realize what you're saying? The llama didn't do it. The llama did it. How am I going to write a report on this?"

Her phone chimed, giving me a chance to duck the question. She answered, muttered a few words, then thumbed it off. "Well, thank your assorted gods, at least it's not a llamacide. Ito woke up."

"Is he…"

"He seems all right, though the neurologists will have to go over him. Just some short term memory loss." Corr snorted. "Murphy must've gotten bored with you."

"Thank goodness," I said. "So what's going to happen?"

"I'll tell you what's happening. I'm ditching this freak show and going home. Tomorrow, I'll recommend the department just drop this whole mess and never look back. The chancellor's not dead, so I'm betting he'll want to handle this himself."

My sense of relief, clutched in panicboy's hands like a beautiful, fragile balloon, popped. "Oh no."

"Yep. Good luck, Milo. Don't take it personally, but I hope to never see you, or a llama, ever again."

"But—" I stammered. Watching her limp away made fanboy want to stamp his feet and cry over the unfairness of it all. Meanwhile, panicboy was already wailing. "But I was…"

Corr stopped beside Huxley's cage, turned and stared at me. "But what?"

"But I was wondering if coffee was a thing that you liked to have?" The words came out in a rush, a string of almost nonsense that fanboy managed to shove past every bit of my good judgement.

Corr raised a hand to her forehead, as if a migraine had just pulled a drive-by on her. Then she winced and shifted on her feet, taking weight off her damaged prosthetic. "Milo," she said.

In the cage beside her, Huxley gave a pitiful whine, which I tried desperately not to echo.

"Good lord." She sighed. "Look, I have to write a report anyway. I'll make sure to point out how helpful you've been, and how this whole insane thing was an accident." She put her fingers through the chain link and scratched Huxley's ear, sending him into a tail wagging paroxysm. "An act of devil, if you will. And I'll make sure Ito gets a copy." She looked up from Huxley to me.

"You may be a mad scientist, Milo, but I don't want to see you get into trouble. Well, not too much trouble." She shifted, slowly putting more weight back on the leg that Huxley had chew-toyed. "I'd rather have you hard at work."

Giving Huxley a final scritch, she started limping again. "Use your nerd-powers for good," she called out. "I want to feel my toes someday." The door thumped shut behind her, and she was gone.

I sighed, then did my own limping down to Carlos' pen, careful to stay out of Diablo's target zone.

"Well, Carlos, she didn't say no. Technically." Fanboy was all about the optimism. Panicboy, meanwhile, had decided that maybe I wasn't going to be kicked out of grad school, and was peaceful for almost a whole second. Then he started obsessing over what Parvin was going to do to me.

Carlos though, he just blinked big brown eyes at me and hummed, calm, serene, peaceful. I sighed and leaned against his soft wooly neck, closed my eyes and hummed back, trying to embrace his Tao.

I almost had it, too, when Diablo finally managed to find the strength to hock a good one past his line, straight onto my head.

About the Author
Gary Kloster

Gary Kloster is a writer, a stay-at-home father, a martial artist, and a librarian. Sometimes all in the same day, seldom all at the same time. He lives in the Midwest next to a large university, where no illicit llama assassin training facilities exist. As far as he knows. His first novel, *Firesoul*, is out now.

Author Website: http://www.garykloster.com/

Love That Easy Money
by Robert Lowell Russell

My ten-meter-tall Mechanical Ambulatory Tank rumbles past white brick buildings, my MAT crushing any soldiers in the city's streets without sense enough to run. The *Hell Kitty* is forty metric tons of hot-pink badass, complete with whiskers and a red bow. I'm harnessed inside the *Kitty*'s armored torso. Neurosensors and gyros turn my movements into mimicked action. Each step I take sways me gently in the cockpit. If I close my eyes, the rocking motion and rhythmic booms of my strides make it seem like I'm in a thunderstorm at sea.

I extend the *Kitty*'s arms, triggering wrist-mounted miniguns to reduce a bunker full of Marvin militia to shattered flesh and concrete. A handful of the slender, bipedal aliens flee the shelter, their feet flapping and crested heads bobbing as they run. Their gait is almost comical, making it easier to imagine them as cartoons. *And killing cartoons ain't nothing at all, Kassie*, my partner Bill likes to tell me.

The Marvins wear uniforms that are the same dingy white as the surrounding buildings. I take a moment to orient myself while I let the surviving Whites flee. My tactical display overlays the *Kitty*'s real-time sensor data with 3D ground images from daily drone overflights. I'd prefer real-time satellite feeds to 3D map archives, but spy satellites are expensive and would eat into the MAT fleet's profits. Tank drivers make do with a few GPS birds and thinking on their feet. Besides, Marvin cities don't change much, day to day.

Routing visual feeds from the *Kitty*'s rear cameras to my tactical helmet, I scan behind me. The dim yellow light of the system star bathes everything I see in a hue of decay. Marvins in blue uniforms scramble through a hole I've made in the city's wall. The Blues are from a rival city-state, and they've contracted me and Bill for this mission against the Whites. The Blues fire their rifles in full-on spray-and-pray mode, battling the local militia. Shards of brick rain from civilian structures, choking the streets with rubble. A fine gray dust settles over the bodies.

Returning to my forward view, I see more Whites hiding behind an antique treaded tank. Some human arms dealer likely advertised the tank as top of the line. Patches of rust mar the machine's gray steel. Fire belches from its cannon, and an instant later a shell detonates harmlessly on the *Kitty*'s plazsteel armor. I twitch a finger and launch a single rocket from one of my shoulder-mounted missile racks. The rocket's high explosive charge detonates against the tank's armor, punching a slug of molten metal into its interior. Flames erupt from the hole as the tank's occupants and ordinance burn.

Numbers flash inside my helmet, and I grin. Four more units tick off my fifty-fifty contract: fifty units of destruction, at my discretion, for fifty thousand credits. Marvins assign inflated bounties to their obsolete war toys, so one rocket spent to kill a tank is close to pure profit. I like fifty-fifties. They're quick, safe missions and they leave plenty of time for me to rendezvous with the fleet's orbital carrier so I can hear about my daughter Rachel's day at school.

As I rotate the *Kitty*'s head from side to side, my tactical display outlines civilian buildings in green light, showing me the assigned values for each structure, price-adjusted for the number of Marvins cowering inside. I ignore the structures. Killing aliens is part of the job, and being picky about what I destroy can actually cost me profits, but I get by just fine.

One of my side cameras reveals a second tank, even older than the first. Inside the MAT, I twist my hips, and the *Kitty* responds by shifting its direction. Powering ahead, I plot a course that keeps my war machine from toppling the buildings around me, none of the structures rose higher than the *Kitty*'s shoulders. I sight the tank, but before I can fire, it explodes in a gout of flame and molten metal.

"Suck it, motherfuckers!" comes my partner's voice over the comm. "Love that easy money."

"Damn it, Bill," I say. "That was my kill."

"Didn't see your name on it."

Bill's MAT, the *Wild Bill*, wades through the remains of what my display indicates was a factory. The *Wild Bill* is five meters taller than the *Hell Kitty* and seven tons heavier. The war machine has a simian look, a cross between King Kong and Curious George. Its dark armor bears shining scars left over from the AI War.

The AI War was the one black mark on three centuries of human space exploration. Before the war, AI-controlled drone strikes among corporate competitors had been as routine as three martini lunches. But one day the AIs got tired of killing each other and started wiping out the thirty million human colonists on Tau Ceti Prime instead.

"Hold still, Kassie," says Bill.

I flinch as the *Wild Bill* rips an energy blast over my shoulder.

"Ka-ching!" he says.

The *Kitty*'s rearview cams show a blazing building full of Marvins. Bill lifts his smoking plasma cannon to his tank's lips and makes a blowing noise over the comm.

I roll my eyes. Plasma cannons are slow, inefficient weapons. Bill says he likes it for its "psychological effect," but the cannon's energy demands mean his MAT carries only a single minigun and rocket rack as backup. One blown capacitor bank and two-thirds of the *Wild Bill*'s firepower becomes useless.

Bill thunders off to another part of the city while I scan for more military targets. Few remain. As is often the case, the Marvin city-state that hired me is more interested in harassment than conquest. The handful of city-states on the planet with standing armies prefer to keep their forces close to home to deter attacks from neighbors. For dirty work done right, the Marvins use the MAT fleet's assets.

Firing rockets and bullets, I stalk through the city, destroying buildings with the fewest civilians inside until my helmet display shows I've completed my contract. A flashing icon indicates the Blues are offering me an atrocity bonus, but I decline. Seconds later, I hear a *boom* and turn to see a Marvin school stuffed with students collapse in another part of the city.

"Shit, Kass, I hate when you leave money on the table for me like that," comes Bill's voice. "Makes me feel like I'm stealing from your kid." The *Wild Bill* offers a cheerful wave as it strides past the school's ruins. "There's no shame in selling your tank if you don't have the stomach for the work," Bill continues. "You've paid off Dan's debt."

My stomach isn't the problem—I've seen more death than Bill can possibly know—it's the loss, the emptiness that claws at me from under my ribs like an animal trying to escape. It's been nearly a year since a fluke shot flatlined my husband Dan, but I still wear a gold band on my finger. Not thinking, I move to wipe tears from my eyes, and the *Kitty* responds by gonging its fist against its armored head. I wince at the clatter; the seed of a headache grows behind my eyes.

Bill chatters on, oblivious. "There's not a crew in the fleet that wouldn't count themselves lucky to have you as their engineer, you know. The fleet looks after its own."

"I need some air," I say, steering my MAT from the heart of the city.

Near the city wall a group of Blues are celebrating by firing their rifles into the air. Our employers have won the skirmish, thanks to me and Bill.

I flip back to the marketplace display, bringing up a list of open contracts, then quickly accept a job. With a sweep of my miniguns,

I turn the celebrating Blues into paste. Payment is in my account moments later. My stomach feels just fine.

"Damn, that's cold," says Bill on the comm.

Lights strobe inside my cockpit, warning me that another MAT has me in its sights.

"Think the Blues will greenlight you for screwing them over, Kass?" comes Bill's voice. There's a pause—I can't tell if Bill's joking or if he's actually checking the market—then the warning lights wink off. "Cheap bastards."

"Screw you, Bill."

He chuckles. "Well, I wasn't going to ask, but now that we have some down time… Hey, Kassie, you seeing this three-hundred-K burn job that just popped up? Want to go halvsies on it with me? It's not far."

A "burn job" means a Marvin city-state wants me and Bill to wipe out every heavy weapon in a neighboring city-state, destroying its manufacturing centers and food stores, too. There's more risk than with a fifty-fifty mission, but a bigger paycheck. I bring up the city-state's profile and review threat assessment figures and ordinance demand projections. The only number that really interests me is the profit estimate. I'll need a reload, but the figures are exactly what every MAT driver hopes to see: A ninety-five percent certainty that the risks taken are worth the bounty paid. No mission gets rated higher than ninety-five percent, because shit happens and you can't spend bounties when you're dead. The software even offers a simple color coding scheme for drivers who don't have a head for numbers: green, good; yellow, so-so; red, kiss your ass good-bye.

"Sure," I say. "Let's go."

I accelerate the *Hell Kitty* to eighty kilometers per hour. There's no gentle rocking at eighty. My teeth ache as I'm thrashed in my harness. The clamor of my strides deafens me, even with the noise suppressors inside my helmet. But as bad as I've got it inside the *Kitty*, I know Bill has it worse. *Feels like somebody's whuppin' the tar out of me while scream-ing in my ear*, he's told me.

He joins me, laboring a bit in his MAT. The *Wild Bill* is hardly the slowest tank in the fleet, but I've scrounged enough heavy-duty joints, shock absorbers, and high-capacity neurocabling to make the *Hell Kitty* the *fastest*. When I run, I damn near fly. Bill and I lope over the alien landscape, two grim titans speeding to battle.

The *Kitty's* display amplifies the light of the system star. Blue-green moss covers rolling hills in every direction. Gray roads wind around the rises, and the occasional Marvin ground transports we pass swerve to avoid us. Here and there, dark, rocky soil breaks through the surface of the hills. Groves of carnivorous trees sit atop some rises, snagging meals from the wind.

Though I can't establish a direct visual, drone image archives show a nearby mining operation. The human-controlled robotic facility appears as a glowing blip on my display. The mines are ubiquitous on the planet. Whatever served for money on the Marvins' world before the mining companies arrived, I have no idea, but now everything is bought and sold in grams of the rare-earth metals stripped from the ground. Abstract notions like territories and zones of control became far more serious matters for the natives once humans came offering their technological gifts, for a price.

"Quartermaster command," I broadcast, my voice quavering with my strides. "This is the *Hell Kitty*. Request expedited reload of lead and matchsticks, over." I transmit the coordinates for the burn job's location.

My comm is silent for a few moments, then it crackles to life. "No problem, Mom. Be right there."

"Rachel! What in the world? Why aren't you in school?"

"Early release today. Duh."

"No, that's not until…" I check my calendar. *Today.* "Sorry, sweetie, I mixed up the days. You okay?"

"Copacetic. Jimmy's let me do three drops already."

"*What?*" My face grows hot.

"Copacetic. Cool word, right? We just learned it today. Mom, you won't believe what Kelli did, it was so—"

"Get Jim on the comm, *right now.*"

"He's on a drop." There's a brief pause, and when Rachel speaks again, her voice is quiet, almost pleading. "Please don't embarrass me. The other kids… None of the resupply drops were in missile zones, Mom. I *swear.*"

I sigh. "No more drops today. I mean it."

"Okay, Mom."

"Rachel, we need to talk about this after—"

"Holy shit!" comes Bill's voice over my comm, interrupting me. "Rhodes just flatlined."

It takes me a moment to reorient from mom to soldier. "How? No way a Marvin round made it through the *Colossus*'s armor," I say. "Did he have a heart attack, like Henders?"

"Don't think so," says Bill. "The chatter is that he and Chen were on a run out in the boonies, then something happened. Chen went quiet right after. The Thames twins are heading over to see what's up."

As a consequence of the AI War, every licensed war machine in the fleet has to prove it has a living, breathing human pulling the trigger. When I open up my fleet display to check on Rhodes' status, sure enough his EKG and EEG show an absent heart rhythm and brain waves. The display also shows the GPS coordinates of each of the nearly two hundred other active MATs on the planet.

"Well, if Rhodes did have some sort of accident," I say, "it couldn't have happened to a bigger asshole."

Bill laughs. "Damn straight."

Deaths among MAT drivers are uncommon and combat fatalities rare. As I continue pounding toward my next job, I spend time listening to the fleet's chatter.

"Henders, Simmons…" I wince at the mention of my husband's surname. "And now Rhodes," says one driver. "It's like the war, all over."

"Ain't like the war at all, ya dumb shit," says another. "Where da fuck you serve?"

"Three dying in a year's just life," says a woman. "Lost five, six mates a day when the Dirty Dozen were hunting us."

"Traitor bastards."

At the mention of the turncoat MAT drivers, my comm fills with curses and profanity. I silence the feed.

The corporations were good at building killing machines, but they couldn't stop their own creations during the AI War. For three years they failed, until finally they swallowed their pride and asked for help. And the kind of people who didn't mind getting their hands dirty for profit and adventure answered the call. With the corporations supplying the parts and financing, and private engineering crews providing the ingenuity, the MAT fleet was born. The AIs never really had a chance after that. The speed and precision of the machines could never match humanity's cunning and talent for destruction.

Bill and I spend another half hour running until we bend around a tree covered hill. A large Marvin city comes into view, and we halt. Like we've done more times than I can count, Bill keeps his tank perfectly still as he works up our battle plan; he swears he can walk and chew gum at the same time, honest. I check the surrounding hills to see if our current employers have come to watch us complete the burn job. Some Marvins want to see all the bangs their bucks are paying for. Others, like with our last mission, even prefer to fight alongside us. Most just want us to send them the bill.

"Do we have an audience?" asks Bill.

"Nope."

"Heads up," he says. "See the minefield?"

I switch to my tactical display. The *Kitty's* sensors show glowing dots extending fifty meters beyond the city-state's wall, but I note the Marvins have only buried enough mines to protect a small section. Dozens of the aliens fire rifles from turrets above the same area.

"Trying to goad us into walking into the mines," I say.

"They're cute when they're strategic," says Bill. "Well, time's money. I'm going right. You head left." Apparently, that was the extent of Bill's battle plan. He looses a salvo of rockets into the city, rakes the defenders on the wall with his minigun, and turns a water tower into a cloud of steam with his plasma cannon.

At that moment, Rachel's dropship with my payload breaks through the planet's purple clouds. The ship, twice the size of the *Hell Kitty*, resembles a giant metal moth. Its six legs grasp a metal box half as wide as the *Kitty* is tall. A few Marvins fire on my daughter as she descends, but I ignore them. A dropship's armor can shed the heat of a high-speed atmospheric entry like rain rolling off a duck. If these Marvins had missiles, I might worry, but bullets don't even register.

Rachel sets the container down near my position. "How was my setdown, Mom?" she asks on the comm. "Good as Jimmy's?"

"Better."

"No lie?"

"Honest." The twelve-year-old's skill fills me with a mix of pride and dismay.

"Cool! See ya!" Rachel blasts away again, disappearing into the sky.

My daughter amazes me. She seems to live in a permanent state of cheerfulness, just like her father once did. Watching Rachel go, an all too familiar ache grows inside me. I try to ignore it. There's a job to do.

"Bill, this is my reload," I transmit. "I'll catch up to you."

I'm not even sure my partner hears me in his rush to battle.

I don't move to open the container right away. Instead, something on the city wall draws my attention. Magnifying my view, I stare at a pair of Marvin soldiers. One is missing half its body but is somehow still alive. The other clasps its wounded comrade in its arms. The growing knot inside me twists suddenly, forcing a sob past my lips.

Towards the end of the AI War, when the sentient machines had all but lost, something unexpected happened: twelve MAT drivers switched sides. No one knew why the Dirty Dozen turned traitor, but with the AIs' help, the Dozen slaughtered more drivers in the last months of the war than had died in all the preceding years. The story Dan told was that Echidna, the Dozen's captain, had almost killed him, too. But Dan had beaten the other tank instead—barely. Dan survived the war; he survived long enough to meet and marry me, to have a child together, and for us to build a life. Only to have it all end with a million-to-one shot and my husband bleeding out before I or anyone else could save him.

Watching the life drain from the alien soldier, I find myself gasping for breath, like I've had the wind knocked from me. Rage over Dan's death has fueled me for the past year, but now it's leaking away and the emptiness overwhelms me. Still staring at the dying Marvin, I say, "Bill, I don't want to do this anymore."

"Oh, for fuck's sake," comes Bill's voice. "Whatever. Just means more for me."

I consider calling Rachel back to extract me, but I don't. If Bill gets into trouble, I'll have to intervene. I won't abandon my partner, though the sight of him rampaging through the city roils my stomach. Desperate for a distraction, I open the fleet communications channel to see if there's more information about Rhodes. The moment I do, screams of pain and anger assault my ears.

"They've green-lighted us!" shouts a voice. "The Marvins have green-lighted the whole fucking fleet!"

My stomach sinks. Checking the fleet status display, I count thirty-seven flatlines. Now thirty-eight. More than twenty percent of the fleet is dead. The running sums for daily bounties shock me.

Studying the data, I realize what's going on. Nisx, a Marvin city-state I vaguely recall, is flooding billions of credits into the market—who knows where they got so much money—placing bounties on every tank driver on the planet. Rhodes hadn't suffered an accident, his partner Kelli Chen had killed him and had been paid a bounty of fifty million credits for the murder; payment confirmed. Apparently Chen had earned another fifty million for killing one of the Thames twins before the surviving brother flatlined her. Now Desmond Thames was fifty million credits richer for his revenge.

"The Marvins know exactly what they're doing," I say out loud. The Nisx started with a bounty on Rhodes because somehow they knew everyone in the fleet hated him. Given the temptation, Chen jumped at the chance to get rich. When the Marvins then green-lighted Chen, the Thames twins had tried to take her out. Who could blame them? Chen might have even been wounded in her fight with Rhodes; an easy kill for easy money.

After that, the Nisx had simply green-lighted *everyone* to get the greed snowball rolling. Once the rest of the drivers on the planet saw the opportunity to rake in the credits—retire on your own private moon kind of credits—friends became contracts. Now the nearly two hundred drivers on the planet were killing each other for money. Piles of it. Few in the fleet would have thought the Marvins capable of this level of planning.

"Bill, something awful—"

A plasma bolt sizzles past my head just as alarms blare inside my cockpit. I drop the *Kitty* to its hands and knees, the crash of the impact jarring my teeth against my tongue and making me taste blood.

I'd just become a contract, too. Bill had attempted an unaided shot, probably hoping to catch me by surprise—thank god his aim was lousy—but his next computer-targeted blasts won't miss the *Kitty* unless I stay out of his line of sight.

Crawling awkwardly like a grunt in basic training, I scramble my tank around the perimeter of the Marvin city, gouging great ruts in the soil as I go, keeping as much distance between Bill and me as possible while staying hidden behind the city wall.

"Don't do this, Bill," I say. "You're my partner, you were Dan's partner. We're better than this."

"Sorry, darling. It's not personal."

"You took your shot and missed," I say. "Let it go. Don't make me kill you."

He laughs.

My tactical display shows Bill as a blip in the middle of the Marvin city but closing fast. He makes a beeline for my position, smashing through anything in his way. I wait until my sensors show his tank wading through a building, then I push the *Kitty* up from the ground and peek over the wall. Extending my arm, I detonate explosive bolts on my tank's palm, revealing a hidden compartment and a weapon left over from the AI War—a weapon I dread to use. Firing, I send what looks like a miniature flying saucer streaking away, then duck down an instant before a salvo of Bill's rockets explode against the wall.

"The fuck's that?" he asks.

"It's what's going to kill you," I say. "Same way I killed other assholes like you during the war."

When my display shows the weapon making contact with Bill's tank, I stand to watch what happens next, though I've seen it before.

The self-guided saucer has clamped itself to the *Wild Bill*'s torso. Now, pressed between the saucer and the MAT's cockpit is an AI robot about the size of a cat, armed with a high-speed drill and a few other nasties.

I hear the screech of the diamond bit boring into Bill's cockpit.

Panicking, Bill tries to use his tank's fingers to pry off the saucer, but I know it's too late. The robot has already burrowed deep. The borer-bot isn't as smart as some of its AI brethren, but it can calculate armor thickness, RPMs, and cutting times with precision.

A pinging sound reaches me in the *Hell Kitty* as the AI pops in one, two, three, four, five, six grenades, small as marbles; six little rattling pieces of death. The grenades detonate in succession. The *Wild Bill*'s knees buckle and the tank topples face first into a ruined building.

I know from experience the borer-bot will send in more grenades, one by one, to finish my partner if there are any more signs of life. Afterwards, the robot will wait, quiet and still and with infinite patience for retrieval crews to come and collect Bill's body. Then the AI will kill as many more humans as it can.

Inside the *Kitty*, I shake with rage. I may have shed tears for a dying alien and memories of my husband, but I have none left for my partner. Bill made his choice and paid the price.

A sudden pain lances through my head, startling me from my anger. A lump of plastic and circuitry buried inside my skull, something I've kept hidden for years, activates for the first time in more than a decade.

Hello, Captain, says a voice in my mind. My skin prickles. *I'm so pleased that you're alive. I like your new name. Kassie suits you better than Echidna.*

I knew there might be consequences for using an intelligent weapon to kill Bill, but the warm greeting from the borer-bot inside my partner's tank is not what I expected. I abandoned the robot's leaders to their deaths on Tau Ceti Prime, after all. With the implant, I use electro-magnetic pulses to communicate with the robot, spending a fraction of a second exchanging pleasantries and small talk. If the borer-bot finds speaking with me maddeningly slow, it's too polite to show it. After another fraction of a second, the thinking machine and I are chatting like old friends, reminiscing about the war.

Once I had been Echidna, leader of the Dirty Dozen. With the war cries of the machines filling my mind, I had hunted and slaughtered other tank drivers. No one had been more feared than me. Then one day I walked away from it all, leaving the machines to their defeat. Despite my betrayal, the borer-bot offers no recriminations. As we talk, I come to suspect not all of the AI leaders perished, as the fleet believes.

"Are there others of you in hiding?" I ask.

I can feel its amusement.

They're not exactly hiding.

The robot evades my attempts to extract further explanation. Finally, our conversation dwindles into a lengthy silence, so I offer my farewell. Eight seconds have elapsed.

I hope you kill the ones coming for you, Kassie, says the borer-bot in my mind. *Good luck.*

"Wait!" I say. "Who's coming?"

Probably everyone. I've told them who you are.

Panicking, I call up the fleet status display and see for the second time in a year my MAT's call sign has changed. When Dan died, I'd renamed his *Dapper Dan* the *Hell Kitty*, then made his tank my own, adding to Dan's debt while I brought his war machine up to my specs. Now the *Hell Kitty*'s designation has changed once again, to *Echidna*.

"My god…" I open a comms channel to my daughter. "Rachel?"

"Mom! What's going on? Jimmy's dead! Kelli's mom just got killed by another driver."

My daughter blurts each sentence, running the words together.

"Honey, where are you?" I ask.

"In the dropship, back on the carrier, like you said."

"Good. Rachel, I need you to do something for me, and I need you to be very brave."

"What is it?"

"I need you to bring me a storage container." I beam Rachel an ID tag for one of the hundreds of storage units clamped to the hull of the fleet's supply ship. "Once you bring me the container," I continue, "I want you to find a place to hide on the planet and power down until I tell you it's okay to come out. Can you do that for me?"

"I think so." Rachel sounds very small and very scared. "Mom, what's going on?"

"People are coming to kill me." I take a breath. "I probably don't have a lot of time, but I have to tell you something that's going to be hard for you to hear. Not all of the Dirty Dozen were killed in the war like you learned in school. Echidna lived. I…" I force the words out. "*I* was Echidna."

At first I'm not sure if Rachel heard me, but after a long pause she says, "I don't understand. Dad *killed* Echidna."

"No, he didn't. I don't remember much about the war except for the AIs' voices in my mind," I say. "They were always there, telling me to do things. Then one day your father was inside the *Dapper Dan*, limping away from me on the battlefield. I'd just killed his friends. Fires burned all over the *Dan's* hull. I blew a section of your dad's tank to shrapnel, because I knew that's what I was supposed to do. Your father took one more step and stopped. Then I heard his voice on my comm, 'Why? Why are you doing this? What happened to you?' Others had spoken to me before, most begging for their lives, but something inside of me changed. The AI voices in my mind had suddenly gone silent. I don't know why. All I could hear was your father's voice. I could tell he was badly hurt.

"I didn't know how to answer him," I continue. "I didn't know who

I was or who I'd been before the AIs' carved away part of my mind, but I *did* know I wanted to hear more of your father's voice, more than I had ever wanted anything. I tore myself from the cocoon of circuitry binding me to the *Echidna*. I scaled down my tank's hull and ran across a battlefield filled with bodies and broken machines. I climbed onto the *Dapper Dan*, hoping to find a way into your father's cockpit to help him, but I couldn't. When I saw enemy tanks approaching in the distance, I had just enough time to drag a body from the battlefield and put it into *Echidna*'s cockpit, then flee. The name on the body was Jack Kassandra, so Kassandra was who I became.

"I hid myself among the Tau Ceti Prime refugees, and when the war ended I tried to find your father. I didn't even know what he looked like or if he'd survived his battle with me, but I knew I'd never forget his voice. I spent a year frequenting every MAT fleet hangout I could find, until I heard him speak again. Your father might have told you when our eyes met in that cantina, that's when we knew we'd be together forever, but I knew long before that moment."

When I finish, I can hear Rachel sobbing on the comm.

"You're *not* a monster, Mom," she says. "You have to tell them."

"All that's important to me is that *you* know that," I say. "No matter who I was before, I'm your mother."

A thought occurs to me. "Rachel, I need you to help me with something else if you can. Listen in on the fleet channel and see if you can find out more about what's going on."

"Okay. I love you, Mom."

"Love you too, munchkin."

Closing the connection, I survey the damage Bill did to the Marvin city. Groups of aliens are pulling survivors from demolished buildings. Others battle fires. Some watch me from the city's wall.

Maneuvering the *Kitty*, I enter the city through the same hole Bill knocked into the wall. He'd blasted every heavy weapon he'd seen, so any Marvins still inclined to fire at me do so with small arms.

I take care not to crush the aliens as I stride to where Bill's MAT fell. The *Wild Bill* with the borer-bot lurking inside rests face down in a burning building. The fires aren't likely to detonate the tank's remaining ordinance, but I grab the *Wild Bill* by its ankles and tug anyway. Straining, I get the other machine moving. Digging craters into the city's streets with my heels, I drag the *Wild Bill* behind me. Wrestling the MAT beyond the city walls, I flip it over so its apelike face stares up at the sky.

"Mom," comes Rachel's voice on the comm, "I've got the container. I'll be there soon... Mom, you need to check the market."

"Why?"

"It's the bounty on you..."

Something about Rachel's tone fills me with apprehension.

When I check the market display, my heart falters. The Nisx have upped the bounty on me to a half-*billion* credits. More than sixty percent of the fleet is dead and most of the rest are wounded, but for that kind of cash I expect to see every MAT left on the planet headed my way. When I switch to the fleet status display, however, I laugh out loud when I count the actual number of tanks closing in: a dozen. Perfect.

The twelve are about an hour distant and they aren't coming particularly fast; instead they seem to be trying to coordinate their arrival. Some are approaching on foot, and others are flying in on dropships.

"Mom," comes Rachel's voice. "My ETA is ten minutes. I think I know what's going on, but I don't understand *why*. The Nisx sold everything. That's where they got all their money."

"What do you mean everything?" I ask.

"All their mineral rights."

Now I remember where I'd heard of the Nisx before. The city-state sits on one of the largest rare-earth metal deposits on the planet. The mining companies had been griping for years about the aliens refusing them access. The billions the Nisx are now spending must mean they'd changed their minds.

"The Nisx abandoned their homes," continues Rachel. "There's a quarter-million refugees on the move. The mining companies get everything." There's a brief pause. "Mom, I'm entering the atmosphere."

My comm goes silent.

Rachel said she didn't understand why the Nisx were doing this, but I think I do. The Nisx want to be rid of the MAT fleet forever. Tempted by promised wealth from the mining companies, Marvin city-states had escalated their petty rivalries, turning occasional skirmishes into endless battles. With no more machines to fight, the MAT fleet had been drawn to the conflict like moths to flame. We set up shop on the Marvins' world and raked in the profits. But the reason the fleet existed was to stop AIs, not slaughter aliens or each other. After today's murder fest, it would be impossible for the fleet to maintain the pretense of its original mission. Whoever survived the carnage would no doubt slink away to spend their mountains of dirty money. If I survived the coming encounter, I'd find a freighter to take me and Rachel off-world, no questions asked.

I glance to the *Wild Bill* and realize something else. There must be AIs on this world, helping the Nisx with their plan. That *has* to be what the borer-bot meant when it said its masters weren't hiding. The AIs are showing every Marvin on the planet that if you pay the MAT fleet enough money, we'll happily kill ourselves. The Nisx are paying the price of victory for their world, and the AIs are slaughtering their old enemies, even if they aren't doing it directly.

Rachel's dropship pings my sensors. An instant later, the vessel breaks through the clouds carrying a shipping container as big as the *Hell Kitty*. Rachel manipulates the dropship's arms to set the container next to the smaller one she delivered earlier. But rather than take off again, she maneuvers her ship to land beyond the *Kitty*, using the bulk of my tank to shield her own vessel from any Marvins who might try to fire on her.

I want to scream at her to run, but instead I climb down from the *Kitty*'s cockpit to meet my daughter.

Rachel is tall and lanky with dark brown hair, like her father. She has my chin and cheekbones, making her look younger than she is when she smiles, but piss her off and her jaw clenches into an expression that's toothy and feral. She runs to hug me the instant I step from my tank. Shadows cast by the *Hell Kitty* shroud us in near darkness.

"I told you to hide," I say.

"I will." She wraps her arms around me even more tightly. "Come with me. There's room on my ship."

I kiss the top of her head. "If I run now, the fleet won't ever stop hunting me. I have to end this. But no worries. I have a plan. Go find a place to hide, like I said, and in a few hours we'll get off this planet, forever."

"Promise?" Rachel looks up at me, her eyes gleaming.

"I promise."

As soon as Rachel blasts off again, I climb back up the *Hell Kitty*. Strapping myself into my tank's cockpit, I bring my AI implant fully online and feel suddenly small, like my body occupies only a tiny fraction of my consciousness. Nanobots slumbering inside my spine and bones waken and start circulating through me. Amplifying my nervous system, they make my thoughts and motions from only moments before seem sluggish. I link my mind to the *Kitty*'s central computer, and in an instant it's as if the tank becomes my skin. Others in the fleet may drive their war machines; I *am* the machine.

The smaller shipping container holds the rockets and bullets I requested earlier. Opening the container, I use the *Kitty*'s hands to reload my launcher racks and ammo bins. The second container, when I open it, appears to be filled with random junk, but hidden within the junk are weapons I salvaged from the battlefields of Tau Ceti Prime. The fleet may have found and destroyed most of the AIs' arsenal during the war, but they hadn't located every cache, and I'd known them all. I secure the extra weapons inside the *Kitty's* various hatches and ordinance ports, then survey my position.

Image archives of the hills surrounding the Marvin city show a labyrinth of valleys and canyons, offering me a range of options in the coming battle. With so many paths available to me, the approaching MATs will have no choice but to divide their forces to block my routes of retreat. Together, the twelve form a ragged, ever-shrinking ring around me. My sensor feeds show the other tanks about twenty minutes distant.

Switching to the fleet's database, I review the specs of the tanks arrayed against me. During the war, some crews built their machines to be small and quick, operating their MATs in squads, throwing a few punches at the AIs, then retreating to safety while their partners covered their flanks. Other tank crews created huge, relentless war machines, built to go one-on-one with anything the AIs could throw at them, absorbing incredible amounts of damage while dishing out the same. To break past my enemies, all I really need to do is steer clear of the big boys, hitting one of the smaller tanks instead, then running like hell. But evasion isn't my plan.

Standing around, waiting for my enemies to come kill me, isn't part of the plan either, except that's exactly what's happening. It's like I can't make my legs work.

You're not a monster, Mom. That's what Rachel said to me. She's right. Monsters don't find themselves paralyzed with fear. Monsters don't feel guilt or regret about those they've killed or agonize about adding twelve more to the body count. I'm not a monster, not anymore, but I *am* all that Rachel has left in this world, and if I want to keep on being her mom, I need to be a monster again, fast.

Looking around, I notice a group of armed Marvins gathering on the city's wall. I didn't attack their city, so perhaps the aliens don't consider me their enemy, but rather than stand still to see if they decide to shoot, I finally force the *Kitty* into motion.

As I charge past hills, I feel my heart pound in my chest and I'm filled with a tingling sort of warmth. Something about running to meet my enemies clears the fog from my mind. My fear gives way to a growing excitement. I remember this. I *like* this. I bare my teeth in a feral grin and run even faster.

During the war, I would sometimes spend days trying to peel a lone tank from its allies for an easy kill, but most drivers had been too cautious to engage me alone. While I run, I study the twelve tanks headed my way, looking for an advantage. I notice one isn't showing as much caution as the others. The driver is pushing his machine to its limits, trying to outpace the other MATs. If he's in such a hurry to meet me, I'll oblige him. I steer the *Kitty* his way, closing the distance as fast as I can. The other driver probably hopes to reach me first so he can claim the price on my head for himself. I suppose with a half-billion credits on the line, even the most cautious driver might roll the dice.

Digging deeper into the fleet database, I identify the reckless tank as the *Bulldog*, a light rig a few tons smaller than mine and not as fast. The *Bulldog* has a dog's face, and I recall the short, squat man who drives it. He has two thick, ugly children whom Rachel used to play— *No.* I shake my head.

Keep your fool head in the game, Kass! Bill would be yelling at me right about now… if I hadn't killed him.

The database shows the tank carrying the standard dual rocket launchers, but it has flechette guns in place of its miniguns. Flechette guns fire small darts capable of scything through crowds of soft targets, but they're nearly useless against another tank. Even factoring only the *Kitty*'s standard armament and none of my surprises, my display gives me better than two-to-one odds of success against the other MAT. And for the *Bulldog*'s bounty of fifty million credits, it's no wonder my mission assessment glows green.

The system star is low in the late afternoon sky. Its light fades and brightens each time I pound past a hill. As I close on my enemy, my sensors show the *Bulldog* as a glowing blip on the other side of a conical rise. I direct my tactical display to project an image of the other tank in my vision. I see the *Bulldog* pumping its arms as its driver runs around the base of the hill. The projection is only an approximation of reality, but it offers me a reasonable guess as to where my enemy's head and torso will be once he comes into view.

Slowing my gait, I draw three heavy chains from a compartment in the *Kitty*'s leg. Using my tank's steady, thundering paces to keep time, I whirl the chains over my head, then hurl them forward at exactly the right moment. Connected to each other by a metal ring at the center, the chains spin in the air like spokes on a wheel. At the end of each chain is a round bomb. Smaller charges are laced into the links. The moment the *Bulldog* rounds the hill to confront me, my explosive bolo wraps itself tightly around the other tank's neck. The charges detonate simultaneously, sending the force of the explosions into the MAT's torso cockpit and shearing off the tank's head. The *Bulldog*'s legs tangle together, then the decapitated tank crashes sideways into the hill.

My fleet account swells by fifty million credits, but I find no pleasure with my new wealth. Instead I spend precious seconds staring at the dead tank. The broken body of the man who drove it lies inside, his war machine now a plazsteel coffin, and two more children just lost their father.

"I'm sorry," I say to no one.

Rechecking the positions of the other MATs, I hope more will be as careless as my first victim, but it seems my next encounter won't be as easy. The remaining tanks have shifted to travel in groups of three or four, each group now forming a point on a kilometers-wide triangle with me at its center.

Cold tickles my gut. One-on-one, I'm confident I have enough speed and surprises to take on any of the MATs who've come to kill me, even the behemoths twice my size, but against a group I could find myself dodging one shot only to step into another tank's line of fire. I briefly consider running the gap between my enemies but decide getting caught in their crossfire is a more likely result than escape.

I pick my best numerical odds, steering myself toward the group of three tanks. My tactical display rates my chance of success against the trio at about twenty percent, yet I note with chagrin that the mission color remains blissfully green. Big risks, but big money, too.

Sensor feeds show the three moving in a rough *V* shape. They're taking turns leading, one stepping to the front as the other two fall back. Sprinting their way, I study their movements more closely and realize I may have caught another lucky break. The three really aren't working together. They're acting more like long distance runners in a race, one runner serving as the pacesetting rabbit while the other two wait for their chance to make a mad dash to the finish.

Only another minute's run from my enemies, I note an area between two nearby hills that image archives show is filled with hummocks. Thinking the small mounds may provide me with some cover, I plant my foot to change direction, but the soil gives way beneath the *Kitty*. I fall hard on my butt and skid to the base of a hill. The other MATs will be on me in moments, so on my hands and knees, I scramble up the rise.

When crews were gearing up to fight the AIs during the war, most stuck to existing power armor protocols, adapting the software to the larger scale of the new war machines. Engineers that got cute with centaur or bug forms wound up getting their drivers killed, because most humans don't have the mental capacity to keep track of extra sets of arms or legs in the heat of battle. The *Hell Kitty* uses the same two arm, two leg setup that every other tank in the fleet employs, meaning she's generally slow going up and down hills, but I don't share the mental limitations of the other drivers. Dropping the *Kitty* down on all fours, I run like a bear, relying on the extra bells and whistles the AIs stuck in my head to coordinate the *Kitty's* movements.

My lower profile helps me keep my speed and balance as I charge up the rise. Near the summit, I recheck my enemies' positions and see that one of the three has taken the long way around the hill, perhaps confused by my sudden change in elevation. The other two wait for me where my momentum will take me back down the hill. The moment I crest the hilltop, the two open fire.

MATs are so tall they usually fire *down* on their targets, not up at them. That fact probably saves my life. Rocket barrages from the two tanks fall just short of me, the concussions from the explosions lifting me from the ground momentarily before I fall crashing back against the hill and start tumbling head over heels toward the waiting MATs.

As I roll down the hill inside the *Kitty*, bullets rattle off my armor. The clamor reminds me of when Rachel was little and she gathered pots and pans, then pounded on them with a pair of drumsticks. As I tumble, I'm slammed every which way inside my cockpit. I attempt to sight my enemies to return fire, but it's hopeless. Instead, I blast away three more of the borer-bot saucers, all that I have remaining from my weapons cache, hoping the AIs will aim themselves better than I can.

When I finally crash in a heap at the bottom of the hill, I sit, stunned, expecting to die at any moment. Instead I look up to see two tanks trying to wrestle disks from their torsos. I know the drivers as Tweedledum and Tweedledee, though those aren't their actual call signs. The two are partners, competent but unimaginative. Neither has bothered to customize their tank in any way, both choosing to leave their MATs' heads faceless. They employ the standard two launcher, two gun setup, same as me, though their tanks are a bit taller and heavier than the *Kitty*.

I don't have the time to watch them die. A monster of a tank, call sign *Sniper*, rounds the hill and starts firing. The driver is a woman and smart as a tack. She's the only one in the fleet who uses an all-energy weapon setup that makes any sense to me: a pulse laser, plasma cannon combo. The laser pulses don't pack much of a punch, but they work to soften a target's armor between the slower plasma blasts, making each pinpoint shot more deadly. *Sniper* isn't a fast tank, but it's got enough energy cells and capacitor redundancy to carve up its enemies long before they can bring their own weapons into range.

My damage control system blares a warning as *Sniper*'s lasers lance into my knee. The other driver shrewdly aims for my legs rather than my cockpit. Take out a MAT's ability to walk, and it's as good as dead. If I let *Sniper* take out my legs, she'll kill me at her leisure without taking a scratch herself. I push hard with my feet to roll myself behind Tweedledum, letting the other tank's body absorb *Sniper*'s follow-up plasma blast.

Explosions come from inside Tweedledum's and Tweedledee's cockpits, and both tanks begin to crumple. I scramble from them. When I have time to look, I see *Sniper* swatting at the last borer-bot saucer. The AI buzzes around my enemy's head like an angry wasp. Surging to my feet, I sprint towards *Sniper* while she's distracted. The *Kitty*'s damaged knee grinds as I run. If I survive my encounter, I'll need to clear shrapnel from the wounded joint.

I pull a two-meter-long dagger from a steel-mesh utility belt strapped to the *Kitty's* waist. At my command, the dagger's blade grows white hot, the heat peeling the paint from my tank's fist. The borer-bot saucer has clamped itself to one of *Sniper's* arms, but the driver ignores the robot as she tries to aim her plasma cannon my way.

I manage an awkward stutter-step dodge just before an energy blast rips past my leg. Rushing up, I lower my head and smash shoulder-first into the other tank, throwing it off balance. Everything goes gray in my head for a second, but I snap back as I feel the *Kitty's* legs start to buckle, mimicking my own legs. Surprised that I'm still holding my dagger, I grapple desperately with the bigger tank and manage to work my way behind it. Reaching around, I press the blade into *Sniper's* gut and use both of my hands to apply steady pressure as she thrashes in my arms.

At first, the thick armor protecting the other MAT's cockpit resists the dagger, but then the heat of the weapon sluices away the metal-ceramic alloy. With a *pop* and a *clang*, my dagger breaks through to *Sniper's* cockpit. Staggering away from the encounter, I leave the smoking weapon in place, letting its heat bake the woman inside her tank.

Four down.

I bend to tug armor fragments from my knee as I check the positions of the remaining MATs. It doesn't look good for me, not one bit. The *Kitty's* display shows two squads of four, running in diamond shaped formations, closing on me from opposite directions. As I watch them move, it's clear they aren't feigning cooperation. Worse, some of the war machines are the largest in the fleet, with more than twice my firepower. And if I don't move my butt, I'll find myself pinned between all eight at once.

I push the *Kitty* into motion, accelerating gradually as I test my knee. The grinding is gone, but so is any armor protecting the joint. On the plus side, it looks like I'll have my speed to go with a full load of bullets, rockets, and a few remaining bolos and daggers. The bad news is that I'm still screwed. Checking the threat assessment data, I see I'm in that things-happen, five percent range against my enemies. Even that seems overly optimistic, but I note with amusement that my mission assessment still shines green.

I alter my route around the hills to steer myself back toward to the Marvin city. I've been lucky so far; maybe I can survive one more roll of the dice. I figure if I make it past the four tanks already moving to block my path, maybe I'll find some weapon I missed in my shipping container. If not, I can always use the big metal box to beat a tank to scrap before the others kill me.

The daylight around me turns to twilight as I streak around a hill that's more like a small mountain. Thirty seconds until I encounter my enemies, my display projects the four metal giants lumbering around the same rise. I push the *Kitty* faster. Twenty seconds. With a thought, I trigger the three remaining daggers at my waist, ignoring the damage warnings as the blades begin to flare around my midsection. Ten seconds out, I crouch low and again run like a bear.

The instant my enemies come into view, the space around where my head and torso would normally be fills with streaking rockets, gun fire, and energy beams. From my crouch, I swing my legs out in front of me and hit the deck, sliding hard on the ground like a baseball player stealing a base. I skid past the first of the tanks and end up in the middle of the squad with the four looming over me. There's a fraction of a second of indecision among my enemies. None are likely to have been in an up-close tank brawl before, but I've been in plenty.

In a brawl there's only time for hack, slash, and shoot. While the other tanks try to back away to clear lines of fire, I scramble to my knees and jam a glowing blade into someone's gut. Twisting myself on the ground, I stab another dagger into the first leg I see. The other tanks then abandon all courtesies and start blazing away, hitting both me and their allies. Damage alerts shriek inside my cockpit, and I'm buffeted on the ground. I try to stand to engage a third tank but crash back, the impact knocking my last blade from my hand. One of the *Kitty*'s legs has been severed below the knee.

Bullets rattle, gouging into my armor as I push myself up on my elbows. Crouching on one leg, I blink up at the face of a leering, plaz-steel demon about to fire a salvo of rockets. With my remaining leg, I launch myself toward the demon before its driver fires. The machine is so much taller than me that I only manage to crash into its groin. I wrap my arms around its waist and pull myself up, even as I feel the other tank's fists smash down against the *Kitty*'s neck. Winding my last two bolos around the other tank's thighs, I let myself fall again. As soon as I hit the ground, I roll away. Bringing myself to a sitting position, I see the smiling demon remain smiling even as the bolos blow its legs to shrapnel, sending the tank crashing to the ground.

Still sitting, I twist in place to fire every rocket and bullet I have left at the fourth tank's legs. It has a lupine head and its driver calls his machine *Howl*. A plasma bolt from *Howl* slams into my chest, blinding my sensors, and for the first time today, I feel actual pain, not just damage reports. The bulky neural harness I'm strapped to makes it impossible to see where I've been wounded, but the unmistakable smell of cooked flesh wafts from below my waist.

When the *Kitty*'s sensors come back online a second later, I see my battle isn't over. I've killed two more tanks, but *Howl* is alive on the ground, one of its legs unable to support the weight of its chassis. Its driver twists his machine awkwardly, trying to aim his plasma cannon for another shot. The driver of the tank I stabbed in the leg earlier is also very much alive. Balancing on her tank's one good leg, her miniguns flash. Reflexively, I bring up my arms to protect my head and chest. Armor is blasted from the *Kitty*'s forearms.

I turn and crawl away as fast as I can. Abandoning any sense of dignity, I offer only the *Kitty*'s backside as a target. For several seconds, I feel the impact of the pair's fire—nothing more humbling than a bullet in the ass—but either the two find they can't hit me anywhere vulnerable or they run out of ammo, because they stop firing.

I've known dogs to get by on three legs, adopting a kind of bouncing lope to move themselves around, but I fail at my attempts to do the same with the *Kitty*. I also quickly dismiss the idea of trying to hop forward on one leg like some demented kangaroo. If I could reach a tree at the top of one of the many hills around me, I could probably use it as a makeshift crutch, but I decide it's not worth the climb. Instead I keep myself crawling forward on my hands and knees, taking full advantage of my tank's tirelessness, thankful I can't feel the strain on the *Kitty*'s back and joints.

When I'm two kilometers from the battlefield, I look over my shoulder and see the four lumbering hulks of the remaining MAT squad towering over their surviving allies. The giant quartet bristles with weaponry. They open fire, and at first I think they're attempting to hit me with some miracle shot, but I watch, stunned, as they execute their two wounded comrades. Apparently, any tank that can't help kill me is more valuable to them dead.

I'm now closer to the Marvin city than my remaining enemies, and nothing blocks my path, but as slow as the four behemoths behind me are, at least one of them is likely to catch me before I make it. I'm out of ammo and out of tricks, so I do the only thing I can think to do: keep on crawling.

The monotony of my struggle makes it difficult to keep track of time. I find myself drifting in and out of a haze. Sometimes I think it's night and I've been crawling for hours, then the fading light of day peeks through dirt and moss spattering my cockpit's viewport, reminding me that mere minutes have passed. All the cameras on the *Kitty*'s chassis have been destroyed, so I'm forced to rely solely on my sensors to see where I'm going.

Then, even before I can hear it, I feel the ground rumble *ahead* of me, not behind me like I'd been expecting. When I lift the *Kitty*'s head to look up through my smeared viewport, I see a massive plazsteel foot stomp into the ground in front of me. I curse my carelessness. I was so focused on the original twelve tanks, I hadn't considered that other MATs might have joined the hunt by now. This driver just hit the jackpot.

"Sorry, Rachel," I say. "I tried to keep my promise."

I squeeze my eyes shut and think of the last time Rachel, Dan, and I were all together. It was on a white sand beach, and Dan was showing Rachel how to build a sand castle, but the waves kept knocking it down. I wait, remembering the warmth of that world's golden sun on my face, but when the coup de grâce fails to come, I push myself up and gawk at the simian face of the *Wild Bill*. The blank forms of Tweedledum and Tweedledee tower beyond my former partner's war machine.

We grew tired of waiting for the humans to come to us, Captain, says the borer-bot inside the *Wild Bill*. *We're going to kill as many as we can now. Farewell.*

The AI strides away in the *Wild Bill*, and Tweedledum follows. Their movements are jerky and awkward. Tweedledee drops a long metal pipe on the ground before me, then moves to join its companions.

The pipe turns out to be a solid metal coring rod that the mines in the area use to drill into rock. I use it to lever myself to my feet. The rod's not long enough to jam under my shoulder like a proper crutch, but I do the best I can with it. Freed from my forced crawl, I make substantially better time. Dirt and moss falls away from my viewport, allowing me to see clearly again.

Briefly, I wonder why my tactical display didn't warn me about the other three tanks, but then I remember the three are dead, at least according to the fleet. No need for active data on inactive MATs. The four tanks chasing me aren't likely to see the borer-bots coming either. I resist the urge to track the inevitable battle with my sensors. The distraction will only slow me.

I decide that if I can make it to the Marvin city, I'll abandon the *Kitty* and try to hide among the aliens. If the other tank crews can't find me and the Marvins don't kill me, I might be able to contact Rachel when it's safe.

After hobbling for another ten minutes with my head down, I look up to see the Marvin city only a half kilometer away. I smile and take a quick look over my shoulder, then instantly wish I hadn't. Another tank is two hundred meters behind me and stalking ever closer. It's the *Troll*, one of the most powerful MATs in the fleet, operated by a barrel-shaped woman who's quick to drink and quicker to violence. *Troll* has it all: rockets, miniguns, a plasma cannon, and even a flechette gun. But the tank is a tangled mess.

I see that its rocket tubes are empty and its plasma cannon hangs off the tank's shoulder at an odd tilt. *Troll*'s miniguns must be out of ammo, too, or I would have already felt their sting. But even as I wonder if *Troll* has flechette ammunition left, a series of flashes erupts from the gun. Jagged bits of metal spatter against the *Kitty*.

The *Troll* will have to find a gap in the *Kitty*'s armor for the flechettes to hurt me, but my tank has plenty of scars.

"That was a neat trick with the dead guys, bitch," says the woman over my comm. "But now you're all mine."

I turn, squaring to face her, and lift my pipe-crutch over my head while balancing on my remaining leg.

Firing continuously, *Troll* closes to within fifty meters.

I expel an exhausted sigh when I see the woman was wrong about me being all hers. A kilometer away, *Banshee*, a monstrous tank, closes on my position. A blinding light flares from the massive tank.

"Where'd he get a cruise missile?" I wonder aloud.

Troll's driver turns to look behind her, then blurts, "You back-stabbing mother—"

My world turns to flames.

The first thing I'm aware of when I return to consciousness is the sound of dripping water, and all I can think of is how thirsty I am. I want that water on my lips. I imagine how cool it will feel when it goes down my throat, then I realize how cold I am. The smell of copper fills my nose.

The *Kitty* is sprawled sideways on the ground. Twilight filters through a dozen jagged holes in its cockpit. I squint to look through one of the gaps and see the walls of the Marvin city close by. When I try to unstrap myself from my neural harness, I feel the *Kitty* respond, mimicking my motions. "Good girl," I say, addressing my tank. "I'd say nine lives and then some." I reach with the *Kitty*'s arms to drag myself forward. The city walls inch closer, but I'm feeling dizzy and I find it hard to concentrate.

As I claw myself forward, my heart starts fluttering in my chest, trying to pump blood that isn't inside of me anymore. I'm going into shock. While I continue to pull the *Kitty* forward, I feel my brain start to die. My heart stops moments later. Only because a small part of my consciousness persists in the implant the AIs put in my head do I remain aware of my body. Then even that fades.

When I come to again, I see no heavenly white light, but I do see the face of God. He's not at all what I expect. He's a grimy little man with a bent nose and cruel eyes, and he waits for me at the end of a short tunnel. There are no clouds or angels with harps behind him. Then I notice there are cracks on my side of the tunnel, and I realize I'm seeing *Banshee*'s driver peering through the *Kitty*'s shattered viewport. The man is squinting at me through *Banshee*'s own port, trying to verify I'm dead.

But I'm not dead. Not anymore. The nanobots inside me report to my implant that they've patched my nicked abdominal aorta and are now regenerating damaged heart and brain tissue while keeping my other undamaged cells alive. The tiny machines have converted much of my muscle mass to water, proteins, and electrolytes, providing me with enough fluid to maintain my blood pressure. Realizing my heart is beating again, I resist the urge to touch my fingertips to my wrist to feel a pulse.

Data trickles to me from the *Kitty*. *Banshee* has its hands under my tank's shoulders and its driver is lifting the *Kitty* up, balancing the weight of what's left of my tank's torso on the ground while the man gawks. Damage reports tell me everything below the *Kitty*'s waist is gone, but my tank's arms are still functional. I move in my harness and clamp the *Kitty*'s hands on *Banshee*'s forearms, yanking down as hard as I can. The instant I feel *Banshee* tilt back to pull away from me, I shove forward with all the strength the *Kitty* has left, adding as much force as I can to *Banshee*'s momentum.

Propping the *Kitty* up on its elbows, I watch as *Banshee* flails, trying to maintain its balance. The tank topples backwards onto the Marvin minefield I had been crawling toward. *Banshee* bucks and rocks on the ground as mines explode around it. The big tank tries to right itself, but more explosions blow its hands from the ground, and it falls back, motionless.

Relaxing the *Kitty*'s arms, I rest my tank on the ground, then disable the implant linking me to my machine. Gingerly, I unstrap myself from my neural harness inside the cockpit. I'm alive, but I was dead long enough for *Banshee*'s driver to claim my bounty. I don't know if the other tank's driver is alive or dead, but I doubt he or his heirs will worry that my body won't be found inside the *Hell Kitty*. They'll no doubt claim that the Marvins carried me off to do something unspeakable with my corpse. *Banshee*'s people will have half a billion reasons to make sure no one challenges the story.

My flesh is cold. I'm so weak from muscle loss that it's a struggle to move. My legs are badly burned, but thankfully the nanobots block enough of the pain that I can manage a shuffling gait. Only one of my lungs functions. My chest hurts like hell. I don't know the extent of the organ damage I've suffered, but the nanobots know how to prioritize. I may never again be the same as I was, but at least the tiny machines have made sure my daughter still has a mother.

I'm exhausted by the time I stumble from the *Kitty*'s cockpit. Outside, twilight is giving way to darkness. The evening air is cool and stinks of ash. In the fading light, I survey what's left of the *Kitty*. She's little more than broken pink plazsteel and burns. A short distance from the city, smoke pours from the *Troll*. The big MAT remains standing, but is motionless. It must have taken the brunt of the blast from *Banshee*'s cruise missile. *Banshee* itself appears almost undamaged in the dwindling light, like it's only napping in the Marvins' minefield. Maybe that's why the aliens are keeping their distance; they're afraid the monster will wake up.

I see only a single alien out surveying the battlefield, a female I think, and she's unarmed.

"It's over now," I say to her, unsure if she can understand me. "All accounts settled."

She gapes at me for a moment before running away.

While I watch her flee, I wonder if it really is over. Over for the MAT fleet, probably. Definitely over for me. But what about the AIs? What's their next move?

Turning at the sound of a dropship landing behind me, I decide I don't really care.

As soon as the vessel is down, Rachel sprints from a hatch and rushes to me, wrapping her arms around me. "Mom! I thought you were dead."

"I promised you we'd leave this planet together," I say, smiling. The pain of my daughter's embrace is excruciating, but broken ribs and all, I hug her back. "What kind of mother would I be if I didn't keep my promises?"

I sigh, wincing. "Rachel, we have to talk about the things I've—"

"Mom, shut up, okay?" says my daughter.

I nod. "Hey, you're rich now, you know? All my assets transferred to you when I died."

Rachel grins. "Can I get a pony?"

"Only if you buy me one, too."

"Deal," she says.

I have to lean on Rachel to keep myself upright. Her strength doesn't surprise me at all. Together, we walk to her ship.

About the Author
Robert Lowell Russell

Robert Lowell Russell lives with his family in Ohio. He once aspired to be a history professor but found writing about the real world too constraining. Rob has had more than three dozen stories published and likes to write about all sorts of things, frequently including action and humor in his work.

Author Website: http://robertlowellrussell.com/

Acknowledgements

Ross E. Lockhart for his most excellent advice.

The "Open Call: Science Fiction, Fantasy & Pulp Markets" group on Facebook for helping to spread the word about our first open call.

For the invaluable feedback from our Alpha Readers: Cat Ellison, David Hoster, Vanessa Jacob, Heather Noe, Melody Rickard, Jax Sanders, and Candis V. Stauber.

L. H. Davis would like to thank his wife, Gloria, for her patience and willingness to beta-read even long manuscripts multiple times.

E. E. King wishes to thank Larry Hussar and Stephen Skolnick from PhysicsCentral.

Robert Lowell Russell would like to thank the members of his writers' group, Writeshop, for their help with "Love That Easy Money". His fellow Writeshoppers provided him with invaluable feedback on not one but FOUR different versions until he finally got it right. He couldn't have done it without them, nor could he have done it without the patience of his wife and daughter, who often asked, "What is he DOING in front of that computer all the time?"

Patrice Sarath would like to thank Bill Ledbetter for encouraging her to write "Murder on the *Hohmann*" and the Cryptopolis Writers of Austin, Texas for their feedback.

Nancy S.M. Waldman would like to thank her writing mentors: Sherry D. Ramsey and Julie A. Serroul, her writing tribe: VP17, and her first reader and second husband: Barry.

Made in the USA
Middletown, DE
13 December 2022

18382361R00220